WHATEVER IT TAKES

WHATEVER IT TAKES
WHEN DUTY CALLS

Harvey Cleggett

Library of Congress Control Number:		2018907133
ISBN:	Hardcover	978-1-9845-0004-5
	Softcover	978-1-9845-0003-8
	eBook	978-1-9845-0002-1

Print information available on the last page.

Rev. date: 06/29/2018

To order additional copies of this book, contact:
Xlibris
1-800-455-039
www.Xlibris.com.au
Orders@Xlibris.com.au
778175

'To my wife Leanne
who I love and cherish as my companion for life.'

'To my son Steven
who continues to exceed my expectations.'

PROLOGUE

The heavy thump of stun grenades combined with the crackle of automatic gunfire reverberating from the ground floor of Victoria's Parliament House in Spring Street, although muffled, was unmistakable. Detective Senior Sergeant John Henderson stood stock-still, tense, fearful. "Mike, with the assault kicking off downstairs the terrorist holding Sonia has two choices—leave her in the ladies' and try to save his own hide or break into the cubicle and drag her out, using her as a shield." He pressed against the caretaker's door where he had been holed up for three days, peering into the corridor, furious his field of vision was limited.

Detective Inspector Michael Ballard was certain his homicide partner was seconds away from bolting out to mount a rescue mission for his pregnant fiancée who was being held captive along with ninety politicians. The masked terrorists' demand for a staggering billion-dollar ransom was still fresh in his mind; the urgency of the situation punctuated by the brutal manner the group's Spetsnaz-trained leader, Sergey Alistratov had executed four parliamentarians, pressing home his determination to extract the ransom from the federal government.

With his mobile pressed hard against his ear, Ballard demanded that Superintendent Peter Donaldson, the Serious Crime Taskforce OC, provide an urgent update, praying the information would dissuade John from attempting any rash action doomed to fail. "Pete, are you back in the van? What the hell's going on out there?" He visualised the department's mobile communication unit with its electronic wizardry parked at the intersection of Bourke and Exhibition streets facing Parliament House, positioned there soon after the siege had begun.

"Like I said Mike, the driver's still sitting in the explosives rig which is slap bang in the middle of parliament's front steps on the first landing. Two of Tim's team are holding him in their sights but that's *all* they can do. Jesus, can you imagine what forty tonnes of ammonium nitrate and diesel fuel would do if the bastard decides to light up the packs of C4 strapped to the tanks?"

Ballard remained silent.

Peter was heard barking orders to police members in the van before returning. "Tim's and Jordan's teams are miked up and as far as I can tell the terrorists on the ground floor have been taken out by Jordan's four guys holed up in the air conditioning room. Using silencers the crooks wouldn't have known what hit them."

A wave of relief swept over Ballard as it appeared Inspector Tim Robbins and his SOG team, supported by Lieutenant Colonel Jordan Hensley and his elite Special Operations Command military group were gaining the upper hand. To that point the terrorists had been in total control of the situation, forcing the federal attorney general to pay the exorbitant ransom with the threat of ongoing executions of an unknown number of politicians. It was only when the demand for a second billion had been made that the attorney general declared no more money would be paid by the government. This required ACs Thompson and Müller to make the life-and-death decision to mount an assault on Parliament House.

"What about ambulances and medics?" Ballard's question referred to the anaesthetic gas which had been pumped into the legislative assembly by Jordan's team after gaining entry to Parliament House via an old brick tunnel leading from the gardens on the north wing.

"All on standby to administer the antidote Mike, but the explosives rig out the front has complicated matters to buggery. We can't just leave the hostages in the chamber while we negotiate with the driver—not now that we know three of the women are pregnant and how the gas may affect their unborn." The tension in Peter's voice was mounting.

Ballard offered a solution. "All I can suggest is have the medics carry everyone into the lifts then take them out via the south ground floor exit. It'll take a hell of a lot longer than out the front, but hopefully a damn sight safer. Just make sure those still in the chamber are placed in the coma position so their lungs don't collapse. We don't want a repeat of the cock-up which happened in Russia with the Chechen militants."

"You're right, the guys here are in contact with the medics' supervisors, and we'll just have to wing it after Tim and Jordan give us the all-clear. The fire brigade, SES—you name it. Every damn emergency service known to man is on standby. In the meantime we can only pray—" He broke off, total silence persisting.

"Pete . . . *Pete, are you there?*"

"Jesus Mike . . . I've just spotted Sergey." Peter's vision was courtesy of the strategically positioned micro drones flown into the legislative assembly; the units provided by James Patterson, ASIO's senior intelligence officer who was working in conjunction with the state police.

"*Where?*"

"In the chamber."

"*What!* He's gone in despite the gas?"

"The bastard came prepared. He's wearing a mask. He'd have known tear gas or the like would be on the cards at some point." Peter hesitated. "*Shit!*"

"What's happening?" Ballard felt himself straining forward, as though being closer to the action would help clarify what was unfolding. John was equally involved, his head alongside the mobile.

"The prick's just walked up to one of his own guys and put a bullet in him."

"*What?*" Ballard felt John tug at his arm, straining to hear what Peter was saying.

"He's crossing the floor . . . presumably to take out the other two. Now he's out of the drone's vision, but you can bet your balls that's what he's about to do." Peter was heard shouting an order to someone in the van to notify Tim and Jordan of the situation. He returned. "Mike, this bugger's making sure he doesn't leave loose ends. I'd say his next move is to exit Parliament House."

"Has he shot more of the hostages?"

"No, just his own guys from what I can gather."

"Where are Tim's and Jordan's teams?"

Muffled discussions were heard, then Peter replied, "Still mopping up downstairs, but it shouldn't be long before they start their sweep on your level."

Ballard turned to John to relay what Peter had just passed on but was beaten to it. "Mike, with Sergey running amuck shooting all his henchmen, he'll be aware several are missing. He'll know they're guarding a number of ladies and guys on a toilet break. That puts Sonia in *immediate* danger." He pumped a round into the Glock's chamber, the firearm seized along with an Uzi from the terrorist they had overpowered minutes before.

"I have to protect Sonia and the baby." John faced his partner. "I don't expect you to risk your neck Mike. You've done more than your share as it is."

"Fat chance, buddy boy." Ballard barked into the mobile that he and John were about to rescue Sonia and for Tim's team to be on the lookout. He disconnected with Peter's words of *"Don't be bloody fools"* ringing in his ears. "Okay John let's do this, but remember, Sergey's a take-no-prisoner kind of guy and needs to be put down. He won't hesitate if he sees either of us so if you spot him, shoot to kill."

"Mike, you read my mind." With a wrench John yanked the door open at the same moment Ballard flicked the Uzi's selector from safe to semi-automatic.

Both men stole a hasty glance along the corridor, tense, aware Sergey outmatched them in every respect due to his specialist training and physical superiority. The passageway was empty yet felt threatening, eerily foreboding.

Ballard hissed out the corner of his mouth, "I'll go in front John. With the Uzi I've got more chance of dropping the prick than you have with the Glock."

John grunted his reluctant agreement, holding back marginally. "The hallway off to the left Mike—that's where the ladies' is."

Ballard's eyes locked on the doors leading into the parliamentary chamber, weighing up how he would take out Sergey if he appeared without placing the hostages inside in danger of friendly fire. The emptiness of the vestibule and surrounding areas had their nerves jangling, both men aware that in the blink of an eye everything could change. Modern weaponry so rapid-fire and deadly there was no room for hesitation.

Edging up to the door leading into the toilet the detectives positioned on either side. Reaching across so his body remained protected, Ballard eased the door ajar, calling out, "Police! You're trapped. Let the lady come out—*alone. Do it now!*"

Both men waited, their hearts in their mouths, praying the terrorist would see reason, their experience and training cautioning otherwise. They knew there was little time, the possibility of Sergey appearing an ever-present danger.

Ballard motioned to John, signalling they had to go in despite the risk to themselves and Sonia. Breathing deeply they pushed the door open centimetre by centimetre, conscious that any sudden movement might trigger a disastrous reaction from the terrorist, especially if he was an inexperienced Thor's Warrior bikie punching above his pay grade.

What they saw had Ballard drawing breath and John uttering a moan of anguish. The terrorist was pressing hard against Sonia's back, his left arm crooked around her neck, his right hand forcing the barrel of an Uzi against her temple. His mask was discarded, the tattoo on his cheek and neck confirming Ballard's suspicion he was a bikie.

Sonia was on tiptoe, arched backwards, her arms rigid; eyes fearful they widened on seeing John and Ballard. Her smart linen dress suit was wrinkled and awry, her normally sleek shoulder-length auburn hair unkempt.

John exploded. "*She's pregnant you shithead!*" Furious, he blurted the words, each one underscored. To Sonia he added, "Do exactly as he says. I promise we'll get you out of this." She blinked her understanding.

Ballard silently questioned the wisdom of announcing her pregnancy, fearful the man would make a connection between her and John, posing an advantage for the bikie. Rationalising the emotional burden his partner had been subjected to over the past two days had blunted his reasoning, Ballard knew there was nothing that could be done.

John recognised his error but knew there was no way it could be retracted. He addressed the bikie. "Take it easy . . . at least let her breathe." The grip eased marginally, Sonia's feet returning to the floor but the hold around her throat was as savage as ever. Eyes flicking, it was clear the bikie was unsure of his next move.

Seizing control, Ballard ordered John to keep a lookout along the corridor in case Sergey showed, aware that taking him by surprise was their only chance of defeating him. Reluctantly John withdrew his gaze from Sonia whose eyes had locked on to his as she fought to remain calm.

Ballard maintained his aim but knew the Uzi's notorious lack of accuracy precluded him from using it without hitting Sonia. He decided to hasten the bikie's decision-making. "If you step outside you'll die."

The statement generated an immediate sneer but was followed by the faintest trace of indecision.

Ballard continued, "In the last five minutes, Sergey, your boss, shot three of your guys, cut them down in cold blood." Disbelief was apparent in the bikie's eyes but changed to momentary panic with Ballard's next words. "Just as he shot one of your own in the committee room for disagreeing with him. You've got thirty seconds, perhaps a minute *max*, before he finds you—if you're lucky."

Ballard's revelation had an immediate impact, the bikie's indecision now verbal. "I'll . . . I'll take my chances out there. If I agree to let her go I'm walking out of here with my weapon." There was no doubt the man was in over his head—a follower, not a leader.

Both detectives glanced at one another, weighing up the risk to Tim's and Jordan's teams posed by an armed bikie on the loose as opposed to the immediate danger to Sonia. The decision was simple.

John saw his opportunity and grabbed it by the throat. "This is how it's going down. Step over here with the lady and I'll put my Glock to your head. The moment you want to leave, you let her go. Then you're out of here. Make *any* effort to take her with you and I'll put a bullet in your brain just as sure as the sun will rise. *Got it?*"

The bikie blinked, assessing his options, smart enough to realise he had none. Shuffling forward with Sonia still in his grasp, he got to the door with John levelling his weapon. "Okay, on the count of three let her go and step outside. After that, you're on your own, *shithead*."

The bikie's eyes darted left and right.

"One . . . two . . ." There was no need for a *three*. The bikie released his grip and stepped through the open door and into the corridor. Sonia collapsed into John's arms, her composure evaporating as she clung to him. Reaching up she wrapped her arms around his neck. "Is it over?"

John nodded, blinking hard, returning the embrace then drawing back. "Beard rash and stale breath, I'd better ease up."

"The hell you will!" Sonia planted another lingering kiss, pressing up against him in her attempt to reassure herself he was unharmed, the ordeal over.

Ballard peered into the corridor and saw the bikie proceeding along it, glancing behind as well as in front, his movements screaming uncertainty. Within seconds black-clad SOG officers appeared, shouting repeatedly for him to drop down. Whether reflex or an acute act of madness he raised his Uzi and was cut down in a hail of bullets. He fell to the floor, blood pooling around him in a widening arc.

Taking no chances, Ballard pulled out a tissue and waved it clear of the doorway in a sign of surrender. The officers approached, their Heckler & Koch at the ready.

Ballard called out, "Guys! Detective Inspector Ballard and Detective Senior Sergeant Henderson. We're here with a pregnant hostage. We're on your side, okay?" Still cautious, he and John stepped into the corridor. The rifles lowered.

"Team, stand down. I'll take care of this." The commanding voice was familiar and welcome.

Carrying an assault rifle and looking every bit the professional he was, Tim's demeanour was thunderclap. "Am I *ever* going to affect an operation without you two being mixed up in it to your back teeth?"

John maintained a protective arm around Sonia. "Lady in distress Tim. Not much choice."

Half smiling Tim approached Sonia. "Are you sure you feel safe being looked after by these two dinosaurs?"

Planting a brief kiss on Ballard's cheek, followed by a lingering smooch for her fiancé, Sonia addressed Tim, whispering, "With my life."

Watching as a sheet was placed over the body, Ballard queried, "Sergey?" He didn't have to elaborate.

Tim's expression hardened. "Jordan has him under guard in the committee room."

Ballard was perplexed. "What, no shoot-out?"

It was Tim's turn to appear puzzled. "When Jordan's team stormed in he was sitting as calm as you please at the head of the table, all his weapons pushed out of reach."

"He surrendered?" Ballard was disbelieving.

Tim was equally baffled. "Apparently so, Jordan radioed me, pretty chuffed I can tell you. He and three of his team are guarding him. At the same time I got the call you cowboys were off rescuing this charming lady."

"Er, *achieved* the rescue." Sonia hugged John once more.

"What about the hostages?" Ballard glanced along the corridor.

Tim was confident. "The evac's under way big time. There are God knows how many ambos ferrying them out of the chamber. The three pregnant women have been identified and given priority with the antidote." His optimism wavered. "In the meantime the situation with the rig is ongoing. My negotiator is doing what he can." His concern increased. "It's time I got you three out of here. You've played your part. We need to evacuate everyone as soon as possible in case the rig driver decides to press a button and light this place up, although with Sergey sitting pretty inside I'd suggest that's very unlikely."

Ballard and John agreed, with John turning to Sonia. "Tim's right. You need to go, darling."

She hesitated. "But what about you?"

John smirked. "Tim doesn't know it yet but Mike and I are going to pay Sergey a visit one last time."

Tim opened his mouth to protest but both detectives stood firm, with Ballard adding, "You owe us that much Tim. Then I promise we'll be out of your hair. You've got enough on your plate."

The SOG officer contemplated dissuading them but gave up. Turning to one of his men he requested that Sonia be escorted from the building and assessed by a medic.

John squeezed her hand. "It's over, darling. You don't know how proud I am. You were *incredibly* brave doing what you did. Now go and get yourself and our baby checked out—that's an order." Sonia blinked back tears. Reaching up she brushed his face before being led away, pausing momentarily as she passed the deceased bikie.

Tim stood in front of the detectives, shaking his head. "Okay you two, let's go and visit one very nasty Russian."

CHAPTER

1

While heading towards the committee room, Ballard swung around to face Tim, holding out a congratulatory hand. "Well done, old son. This whole operation could have been a cock-up. It had every hallmark of a no-win scenario through and through. I'll bet the AC and the attorney general are breathing a bloody great sigh of relief."

John reached across, crushing Tim's hand. "I'll second that. I just wish you'd arrived a day or two earlier. That way there wouldn't be so many plastic bags full of my doo-doos stacked in the utility room ceiling."

Tim automatically checked his hand, his face screwing up as a less-than-pleasant image flashed to mind.

John laughed. "Don't worry, mate. The room had a sink with soap and all the mod cons." He kept walking, chuckling to himself.

As they approached the committee room the door burst open and Jordan appeared, his grim expression not indicative of someone who had just captured the principal offender of an audacious siege. He gestured for the group to join him off to one side of the vestibule. In the distance they saw multiple ambulance officers carrying unconscious hostages on stretchers, heading towards the lifts.

"Jordan, what is it?" Tim's radar was working overtime, recognising the news wasn't positive.

The army officer began by addressing Ballard and John, acknowledging his relief they were now safe. "Our Russian friend inside has his thumb on a trigger mechanism he *claims* he'll press to set off the rig if we make any move to arrest him. The device looks real enough to me, so Tim, we haven't any choice but to believe him."

Ballard thought back to his discussion with Vladimir Bokaryov, the corrupt billionaire businessman who had financed the Note Printing Australia robbery. He had declared after he was captured that Sergey would never allow himself to be arrested and would choose to die rather than spend his remaining days in a prison cell. "You'd better believe it Jordan. So, what *does* Sergey want?"

Jordan's gaze slid uncharacteristically from Ballard's, unleashing a jolt of unease within the detective. John also registered more bad news was about to be revealed.

"All right Jordan, spit it out." Ballard figured it was time to face the music.

The army officer blurted, "Sergey told me that when he gives the word a chopper will land alongside the rig to pick him up. He then said if *any* attempt is made to stop or track him over the next three hours he'll blow the truck."

"But he'll be out of range by then." John was confused.

Jordan shook his head. "Not so simple John. Detonators can be activated by remote phone calls."

John persisted, "Well, can't the bomb squad disarm the damn thing?"

A shake of Jordan's head followed. "Again not that simple. Sergey maintains he's got someone watching it. By my reckoning, he must have a spotter on one of the high-rise buildings . . ."

"*The bastard!*" John's agitation was exacerbated by days of accumulated exhaustion.

"I agree. In fact Sergey said if *anyone* tries to disarm the charges, drain the tanks, or drive the rig away in the next three hours it'll be blown."

"He's bluffing . . . surely." John's last word was a mere whisper.

Jordan's next revelation disputed John's assertion. "That much explosive would be catastrophic. We simply can't take the risk." He turned to Tim. "How much longer to evacuate the hostages?"

Tim was uncharacteristically hesitant. "I can't see it finishing for at least another hour. Because of the rig we need to take the long route to afford some protection should the damn thing go up. Let's face it—we can't ask the ambos to risk their lives any more than they currently are . . . No, we *have* to keep evacuating via the lifts."

Jordan ran his hands over his face before making a stunning announcement, leaving everyone speechless.

"Sergey then demanded there be a hostage in the chopper . . . as additional insurance."

John exploded, his eyes popping. *"That's just bullshit!"*

Jordan's mouth formed a tight line as he stared at Ballard, again dropping his gaze.

Ballard decided to ease his disquiet. "He's demanding *I* be the hostage . . . am I right?"

The army officer nodded, not trusting his voice.

"*Crap!* The shithead can go and goddamn well jump. It's not going to happen." John grabbed Ballard's arm. "Mate, *surely* you're not contemplating agreeing to this!" He broke off, appearing thunderstruck as he took note of Ballard's expression.

In a lame effort to recycle his partner's favourite joke, Ballard quipped, "John, if I've told you once I've told you a hundred times— stop calling me Shirley." John didn't come close to laughing.

Ballard continued, "This is payback for what he perceives is my cocking up his chance of ripping a second billion out of the federal government. Believe me gentlemen, if there was any other way to resolve this I'd take it. This guy's ruthless but he's also a professional. This is all about giving himself additional insurance we won't blow the chopper out of the sky once he's airborne."

"So, you think he's just going to fly you somewhere, pat you on the head, then disappear into the sunset? Jesus Mike, this is Sergey we're talking about." John's voice rose in frustration. He addressed Jordan, desperate. "What if we call this prick's bluff?"

"John, if I know *anything* about human nature I'd bet my life he'll do just that—blow the rig."

"The trouble is it's not *your* life you're betting." John spat the words then instantly regretted them. "Jordan I'm sorry . . . I didn't mean that."

The army officer planted a forgiving hand on John's shoulder. "It's okay. I'd say the same thing if it was *my* partner being asked to risk his life."

"What if we threaten Sergey as we did Vladimir? That if he doesn't release Mike we make it public he told us everything he knows about the Russian group The Board. It worked with Vladimir, well sort of . . ." John's voice trailed away. "What am I saying? Sergey wouldn't give a stuff, and come to think of it, his knowledge of The Board's inner workings is sure to be less than Vladimir's."

Each of them mulled over the conundrum. Confronting them was a professional team of elite Russian criminals with links to the Kremlin who operated throughout the world, pulling off daring capers netting them a fortune. The siege on Parliament House was a mere blip on the horizon compared to some of their escapades.

Ballard decided it was time to act. "Guys, let's get in there and sound this bastard out." While he did his best to appear positive, the acrid taste of fear was overwhelming. He struggled to control it, knowing dozens of lives depended on him, but his trepidation for how this news would impact his wife Natalie threatened to rob him of the courage he so fervently searched for.

CHAPTER
2

As the four men were about to head into the committee room, Jordan pulled on Ballard's arm. "We can't wire you up or give you a firearm, and I don't have any trackers on me, but we're not letting you go without *some* protection." Reaching down to a scabbard strapped to his thigh he produced what appeared to be a black plastic handle, nestling it in the open palm of his hand. With the flick of his thumb a nine-centimetre dagger sprang into view, the action almost instant. The reverse flick retracted the blade equally as fast.

John gaped. "Jesus, let's hope there aren't too many of those on the street."

Jordan handed it to Ballard who weighed it in his hand. "Hmm, small enough to hide. Even if I'm frisked it's unlikely it'll be found." He bent down, concealing the knife in the side of his shoe. Straitening up he quipped, "Cyanide tablets?"

John exploded. "*Goddam it Mike.* Stop your bullshitting. This is bloody serious!"

Ballard attempted to reassure him. "John, I'm going for a short jaunt in a chopper. I'll be back in time for a shower then breakfast at Nat's." John's expression was pure anguish, words failing him as he imagined having to face Natalie should anything happen to his partner.

"Okay, let's do this." Ballard led the way into the committee room.

Sergey held sway at the head of the table, calm, almost relaxed, as though he had just ordered an expensive meal at a top restaurant.

His eyes were bloodshot, and he had a three-day stubble, but for all intents and purposes he was as sharp and alert as he would have been at the onset of the siege. Near his right hand was a slim silver cylinder with a single flashing green LED, his confidence such he wasn't bothering to hold it. The device appeared authentic.

A mobile rested on the table alongside his semi-automatic, both just outside the Russian's immediate reach. To his rear three of Jordan's team stood guard, their rifles levelled. Sergey ignored them; to him they didn't exist. Taking a chair each the three police officers and Jordan settled, choosing not to address the Russian.

Sergey smiled cruelly. "Ah Mr Ballard, we meet again. You and your colleagues have caused me a great deal of trouble, not to mention deprived me of a *lot* of money." While his accent was heavy, his English was near perfect, almost Oxford educated in its delivery. Here was a highly trained soldier who possessed nerves of steel and operated ice-cold under pressure. Panic didn't occupy his psyche.

Ballard remained silent, struggling to calm his heart rate, registering that despite the countless pressures the Russian had been subjected to, along with the complex coordination the siege would have demanded, the man still had the presence of mind to remember his name.

"As you'll know, the rig parked outside has enough explosive capacity to decimate your Parliament House and most of the surrounding buildings. Over forty thousand litres of ammonium nitrate and fuel oil, which I arranged to be premixed. Many people will die, including myself should you choose to arrest me."

"As I explained to the army officer"—he waved a dismissive hand towards Jordan—"in the next fifteen minutes a Eurocopter will land alongside the rig. I'm imposing a three-hour embargo on being tracked during that time." He locked eyes on Ballard. "You will also be aware I've asked for this fine detective to accompany me. Now if he refuses, any one of you gentlemen may step forward in his place."

Ballard sensed John stirring and instantly struck a backhanded blow against his partner's shoulder. "It's already been decided. *I'll* be going for the ride."

John wasn't to be silenced. Glaring with futile hatred at Sergey, he snarled, "If you so much as lay a finger on this guy, I promise you I'll hunt you down *wherever* you are. You can be certain of that you shithead." The intensity in his voice was staggering.

Sergey appraised him before returning with a cold rebuff. "I'd have assumed you'd be hunting me down no matter *what*."

John was equally combative. "Oh there's a difference. Harm this guy and I'll put a bullet in your brain and stuff the legal consequences."

Sergey maintained his indifferent scrutiny, sensing the man before him had played more than a minor role in placing him in his current predicament. "I've no doubt you may well try to do that." He spoke with the fatalism of a career soldier.

Tim stared at Ballard then Sergey, troubled, desperate for clarification. "After you're picked up, along with the Detective Inspector, how do we know you won't execute him the first opportunity you get?"

"You *don't*. But think about it. I'm a soldier. I kill people to achieve a professional end. Murdering this man is of no advantage to me. In fact, it would only intensify your efforts to hunt me down. He won't be harmed. My sole purpose of taking him with me is to prevent you from blowing me out of the sky." No one believed the Russian, least of all Ballard, the image of him executing his own without hesitation still a graphic memory.

Sergey continued, "Before he steps into the chopper he'll be searched, blindfolded, then cuffed."

John stirred, but Sergey dismissed the objection forming. "This is not open for discussion. After all, we wouldn't want your man falling out in mid flight, would we?" The chill in his voice was like ice cubes fracturing after being splashed with gin and tonic. "I stress again—no one is to disarm the vehicle, drain the fuel, or drive it away in the three-hour period. It's under constant surveillance with orders to blow it if *any* of these demands aren't met. At the three-hour mark I'll make a call to your superintendent." He waved a dismissive hand towards Peter, having taken his mobile number at an earlier encounter. "At that point I'll provide the disarm code for the charges. Are we clear?"

The sustained and piercing glare from the four men was confirmation enough for the Russian.

Stretching forward, Sergey took up his mobile and weapon. "It's time." He speed-dialled a number and pressed the phone to his ear, appraising his audience as he did so. Making contact he spoke in Russian, barking what appeared to be a string of orders. Satisfied he dropped the mobile into a breast pocket. Snatching the electronic trigger he looped its cord over his wrist before standing abruptly, ignoring Jordan's men behind him.

The soldiers appeared uncertain as they glanced towards their commander. Jordan shook his head, indicating they weren't to intervene other than follow as everyone exited the room. Crossing the vestibule, Ballard felt his chest tighten. He forced a smile at John who was beside him.

His partner licked dry lips before blurting, "Mike I almost believe this guy, that all he wants is security while he's in the air."

Ballard chose not to share his opposing view. "John, *not a word of this to Natalie.* Call her and tell her I'm held up at work. As soon as I'm released I'll get to a phone. Christ knows when and where that'll be, but I *will* call her."

John attempted an encouraging smile, but it was too weak to inspire. "Perhaps you could drop *me* a line as well old son. That way I can jump in a car and come and pick you up." Despite the less-than-subtle sarcasm, the words were heartfelt, punctuated by the deepest of emotional pain.

Ballard addressed his partner. "John, we've spoken about this before, when Parnell was holding my sister hostage, remember? Should anything happen to me you know what to do for Nat and the kids. Bradley has a copy of my will so he's up to speed on that score."

Breaking stride John growled, "If my memory serves me correctly my reply to you during the kidnapping was 'Piss off and do what you have to do' or something along those lines. Well, it's ditto all over again."

Ballard laughed, a genuine throaty chuckle causing Sergey to glance in his direction, his expression curious, bordering on mystified.

Ballard quipped, "Such encouragement John. To what do I owe these words of comfort?"

John thought about a reply but choked, unable to voice his emotions. Instead he tightened his grip on Ballard's forearm, his touch spanning three decades of comradeship, the gesture tapping into mutual respect that knew no boundaries.

Emerging onto the head of Parliament House steps, Ballard gazed down Bourke Street, the street lights reminding him of the late hour. He momentarily reflected on his days as a constable on duty at the exact location. What confronted him now was the stationary rig on the lower landing, its sheer enormity and the multiple packs of C4 strapped under the dual tanks highlighting its massive destructive potential.

Without warning a helicopter swooped in low, hovering, positioning itself in front of the rig. The manoeuvre was an impressive display of pilot skill due to the surrounding obstacles, not least of which were the ornate lamps. Several of them shattered from the explosion that killed the politician, a cold-blooded, deliberate execution by Sergey. The scream of jet engines reminded Ballard of PolAir, the sound piercing, shrill. Dust billowed into the night sky, gradually diminishing as the rotor blades swept the surrounding steps clean. The driver in the rig leapt out, approached the chopper and stood beside it, almost to attention.

Sergey descended the steps like a conquering hero, his actions in sharp contrast to the reality that he was a merciless terrorist who killed indiscriminately and had been comprehensively thwarted from extracting a second billion dollars from the government. Reaching the chopper he wrenched open the door opposite the pilot who occupied the right-hand seat. Ever aggressive, Sergey shouted a stream of Russian. Although hesitant, the pilot appeared to understand. Sergey motioned to the rig driver who scrambled aboard behind the pilot, settling in the second row of seats, facing forward, buckling into his full harness.

Spinning around, Sergey gestured to Ballard and skilfully patted him down, looking for anything obvious—a mobile, knives, concealed firearms, or similar. Proving his professionalism he checked Ballard's lower legs for ankle holsters. Collectively his audience held their breath, relieved when he straightened up empty-handed. Next he produced a grey hood with drawstrings. As he went to place it over Ballard's head, clutching it two-handed so it wouldn't be whipped away by the savage downdraft John stepped forward and snarled, *"Not so fast, shithead!"* His words had to be shouted to be heard above the shriek of the jet engines.

Sergey's eyes narrowed as he contemplated his next move. In a conciliatory gesture he stepped back to allow everyone to shake Ballard's hand. Each man solemn, bereft of words, desperate not to imply this would be a one-way flight.

Ballard thanked them all. Turning to Sergey, he allowed him to place the hood over his head. The darkness was total. He felt the cords tighten uncomfortably under his chin. Then his arm was taken, the grip powerful, forcing him into the chopper. His lack of vision was disorienting to his senses. Next a snap of cold steel encircled his left wrist, followed by an accompanying click as the duplicate cuff was secured to an anchor point within the chopper, his restrained arm suspended at chest height. To his surprise his seat harness was secured around him but no effort was made to tighten the straps. He sensed the rig driver alongside him.

The door slammed shut, muffling the jet engines. The pitch of the twin motors intensified as the pilot applied full power. Ballard felt the chopper climb savagely, the sensation akin to an express lift. Turning his head to the left, despite the hood, he visualised the illuminated cityscape dropping beneath him as rapidly as his plummeting hopes of ever holding Natalie in his arms again. Eyes clenched shut he fought to block out the mental image, utter despair engulfing him, blunting his spirit as a shiver of dread coursed through his every fibre.

As the chopper banked hard to the right, a single question bombarded his consciousness again and again: *Will I ever find my way back?*

CHAPTER

3

Ballard fought the mounting panic threatening to overwhelm him as the helicopter levelled off at its cruising altitude. The hood's fabric over his mouth was suffocating, pulsing with every ragged breath which he fought to normalise. He sensed they were travelling in a north-westerly direction. This meant they were heading away from what would be line of sight of Natalie's town house in South Yarra, passing over the Docklands NewQuay marina where his motor cruiser was moored. And if he was correct, they were now proceeding in the general direction of his ranch-style home in Gisborne. He acknowledged his fragmented thoughts were linked to known confidences in his life, a reflex defence mechanism, his awareness of the reality an emotional comfort he welcomed as he assessed his calamitous situation.

Every second in the air increased the physical distance between himself and his loved ones and his desperate longing for them: Natalie his wife; her four children; his younger sister Kathryn; Bradley his son; and Laura his daughter. He imagined the aggravation John and Peter would be experiencing, helpless as to what they could do save for informing his superintendent, Delwyn Peters, of the perilous situation he now faced. John would be railing against the circumstances while Peter worked through various contingencies.

Reaching up with his right hand he eased two fingers under the hood's cord. Drawing outward he released some of the pressure from his neck, praying his action wouldn't result in repercussions from either the rig driver sitting beside him or Sergey directly in front.

He assumed they were flying without cabin lighting to ensure the chopper was less conspicuous.

He continued to assess his options and refused to accept they were minimal at best. Drawing on his extensive training he began analysing his circumstances, thrusting to the background the dark apprehension welling inside him. As Sergey had admitted in the committee room, he was a professional soldier who killed to achieve an objective. Wracking his brain, Ballard couldn't think of a single reason why the Russian would feel the need to harm him or what he might gain from doing so. Attacking those thoughts was the knowledge the terrorist had executed his own men for nothing more than opportunistic expediency.

Again Ballard wrestled to supress the black cloud of hopelessness engulfing him, numbing his mind to the point where his rationalisations lacked logic. It was known at multiple levels within the police force and government that Sergey was the siege ringleader, so he would be mindful of the additional lengths authorities would go to in their attempts to arrest him were he to kill one of their own.

Determined to rid himself of all thoughts associated with personal harm, Ballard concluded it was mere pragmatism for Sergey to take precautions and hence secure a hostage, backing it up with the threat of exploding the tanker. These actions were a clear example of the Russian's prodigious ability to adapt, to survive.

Ballard agonised over the undeniable certainty Sergey wouldn't keep his promise to contact Peter with the disarm codes should he effect an escape within the three-hour period; the potential for countless deaths and immense destruction in the Spring Street surrounds gnawed at his conscience, raising even more doubts regarding the best course of action to adopt.

Reasoning that the evacuation of Parliament House would be complete by now and the widening of the public exclusion zone for nearby pubs, hotels, and office buildings an easier task due to the late hour, Ballard concluded that if any form of freedom presented itself, however slim, he would seize it. He backed his decision with the knowledge that the department would be making every effort to determine which high-rise building the observer was viewing the rig from, almost certainly deploying surveillance drones at an elevated height to reduce the chance of them being detected while they conducted the search.

Racking his brain, Ballard assessed his chances. He recognised that having one arm chained to the chopper while sightless and having the driver of the rig beside him, slim build though he was—all these impediments posed collective obstacles that on the face of it were insurmountable.

Wriggling his toes in his right shoe he felt the comforting shape of the knife Jordan had passed to him, reassuring himself that despite his left arm being secured he could reach the weapon at any time with his free hand. Even without headphones the noise inside the Eurocopter was low level due to its extensive soundproofing throughout—a situation he and John had experienced when they were in Malcolm Ferguson's identical helicopter, the city property developer unwittingly drawn into Vladimir's web. Ballard conceded that even if he could rid himself of his hood he wouldn't be able to subdue the driver alongside him before Sergey reacted, either by knocking him out or by shooting him.

For the next thirty minutes the drone of the twin turbines was almost hypnotic were it not for Ballard's mind racing with conflicting scenarios. He sensed the driver beside him shift forward, speaking for the first time. The conversation was indistinct but the general essence was clear.

"So . . . money will be . . . when we land?"

Sergey's tone and the intensity of his reply was naked anger.

The driver hesitated then shouted back, "*Bullshit!* If it wasn't for . . . be stranded in . . . I want my share!"

Ballard knew his moment had arrived. While the argument raged beside him he reached down with his right hand and extracted the knife. Concealing it in his palm, he prayed his actions weren't being observed by the two feuding men, hoping upon hope the cabin lights were indeed off. Moving his hand to the left side of his face he pretended to scratch an itch through the hood. At the same time he pressed the button to release the blade, sliding it under the cord, slicing through with surprising ease. Leaving the hood in place he retracted the blade and was about to slip the knife back into his shoe when a shot rang out near his head, the sound shocking in its intensity, deafening him on his right side.

Ears ringing he realised Sergey had eliminated what to him was a mere annoyance—namely the rig driver. Thinking he might well be next he snatched the hood from his head while pressing the button on the knife. In a blur of motion he stabbed the blade into Sergey's right forearm which was within reach. The Russian was still aiming his gun at the rig driver who was slumped sideways in his seat, head lolling, his headset awry, blood spreading across his chest.

So great was the force Ballard exerted the blade sank to the hilt. Sergey howled in pain, the weapon dropping from his paralysed fingers, landing near Ballard's feet. Withdrawing the blade produced an equally loud bellow. Scrabbling, Ballard snatched up the semi-automatic and held the hot muzzle against the side of the Russian's shaved temple, having dislodged the man's headset with the barrel. "One move you prick and I'll blow your goddam brains out." The pilot twisted sideways, eyes bulging, desperate for Sergey to provide some form of direction.

Grimacing, Sergey hissed, "You won't kill me. You don't have the balls."

Ballard needed a psychological edge, and quickly. Aiming in front of him he fired a round through the windscreen, unleashing a numbing cold jet of air into the cabin, the glow from the instrument panel the only source of light. The noise from the shot was horrendous. The pilot ducked in shock, causing the chopper to buck violently; even Sergey recoiled to one side. Ballard took a risk and stretching his handcuffs to their limit, fired three shots into the links before achieving their separation, the bullets passing through the chopper's fuselage. Again the noise of the shots in the confined space was thunderous, the smell of cordite sickly sweet. Although his left wrist was still shackled with the cuff, Ballard's hand was free to flick the release on his harness, allowing him to reach further over the seat in front, encircling Sergey's throat in the crook of his arm. Blood dripped from the Russian's wounds onto the centre console.

With his right hand Ballard smashed the butt of the Glock hard against Sergey's head. Reaching around he placed the barrel against the fleshy part of the Russian's thigh, pulling the trigger. Sergey arched back in agony, sucking through clenched teeth as he pressed the palm of his uninjured left hand against the wound.

Ballard struck him again on the side of the head with the Glock, stunned at the man's capacity to absorb what must be excruciating pain. "That's just for starters." The words were hissed in the Russian's ear.

Sergey attempted to twist around but was pinned in his seat by the headlock. He snarled, "*I will kill you. I will kill your family . . . one by one.*" The venom in his voice despite the restriction on his throat was alarming, spittle running down Ballard's forearm.

His heart sinking, Ballard realised the threat was genuine and in his desperate struggle to survive he had unintentionally imposed a death sentence on each of his loved ones.

CHAPTER
4

Glancing out the window, Ballard saw the lights of a small town passing beneath them. Peering harder he could see a mountain range in the distance. Estimating their direction, flight time, and speed, he guessed they were near the Grampians but couldn't be sure. Not being able to look at his watch for fear of releasing his grip on Sergey, who for the moment had ceased struggling, he estimated the time to be between 1 and 2 a.m.

His mind went into overdrive. He knew he had to force the chopper down or face flying into unknown danger where more of Sergey's team would be waiting when they landed, outnumbering him, a certain death sentence. He reached across and ripped off the pilot's headset before striking him on the side of the head with the Glock to gain his undivided attention. "Land the chopper." Crying out in pain the pilot rubbed his left ear as he looked to Sergey for direction. Ballard struck the man a second time, harder, drawing another howl of agony. "Don't look at him. *Land the chopper. Now!*" Once more the pilot deferred to Sergey.

Aiming the Glock at the controls in front of the Russian, Ballard prayed shooting out the circuitry on that side wouldn't result in a crash. He pumped two rounds into the instrument panel only to have the pilot scream at him in English, "*Stop it*! If I lose control we *all* die."

Ballard maintained his chokehold on Sergey as he roared at the pilot, "*You've got three seconds to bring this thing down or I'll shoot you in the leg just as I did your boss.*"

Through gritted teeth, while still compressing his wound, Sergey spat a statement in Russian. The pilot nodded and kept flying, but not before casting panicked glances Ballard's way.

With every second drawing him closer to Sergey's flight destination, and what would undoubtedly be a grizzly fate, Ballard knew he had to act fast. Aiming at the pilot's leg he squeezed off a round but the man swivelled at the last moment, the bullet missing, piercing the floor instead. Desperate, Ballard fired a second round into the controls, praying they wouldn't drop out of the sky but aware crashing the chopper was a safer gamble than landing at Sergey's chosen destination. They kept flying.

Ballard aimed at the pilot's head, hissing, *"Land this thing. Now!"*

The chopper began to nosedive as the pilot complied, uttering a string of Russian. Ballard assumed the words weren't complementary and may even be a prayer. Sergey reacted, struggling to free himself. Applying every ounce of strength to contain him, Ballard managed to maintain his headlock.

Still fighting, Sergey barked an order towards the pilot, his voice distorted by the choke hold. Ballard guessed it was a demand to maintain their altitude. Determined to remove any doubt in the pilot's mind Ballard fired another shot near the man's ear then pointed the barrel at the man's thigh. The barrage of Russian continued from Sergey but the pilot chose immediate self-preservation over what might happen to him at a later time.

Ballard counted the shots he had fired and arrived at ten, alarmed that in his haste to assert his authority he had been too trigger-happy. The weapon was a Glock 17 and he prayed Sergey was using a seventeen-round mag. Thinking back to the shots the Russian had fired to execute the hostages and his own team, Ballard counted at least five. Those plus the ten he had fired meant the semi-automatic was near empty. His heart sank. He wondered if Sergey had conducted his own maths, coming to the same conclusion; if so why wasn't he struggling more? While his wounds would have laid the average man flat on his back, this was Sergey, with the ominous threat of The Board hanging over him as an additional incentive.

Ballard concluded without conviction that the Russian might well have reloaded the magazine at some point. If so, it was possible there were still four or more rounds at his disposal. Knowing he couldn't take the risk to attempt another shot for fear the weapon's slide remained open, demonstrating an empty magazine, he decided to rely on what must be doubt in Sergey's mind, hoping upon hope luck was on his side.

Glancing at the semi-automatic again he was grateful it had a Streamlight laser flashlight attached under the barrel. The torch would be invaluable when they landed, preventing him from stumbling about in the dark, the quarter moon providing scant assistance. He checked the position of the toggle switch for the three-option laser light combination, remembering reading at some point that the battery life was approximately one and a half hours but much longer if the light wasn't used constantly.

Without warning the chopper began to climb. Ballard cursed, assuming the pilot had concluded Sergey was a much nastier adversary after all. He felt the Russian struggling again, almost as though boasting he had total control over the pilot.

Wracked with indecision whether to squeeze off another round, Ballard tightened his grip on the Russian's throat as he wedged the Glock between his seat and his buttock. Taking Jordan's knife which he had dropped on the floor, he exposed the blade, stabbing it into the pilot's thigh, striking bone. A blood curdling scream was followed by a stream of Russian, the man howling in agony as Ballard twisted the blade without remorse. "Land this bloody thing or by Christ I'll slit your goddam throat!" He was alert to the fact that to avoid a crash the pilot needed to use both feet to operate the tail rotor pedals, essential for maintaining the chopper's direction, especially significant during a night-time landing. His latest assault on the pilot made that task more difficult.

Eyes protruding and sweating profusely, the pilot didn't bother to address Sergey. Instead he pushed the chopper's collective down with his left hand, wiping off altitude like a free-falling stone. Fearing the man was about to pass out, Ballard chose to leave the knife embedded until they were nearer the ground.

Peering out the window he saw trees rushing up at him. "Ease up. Ease up!"

The pilot nodded, almost to himself; he was ashen-faced, sweat soaking his collar. He halted the descent then flicking on the search light, hunted for a spot to land. He chose a clearing which appeared out of the blackness off to the right. Sergey renewed his struggle, causing Ballard to make a snap decision. Dragging the knife from the pilot's leg which produced another shriek of pain, Ballard plunged the blade into the thick trapezius muscle covering Sergey's shoulder, then withdrew it, twisting the handle as he did so.

Once again the Russian arched back, shuddering. Through gritted teeth he hissed, "Like I said . . . you don't have the balls."

Ballard's emotions exploded, fear for his loved ones and his own safety swamped his reasoning. Shaking with uncontrollable rage he came to the shocking conclusion he was more than capable of slitting the Russian's throat without giving it a second thought. From somewhere deep within his collective upbringing and years of training he fought to drag his fragmented conscience to the surface, smothering the rampant primeval instincts threatening to overwhelm him.

Unexpectedly the pilot slumped forward, held only by his harness, appearing to have passed out from delayed shock. Ballard wondered if it was from the stab wound to his thigh or because he had struck the man a series of violent blows to the temple with the butt of the Glock. Glancing out the window he estimated they were less than fifty metres off the ground, the chopper spiralling as it pitched forward.

Ballard noted with alarm that the pilot still had hold of the collective and in his near-unconscious state the weight of his arm was pushing the lever down, causing the chopper to lose altitude fast. Sergey saw what was happening and demanded to be freed. "I'm a pilot!" He scrambled to reach his own collective but Ballard tightened his grip around the Russian's throat, forcing him back in his seat. It was clear Sergey saw taking control of the chopper as an opportunity to arrest the unchecked descent then continue flying to his original destination, the threat of the chopper crashing affording him the upper hand.

Reaching around Ballard flicked the release on the Russian's harness, deciding to allow the chopper to nosedive into the ground rather than let Sergey take over. He figured the impact would sling the man forward onto the instruments and would hopefully knock him out or at the very least, injure him to the point where he couldn't put up a fight. The bullet in his thigh and the knife wounds to his forearm and shoulder contributing to that outcome.

Using the back of Sergey's seat as a brace, Ballard looked out the window at the ground rushing up at a sickening rate as they rotated towards it. He knew he would have to release his vice-like grip on the Russian's throat just before impact, hoping to survive the crash himself so he could escape should Sergey not be knocked out.

With the pilot unconscious and Sergey continuing to struggle to reach the collective, the multiple warning lights and audible alarms signifying a pending crash meant the last seconds of the descent were chaotic. The impact when it came was brutal, far more severe than Ballard could have imagined.

Initially the rotor blades sliced through the light foliage of several gum trees before carving into small limbs, finally embedding in a solid trunk, lurching the chopper's cabin hard to one side. Dropping straight down it crashed with jarring force onto the ground. The noise horrific as the cabin folded in around them. Sergey's effort to brace with both hands was to no avail, the force of the crash hurling him into the front screen. In turn, despite Ballard wrapping his arms around the seat with all his strength, the angle of the impact was so steep he pitched over the top, crashing hard onto Sergey who lay motionless, clearly stunned. For an instant Ballard thought his left arm was broken, but after moving it and flexing his hand several times he concluded it was only bruised muscle.

Least scathed was the pilot strapped in his seat, his head lolling on his shoulders, his tongue protruding from a lax jaw. Ballard managed to crawl off Sergey who remained slumped over the instruments, his shuddered breathing signifying he was still alive but far from the all-powerful soldier he had proven to be moments before. Ballard was desperate to find anything that would bind the Russian's hands, but frustration swamped him as he concluded there was nothing in the cabin that would be strong enough; even the cord from his hood was of no use, the previous knife cut having reduced it to two short lengths.

Searching for the Glock he discovered it lying under Sergey's seat. He thrust it in his waistband then returned Jordan's knife to its original hiding spot in his shoe. Smelling aviation fuel he set about determining the best means of exiting the wreckage but not before attempting to locate Sergey's mobile. After precious seconds he gave up, frustrated that it wasn't in any obvious pockets, including the breast pocket where he had last seen it.

Relieving the Russian of his black-handled army knife strapped to his thigh, Ballard lay on his back as he kicked at the cockpit door on the left side. Smashing the heel of his shoe repeatedly above the handle he managed to force the door open. Reaching across he released the pilot's harness and drawing on every ounce of strength, hauled the man across the cabin and out the door, slumping the body onto the ground, grateful of his slim build.

With the smell of aviation fuel increasing by the second, Ballard dragged the pilot thirty metres across open ground before collapsing, his heart pounding, sweat soaking his shirt. Rolling the man over, Ballard went through his pockets and almost cried out in joy when he discovered the prize he was seeking, a mobile phone. Checking for a signal he was rewarded with three bars. Next he took out his Glock and released the magazine; with a sinking heart he discovered he had one round left. He double-checked, willing there to be more.

After glancing at the quarter moon and the deep shadows formed by the surrounding trees and shrubs, Ballard took note of the pilot's boots and their thick laces, astounded at his own stupidity for not thinking of using Sergey's to bind his hands and feet. Pouncing, he quickly untied the laces, extracting the man's belt for good measure.

Leaving him lying in the coma position, Ballard retraced his steps to the chopper, Glock at the ready, aware that should he need to use it he couldn't afford to miss. Approaching as silently as the dry underbrush would allow he sidled up to the cockpit, realising the risk he was taking, the pungent smell of spilt fuel now stronger than ever.

Pointing the Glock into the cabin he flicked on the flashlight. The hair on the back of his neck prickled as he came to the gut-wrenching realisation the chopper was empty. Resisting the urge to glance over his shoulder, his skin crawling, he switched off the light, cursing inwardly that his night vision was now impaired.

Moving fast he retreated from the helicopter which less than a minute later erupted in a ball of flame, aviation fuel ignited by the hot metal. The light from the flames reached into the night sky, clawing at the inky darkness. Birds in nearby trees scattered in all directions, their wings beating the air in their panic to escape. The gum tree the chopper blade had sliced into exploded in a eucalyptus-fuelled fireball, showering sparks skyward, lighting up the undergrowth but thankfully not spreading beyond the immediate area which was almost bare from what appeared to be a previous grass fire. The light from the crackling flames failed to reveal Sergey's whereabouts, and despite the random eruptions of combusting fuel fanned by the slight breeze, the area soon returned to semi-darkness other than for the smouldering trunk and wreckage.

Ballard forced himself to be disciplined, aware that in his stressed state and with the threat of the Russian potentially behind every tree or bush, he needed to resist the overwhelming impulse to squeeze off the last round were he to be spooked by a startled bird or animal. Sergey's right arm might well be incapacitated and his right leg less than 100 per cent, but Ballard was cognisant that even in Sergey's reduced physical state the soldier possessed the elite skills to overpower him. Sergey had been trained to adapt, and Ballard knew the Russian would have armed himself with a stick to stab him in the neck or eye or perhaps a rock to club him over the head, the man equally comfortable using his left and right hand. Night combat would be as natural to him as daylight fighting, with the required skills drilled into him to the degree he would be accomplished operating in either state. Perhaps more so in the dark due to the element of surprise it offered.

In turn, Ballard reasoned that if he missed with the Glock or lost his two knives in close-quarter combat, with his left wrist still encircled by the handcuff he might be able to rake the cuff and its remaining links across the Russian's face, but he acknowledged his chance of surviving any form of one-on-one struggle to be near zero.

He forced his thoughts to more specific issues, prioritising them, acutely aware his next decisions could well mean the difference between life and death. His immediate task was finding a location which would afford him a degree of security, one where he couldn't be approached from all sides. Then he had to determine his current latitude and longitude using the pilot's iPhone, assuming he could activate the device, praying it didn't have a security lock.

Checking the position of the moon he waited until a series of clouds scudded past then made his move to a more secluded area. Crouching low he ran, tense, each shadow a Russian killer about to pounce. He spotted an outcrop of rock shaped in a rough semicircle which had an escape route over the top. Flattening his back against the jagged confine, breathing hard but desperate to be as silent as possible, he peered into the darkness, hoping he had traversed the open ground without being spotted, alert for any movement within the shadows.

Taking the mobile he drew across the screen and was dismayed at the immediate request for a digital scan. His mind raced. He knew he had no alternative but to retrace his steps to the pilot and hope he could pick the correct finger before five false attempts locked the phone, demanding a password. The mobile's battery level indicated 50 per cent, enough for his immediate needs. He kept the screen low, ensuring its illumination couldn't be seen, waiting several seconds for his eyes to adjust to the blackness surrounding him.

He sucked in a lungful of air then stooping to minimise his silhouette against the skyline, moved with stealth back to where the pilot lay, Glock at the ready. A wallaby broke from the bushes, bounding away, unaware how close it had come to being shot; as if to punctuate Ballard's pounding heart, two owls hooted in the distance, normally a comforting sound but under the circumstances a potent omen.

Reaching the still-inert body, he saw the pilot was now lying on his back. Taking the man's hand he identified a limpness that registered far more than mere unconsciousness; he was dead. Peering closer he felt his skin crawl as he touched sticky dampness on the man's forehead, discovering the front of his skull crushed. This meant one thing, Sergey was hell-bent on continuing his ruthless rampage, ensuring there were no loose ends.

Spinning on his heels, senses screaming, Ballard expected the Russian to appear from nowhere, rock in hand, raised to smash his skull with one mighty blow. Mercifully nothing but darkness surrounded him on all sides.

Drawing ragged breaths he knew he had to press on, desperate to unlock the phone as it was his only means of rescue. Steeling himself to concentrate on his immediate task he took the pilot's hand and pressed the man's thumb onto the screen. To his distress the scan was rejected. Taking the forefinger he tried again. Once more the scan was disallowed. Ballard's anxiety deepened as he knew he had just three more attempts before the phone locked.

Tensing, he placed the pilot's middle finger on the screen and almost collapsed with relief when the scan was accepted, the mobile's functions coming online. More rustling in nearby bushes had him frozen on the spot, yet again an unknown animal was heard scuttling into the undergrowth. The moon appeared from behind clouds and despite its infancy, shone like the headlights of a car. Ballard retreated to deeper shadows and with shaking hands, dialled John's number, praying there was adequate signal strength to make the call.

John's voice was hesitant, Ballard aware the caller ID would be displaying an unknown number.

"Henderson."

Experiencing a wave of emotion, Ballard felt his legs buckle. In a hoarse whisper he declared, "John, it's me!"

There was total disbelief in his partner's reply. "*Mate!* Is it *really* you? I . . . I . . ." He broke off, choked for words, before demanding, "Are you okay?" It was clear his professionalism had kicked in.

Ballard checked around him. "I'm fine John, but no time for details. I'm on the ground. The chopper crashed. The pilot and the rig driver are dead. Sergey's wounded but on the move. I've got two knives and a Glock with just one round in the clip."

His partner's expletive was copybook John.

Ballard pressed on while staring into the darkness, his eyes now fully adjusted. "I'm going to bring up my latitude and longitude . . . I think I'm somewhere in the Grampians. While I'm doing that get Tim and his boys to rustle up PolAir." He heard John barking orders while he opened the application to pinpoint his position, grateful Natalie's son Josh had taken him step-by-step through how this was achieved months prior. Tapping in the necessary commands he was staggered at the speed of the reply. "John write this down."

His partner's reply was instant. "Yes Mike, shoot."

Ballard winced at the image the innocent remark conjured. "Minus thirty-seven dot one-four-one-three-seven-two-six-eight-zero-seven latitude, one-forty-two dot five-one-eight-nine-five-one-four-one-six longitude."

John repeated the coordinates, passing them to a colleague with the demand for Tim and his rescue team to get a move on and that he was coming along for the ride. He came back. "Mike, we're on the way but at best we'll be over an hour, perhaps ninety minutes before we touch down. How will you let us know where you are?"

"The Glock I ripped off Sergey has a flashlight. When I hear you overhead I'll flash an SOS."

"You took the Glock *off* Sergey?" The incredulity in John's voice didn't call for an answer. "Mike, keep your head down, and if you have to pump your last round into the bastard, do it!" He paused before adding, "Mate I didn't think we'd be having this conversation. I . . ." He broke off once more.

Ballard felt his partner's emotion. "Just get the cavalry up here John. I'll do my best to stay out of Sergey's clutches and afterwards we can swap war stories. Again, say nothing to Nat. Have you been in touch?"

"Yep, she thinks you're still here, grinding away. Keep safe buddy."

Ballard disconnected, feeling his spirits nosedive the moment contact with his colleague ended. Their years of working together had formed an unbreakable bond akin to military personnel who shared combat action. He looked about him, wondering if Sergey was nearby, waiting for the right moment to strike. Conversely, was the Russian making distance due to his injured state, choosing a tactical retreat?

Ballard did his best to ignore the naked fear gripping him like a vice. Death dealt by Sergey would be slow and excruciating, and Ballard was aware that at the end he would beg to be put out of his misery. Forcing himself to overcome the wave of panic welling inside him he checked that his access to Sergey's knife was immediate. Grasping the Glock he promised himself he wouldn't go down without a fight, thoughts of Natalie and his children bracing him for what lay ahead.

Without warning two torchlights pierced the darkness, sweeping side to side, searching. Ballard crouched lower, positioning behind a bush. Was this Sergey's men coming to find him or innocent locals stumbling about in the undergrowth, keen to assist, having seen the chopper crash or perhaps observed the fire, limited though it was? The lights illuminated one of the visitors for a brief second, long enough for Ballard to recognise they were police officers.

Heart in mouth he rose to catch their attention but instantly froze. Approaching from the shadows was a single figure. The police torches swung and to Ballard's horror they confirmed it was Sergey, his right arm hanging awkwardly as he walked with a considerable limp.

The two officers lowered their beams as he approached, assuming he was injured from the crash. Despite Sergey's impaired state, Ballard feared for the officers' safety, knowing the Russian would be intent on securing their weapons.

His mind in overdrive, he evaluated his options before choosing the only one that would ensure both policemen drew their firearms. Aiming into the ground he fired his remaining round. The two officers dropped to a crouch, reaching for their weapons. But it was too late; like a lion Sergey pounced, chopping his left hand in a savage blow across the throat of the closest policeman. The torch slipped from the man's lifeless fingers as he lay motionless, the beam casting a ghostly arc across the ground.

Sergey lashed at the second officer with his foot, connecting with the man's shin. As the policeman doubled forward in agony Sergey shot out his left arm, connecting the heel of his hand with the bridge of the man's nose. The officer slumped to the ground and in one blur-filled motion Sergey ripped his weapon from his grasp then shot both men in the head. The entire action from Sergey pretending to be wounded to him firing the two fatal shots took less than fifteen seconds—elite training at its most lethal.

Ballard felt utter bleakness engulf his reasoning, overwhelming him as to what he should do next. The Russian crystallised his thoughts by sweeping his torch in the direction he had heard Ballard discharge his round, holding the light in his injured right hand. Ballard noted the police officer's weapon was in Sergey's left; without doubt the soldier equally accurate with either hand.

Every instinct Ballard possessed screamed for him to head in the opposite direction but he knew that was too obvious. Sergey would be expecting him to do that. Tucking the empty Glock in his belt he grasped the Russian's knife, more comfortable with its longer blade. Assessing his options he made the difficult decision to move laterally to his left before creeping forward, something he prayed Sergey wouldn't expect; with luck he would pass the Russian without him knowing, the latter continuing in the wrong direction.

His mouth dry and breathing shallow, Ballard crept sideways then ahead, utilising every available bush as cover. Reaching down he grabbed a handful of dirt which he rubbed over his sweating face and hands to minimise his skin's contrast with the surroundings. The ongoing sweep of Sergey's torch almost caught him. Ducking his head to hide his face he prayed his hair would blend into the background.

Feeling a stone underfoot he snatched it, hurling the rock in the direction he wanted Sergey to follow. The beam focussed where the stone landed then darted into the darkest shadows, seeking him out. Sergey called out, sending a chill down Ballard's spine, "I don't need to kill you. I just have to get away. Tell me you won't try to stop me." The beam from the torch remained static. Clearly the Russian was motionless, hunting for any sound which might reveal his quarry.

Ballard was stunned at how matter of fact Sergey appeared, as though all he was suggesting was a trip to the supermarket.

Holding his breath Ballard waited, hoping his foe would believe he wasn't within earshot and that the stone would draw him further in the opposite direction. Before either party could move the sound of an approaching helicopter drew Ballard's attention skyward. He calculated the elapsed time since his call to John and came up with thirty minutes, far too soon for this to be PolAir.

A sudden revelation had him amazed at his own stupidity. The severity of the chopper's crash would have triggered an emergency location transmitter, almost certainly one monitored by Sergey's support team. With a sinking heart Ballard knew it was more than an even chance the cavalry had arrived, but they were here to rescue the wrong team.

CHAPTER
5

The chopper circled, and it was clear the glow generated by the smouldering tree alongside the wreckage was the focal point. The pilot continued looking for a suitable landing site, the helicopter's searchlight cutting a swathe through the darkness. Ballard's mind flooded with opposing scenarios. Should he remain close by to see what unfolded which may assist in a subsequent arrest? Alternatively, was his prudent option to choose discretion, placing as much distance between himself and his foes as possible? Outgunned and outnumbered, he was aware dawn was less than an hour away, at which time concealment would be almost impossible in the sparse undergrowth.

With the chopper landed and the dust storm it created subsiding, Ballard spotted Sergey being embraced by two men who had jumped from the cabin. Furious discussion ensued with the men drawing their weapons. Taking Sergey's torch they made to head into the scrub.

Ballard's heart sank, knowing he couldn't outrun either man, both hell-bent on avenging Sergey's current situation and sustained wounds. Before they had gone ten steps Sergey held up a hand, calling out something which halted the men in their tracks. Reluctantly they returned to him. After another brief discussion they trekked back to the chopper, assisting the Russian into the cabin.

His heart rate subsiding, Ballard assumed Sergey must have reasoned it wouldn't be long before additional police and emergency services arrived, making escape without a gun battle impossible. Having murdered the pilot it was probable Sergey knew the man's mobile was missing and assumed it would be utilised by Ballard to contact a rescue team. He would also be mindful that trained SOG personnel were a much tougher obstacle to overcome than two police officers innocent of the fact the injured man approaching them had lethal intentions.

Within seconds, the cabin doors slammed shut, the chopper's twin motors increasing in intensity. Dust swirled in rolling clouds, and debris scattered as the machine rose into the night sky, its cabin and navigation lights switched off. Watching the helicopter rise, Ballard noted how the earlier canopy of stars overhead had diminished, heralding a fast-approaching dawn.

A sense of relief swept through him but was countered by his distress for the two slain policemen. He waited until the chopper disappeared over the horizon to the north-east then taking his Glock and switching on the flashlight, retraced his steps to where the officers lay.

Blood had soaked into the soil around their heads, making the test for a heartbeat mere professional formality. Searching about him he broke off clumps of grass, covering the officer's faces from the flies that would swarm at daybreak; in a vain attempt he kicked away the trails of ants already feasting on the pools of congealed blood. Staring down he recognised his efforts were inadequate but knew they were the best he could achieve under the circumstances, his jacket having been discarded earlier at Parliament House.

Shame filled him for not preventing the officers' deaths. A black cloud of grief threatened to engulf him as he struggled to come to terms with what he now felt was a futile firing of a warning shot. Deep down he knew Sergey's murderous intent was unstoppable, the distance between himself and where the executions took place too great to cover before the Russian was able to complete his lethal attack. Despite this, Ballard's mind was numb with culpability for not doing more to assist the two young men, robbing him of any sense of relief he had survived what were impossible odds.

Grim-faced, he slumped to the ground alongside the two bodies to protect them from the ravages of wild animals. The twenty-six-hour long-haul return flight from a European holiday with Natalie after having learned of the siege at Parliament House while on a Rhine river cruise, plus his emotionally taxing input into the rescue operation, and then his subsequent captivity by Sergey were proving too much even for his considerable stamina. He sat with his head bowed, too exhausted to contact John, his breathing shallow, emotions raw.

Minutes passed before he staggered to his feet, drawing on his last vestiges of inner strength to make the call, praying John would hear his mobile over the din of the Dauphin's jet engines. Voicemail was his partner's unwelcome response. With sinking spirits Ballard left a message requesting a return call, adding he was safe but that Sergey was heading away from the crash site in a second chopper.

No sooner had he disconnected than his mobile burst to life. "Are you okay buddy?" John's voice was tense. The background noise was considerable but not to the point he couldn't be understood.

Ballard attempted to run his fingers through his matted hair. "Well I'm breathing and blinking. Yeah . . . never felt better. How long until you get here?"

Background discussion was heard. "Fifteen minutes, tops."

"Sergey and his goons took off about ten minutes ago. The chance of Tim and his team catching them isn't great, but I guess he hasn't any choice other than to try." Ballard stared at the mountain ranges materialising in the orange glow of the morning's half-light, their peaks encircling him, confirming he was indeed in the Grampians.

"John, bad news, two coppers turned up earlier. I'm assuming they were stationed at Halls Gap. Well . . . Sergey got to them before I could warn them."

"Jesus, don't tell me he . . ."

"'Fraid so, the bastard took them out in a matter of seconds, put a bullet in each of them with their own weapon."

"*The shithead!* I can't believe the trail of bodies this prick's leaving behind."

"I can John, and I've no doubt it'll continue."

"Mate are you still near your original coordinates?"

Ballard looked down at the two bodies, feeling the grief rising in his throat. "I'm about forty metres away, guarding the men from any wildlife."

"Christ, you poor bastard. This all makes sense now. I contacted the cops at Halls Gap after you rang the first time, explaining about the chopper crashing and the fire. They said they'd send units your way once I gave them the all-clear. Now I know what they meant when they told me they'd lost radio contact with two of their general-duties guys. The poor buggers must have seen the chopper come down and checked it out without radioing in what they were doing. Damn inexperience that ended up costing them their lives."

Sounding frustrated he changed subjects. "The Halls Gap guys have offered me a car so I can drive you back to Melbourne—after you've had something to eat in town that is. You can fill me in on how in hell's name you got away from the murderous bastard over brekkie."

There was a pause. "We should be there in ten. I'll ring Halls Gap in the meantime and pass on the bad news." He hesitated. "Mike, I can't imagine how you must be feeling right now but they came up against Sergey. They didn't stand a snowball's chance in hell of overpowering him, not with what he had in mind."

Ballard felt a second wave of fatigue wash over him, his legs buckling beneath him, dropping to his knees. "It's light enough now so when you get here you'll see where I am. And John . . .'"

"Yeah?"

"Thanks for coming along."

"The least I could do old son.

"One more thing."

"Yes?"

"Tell Halls Gap to bring bolt cutters. I need to get this bloody handcuff off me."

John chuckled as he disconnected.

True to John's prediction, PolAir appeared on time, initially as a speck in the distance, heading in from the south-east. Feeling like an octogenarian, Ballard struggled to his feet once more, unnecessarily waving a hand as the chopper circled overhead. Positioning over the same location as Sergey's rescue helicopter, PolAir's pilot chose the semi-cleared area created by the downdraft of the previous landing.

John burst from the cabin and rushed up to Ballard, wrapping him in only the second bear hug he had ever given his colleague, the first being at Ballard's property in Gisborne when his sister had been held captive by a deranged gunman. "Jesus Mike! When are you going to stop stressing me out like this? I'll be dead before I reach fifty."

Rearing back he gripped Ballard's shoulders. "Mate, you look like you've fallen face first in the mud!" He returned to the chopper and came back with a bottle of water and a cloth; in no time Ballard had scrubbed most of grime from his face and hands.

The spruce-up complete, both men stood staring down at the dead policemen, with John hooking a comforting arm around Ballard's shoulder. "There was nothing you could have done Mike. You *have* to believe that."

Ballard nodded, staring at the deceased officers, kicking angrily at the persistent lines of ants marching towards the pooled blood.

Tim hopped down from the chopper after being engaged in animated discussion with the pilot. Looking tired but relieved that Ballard had evaded Sergey's clutches, he shook his future brother-in-law's hand. As usual he got straight down to business. "Which direction Mike?"

Ballard pointed over the range towards the north-east. "He headed out just over twenty minutes ago."

Tim grunted his displeasure. "How many on board?"

"A pilot, two goons, plus Sergey. The Russian's pretty banged up."

Tim glanced at John. "You okay to babysit until the Halls Gap boys get here?"

John grinned, warming to his newfound role. "Tim I've got nothing better to do. Besides, someone's got to stop this guy from getting into any more shit than he's already been in."

Tim fixed Ballard with a hard stare. "I'm stuffed how you got away from the bastard, but now's not the time. Don't forget to call Natalie." He rotated a forefinger vertically at the pilot before climbing on-board, waving at his colleagues as the jet engines rose to full power. With considerably less dust and debris being flung about than that created by Sergey's chopper, PolAir lifted off, heading in the direction Ballard had indicated.

John looked up at the sun peeping over the eastern ridge. "Let's hope the Halls Gap boys get here soon with a tent so we can keep the sun off these two poor lads." He knelt, touching each on the shoulder, a sign of respect, his face displaying the sadness he was experiencing. Standing, his features assumed the fierce determination Ballard had witnessed countless times over the years. "We'll catch this bastard Mike. I don't know how, when, or where, but we'll catch him, and when we do, we'll throw the bloody key away."

He took his mobile and rang Halls Gap police, explaining the current situation. Heavy of heart he reconfirmed the sad fate of the two officers. He was told other police and several detectives were minutes out, along with the local fire brigade.

Hanging up, John pointed to where the undergrowth was much thicker. "Thank Christ you didn't crash over there Mike or most of Halls Gap would be up in flames by now."

Ballard went to reply but his attention was taken by a convoy of four-wheel-drive vehicles heading their way. Behind them were two Country Fire Authority trucks. They pulled up and officers began spraying foam onto the wreckage, the tree alongside still smoking at the base.

Both detectives approached the group. With Ballard watching on John assumed control, introducing himself and his partner before elaborating on the tragic news of the policemen's deaths. He explained Ballard's desperate attempt to warn them of the immediate danger they faced from Sergey, describing the Russian's elite Spetsnaz training and how that made him lethal even when wounded.

Moving over to where the bodies lay they stood with heads bowed, Ballard apologising for not being able to cover the men with more dignity. The taller of the officers, a sergeant, declared in a solemn voice, "Considering the circumstances you did your best sir. I'll see to it their families are made aware of your efforts to protect them."

Ballard's eyes moistened, his emotions flatlining as fatigue had him near collapse. In an exhausted voice he requested, "Let me know the funeral details. I want to attend." He and John looked on as a tent was erected over the two bodies.

Ballard then led the way to where the dead pilot lay in the undergrowth. The man's face was grotesque from his injuries and the resultant congealed blood, the swarming flies a pulsating black mask. The officers stared open-mouthed, fully registering the ruthless brutality of Sergey against anyone who got in his way.

Ballard explained how the Russian would have crushed the pilot's skull to prevent him from talking to police and passing on details which might compromise Sergey's location. As an aside to John he added the killing was possibly to prevent light from being shone on The Board's members, as unlikely it would seem that the pilot had that degree of inside knowledge. He informed the officers he had the pilot's mobile and would be taking it to the department's analysts to have the calls and texts assessed.

After exchanging contact details with the two detectives, John accepted the keys for the police vehicle which he was told was parked half a kilometre away on the dirt track leading back to the highway.

John took in his partner's demeanour as both men trudged through the undergrowth. "You need food in you before you even *think* about ringing Nat. Otherwise she'll freak out hearing how stuffed you are."

"Yeah, thanks for the heads-up." Too tired to argue, Ballard accepted that waiting another thirty minutes was a wise move, knowing how perceptive Natalie was and how worried she would be thinking all was not well. "John there's another complication."

The tenor of Ballard's voice had his partner halting in mid stride, his stare probing. Ballard continued, "Sergey threatened to kill me—which is par for the course I know—but he's also threatening to kill my family . . . *and the bastard meant it.*"

"*Jesus.*" John tried to look unconcerned but fell short. "Not a threat to ignore that's for sure, but first things first Mike. We need to get your sugar levels up before we start making crucial decisions."

CHAPTER

6

Forty minutes later, after wolfing down a bowl of cereal topped with diced fruit, followed by a plateful of scrambled eggs, bacon, and several slices of toast and jam, Ballard sat back, sipping on a glass of pineapple juice, his spirits lifting.

Sporting a Milo moustache on his upper lip, John stared at his partner, his eyes piercing, demanding a further explanation as to how it was possible to escape from Sergey's clutches.

"Jordan's knife saved me, as simple as that." Ballard pointed to his own lip and made a scrubbing motion which John mirrored with his serviette. "The other saving grace was Sergey's penchant for killing anyone who gets in his way, or disagrees with him."

Ballard went on to describe how the Russian shot the driver of the explosives truck and how this presented the opportunity to stab him in the forearm before snatching his Glock.

"*Then you put a bullet in his thigh?*" John ceased masticating his mouthful of toast, amazed at Ballard's life-and-death actions.

"Tough as old boots John. You and I would be rolling about screaming in agony, but the bastard just grunted and sucked it up. I don't know what training the Spetsnaz guys go through, but it *has* to be horrendous."

John inspected Ballard's left wrist now the cuff had been removed. "How many shots to separate the links?"

Ballard was sombre. "That's just it. I fired too many all up, finishing with only one in the mag." He stared into the distance. "If I'd had four or five shots left those poor coppers may still be alive."

John wasn't having any of it. "How far away from Sergey where you when he attacked the Halls Gap boys?"

"Thirty . . . maybe forty metres."

"Well there you have it. You'd have to be a bloody crack shot to put Sergey down with a handgun at that distance without hitting the others, and in your condition there was *no way* you could have covered the ground in time even if you *were* able to overpower him, which I very much doubt despite him being pretty banged up."

Ballard looked at his partner, his eyes haunted. "You and I have seen just about everything there's to see in our time John, but watching those poor buggers getting shot in the head and not being able to do a damn thing about it, Christ, that's the worst experience I've *ever* had."

John returned the look. "I won't lie to you Mike. You're going to have sleepless nights before you come to terms with this. If you ever need to talk about it, just come out and say so, day or night."

"Thanks for the offer. I've no doubt Delwyn will be lining up a stint with Marjorie in double quick time." Ballard's reference was to the police psychologist who had conducted a number of sessions with both detectives over their recent hair-raising adventures. John snorted in agreement.

Ballard pointed an accusing finger at his partner. "And don't think *you'll* escape the inquisition old son. Considering you spent three days hiding in the cleaner's ceiling dodging Sergey's goons, you're in for a grilling as well."

John's eyebrows shot skywards as he contemplated fronting the psychologist who possessed an uncanny knack of knowing what he was thinking, often before he did.

Ballard leaned to one side as a waiter gathered his dishes. Ensuring the young man was out of earshot he asked, "Now John, what about the explosives truck on Parliament House steps? What's the go there?"

Flicking hair from his eyes John's tone was upbeat. "Done and dusted my good man. The surveillance drones the boys sent up did the trick. Would you believe the spotter was propped on top of Nauru House, or whatever the hell it's called now, direct line of sight to the truck. God knows how he got up there. Tim's lads went to confront him and the silly bastard pinged off a couple of rounds, so they had to put him down."

"Did he have a trigger device to set off the explosion?"

"You bet your fortnightly pay cheque he did, along with tripod-mounted binoculars and a two-way radio."

"Jesus!" Ballard shook his head, amazed at how thorough Sergey's escape plan had been, meticulous in every aspect.

"Where's the truck now?"

"The bomb squad moved in and disarmed the C4 . . ." John looked and sounded in awe. "I'm telling you Mike, those buggers can have their job. There's no way on God's earth I'd have the nuts to do what they do, and to them it's just a training drill. With their protective suits on they looked like overgrown Michelin tyre mascots."

"What about the ammonium nitrate?"

"One of the bomb disposal guys drove the truck with a police escort front and rear. They dumped the load onto vacant land under the Westgate Bridge as it was the closest open space they could find. Obviously they couldn't traipse all over the suburbs with it. The fire brigade then set about neutralising the stuff with foam and water. Not sure where the EPA guys were but I'm guessing this was something that had to be resolved in a hurry. Choosing somewhere which kept the stuff from seeping into drains and waterways was their top priority."

"John, you don't know the guilt trip I had wondering if I should even *try* to escape, knowing it might set Sergey on a payback mission, blowing the truck and bringing down Parliament House and everything around it."

"Like I said Mike, it's going to take a hell of a long time before you get over this." He grinned suddenly, nudging his partner. "It's a bloody miracle what you did, and it'll be the stuff of legends when the story gets out."

Ballard muttered his displeasure at the revelation as he took out the dead truck driver's mobile, looking to John. "We need to have the calls and texts on this analysed as soon as we get back. Who knows what they might pick up? Now on a personal note, what have you told Natalie?"

John shrugged. "Just what you told me to say, that you were up to your armpits and would call her back when you could."

"Did she believe you?"

John looked helpless. "Have you *ever* managed to put anything over her?"

Ballard confessed, "Not that I can recall." His troubled look returned. "John I've got to warn her about Sergey's threat. While he may not be in a condition to do anything himself, I've every belief he'll have any number of goons willing to do his dirty work for him, and if not, some pretty keen Thor's Warriors out to make a name for themselves." Ballard referred to the motorcycle gang Sergey had a major influence over.

John tried to look positive. "Mike it's a difficult one, the probability of Sergey knowing about Nat and the kids is near zero, but I understand you can't take any risks with this bastard. What do you have in mind?"

Ballard didn't hesitate. "She'll have to move in with her parents for the time being. The kids can get to school from there. Thankfully their bus goes past just a few streets away."

Ballard visualised the forty-five square, double-storey mansion in Hawthorn which Robert and Barbara rattled about in, knowing they would be overjoyed to have Natalie, Josh, and Kayla stay with them. His only concern was the inquisition the Vietnam veteran would subject him to regarding his work, which yet again had placed Natalie and her family in harm's way; the ex-army colonel not renowned for his subtlety.

Ballard dialled Natalie's number as he made an aside to John. "This should be good, especially with an unknown number coming up on her phone."

He held the mobile to his ear and waited four rings before Natalie's hesitant voice came on the line. "Yes . . . hello?"

"Perhaps not the warmest greeting I've ever had."

"*Michael!*" Her cry of joy had him wrenching the mobile from his ear as he broke into a broad grin. Natalie wasn't about to let up. "Are you okay? I was *so* worried. John rang me several times to tell me you were busy, but with you two always in cahoots I knew there had to be more to it than that. *Where are you?* When are you coming home? Whose mobile are you calling from?"

Ballard chuckled, winking at John. "Now let me see. That's yes I'm okay, and yes John did tell you the truth. I really *was* tied up." He lifted his left wrist which Sergey had handcuffed, inclining his head towards his partner who rolled his eyes. "As for where am I, well, I'm at Halls Gap with Johno. We—"

"*Halls Gap?*"

Ballard extended the phone once more, hesitating before broaching the subject he was dreading. "Darling, I need you to do something for me without asking too many questions. A threat's been made against me by one of the Parliament House crooks, and by default it may involve you and the kids." An audible gasp was followed by a lingering silence. "Nat . . . it's one of those situations where it's *very* unlikely anything will happen, but we can't take the risk, not until a particular offender is caught. So you and the kids need to move in with your parents, *tonight*."

"*Tonight?* Where are you going to stay?"

Ballard thought hard as to what the best answer would be. "The farm's too far away from work while all this is going on. I need to be close to the office." He winced, knowing what Natalie's next reaction would be when he revealed his intentions. "I, er, I thought—"

"So you're going to stay at the town house." Natalie's statement was direct, her tone brooking no nonsense.

"Well it crossed my mind."

"Why not stay at my parents? They wouldn't mind."

Ballard shook his head as he answered, "Love to Nat, but like I said, I need to be close to work—"

"Nonsense Michael. You're just nervous being around my father." Her voice lowered. "And I don't blame you."

"Guilty as charged, I'm embarrassed to admit."

"In that case I'll take half a day off work and drop some clothes and toiletries at Mum and Dad's for the kids. Then I'll ring and have them go straight to their grandparents after school. Emma and Tricia are working interstate for the next week. They call me every day so I'll make sure they only visit their Gran and Pop when they get back." A silence ensued such that Ballard could almost hear her mind ticking. "Just let me know when you're ready Michael. I'll come back to the town house and rustle something for you to eat."

Ballard recognised he was wasting his breath, but he knew he had to make the effort. "Nat this is serious. I don't want you taking any risks by being with me."

"Michael! You sound exhausted and need looking after. Besides, the kids prefer being at their grandparents without me because they get spoilt rotten. Do you have any idea when you'll be free?"

Checking his watch Ballard looked to John, voicing his estimate as much for his partner as for Natalie. "It's just after nine thirty. The drive back to the office will take upwards of two and a half hours. Delwyn's sure to want a debrief, so Nat, I can't see myself getting off until well after three, perhaps four this afternoon."

"*Michael*, you'll have been awake for nearly three days! Well apart from the few hours' nap you got on the plane coming home." Natalie was aghast.

Performing arithmetic, Ballard had to agree with her shocked declaration, but he knew there was no alternative. "I'll snooze in the car. By the time I lob at the office I'll be bright-eyed and bushy-tailed." John rolled his eyes once more.

"Nonsense Michael, but I know there's nothing I can say that will change your mind. Just give me plenty of notice before you come over."

After blowing her a noisy kiss, which he prolonged to annoy John, he hung up, sporting his first genuine smile for days.

CHAPTER
7

Once on the road, with John cruising a scratch over the speed limit, Ballard realised just how exhausted he felt. With the morning sun rising over his left shoulder they headed down the Western Highway. The traffic was sparse but punctuated by more than a fair share of thirty-two wheelers thundering towards Melbourne, John booting the police vehicle to scenery blurring surges as they passed each rig.

Ballard scrutinised his partner. "Come to think of it John, you haven't had too much shut-eye yourself over the past few days, worried sick about Sonia as you would have been."

John contemplated his answer. "I caught an hour or two here and there." He grinned. "Actually that's horseshit. As soon as I dozed off my subconscious kicked in and dumped another squirt of adrenaline down my pipes." He changed subjects. "Mike, you've no idea how grateful I am you came up with the brainwave of Jordan's boys accessing Parliament House via the old air conditioning tunnel. Once that scenario slotted into place the guys were able to release the knockout gas and the rest is history." He shook his head without taking his eyes off the road. "A full-blown assault would have ended in a massacre, and there's every likelihood Sonia would have been caught in the crossfire. Mate, we all owe you a big one."

Ballard sat reflecting. "It was all or nothing. I think I aged ten years waiting to see if everything went to plan. Carfentanil isn't something to be messed with. Tim and his crew were top shelf as usual, and Jordan's lot lived up to their reputation. They sure know how to lay down heavy-duty firepower."

Ballard faced his partner, serious but relieved. "The whole thing could have turned to poop John. Thank God it didn't, or you and I wouldn't be hotfooting it back to Melbourne in one piece as we are now."

He dragged out the truck driver's mobile. "Time to make some calls." Contacting Alan Dempsey, his neighbour who had project-managed much of the building of the B & B and squash court at the farm, he asked him to keep an eye on the place while he was away. Next he left a voicemail for his housekeeper, Vera, explaining his circumstances and that he hadn't sold the property and forgotten to tell her.

Hanging up he growled, "Considering the little time I spend there these days, I may as well sell it." He shrugged. "I guess the B & B will be something to do when Nat and I retire, whenever that is."

John swerved in his lane as his head spun sideways, eyes bulging, his lips curling over bared teeth. "Jesus Mike, your lack of sleep has addled your brain. For Christ's sake stop mentioning the *R* word. *That's an order.*"

Ballard laughed. "If my memory serves me correctly Johno Marjorie gave us both a fair old pasting for involving ourselves in some pretty hairy capers, stockpiling memories to tide us over in old age."

John agreed. "How could I forget it? And truth be known, neither of us can deny there's an element of reality in what she said."

"'Fraid so, buddy, and without a doubt, when things settle down after this latest episode we're going to be ordered by Delwyn to participate in a few more of our favourite psychologist's grilling's." Looking hopeful, Ballard asked, "Now tell me, the last I heard Sonia and the baby were being checked out by medicos. What's the prognosis?"

John glanced at his partner. "Thankfully, no issues at all, so that's a load off my mind. Sonia's conscious her age is a crucial factor, and the pregnancy will need to be monitored throughout. Were she to have lost the baby, the chance of her falling pregnant again aren't all that good. That's why I was so worried about her being exposed to the gas in the first place."

"Weren't we all John?"

"What about Kathryn and Laura? Are you going to tell them about Sergey?"

Ballard considered John's concern for his sister and daughter. "Kathryn spends more time at Tim's digs than at her own place these days and being with a guy who's in charge of the SOG is about as safe as she's going to get. As for Laura, well, I guess being estranged from her for over two years means there's little possibility Sergey's going to link her or her mother to me. I think I'll let sleeping dogs lie on that front. Bradley's in Canberra at the military academy, surrounded by soldiers with rifles, so I'm not concerned there." Taking a deep sigh, he confessed, "All in all, I'm praying Sergey's threat against my folks was an impulse thing. That's not to say I have any doubt he'll try to finish me off the first opportunity he gets."

John cursed. "It might have been better if you *had* put a bullet in his head rather than his thigh."

"Don't think I was too far off doing it John, believe me." Ballard relived the crucial seconds when he was within a hair's breadth of murdering the Russian. Dredging up dark demons, he recounted his near-career-altering thoughts prior to sanity hauling him back from the brink. John agreed, indicating his appreciation of the pressure situation that had confronted his partner.

Both men sat in silence, the kilometres rolling by, each contemplating random scenarios had the siege and kidnapping taken an alternate path. As if guessing the other's thoughts they glanced at one another, with Ballard stating, "Time to get stuck into the nitty-gritty John." Recognising they had been avoiding discussing the current host of challenges confronting the department and government, as a result of the siege, along with the trauma and anxiety they and their loved ones had been subjected to, they mentally braced themselves.

Ballard kicked off proceedings. "Have you heard anything regarding the political fallout the government's bound to face for coughing up the billion dollars?" Before John could respond, Ballard added, "Christ, can you imagine the outcry from the Americans and the Brits right about now, especially as all we achieved by forking over the money was a demand for a second billion? The Yanks will see it as sign of weakness on our part. Everything is black and white to them."

John shook his head, unconsciously increasing speed as he contemplated the rock and the hard place the attorney general and his representative, Damien Harcourt, found themselves in as Sergcy ramped up the pressure by executing more politicians to secure the money transfer. "It's all very well for Uncle Sam to claim the moral high ground Mike, but with the body count mounting by the hour it was plain to see if the deaths had continued the federal government would be in the political wilderness for the next twenty-odd years, I've no doubt on that score."

"Any public statements yet?"

"Not sure what the chief and the premier have in mind for the long term. They both made nonspecific announcements to the press yesterday, spruiking the need for understanding as the situation is currently being investigated by multiple agencies. Also, I think the various authorities were holding off on announcements until the explosives truck was moved. Now their hesitation is linked to whether any pollies might die from their exposure to the gas, which is a genuine concern by the way."

Ballard's head swivelled. "Why? What's the issue there?"

John blasted the horn at a motorist weaving in front of him. "A few have had respiratory issues, but we're hoping it's nothing life-threatening. The good news is the three pregnant ladies are okay, and let me tell you, our resident intelligence officer, James Patterson, he's breathing a bloody huge sigh of relief that his department's antidote did the trick without apparent side effects. Still, it's early days."

"How's the AC holding up?" Ballard visualised the thirty-year veteran gritting his teeth, his cobalt-blue eyes boring into anyone he believed wasn't pulling their weight as the crisis unfolded.

"Tough as old boots as usual, but worried sick about the predicament you found yourself in. He was amazed when Peter passed on you'd survived the ordeal."

"How about your guys?" Ballard knew John's three youngest detectives—Ken, Bobby, and Susan—would be chomping at the bit to assist. Ken would be offering profiling advice which would not be welcomed by John who wasn't a fan of the technique.

"Susan was beside herself. Mate, I'm telling you, she's fast becoming your pseudo daughter."

Ballard agreed. "Perhaps the only one I'll ever have, despite my efforts with Laura."

John pushed on. "Hmm, well, my guys are head down and arse up, grinding away on the briefs for Vladimir and now Sergey, assuming the mad bastard is caught at some point." He wriggled into a more upright position. "Which brings me to the million-dollar question. How the Christ are we going to track the bugger down? I know Tim's doing his damnedest, but a twenty-minute head start in a chopper means the prick could be more than a hundred and fifty klicks away in any one direction. With The Board's contacts they're certain to have corrupt medical guys on standby to take out the bullet and patch up his arm. My gut feeling is Sergey will lay low to mend for at least a week or two. That'll give us *some* breathing space before he starts his murderous rampage again. It's in his DNA Mike. He can't help himself, 'specially as it's clear he wants to improve his standing with The Board."

"Well, he's made a pretty solid start by raking in a billion dollars for them, and it took a fair degree of luck on our part he didn't turn that into two big ones." Ballard appeared thoughtful as he asked, "Do we chance our arm twice and utilise Bernard Junior's private agency again to track Sergey down?" His question referred to Bernard Winters, an ex-CIA operative whose son ran a private detective agency in Melbourne and who had successfully tracked down Vladimir when he went into hiding. Ballard and John were aware they had taken a huge gamble stepping outside the police department's protocols by employing the agency's services without seeking formal approval.

John contemplated the risks, shrugging as though shedding a load from his shoulders. "It worked once. Can't see why it shouldn't again. I guess we'll get a better idea of the lay of the land at the AC's briefing. I'm assuming you'll want to attend even though you're in a semi-comatose state. Delwyn will be fighting tooth and nail for you to go home and rest." He laughed suddenly, causing Ballard to eye him with a degree of suspicion. "Mike, you realise Delwyn's going to *insist* you take time off because of this little caper?" He blew the horn twice to warn a driver who was wandering across the median strip that he was about to pass.

Ballard glanced across as they shot past. "Yeah, just as I thought, the silly bugger's texting. Flick the siren John, that'll wake the dopey bastard up."

John did one better, operating the light and siren for several seconds, causing the driver to fling the mobile onto the seat alongside him before decreasing speed dramatically, moving to the extreme left of his lane. Both detectives laughed as they continued, certain the driver would be relieved he only received a heart starter and not an expensive ticket.

The sign indicating five kilometres to Ararat flashed past. Minutes later Ballard pointed to the swing set and slide he and Bradley used to play on when they drove over to Bordertown in South Australia to visit his parents on the farm where he grew up with Kathryn. "A long time ago John."

"How's Brad coping at the military academy? What year's he in now? Three?"

Ballard chuckled. "Time flies John. Four. And it's Duntroon this year." He twisted sideways, hefting his right leg partially onto the seat to better face his partner. "I've told you some of the stories about Bradley and how I was juggling custody of him while working homicide. You'll never guess what he told the Duntroon psyche major." John punctuated his interest by leaning his head closer. "Bradley's got a small lump in the middle of his left palm. I had it checked out years ago and the doctors said to leave it alone as it was near nerves and benign. Well, the little bugger informed the psych major it grew because of me whacking him with a wooden spoon whenever he misbehaved." John whooped his delight at the revelation, silently requesting more information. "When I went to Canberra at the beginning of the year with Nat for a visit, the upstart major called me over and demanded we chat about how I'd brought up my son."

"*No way!*" John burst out laughing. "What did you say?"

"I told the guy to get stuffed then asked him if he was married and whether he had children. After he'd said no to both I suggested he spend time achieving those events in his life then come back and talk to me."

"How'd he take that?"

"On the chin to his credit, but Bradley was mortified I'd spoken to a major that way."

John laughed again. "I remember you telling me Bradley had bucketloads of willpower."

"He did. Still does. And it needed to be guided when he was younger. The funny thing is it was only half a dozen times he ever got a whack on the hand, but John, it was *always* after I'd warned him not to do something. I'd even sit him down to explain why he shouldn't do it. Well, every now and then he'd defy me and do it just for the hell—to test me I guess. I've no doubt my treatment's a no-no these days, with all the do-gooders shouting from the rooftops that children should be free to explore their boundaries."

John snorted. "I wouldn't get too stressed about it Mike. Whatever you did worked a treat. A scholarship from the Ivanhoe Boys Grammar slotted him straight into the army. That's got to be worth millions to him over the years."

"Thankfully he's got his mother's brains and my willpower."

Ballard settled back, clearly proud of Bradley's achievements. Moments later he responded to his partner's previous statement, praying John's prediction wouldn't amount to a direct order from his superintendent. "Come to think of it Delwyn *will* be pushing for me to take time off, right in the middle of this damn case. I guess she's between a rock and a hard place, ensuring I don't add to the department's ever-mounting compo' bill."

John agreed. "Even I admit the job's getting harder. There just doesn't seem to be any honour in today's crooks, and as for the youth of today, Jesus Mike, it's nothing for them to walk up to coppers and openly abuse them or smack them in the mouth. Incredible. Never happened in our day down at St Kilda."

"No John, indeed it didn't."

Ballard shuffled into a more comfortable position as they slowed for the roadworks which were part of the Western Highway duplication. "My friend, I think I'm going to take my own advice and have a catnap for the next hour or so. Wake me up if you come across any bad guys who need locking up." He slid further down and in a matter of minutes was fast asleep, his expression that of a man without a care in the world.

CHAPTER
8

The persistent jangle of a tram bell warning a motorist his vehicle was blocking the tracks brought Ballard back to consciousness with a jolt. "Bloody hell John, that was quick. How many speed limits did you break?"

His partner shook his head. "Actually, very few. You've been out like a light for over an hour."

"*No way.*"

"Yep, and you snored through most of it."

"Get out! Nat reliably informs me I *don't* snore."

"She's your wife Mike. I'm your partner. I tell it as it is."

Ballard reflected on the statement as John manoeuvred through the car park entrance of the new Crime and Intelligence building located on the corner of Spencer and La Trobe streets, metres from where Sergey had made his daring escape over the wall of the Melbourne Assessment Prison on the opposite side of the road several weeks prior.

Glancing over his shoulder, Ballard commented, "It took balls for The Board to pull off what it did." His reference was to a tray truck with a cherry picker bolted to the back, pulling up alongside the prison's exercise yard. From there a Thor's Warrior bikie swung over the razor wire in the bucket, shooting two guards as Sergey climbed a rope ladder to make his audacious escape. Just twenty-four hours prior he and Vladimir had been arrested by Tim and his SOG team. Both men attempting to extort money from Malcolm Ferguson and his wife Teresa, at their Eureka Tower penthouse.

John looked thoughtful. "You're telling me, and I don't need to be reminded how unsuccessful we were chasing after the bastard in the railway yards with Delwyn hot on his heels. Pretty embarrassing that she managed to outrun us every step of the way. Built like a bloody greyhound she is." He grunted. "Never did figure out how Sergey managed to disappear into thin air once he reached the shunting yards."

After parking the car both men got out and stretched their aching limbs. Ballard pointed to the toilets. "John before we get to the office, let me clean up a bit. If nothing else I need to wash my face again so I don't frighten the kiddies."

"Sure thing. I think I'll join you."

After scrubbing the last of the grime from his face and hands, Ballard straightened his tie, noting the bloodstains and smudges of dirt on his white business shirt. Next he borrowed John's comb, flattening his hair into some form of respectability. He cupped a mouthful of water then gargled, spitting into the sink before drinking several mouthfuls straight from the tap.

He inspected himself in the mirror. The image staring back at him resembled that of a tired and somewhat dishevelled Sting, perhaps recovering from an all-night bender. Aware he was taller and appreciably more muscled than the famous singer, Ballard was nonetheless satisfied with the result considering the ordeal he had just been through. "Okay John, time to face the music."

Stepping onto the fourth floor, now the new home for the homicide squad, Ballard was greeted by his colleagues expressing a jumble of emotions, the reactions ranging from acute astonishment to utter relief, notwithstanding the odd moist eye which wasn't limited to the female officers.

"*Boss!*" Bobby was the first of John's younger detectives to greet him, the pumping of his hand hinting at an impending hug. A trace of uncertainty spared Ballard from what would have been a rib-crushing embrace. Ken approached next but was unceremoniously shoved out of the way by Susan who rose on tiptoe, planting a warm kiss on Ballard's cheek, unashamed tears welling but not breaking free.

Ken reached around Susan to shake his hand. "Welcome back Mike. It's good to see you're in one piece." His voice faltered as he inspected his feet, embarrassed yet relieved at the same time.

Additional colleagues gathered, clapping him on the shoulder and shaking his hand. Everyone was eager to hear how he managed to evade Sergey's clutches. Disbelief was evident on their faces that he had achieved such a feat since all were aware of the Russian's formidable reputation.

"Michael! John!" An authoritative voice carried across the room. Spinning around the detectives spotted Delwyn framed by her office doorway, her steel-grey short back and sides haloing in the overhead lights. She beckoned them over. Ballard and John complied, excusing themselves from the throng.

Approaching her office John quipped under his breath, "Two minutes Mike."

"Come again?"

"Two minutes max before she insists you take leave." John checked his watch as they entered Delwyn's office. The superintendent embraced Ballard with a lingering hug, punctuated by several contented but unintelligible mutterings, all followed by an audible sigh.

"And here I was convinced Marjorie had persuaded you both to ease up on risky ventures. It's never going to happen is it?" She broke free, not expecting an answer, certainly not one that would reassure her.

John, embarrassed and looking contrite pulled out a chair and pretended to help Ballard into his as though he were an arthritic old man.

"Ham it up you two. I can't guess how many years you've chopped off my life." She became serious. "You know what this means, don't you?"

John inspected his watch with an exaggerated sweep of his arm, declaring triumphantly, "Ninety-four seconds. *Yes!*"

Delwyn looked perplexed but gave up attempting to fathom what John's outburst was all about. "First things first, you've been awake now for how long Michael? Almost three days?"

Ballard muttered, "Something like that, but I slept on the way back in the car, so I'm—"

"I know, I know . . . bright-eyed and bushy-tailed." Delwyn mimicked one of Ballard's favourite sayings, not buying any of it. "I'll get one of John's team to drive you home." She hesitated. "The town house?"

John and Ballard glanced at one another, the exchange not escaping Delwyn who instinctively knew something was afoot. "Okay, spit it out."

Ballard braced in his chair before commencing a summary of events from the moment he lifted off in the chopper to when John, Tim, and his team landed at Halls Gap. Delwyn scribbled notes throughout, interjecting with the odd question but in the main absorbing the information like a sponge, wincing at the point where Sergey made the threat towards Ballard's family.

"Banged up though he is Michael, you're wise to have Natalie and the children removed from any immediate danger." Ballard decided not to mention that Natalie was hell-bent on returning to look after him. Delwyn continued to probe. "You're sure you want to stay at the town house? The quarters here in the building are for this sort of contingency."

Ballard shook his head. "No thanks Delwyn. When I analyse it I'd just shot Sergey in the thigh and plugged him twice with Jordan's knife, so I'm not surprised he made the threat. It was more reflex rage than anything premeditated."

"Maybe so but I'll arrange for some uniforms to cruise past throughout the night. It can't do any harm to fly the flag that there's a police presence nearby."

Ballard stared hard at his superintendent. "Susan mentioned the AC, the chief, and the premier are holding a press conference in half an hour . . ."

"Michael, Michael, what will it take?" Delwyn sighed in exasperation, glaring at John for allowing one of his staff to offer Ballard a further excuse to hang about when he should be resting. John swallowed, inspecting the back of his hand like he'd just discovered it.

In all sincerity, Ballard commented, "You may not believe this but it'll ease my mind to hear what the brass have to say before I call it a day. I've already warned Nat I won't be getting to the town house until later this evening for a meal." The moment he uttered the words he regretted them.

Delwyn pounced on the slip. "I thought you said she was staying with the children at her parent's place!" Her expression predicted the answer.

Ballard shrugged. "She is, but she wants to give me a home-cooked meal first."

"I don't need to tell you Michael, Sergey isn't your average crim and shouldn't be trifled with."

"Indeed you don't Delwyn." Changing subjects he asked, "When's the conference scheduled?"

Everyone glanced at the wall clock.

"Twenty minutes." Delwyn's features relaxed, resigned to the inevitable. "It's being held in our spanking new corporate media room. You'll be impressed Michael. I guess the powers that be figured most press releases centred around crime, so they decided to put one in the building. It's heaps more high-tech than the old one at headquarters."

"Is the current media room still there?"

"For the time being. And for your information the lease on the building expires in just over two years so they're planning to build a thirty-nine-storey complex right alongside us, fronting Spencer Street."

"Praise be to God Delwyn. Talk about all our eggs in one basket." John shook his head in disbelief as he turned to Ballard who had leapt to his feet, his action as much to prove to Delwyn he had recovered from his ordeal.

"Come on John, I've just enough time to have a shave and shower before I jump into some clean clothes. In the meantime rustle me up a sandwich and a hot chocolate from the canteen."

"Jesus Mike, how many of us have a spare Van Heusen business shirt, a Morgan silk tie, and a charcoal-grey pinstripe Armani wool suit in our locker, not to mention Grenson Nubuck brogues, *just* in case our current glad rags happen to get soiled?" John gazed at his partner with more than a degree of envy, tinged with open admiration.

Grinning, Ballard muttered out the corner of his mouth as he, Delwyn, and John settled in adjacent seats at the back of the media room, "I'm impressed by your fashion acumen old son. Well spotted. Let's just say these glad rags make the tough times feel a whole lot better."

Looking about him he was surprised at the size of the room, catering for at least fifty press reporters in comfort. A much greater number were currently crammed in the space, all jostling for a vantage point, shoulder-mounted and tripod cameras positioned at the ready. Large screen TVs were strategically located along the walls, together with the latest electronic whiteboards. Three podiums were placed side by side in front, each fitted with microphone bouquets so every word could be captured. The expected VIPs were not yet present so the hubbub of chatter was considerable and laced with anticipation as the siege was a national and international sensation, many of the reporters representatives of overseas networks.

A heavy hand descended on Ballard's shoulder. Glancing up he was delighted to see Peter beaming down at him. "About time you got back to work Mike instead of gallivanting all over the countryside." Peter's expression echoed his relief that his partner was safe. Grabbing a spare chair he plonked down alongside his colleagues, resting an ankle over one knee as he leaned back. Glancing around he was amused at the frenzied manoeuvrings of the media milling about, jostling for an uninterrupted view. "Is Jordan going to be here?" He addressed the question to Delwyn.

"No, he told me his team rely on anonymity. He said I could brief him afterwards."

A door opened at the far end of the room and the Premier, the Chief Commissioner, and Assistant Commissioner Thompson strode in, displaying understated confidence. Standing behind the centre podium, resplendent in a dark-navy suit, white shirt, and grey silk tie, the premier waited until the two police officers were in position before sweeping everyone with intelligent eyes that missed nothing, a master at painting a verbal picture with an economy of words. The surrounding buzz lowered to an expectant, tension-filled hush.

In an authoritative, controlled voice, the premier addressed the gathering. "Ladies and gentlemen, I'm going to begin by quoting a *very* famous politician." He paused for special effect. "Never was so much owed by so many to so few." Focussing on the bank of cameras he explained, "Three days ago, a group of—for expediency I'll refer to them as terrorists even though this hasn't yet been established. Three days ago a group of terrorists took control of our state legislative assembly, holding hostage 108 sitting politicians, their support staff, media representatives along with members of the public viewing the everyday running of our democratic Westminster system. It must never be forgotten that the foundation of our legal authority to govern is our parliamentary process, ably supported by an impartial public service, a dedicated police force, together with our armed services, each operating under the rule of law, all these authorities underpinned by an independent judiciary.

John drawled out the corner of his mouth, "Buckle up folks. We're in for a history lesson."

Delwyn kicked his ankle without taking her eyes off the premier, this despite a ripple of discussion breaking out amongst the reporters.

The premier made it clear he would only continue once the verbal asides ceased. "The attack on our state parliament struck at the very heart of our democracy. We in Victoria have been subjected to two major criminal atrocities in the past months. Firstly, the robbery at Note Printing Australia in November last year in which many innocent lives were lost and a hundred and twenty million dollars was stolen. I can inform you the principal perpetrators have been caught and a significant proportion of the money now recovered." Ballard's eyes opened wider as he took in his colleagues, conscious the premier was choosing not to divulge that seventy million had passed to The Board and would almost certainly never be seen again.

The premier swept his audience with piercing eyes once more, aware of everyone's attention, even note-taking dropping away. "Are there links between those who performed the robbery and the attack on Parliament House?" He addressed the question to the chief commissioner. "I'll leave that for you to expand on Glen." The chief inclined his head, acknowledging the request.

"A robbery is a robbery, albeit one which resulted in a number of deaths. The attack on Parliament House was an assault against our very way of life, our values. It struck fear into the hearts of everyday citizens that the rule of law no longer protected them, that armed thugs were free to act as they pleased, with impunity. The very fabric of our great democracy appeared to be in jeopardy."

The premier drew himself to his full height. "I'm here to emphasize how my opening words weren't idle rhetoric. We do *indeed* owe an incredible debt to the remarkable men and women who put their lives on the line and stood up to the terrorists, preventing a major catastrophe in the form of significantly greater loss of life and the potential destruction of irreplaceable historic buildings. Indeed the effort wasn't without fatalities, and for those politicians who were murdered in cold blood, brutally cut down in the prime of their lives, my heart and condolences go out to their families and loved ones. Nothing will bring them back, but I make this promise to all Victorians, to all *Australians*, we who possess the authority and expertise to bring these criminals to justice will *never* rest until every one of the perpetrators are captured, brought before the courts and suitably punished. In honour of those who died I'll now ask everyone to observe a brief silence as a sign of respect for their shortened lives."

Standing with his head bowed, the premier closed his eyes, his demeanour one of dignity and reverence, the image powerful.

Everyone followed suit, the atmosphere in the room in sharp contrast to the general thrust and parry of typical media briefings.

Ballard reflected on the fine line the premier was treading—on the one hand ensuring he wasn't diminishing the enormity of the attack, while on the other, reassuring the public that the respective law enforcement agencies were sufficiently equipped and trained to negate any future threat which might be brought against the state.

As if reading Ballard's mind, the premier continued, "Thank you. I'd like to conclude by repeating that the cooperation between the various agencies in thwarting the terrorists' actions was outstanding, so much so that despite the ruthless professionalism of these criminals we were able to nullify their brutal efforts and prevent greater bloodshed." Turning to his right the premier concluded, "I'll now hand you over to the Chief Commissioner of Police, who will detail the mechanics of the siege which took place."

Peter leaned across and whispered to Delwyn, "All very calculated. The bugger's lumping the thorny issue of the ransom payment for the chief and the AC to explain." He appeared uncertain how the officers were expected to answer the inevitable questions that would be raised by the media.

After coughing into a closed fist the chief commissioner acknowledged the premier prior to commencing his address. "Ladies and gentlemen, the past few months have been a testing time for our law enforcement agencies and emergency services. As the premier stated, they all performed spectacularly. Their courage, training, and endeavour were exemplary. On Tuesday morning ten offenders entered Parliament House and within minutes held over a hundred people hostage in the legislative assembly. All entry doors into the chamber were armed with explosives. Antipersonnel mines were placed strategically throughout the building and on the front steps. This made any rescue mission extremely dangerous for the hostages and almost impossible for the specialist teams." There was a ripple of disquiet throughout at the mention of the deadly mines employed by the terrorists.

"Tragically, four politicians were executed before a liberation mission could be mounted. Due to the complexity and critical nature of the operation in terms of potential loss of life, it was decided to support our very capable Special Operations police with the Australian Army's special forces personnel."

This drew another round of animated discussion which the chief commissioner cut short by his next comments. "The combined expertise of these teams enabled them to infiltrate Parliament House and secure the hostages without further deaths. However, due to the aggressive nature of the offenders, all of them resisted arrest and were killed, except for the leader who later escaped in a helicopter which landed on the front steps of Parliament House."

John stared at Ballard, his eyes narrowing, making it clear he understood that while the chief's words were true, pertinent facts—such as Sergey's identity and that he executed four of his own men—was not something to be shared with the public. It was also clear the press were becoming restless as to the limited details being provided. The TV footage of the chopper landing and taking off minutes later now common knowledge, the images transmitted throughout the world.

Sensing everyone's disquiet the chief commissioner suppressed a tight smile. "Before I throw this briefing open to questions, I need to add that just prior to the chopper landing a rig fully loaded with forty tonnes of ammonium nitrate and diesel fuel was driven onto Parliament House steps. Following this a very real threat was made by the terrorist leader that the unit would be remotely exploded if he wasn't permitted to leave. Due to the certain loss of life and extensive property damage which would have ensued, a collective decision was made to allow him to leave Parliament House via the chopper."

He had foreseen this revelation would be the catalyst to tip the media over the edge and he wasn't disappointed.

"Chief Commissioner, do you know the identity of the terrorist who got away?"

The officer's eyes bored into the reporter asking the question. Without the slightest hesitation he declared, "Yes we do, but for operational reasons I won't be disclosing it." With a meaningful stare which shrieked "Don't bother pursuing this" he added, "A necessary precaution, as you would appreciate under the circumstances."

A brunette reporter sitting in the second row held up her hand and without waiting to be asked, called out, "Were the public in any danger during the disarming of the truck?"

The chief commissioner deferred to AC Thompson who flashed a boyish smile in the reporter's direction. "Our bomb disposal squad was faced with the difficult task of disarming the multiple explosives strapped to the exterior of the rig. That operation proved very complex, not to mention dangerous. I must stress this phase wasn't undertaken until every one of the hostages had been moved to a safe location to receive a thorough medical assessment."

As he took in his audience the AC reached for a glass of water on the lower shelf of his podium, taking several mouthfuls. "Once the charges on the rig were removed, because the fuel load had been premixed and was therefore extremely volatile, it was then a matter of escorting the unit to a location where the load could be safely neutralised."

The reporter raised her hand again. "Where did this take place?

The AC flashed another high-voltage smile. "Nice try, but sorry that's an operational need-to-know."

"Was there a ransom demand?"

The question wiped the smile from the AC's face, but to his credit he chose not to defer to the chief commissioner. "Yes, a demand was made."

For several seconds a hushed silence filled the room. The detectives looked at one another, unsure where the AC was heading. They knew the next question would reverberate around the world, the answer sure to have political ramifications for years, even decades to come. It didn't take long for the request to be made.

"Was a ransom paid to the terrorists?" There it was, plain and simple, begging to be answered, demanding an uncomplicated yes or no response. There was collective wisdom throughout the audience that this wasn't going to eventuate.

With calmness and a steady gaze the AC answered, "It's a long-standing government policy not to pay ransom demands."

"I'm aware of the government's policy sir, but my specific question is *did* the government pay a ransom to secure the release of the hostages?" It was clear the reporter wasn't going to let go and knew she was pursuing what was on the lips of every one of her colleagues.

The chief commissioner and premier glanced across at the AC, content to allow him to continue, a task which Mr Thompson appeared untroubled by. His more than thirty years of operational experience had engendered a steely resolve which was now serving him well. "The successful release of the hostages was effected *solely* by the incredible skill and bravery of the rescue teams that breached Parliament House, nullifying the threat from the terrorists."

The reporter opened her mouth to continue her inquisition but was beaten to the punch by a female colleague who appeared to be in her teens, her youthful appearance offset by abundant confidence. "Mr Thompson, when the hostages were freed they appeared as though they were unconscious or near unconsciousness as the ambulance teams stretchered them out. Can you explain why this was the case?"

Again, without the slightest hesitation the AC flashed a disarming smile prior to his response. "The siege lasted just over three days, and while *some* food and drink was made available during the ordeal, the unbelievable tension and lack of sleep the hostages endured throughout that period would have placed an incredible strain on them physically and emotionally. Clearly it took its toll in the form of near or actual physical collapse. The ambulance officers would have been aware of this and reacted accordingly to ensure the well-being of the hostages was their top priority." His broad smile underscored the statement.

John nudged Ballard and hissed, "Take a look at him. The bugger's actually enjoying this, ducking and weaving through the political minefield as he gives only those facts he cares to pass on. Jesus, I wish I could think that fast on my feet." His admiration for the AC was stamped across his face. Peter and Delwyn agreed, impressed by what was fast becoming a tour de force by the AC.

Ballard leaned across and whispered in John's ear, "Let's hope he doesn't get *too* cocky. I've seen that before today, then watch the reporters turn into snarling, rabid dogs."

John chewed on his lip as he contemplated the possibility.

The questions flowed thick and fast, the majority thoughtful, all probing, save for a number which were just plain banal. The premier and chief commissioner shouldered their share of the answers then the premier held up a hand to end the session. "Ladies and gentlemen, there's much work to be done as we continue with our multiple investigations. Again I thank all those who were involved in bringing this crisis to an end as effectively as possible under the circumstances. The chief commissioner and I now have the arduous task of meeting with the deceased's relatives to offer our condolences. We can't imagine their collective pain and sorrow, and while we'll answer their questions as best we can, we know nothing will satisfactorily explain why a loved one going to work with the best of intentions is brutally and senselessly murdered hours later. Life is not always fair or fathomable." He raised his hand again. "Thank you everyone."

On that sombre note the premier, the chief commissioner, and the AC turned and with heads held high, left the room without a backward glance. As though a grenade had been tossed amongst them the reporters dashed for the exits, desperate to file their reports. Their frantic actions were almost comical were the context of their transcripts not so serious. The public was about to be enlightened regarding what took place at Parliament House, however the detectives were conscious how heavily censored the facts to be revealed really were.

They sat in the now empty room, the ensuing silence in sharp contrast to the palpable tension which had flowed about them moments before. Delwyn looked at her two colleagues. "Thanks to the AC being an old hand at handling the press I think we've dodged a bullet, but it's only a matter of time before the premier or someone else in the government lets slip we forked out a billion dollars for zero gain. Then watch the media explode into a frenzy."

They sat in silence, each contemplating the verbal post-mortems now under way. Armchair experts would be pontificating what should have occurred, wise after the event, comfortable in the knowledge they would never have to make life-and-death decisions in a matter of seconds then live with the consequences.

Standing abruptly, Delwyn pointed to Ballard and John, ordering, "Downstairs so I can arrange for you both to be driven home." John began to protest. "Not an option John. Ken can drive your unmarked and after Bobby's dropped you off he'll pick up Ken. As for you Michael, Susan will take you around to the town house." She hesitated. "You're sure you want to stay there considering what Sergey . . ."

"I can't dodge shadows for the rest of my life Delwyn. You know threats like this go with the territory."

"Yes but they rarely come in the form of a pathological Russian soldier."

"Maybe, but I'd suggest he's got one or two injuries that'll occupy his thoughts for the next week or so. Tough as he is what I dished out has to slow him down for the short term."

Delwyn, while not convinced was resigned to the situation. "Like I said, I'll have uniforms cruise past at regular intervals during the night. Now I don't want to see either of you tomorrow—that's an order. I've contacted Marjorie and she'd like a brief session with you both the day after, say around eleven." John gave Ballard an "I told you so" glance.

Thanking Delwyn, Ballard stood to one side so she could leave the room. John pretended to wait for his partner then at the last moment pushed him sideways as he bustled in front. Turning and staring at both detectives Delwyn went to say something but changed her mind, a faint smile tugging the corner of her mouth as she led the way downstairs to their new digs.

CHAPTER

9

Pulling up outside Natalie's clinker brick town house, Susan cocked her head as she gave Ballard a wry smile that spoke volumes, displaying her relief he was still in one piece. After dropping him off she reversed down the driveway, waving briefly as she did so. Not expecting Natalie to have arrived, he was surprised to be welcomed by her bursting from the front door, flinging her arms around his neck, hugging him with all her strength.

"Hmm, I see you ignored my advice Nat and decided not to stay with your parents." He returned the hug, attempting to ignore the fatigue threatening to overwhelm him.

"Try keeping me away, buster! Wild horses . . ." She didn't bother to finish, instead encircling his waist as she ushered him inside. Stopping to appraise him under the hallway light she admitted, "Gosh, for someone who's been awake for three days you've scrubbed up rather well Mr Ballard." She grew serious. "John contacted me a number of times so that had me suspicious you were up to something dangerous and couldn't ring me. *Were you in any danger?*" Her demand was so forceful she appeared angry, defying him to brush off her concerns.

Ballard knew now wasn't the time to explain what had happened, deciding a white lie was his best option. "Ah, you saw through our deception." Just as Natalie's expression changed to one of "I knew it", he added, "but I have to disappoint you darling and say I *was* tied up while following a lead at Halls Gap and yes, the threat from the main terrorist needs to be taken seriously. I promise I'll give you a full rundown in the morning when I've got more get-up-and-go in me." He pointed to his clothes. "The new digs Nat, they're quite flash under the circumstances, and as you can see I was able to freshen up before coming here." He cocked his head as the aroma of a home-cooked meal drew his attention.

Natalie caught his appreciative glance. "Yep, ready to serve, piping hot lamb and minestrone soup with crusty bread for starters, then apple crumble and ice cream for dessert. Afterwards it's off to bed with you."

Ballard took her in his arms. "I may have to disappoint you tonight darling. I'm not sure I'm up to our usual after-dinner activities."

"Ha! You know *exactly* what I mean Michael. I'll be amazed if you're still awake at the end of your meal."

"I've never fallen asleep during one of your culinary delights and I certainly don't intend to start now." His bloodshot eyes contradicted the veracity of his words.

Taking his coat Natalie pushed him towards the dining table. "Good, go and sit down and I'll dish up. Prepare to be amazed."

Thirty minutes later, wiping his mouth with a napkin he sat back and declared, "You didn't disappoint Nat. This was just what the doctor ordered."

Eyeing him Natalie watched his eyelids droop as his last vestiges of energy drained away. Fearing he may fall asleep she was mindful of the fact she wouldn't be able to carry him upstairs. "Come on darling, the last thing I need is for you to pass out and I have to bunk you down here in the lounge."

Stumbling upstairs to the bathroom he stripped down, wearily performing the most basic of ablutions before Natalie eased him into bed. The moment his head hit the pillow he fell into a deep slumber. Sitting beside him, lost in a jumble of thoughts Natalie stroked his forehead over and over.

7 a.m. saw Ballard's internal clock kick in, despite being two hours later than usual. Wide awake he sat up, careful not to disturb Natalie who was slumbering beside him. As quietly as he could he slipped into his dressing gown and after disconnecting his mobile

from the charger, padded barefoot downstairs to the lounge and flicked on the twenty-four-hour news channel.

He wasn't disappointed. The prediction of armchair experts engaging in an orgy of opinion conferring was underway. A former chief commissioner of police, a professor of criminology, and a social science commentator were all offering their views, adjudicated by one of the station's stalwart reporters. Ballard increased the volume as he listened to the commissioner expound on the difficulties the authorities faced from such an expertly led group of terrorists. His reasoning was angrily countered by the strident declaration from the social science commentator that paying a ransom was a catalyst for further attacks, the assessment rammed home with shrill indignation.

The reporter asked whether there was firm evidence of a ransom being paid, to which the social commentator replied, "A substantial rumour is doing the rounds that a *billion dollars* was handed over by the federal government."

Shocked, the reporter's eyes widened, and for several seconds he was speechless. Recovering and to his credit choosing the prudent route, he stated, "I think we need to be circumspect whether *any* money let alone such a huge sum actually changed hands. Without firm evidence this claim appears to be supposition at best." Having protected himself and the station from potential legal challenges, he posed to the professor, "*Hypothetically* speaking, were such a demand made, taking into consideration the horrific incidents that occurred over the past three days, would a payment by the government be justified?"

The professor hesitated, fully aware he was being asked to expand on a politically sensitive subject. "Another way to pose that question would be to ask how many brutal murders—no, let's call them for what they were—how many *executions* would need to occur before public outrage overwhelmed *any* possibility of copycat actions." He grimaced. "There were over a hundred people in the legislative assembly. Would a humane government anywhere in the world sit back and watch them being slaughtered by the dozen and do nothing to halt it?"

The commentator lurched forward in his seat, eyes bulging. "Of course not. That's why the elite forces should have gone in earlier and got them out."

The commissioner didn't wait to be asked, growling, "*It's not that simple.* The legislative assembly was heavily fortified with explosives arming each of the entry doors along with an unknown amount of C4, or equivalent, *inside* the chamber. A full-on assault could have resulted in every one of the hostages being killed, and we'd be sitting here now lamenting the inconceivable loss of lives, questioning why the assault teams acted so hastily."

Caught up in the exchanges, Ballard reflex-punched the air as he called aloud, "Damn right! Try making decisions that important in real life!" Embarrassed, he looked over his shoulder, relieved Natalie hadn't witnessed his outburst.

The reporter stared down at his prompt sheet, riding the high of a sure-fire ratings winner. "Were the army's special forces brought in to assist the police Special Operations Group because of the degree of difficulty of this mission?"

While the question was thrown to all three experts, the commissioner was the only one experienced enough to answer with any degree of credibility. "Correct. To engage the army is very rare. In fact I can't ever remember it occurring in the past, not for a civilian siege situation. A number of legal hurdles need to be cleared before the military can be commissioned to undertake a civil rescue."

His eyes focussed on a point in middle distance. "For starters the Australian Defence Force Special Operations Command personnel can only be deployed at the request of the governor general, the state or territory jurisdictions, or by the Commonwealth. So a decision to engage them had to be made at a senior level within government ranks. This takes time."

A pause was followed by, "Again I stress this is no reflection on the skill or resolve of our state police SOG members. They're world-class, but in fairness the group who attacked Parliament House had exceptional skills and were led by a very professional soldier who undoubtedly had years of military training."

Ballard found himself nodding in agreement, impressed by the commissioner's grasp of the situation, reflecting back to when Jordan had briefed the AC and a roomful of anxious faces, all praying the lieutenant colonel's services wouldn't be required.

The commissioner continued. "When the ADF is engaged the level of force used by the military is guided by four major principles: primacy of the civil authority, proportionality, and equally important, necessity." He paused, staring directly into the camera lens to emphasise his next point. "Fourthly, it's imperative the army retain command over its own troops at all times—this is paramount. It must also be remembered the SOG takes its principal directions from the chief of the army." Ballard's admiration went up several notches, and it was clear the reporter was equally impressed.

The professor and the social commentator shuffled in their seats, annoyed at their apparent exclusion from proceedings. The reporter sensed their disquiet and skilfully posed a question which drew them into the discussion. "Up to this point the attackers have been referred to as terrorists, as much for expediency as reality . . . *were* they terrorists in the true sense?"

The professor opened his mouth but was beaten to the punch by the commentator. "There are multiple definitions for *terrorism*, but the simplest includes 'any person or persons who use violence and intimidation, especially against civilians, in the pursuit of political or religious ideals'. Well the violence and intimidation was evident in spades, but I'm not aware of any political or religious commentary at any point throughout the siege."

He deferred to the professor who shook his head. "I agree. It appears these particular individuals were driven solely by the desire for money, which they may or may not have received from the federal government."

The reporter placed his prompt sheet to one side, a clear indication the segment was drawing to a close. "Well gentlemen, one last question. What have we learned from this tragic incident?"

The question had all three hesitating before the commissioner stated in a soft voice, "Australia's long-held innocence from such acts of violence is now over, never to return. This is a wake-up call and one which authorities in this country will from time to time be confronted with by similar acts of brutality. As such they'll need to be even more vigilant than they currently are."

On that sobering note the reporter thanked each of the guests then eyeballing the camera, uttered in his celebrated baritone voice, "This is Phillip Sanders on behalf of *The Forum* . . . until next time."

Ballard sat motionless for several seconds then angrily thrust the remote towards the TV, muting the sound. Frustration building, he castigated himself that had he thought of the tunnel option sooner at least two of the murdered politicians might still be alive. His aggravation intensified, guilt wracking him before logic struggled to the fore, reminding him that had he not conceived the action, many more lives would have been lost.

He dialled John's number.

Three rings had his partner answering. "Mate, why aren't you still asleep?"

Ballard snorted, dismissing the notion. "Did you see the interview on channel 24 by any chance?"

"I certainly did, and what a pair of bozos the professor and the commentator turned out to be. Intellectual twits with blisters on their backsides who've never experienced reality in their lives. Pretty chuffed with how the chief handled himself though. Hasn't lost any of his street smarts since he retired."

Ballard agreed. He and John had discussed numerous murder cases with him over the years, primarily those which threatened to become political or major headlines; the AC often joined them in the chief's office to thrash out the most suitable course of action. Throwing caution to the wind Ballard mentioned his feelings of regret at not acting earlier, drawing a predictable rebuff from his partner.

"*Bullshit Mike*. Seriously, how many lives did you save by coming up with the tunnel option in the first place? Sergey's a bloody psychopath of the tallest order. People were going to die no matter what, something I'm sure we'll be reminded of when we have our session with dear Marjorie." He paused. "I take it we're still on for tomorrow morning?"

"Yep, and I'll bet you're really looking forward to it." Grinning, Ballard shook himself from his temporary funk before asking, "Changing subjects, how would you and Sonia like a short jaunt in the Riviera this morning, perhaps down to the new Wyndham Marina in Werribee? A BBQ at the clubhouse then we can tootle back in the afternoon. An hour and a half each way, tops. I checked the weather forecast and you'll be pleased to know there's no wind so the bay's going to be a millpond. I promise not to frighten the life out of you Johno." Knowing full well his partner's fear of anything nautical, along with heights, Ballard was chuffed by his response.

"You know something Mike? I think that might be just what the doctor ordered. Sonia's home for the next few days and she enjoyed the last trip we took with you guys. What time do you want us at NewQuay?"

The mantle clock showed 8 a.m. "Nat's not up yet but I believe she's got minute steaks in the fridge. We can marinade them while we're motoring down. Say elevenish at the dock?"

"Great. We'll be there with dessert." The disconnect beeps signalled John was gone.

Ballard sat staring at the muted TV, his mind trolling through the events of the last seventy-two hours, desperate to make sense of what had transpired but experienced enough to know time was needed to lessen his disquiet. His mind ached as to how and when he would reveal to Natalie the events leading up to and during the chopper ride and the tragic loss of two policemen, turning over in his mind what he would say.

"It helps if you turn the volume up, unless you're practising your lip-reading skills."

Swinging around Ballard saw Natalie propped against the door, her robe doing its best to cover delicious patches of flesh but failing miserably. Springing to his feet he took her in his arms, kissing her as his hands roamed beneath the multiple layers of silk.

"Isn't it marvellous how a few hours' sleep perks one's batteries?"

Mumbling a reply, Ballard's lips advanced to her breasts as he pulled her closer. "Just making up for falling asleep on the job last night."

Delighting in the exchange, Natalie returned his affection before slipping away. "Was that John I heard you talking to?"

Watching her rearrange her robe, Ballard nodded. "I suggested we take the boat down to the new marina at Werribee. Sonia's coming along as well."

Natalie's face lit up. "That's wonderful. We've got a lot to catch up on. Do they have a restaurant down there or should I rustle something up?"

"They do, but I thought with the weather as it is we could have a BBQ then head back to NewQuay in the afternoon."

Natalie completed tying the sash on her dressing gown in a businesslike manner, heralding "Your fun's over buster. Let's start preparing for the trip". Gazing up at him she asked, "When do you want to head off?"

Resigned, Ballard stepped back, smiling. "Is ten thirty too early?"

"No, just let me throw a few things together."

"You *never* just throw things together Nat, but it's good you didn't freeze the steaks."

"No brain surgery there darling. With this fantastic weather a BBQ somewhere was always on the cards." She reached up, pressing her lips against his forehead before hurrying to the kitchen.

Taking his mobile Ballard called out, "I'll ring the marina and book a berth."

CHAPTER
10

Stepping onto the swim deck of the Riviera, Ballard unzipped the canvas awning and pushed open the half-swing door leading into the cockpit. Helping Natalie on board with her cool bags stacked with food, he was thrust aside unceremoniously by John who positioned himself so he could assist Sonia, almost carrying her aboard.

"Er John, I'm only eleven weeks along. Women still ride horses at this stage, play tennis, even step onto boats without ill effect, but thank you for being so caring." Reaching up she kissed him on the cheek which was reddening by the second under Ballard's amused gaze. Smiling at Natalie Sonia relieved her of the bags of food, freeing her to unlock the sliding canopy which led down to the saloon. Both women disappeared to stock the fridge.

Ballard turned to his partner. "Sooo Johno, care to take this baby for a spin?"

John growled his reply, "Are you crazy? No, I'll leave the captaining to you, thanks all the same."

Ballard couldn't resist. "This thing's only twelve metres long and eight tonnes." He hooked a thumb towards Cinderella located on the outer berth. "Now if I was asking you to take *that* sucker out, 35 metres and 180 tonnes, well, I'd understand your reluctance."

Glancing over his shoulder to check that the ladies couldn't hear him John hissed a predictable two-word pithy response. Chuckling, Ballard took a set of keys and inserted them in the ignition before switching on the air extraction blower to remove possible petrol fumes from the engine room. He then activated the marine digital throttle system which turned over the twin MerCruiser motors.

The heavy-duty 640-horsepower V8 rumble produced the same appreciative grin from John as it did the first time he heard it.

Cocking his head he analysed the motor's pitch. "Music to my ears Mike. I just love it."

Ballard became serious. "As you said John, this is just what the doctor ordered. We've all soaked up our fair share of stress over the past few days. We need to back off a tad and smell the roses, even if it's just for a couple of hours. I'm glad you and Sonia could make it." Both men shook hands, solemn, in tune with each other's emotional needs.

"My, my, that looks formal." Natalie poked her head up from the saloon, followed by Sonia.

"Secret men's business." Ballard placed an arm around her, hugging her to his side. "Time to cast off." While the engines warmed he unlocked the rear storage hatch on the swim deck, extracting the boat hook which Natalie employed to help guide the Riviera while manoeuvring in and out of the pen.

After placing the fenders along the gunnels, he untied each of the securing ropes before hopping back on board, returning to the helm. Easing the Riviera out of its mooring he swung to starboard in one smooth arc, heading for the Bolte Bridge. As on the previous trip Sonia and Natalie stood side by side, taking in the scenery.

In the distance the Portarlington Ferry was seen pulling away from its berth. Ballard nudged the throttles forward, adding 500 revs which increased his speed to 7 knots. "That should get us under the bridge before the ferry." He half-smiled at John. "If we get nailed by the Water Police for speeding I'll let you do the talking."

"The hell you will Mike." John scoffed. "Like I said, you're the captain. The buck stops with you, boyo."

Natalie tutted. "Now, now, gentlemen. Let's not have a mutiny between the captain and the first mate."

Ten minutes later, having passed the container ships unloading at the docks, they swept under the Westgate Bridge where Ballard opened the throttles, increasing the speed to twelve knots. The bow of the Riviera rose out of the water as it began to plane. "I don't think two or three knots over the limit should trouble anyone."

Sonia interrupted her in-depth conversation with Natalie, delighted at the increase in speed, as minor as it was. "Isn't this fun John?"

Mumbling John replied, "Just as long as we don't go any faster or hit rough water."

"You know, for a speed fiend on the open road you surprise me." Ballard shook his head, curious.

"Yeah, yeah, in a car I put my foot on the brake and the damn thing comes to a stop. This beast just keeps going, bobbing about like a bloody cork."

Natalie sprang to her feet. "Speaking of which Sonia, I've a small bottle of champagne we can pop." Querying both men, she asked, "Apple juice?" They nodded.

Nearing Point Gellibrand, Ballard motioned to the Navman. "Keep an eye out John. While our hull depth is only a bit over a metre, this spot is notorious for sandbars."

John's eyes widened as he envisaged running aground and being asked to hop overboard, pants rolled up, having to push the Riviera free. Navigating a wide berth from the shoreline, Ballard reduced speed, also peering at the screen. Just when he thought he was past the shallowest point John reacted with a "*Careful!*" At the same moment everyone felt the faintest of nudges under the hull.

"*Bugger!*" Looking at his wide-eyed passengers, Ballard stated with exasperation, "Would you believe it? We just touched the bottom." Annoyed with himself for not sticking in the shipping channel for longer, he swung the wheel to port, heading for deeper water. As soon as he saw four metres beneath the hull he resumed cruising at twelve knots.

Natalie gave him a comforting squeeze, knowing how cautious he was and how even the slightest miscalculation annoyed him, having declared on more than one occasion, "Only amateurs scrape the bottom."

"Darling, that's almost the identical spot we touched six months ago."

Ballard grinned ruefully. "I know. I must be a slow learner. Oh well, no damage done so that's the main thing."

Natalie escorted Sonia to the rear of the boat where they settled on the couch. With their heads together, their light-hearted mood turned serious, the topic clearly Sonia's ordeal at Parliament House. Ballard and John guessed details of her pregnancy would follow a close second.

In the distance fishing and other pleasure craft cut a swathe through the remarkably still water, with several container ships anchored further out in the bay, waiting for their turn to enter the docks to unload.

Ballard signalled for John to move closer. "Any news from work?"

His partner stole a glance behind him. "I hear the AC's going to gather all the players together for a briefing tomorrow morning. Hopefully we can slot into the session before we get an earful from Marjorie."

Ballard stared ahead, ensuring his course was a straight line towards Werribee, his expression contemplative. "You know, effectively The Board won John. I mean they raked in a billion dollars despite pushing for two. Add to that, all the players except Sergey are dead, so there's no leaks back to *head office* so to speak. That being the case what the hell are they planning to do next?"

John's face screwed into a pained expression. "Well, Vladimir's behind bars thanks to Malcolm's pretty gutsy citizen's arrest, and the Russian embassy guy, Ola . . . Ole . . ." He shrugged in frustration.

"Olegovich."

"Yeah, *that* guy. He's the key to us ferreting down the burrow and exposing some of The Board's members." He shook his head in disbelief. "You could have knocked me over with a feather when James confirmed Olegovich was The Board's Australian cell leader—and living it up big time in a mansion in St Georges Road no less where all the Toorak heavies hang out."

"Hmm, working at the Russian embassy is a sting in the tail we never saw coming." Ballard leaned towards the Navman, checking his speed, direction, and depth beneath the hull. "Think about it John. Could there be a more perfect cover—complete diplomatic immunity which protects not only himself but his family and his residence from prying eyes? The AC stuck his neck out bringing him in for questioning and deserves full marks on that score. I guess the international ramifications for shooting our politicians has even the Kremlin sitting up and taking notice. As for pressuring Russia to cut Olegovich loose from the diplomatic immunity he's hiding behind, time will tell how far we get on that front."

Two jet skis shot either side of the Riviera, hurling dual wakes against the hull, spraying the windscreen. Sonia and Natalie jumped to their feet to witness the commotion while John waved an angry fist. "*Dickheads!* Don't they realise how dangerous that is?"

Ballard switched on the windscreen wipers, restoring the field of vision. "Er, probably not John. Enforcing rules for jet skis is pretty much pot luck. The buggers know they can make it like the Road Runner out there because this thing isn't fast enough to catch them, so it's a free hit for the young and the restless." Clearly aware of the disturbance they had caused, the two shirtless riders waved a dismissive hand each as they zigged and zagged into the distance. John continued to mumble his discontent as the ladies resumed their in-depth discussion.

Returning to the case John snarled, "I can't *wait* to grill Vladimir. How on earth he thought he could get away with removing the locator chip James had surgically inserted beats me. Let's face it. If not for Bernard Junior's private agency he might still be on the run." He appeared perplexed. "The AC went out on a bloody long limb releasing Vladimir, considering all his indictable offences, but it shows the political heat our brass must have applied to insist on it.

"In fairness, at the time he was the only person who had even the remotest chance of being able to prewarn us about the attack on Parliament House as well as *perhaps* give us a heads-up who some of

The Board members might be." He frowned. "Not that the bugger was too forthcoming when you think about it."

Both men contemplated the AC's earlier decision to free the Russian on the slim chance his links to The Board would provide vital information regarding the rumour that a number of politicians were going to be held hostage. The decision was a career-defining moment for the AC, underpinned by technical wizardry care of James who promised Vladimir's every move would be tracked electronically. Despite this precaution the gamble didn't pay off, with Vladimir disappearing for several weeks only to be rearrested at Portsea at the midpoint of the siege.

As though able to read his partner's mind John questioned, "How is it we find ourselves mixed up with professional crooks who have their own executioners able to be unleashed at a moment's notice to clean up any mess that even *hints* at exposing The Board's membership? Christ, this is Australia Mike—sunshine, beer, beaches, and bikinis. What the hell has happened to this country?"

Ballard matched his partner's angst as he nudged the throttles, increasing the speed to fifteen knots. "We became part of the global village John. It has its advantages, but in our line of business it muddies the water—*a lot*."

Agreeing but not liking the reality, John glanced once more at Sonia and Natalie whose heads were almost touching. "How's Nat handling the Sergey threat?"

Ballard's cheeks ballooned. "Like it isn't a threat, and that's a real concern."

"She's a tough cookie Mike, mentally and physically. I wouldn't worry too much."

"As I said to Delwyn, we can't dodge shadows forever, but Sergey isn't someone to be trifled with. The kids are safely with their grandparents, so that's one problem out of the way. I'll just have to keep on suggesting that Nat stay with her folks until he's caught." His features hardened. "When that happens I'll personally make sure Corrections take him seriously this time. What a cock-up his escape turned out to be."

Both men reflected on previous events before Ballard shook himself from his reverie, announcing, "Enough of this thrashing over work John. The whole purpose of today is to get *away* from it all."

Turning to face Natalie and Sonia, he grinned roguishly. Natalie caught the look and stopped in mid sentence.

Ballard inclined his head, inviting the two women to move closer. "I thought I'd entertain you good folk with a few specifics regarding the bay. It's fascinating when you delve into its history."

A comical groan from John momentarily drowned out the V8's rumble.

Both ladies approached and kneeled on the couch behind the helm. They directed looks of sympathy squarely at John, with Natalie whispering, "Now play nice Michael."

Feigning confusion, Ballard led off. "*Did you know* the bay was only formed about ten thousand years ago? Prior to that, what's known today as the Yarra River flowed down the middle in a depression. At the southern end the river formed a lake which ran into Bass Strait." Ballard was reflective. "The first Aboriginals would have hunted and fished all along the shoreline prior to the bay flooding at the end of the last Ice Age. During a prolonged dry period around three thousand years ago, the bay drained for a second time before reflooding. Can you imagine the chaos if that were to happen today?"

While John's face assumed an expression more akin to having his wisdom teeth extracted, both women appeared amazed at the revelation. Ballard took this as an open invitation to press on. "Now, the deepest point in the bay is around twenty-four metres. However, over half of its area is eight metres or less." He fixed Natalie with a meaningful look before blurting in exasperation, "Something I discovered yet again this morning near Williamstown."

Natalie pretended to be sympathetic, but her effort was short-lived.

"Geographically the bay covers nearly two thousand square kilometres, with a shoreline of just over two hundred and sixty. Despite being very shallow in the majority, the volume of water is a mind-numbing twenty-five cubic kilometres in total." Once again the ladies' eyes widened.

John began muttering unintelligibly, with Sonia attempting to appease him with a gentle hug. "This is all so *fascinating*." The mutterings grew in intensity.

Refusing to be discouraged, Ballard checked the Navman while performing a three-sixty-degree sweep for nearby craft. "The first Britons to enter the bay were John Murray and Matthew Flinders in 1802, but it wasn't until 1835 that Melbourne really began to take shape. And of course it took off big time in the gold rush." Realising he had pushed John to his emotional limit, his partner's face turning a mottled shade of red, he relented. "And as they say in the classics, the rest is history."

Just as John began to relax, Ballard raised a forefinger skyward, eyes widening dramatically. "*Oh, I forgot to mention*, Port Phillip is the most densely populated catchment in Australia with a population of over five million living around its shoreline."

John mouthed a crude word, causing Sonia to back him to the far side of the boat. She pressed her lips against his cheek, her Estée Lauder imprint remaining on full view. Natalie moved alongside Ballard. "That was very naughty Michael, but fascinating all the same."

Hooking an arm around her waist, he pointed in the distance.

"If I'm not mistaken that's the breakwater for the Wyndham Marina."

Natalie took up the binoculars and confirmed his sighting.

Thirty minutes later they berthed in the pen allocated by Darren the marina manager which had been arranged during Ballard's early morning phone call. They traipsed into his office, exchanging handshakes, Darren's broadening smile working its way to intelligent eyes framed behind black-rimmed circular glasses. "You mentioned you were down for a BBQ?" Nods ensued. "Well, you picked the perfect day for it." Everyone concurred, having commented on the almost cloudless sky as they approached the marina office, appreciating the expanse of manicured lawn out the front dotted with huge palm trees, the ground floor offices, club room, and restaurant topped by two levels of residential apartments.

"How many boats do you have moored here?" Ballard was surprised at John's apparent interest.

"Just on sixty, but we have an application with the council to extend the berths by another two hundred. The government plans to spend billions on an education city development just up the road from us which should inject much-needed interest in the marina." He expounded on the plans for the harbour, his enthusiasm infectious. He eventually paused, appearing embarrassed. "Sorry, as you can see, I get carried away at times. I'll fetch the BBQ, and you can set it up wherever you like." He waved an expansive hand, taking in the marina's entire water frontage.

Natalie and Sonia thanked him, reconfirming the security gate code to access the berth before heading back to collect the food, leaving Ballard and John to set up the massive stainless-steel monster which Darren rolled out of the club room. Selecting a spot near an outdoor table they fired up the hotplates as they waited for the marinated steaks to arrive, along with everything Natalie had prepared in the town house—namely, enough mouth-watering side dishes to feed an army.

The tantalising smell of searing filet mignon steaks, along with mushrooms, onions, corn on the cob, and potato wedges wafted across the marina, causing several passers-by to nod appreciatively. Natalie and Sonia busied themselves setting the table then added the final touches to the accompanying dishes. The air was so calm even the serviettes lay undisturbed.

Taking a plate each they piled on food before tucking into the eagerly anticipated feast. Darren called by to ensure all was well, and although invited to take a plate, he declined the offer with thanks.

Natalie smiled across at Sonia, waving her fork in mid-air. "All good protein for the baby. How are you coping with morning sickness?"

Swallowing her mouthful, Sonia announced, "Surprisingly well. Bub must have a mild temperament like its dad."

Ballard appeared to choke on a piece of steak. Eyes watering, he asked, "So you don't know the baby's gender?" Natalie continued to eat while fixing him with a firm stare.

Both John and Sonia shook their heads in unison, with John sighing. "Just give me ten fingers, ten toes, and a brain as sharp as its mother's and I won't have any complaints." Sonia snuggled alongside him, eyes shining, leaving him in no doubt she was in total agreement.

Ballard opened his mouth to pursue his long-held belief that parents were crazy not to determine the sex of their baby, but Natalie's unblinking gaze left him in no doubt she was demanding the matter be dropped.

"Not *everything* in life has to be regimented, darling." Her tone was dry.

Ballard nodded with considered deliberation, fully aware Sonia was eternally grateful she had fallen pregnant, which was a blessing as she was in her early forties, notwithstanding being fitter than most women half her age.

Raising his glass he toasted the couple. "Here's to you both. Nat and I couldn't be happier. Boy or girl, the baby's blessed to have you as a mother Sonia, and well, he or she's just going to have to suck it up and accept John for what he is."

"*Michael.*" Natalie elbowed Ballard while John sported a lopsided grin, still coming to terms with his good fortune at becoming a first-time dad. Natalie followed with "Don't worry John, you'll be a fantastic father."

"I'll do my best Nat." He rested a hand on Sonia's belly, channelling his love for the young life developing within. Ballard marvelled at the transformation in his partner who was regarded by his colleagues as one of the last real hardmen in the job, happy to run towards danger to protect others or, as on countless occasions, persevere long after others had given up in their endeavour to solve a complex case.

Finishing their main course they sat chatting, basking in the sunshine, allowing overloaded stomachs to digest the food just eaten before tackling Sonia's still-warm date scones topped with jam and whipped cream. Despite his brain cautioning him otherwise, Ballard tackled a second helping. Even John appeared astounded by his partner's seemingly limitless capacity.

Ballard saw the look and quipped, "Yep, but I'm approaching FF to B Johno."

Sonia was perplexed before Natalie came to the rescue. "That's Michael's way of saying 'full fit to burst'." This produced a round of laughter.

With the BBQ cleaned and returned to the club room, and the mountain of leftover food stored in the motor cruiser's two fridges, Ballard was once again at the helm as they headed back towards Melbourne. The bay was equally calm as in the morning, and this went some way to convincing John that sea travel could be relaxing and enjoyable, producing a firm stipulation, "Providing there are no thunderclouds on the horizon."

Entering the Yarra River precinct they watched a monster container ship shepherded by two tugs pass beneath the Westgate Bridge. Keeping a wide berth they stopped off at the Pier 35 fuel depot, everyone standing clear while Ballard pumped a quick 150 litres of premium petrol into each tank. In the distance, propped beside one of the marina's restaurant tables with a group of people was Terry, the salesman who had sold Ballard and Natalie their boat and took them out on their first nerve-wracking nautical run.

Ballard called out, "Best thing I ever did." Terry raised a hand, smiling his acknowledgement. Ballard followed up with "Say hello to Chris for us." Following a brief wave, Terry escorted the group towards his office, almost certainly to clinch another well-crafted business deal.

An hour later, *Whatever It Takes* was back in the pen at NewQuay and washed down, with everything stowed and shipshape. John shook his head as he took in Ballard and Natalie's disciplined routine, his arm encircling Sonia's still-slim waist. After a final check, Ballard led the way up the ramp to the promenade where they all said their goodbyes, agreeing the day on the water had been wonderfully therapeutic and should be a more regular occurrence.

Ballard and John spoke briefly, confirming they would be at the office by 7 a.m.

Just as Ballard and Natalie were about to head to the car park, Ballard spotted a powerfully built man in the distance who maintained a direct gaze for several seconds before turning and walking with purpose along the promenade in the opposite direction. An alert registered with Ballard which he struggled to bring to the fore. Realization suddenly hit him like a sledgehammer. The man was the Russian sailor he and John had attempted to arrest at the docks several months prior with no success. The deckhand had dived off one of the container ships clutching an iPad which contained what was believed to be revealing information about The Board. The sailor disappeared in the murky waters along with the iPad which was thought to be buried in metres of soft mud at the bottom of Swanson Dock.

Ballard spun around, aggressive, preparing to give chase, startling Natalie. A visual search of the promenade confirmed the sailor was nowhere to be seen, having merged with the strolling tourists.

CHAPTER
11

AC Thompson, in full uniform and looking every bit as commanding as his rank, fixed everyone at the Critical Incident's conference table with cobalt-blue eyes, his gaze so steadfast several of the attendees looked away, peering down at their folders. The multiple screens mounted on the walls were switched off, and the electronic whiteboards were scrubbed clean; it was clear the meeting was limited to a specific need-to-know audience.

"We dodged a catastrophe ladies and gentlemen, despite the tragic deaths of four of our finest politicians. The reality is the incident *could* have ended up being a massacre which doesn't bear contemplating. The successful rescue of the remaining hostages is directly attributable to the courage and expertise of everyone in this room. Something the premier and police minister on behalf of every one of the impacted politicians and their families have acknowledged with a heartfelt thank you, which they've asked me to pass on." A ripple of appreciation circulated. "The minister believes parliament will resume as early as tomorrow. He said it's as much to fly the 'we're the government and back in charge' flag as anything else, demonstrating to the public *and* other would-be crooks the rule of law is alive and well."

Ballard, sitting between John and Delwyn, with Peter to her right, was still recovering from the shock of seeing Bernard Winters was in the room, rubbing shoulders with James Patterson. The retired CIA agent and the ASIO intelligent officer cheekily acknowledged with a wry smile Ballard and John's open-mouthed amazement. Bernard's eyes were twinkling, accompanied by his trademark mischievous grin. What appeared to have been a serious conversation between the two men was halted by the AC's opening remarks.

Damien Harcourt, the federal attorney general's representative, was ensconced to the left of the AC, with Gerhart Müller, the counterterrorism commander on his right. Observing around the table, Ballard waved to Superintendent Mark Oldfield who was heading up the dragnet bikie taskforce, wedged between an exhausted Tim and a uniformed Jordan Hensley. Alongside them was a debonair Robert Mayne, the forensic ballistic expert as resplendent as ever in a grey pinstripe suit, white shirt, and sapphire-blue bow tie. Robert was a self-confessed ladies' man and Ballard was surprised he wasn't sitting alongside Marjorie Otterman from the Psychology Unit. Her presence reminded Ballard of the scheduled session with John and himself later that morning.

Sitting in deep reflection Marjorie was elegantly attired in a pale-cream pin-tucked blouse, its delicate lace collar framing a pearl pendant nesting above a hint of tanned décolletage. Her ebony-black hair was pinned to perfection by a filigree gold clasp. On cue Robert leaned forward and acknowledged her presence with an enthusiastic nod and a perfect smile which generated an equally dazzling response. Marjorie was fully aware of the ballistic expert's Casanova-like reputation. Glancing across at Delwyn who had witnessed the exchange, the psychologist gave the superintendent a knowing incline of her head.

Rounding out what was an overcrowded conference table, Commander Roger Crimmins, the federal police representative who had provided essential information on money laundering after the Note Printing Australia robbery, sat shoulder to shoulder with Captain Dennis Nelson, the army officer who was an expert in explosives.

AC Thompson took several sips of his tea, a cloud of steam rising from his cup, causing Ballard to reason the man must have an unbelievable pain threshold. Taking in his audience, the veteran officer introduced everyone before dropping a bombshell. "It's with growing misgiving I'm here to inform you that The Board's raid on

Parliament House appears to be nothing more than a common cash grab to help finance their true objective, an objective infinitely more disturbing than we could ever have imagined—that being, taking control of the ports here in Melbourne and in Sydney."

The stunned expressions around the table were a clear indication that everyone was aware of the implications should the group ever achieve their goal—a free hit to move contraband in and out of the country virtually unchecked. This was a nightmare scenario which would generate them billions of dollars over decades to come, not to mention trigger countless deaths as a result of the ensuing drug trade.

John leaned across to Ballard and hissed, "There's no end to what these bastards think they can get away with."

In his trademark considering manner Peter sought clarification with the simplest of questions. "What are the facts sir?"

Understanding the superintendent's request was for the benefit of those present, the AC waved a directing hand at James who stood to take up the commentary, tugging the cuffs of his pale-blue business shirt so they were a fashionable length beneath his navy suitcoat, an unconscious action all present had witnessed at prior briefings. "Ladies and gentlemen, it'd be fair to say most of you wouldn't have met Mr Bernard Winters." He hesitated, straight-faced, directing an extended stare towards Ballard and John, who produced an almost convincing "I know nothing" expression; it fooled the majority in the room but not the AC or Delwyn whose suspicions were growing by the minute. The giant Texan half rose in his chair, nodding to the attendees but said nothing, his intelligent eyes continuing to assess and catalogue his audience.

James sipped from his water. "Mr Winters and myself will detail what has now progressed from suspicion and supposition to measurable certainty regarding a criminal takeover of the ports. That said, before I proceed on that front, the AC would like to run over more immediate issues associated with the raid at Parliament House." With a brief nod he handed the meeting back to the AC who addressed Damien Harcourt. "Mr Harcourt, I'm aware your time is limited but you mentioned you wished to address the group?"

With his silver hair slicked down to the point it defied movement save in a hurricane, Damien Harcourt rose from his chair, appearing tired but defiant. While heavy set there was underlying muscle which spoke of athletic endeavours in his youth. "Thank you, Kevin. On behalf of the attorney general and with special mention from the prime minister, the federal government is in your debt ladies and gentlemen, for everything you achieved throughout the siege. Australia generally and specifically Melbourne have copped a battering over the past four months—first the Note Printing Australia robbery and its aftermath, and now the most audacious attack on our democracy since the Second World War, as dramatic as that may sound."

He studied everyone, much as the AC had done, determined that they appreciate the value of what they had achieved and the consequences had they failed in terms of additional lives lost and the political implications that would have ensued. "The federal government now finds itself in a maelstrom of criticism regarding the payment of the ransom."

This generated a round of muttered comment which he allowed to run unchecked before adding, "There was no way *any* of us could have known for certain whether the ringleader of the group was going to continue slaughtering politicians, but witnessing the bloodshed that *did* occur, it convinced me as a senior federal government representative that we had a duty to act. Accordingly, I advised the attorney general there was no choice but to pay the ransom. It was mine and ultimately his decision to do so, and we take full responsibility."

He drew a deep breath. "Of course had we known the moment we paid the first billion that two more executions"—he hesitated, his brow furrowing—"two more executions along with a demand for a second billion would follow, well, we wouldn't have gone against our hard-and-fast protocol which mandates we *never* pay. Instead we'd have made the agonising decision to commence rescuing the hostages under the high probability of catastrophic casualties."

Ballard winced at the statement which continued to pick away at his scab of guilt for not coming up with the tunnel solution earlier; John fixed him with a hard stare and a firm shake of his head.

The representative's countenance grew darker. "Well, that's all water under the bridge. The payment was made under duress. It didn't achieve a damn thing, and the Yanks, the Brits, and even the French are putting us through the ringer which brings me to the point I need to make before I leave." His gaze was piercing. "It's vital there be *no* comment made regarding the ransom payment—not to TV reporters, the press, friends, family . . . *nobody*." The last word was uttered so forcefully even Delwyn shuffled uncomfortably in her seat. "This is vital to minimise the potential for copycat ransom demands in the future."

Peter whispered out the corner of his mouth, "And I'll wager to save his and the AG's hide." Delwyn appraised her colleague, agreeing with the faintest of nods.

"Our official response must always be 'It's government policy *never* to pay ransoms'. End of story." Damien's fierce gaze was like a laser beam, cauterising any trace of disagreement.

Satisfied his entreaty with the attendees would hold fast, he turned to ACs Thompson and Müller, shaking their hands before acknowledging everyone with a brief nod. As he walked to the door his head was held high but undoubtedly his spirits were weighed down by a troubled heart.

Peter took in his companions. "Can you imagine the grilling he and the attorney general will face from their *own* camp let alone the opposition and the press, not to mention from government representatives around the world?" He added as an angry aside, "As if the other countries don't pay ransoms for so-called important hostages, writing them off as foreign aid or the like."

Delwyn agreed, her expression sympathetic, her rank having versed her well how sustained public and political pressure generated crushing burdens which often proved fatal for careers. "Let's hope those broad shoulders of his are as strong as they appear."

The AC resumed control of the meeting. "Every one of you is experienced enough to know even the slightest slip of the tongue in the wrong quarter could set off a wildfire of rumour and supposition regarding the payment of the ransom and what that would entail." He glanced down, reflective, almost apologetic. "Considering the strain you've all been under these past days I realise this is yet another impost on you, but it's one you will need to take to your grave.

"Speaking of ransom payments, I guess this is as good a time as any to hear the latest on the matter." Turning to Roger Crimmins he invited the commander to provide an update on the billion dollars paid by the federal government to The Board.

Rubbing a hand across his prominent jaw it was evident Roger's news wasn't positive. "As I advised during my previous briefing, the money was moved from the Fed Reserve account via RITS, the Reserve Bank Information and Transfer System. That was after the governor and The Board gave their approval which under the circumstances wasn't even questioned."

The AC growled, "You're damn right it wasn't."

"Because the funds were transferred from the Australian government, the usual processing delay was avoided, so it didn't take us long to determine the transaction was made to a Swiss account. We've been in touch with the bank for nearly two days now and they're still coming to terms with the reality their senior officer who handled the payment was shot dead in the street forty minutes after the transaction passed through their system."

Despite the execution-style murder being common knowledge amongst the group, the expression on many faces was one of disquiet, with Mark posing the obvious question, "And because of that none of the bank officials are cooperating?"

Roger's head shake forewarned his reply. "Not one, and deep down I don't blame them. It's all very well being hairy-chested on something like this but when you or, worse still, your family is under threat by The Board, logic comes to the fore and demands 'It's only money'."

Studying the two ACs and observing their troubled expressions, Roger followed up with "Of course we'll be pursuing this to the end. Two of our investigators jumped on a plane yesterday to speak first-hand with the Swiss bank executives, but clearly the money's been transferred to God knows how many accounts around the world." Looking exasperated he added, "I'll keep everyone posted as updates come to hand."

Assessing the group much the same way Damien Harcourt had done, the AC appeared to mentally steel himself in preparation to tackle the immediate issues which needed to be addressed. "I've been briefed by the crime scene team prior to coming here today and they confirmed the gathering of forensic evidence for impending charges has now been completed." A tight smile was followed by "Not that any of the terrorists survived once Sergey began his take-no-prisoners killing spree. The guy's proving to be very, very elusive." He waved a hand towards Tim, inviting him to provide an update.

Responding, the SOG officer braced both hands on the table to help him get to his feet, fatigue lining his face. "As the AC indicated, Sergey shot a total of four of his own men at Parliament House." He glanced at Jordan. "There were ten attackers in all, eleven if you count the spotter on Nauru House who made to shoot one of my guys when he was confronted and had to be taken out. Our snipers also shot the guy manning the claymores positioned on Parliament House's steps, the guard on the roof and finally the bugger holding John's fiancée." All eyes swung in the direction of the veteran detective who appeared grim.

Tim looked towards Mark Oldfield. "I'd be correct in saying at least three or four of those shot were Thor's Warriors?"

Mark didn't hesitate. "I've seen the photos and shown them to my guys and yes they've corroborated they were. Also, there's a lot of online chatter coming out of their headquarters which we're monitoring to see if we can pick up anything that might be of use."

Tim was reflective for several seconds before continuing, "I'll give a brief update on our efforts to recapture Sergey in a minute, but first I'd like Jordan to give his thoughts on the rescue. Jordan?" He passed the briefing over to the lieutenant colonel, clearly impressed by what the professional soldier and his team had achieved.

Replacing his cup onto the saucer with a clatter, the army officer took up the commentary. "As you know a number of my team accessed the Parliament House ground level via the disused 1889 air intake tunnel, as proposed by Michael. Once in position they were perfectly placed to take out the remaining terrorists who were guarding the south entrance. Thankfully we didn't have to use the Browning heavy machine guns we had mounted on the Balkans." He shrugged, appearing embarrassed at what could have been construed as overkill. "At 500 rounds a minute, firing 12.7-millimetre slugs it would have made a fair old mess of the building's bluestone walls."

The AC permitted himself a rare smile, aware of the firepower the army had on tap and grateful it wasn't used as there would have been the need for a lengthy explanation as to why so much damage was wreaked on the heritage-listed building

Jordan matched the AC's aside with his own tight smile. "Okay, that left us with Sergey handing himself in but with a very nasty sting in the tail: 40,000 litres of ammonium nitrate and diesel fuel premixed in a rig parked out the front of Parliament House." His eyebrows peaked as he nodded to Dennis Nelson. The officer sprang to his feet, standing almost to attention.

Licking dry lips, the explosives expert began with a jaw-dropping revelation. "Worldwide about two hundred million tonnes of fertiliser are produced annually, the perfect ingredient for making bombs and it's very, very accessible to criminals of all persuasions." He paused to see what reaction his statement had and was rewarded with everyone's fixed gaze. "Now this brings me to Timothy McVeigh, the anti-government extremist who used about two thousand kilograms of ammonium nitrate mixed with three thousand dollars' worth of motor-racing fuel to blow up a US federal government building in Oklahoma City in 1995. A hundred and sixty-eight people died, and the front half of the nine-storey building was destroyed. Substitute the motor-racing fuel for everyday dieseline and three thousand dollars' worth comes to about two thousand litres. All up, the ammonia nitrate and the fuel McVeigh used weighed around four to five thousand kilograms. I'm sure you all remember the graphic photos of the destroyed building." Heads bobbed, with several unconsciously leaning forward, pre-guessing where the captain was heading.

"The rig parked outside Parliament House had *40,000* litres of ammonium nitrate mixed with diesel fuel, almost ten times the explosive power of the Oklahoma bomb." Running his fingers through his sandy-blonde hair he elaborated, "As I said, the rig was premixed and to top it off, it had 6 kilos of C4 strapped externally to ignite the fuel load. When I briefed you after the NPA robbery I mentioned that the shockwave from a C4 explosion travels at 8,000 metres a second."

The officer warmed to his subject, punctuating his points with a forefinger stabbing the air. "Were the rig to go up, the shockwave wouldn't have had much purchase travelling across the front steps, *but*"—again he thrust his finger—"once the wave reached the alcove, because the structure is enclosed at both ends there *would* be significant resistance, the build-up of forces extreme." He shook his head as though imagining the scenario for real. "The best way to describe the kinetic energy generated is to equate it to twenty fully loaded freight trains slamming into Parliament House simultaneously. The damage would be nothing less than catastrophic, and I'm certain *some* of the fourteen colonnades at the head of the steps would collapse, at the very least dropping the front half of the building, if not more."

Delwyn interjected, caught up in the moment. "This would have been fatal for the hostages and the ambulance officers stretchering them out." Her comment was met with bleak expressions.

Dennis agreed. "Without doubt Delwyn." He shook his head. "It's hard to imagine we came so close to this happening. The carnage would have been indescribable."

Fearing the mood was becoming introspective the AC resumed control. "Thank you Dennis, Jordan. Questions anyone?"

Ballard raised a hand. "How was the truck stolen?"

Peter rocked forward, slapping a hand on the table causing Marjorie to jump in her seat. Apologising, Peter continued, "My team has been following up on this, so I can provide the current state of play. The rig originated from a company located in Laverton. The CEO is currently being grilled how one of his units was casually driven out of the yard fully laden without police being notified until it was too late. Apparently it's common practice to preload the trucks then park them overnight so they can be moved out first thing in the morning to the various mine sites. Considering the damage one of these babies can deliver I'd rate the security at the compound as one out of ten, at *best*. Looking at this from another angle we're following up on whether it was an inside job."

The AC addressed AC Müller. "Gerhart, may I leave you and Peter to lean on the company and straighten them out?" AC Müller required no encouragement. "I'll liaise with Peter. However, knowing his bulldog ways I've no doubt he's already got the message across loud and clear." A meaningful look was directed towards the superintendent.

The AC turned back to Tim. "Would I be correct in assuming you've had no luck tracking Sergey after he was choppered out of Halls Gap?"

"None whatsoever sir, his lead was over twenty minutes. As Michael stated at the time he could well have been 150 kilometres away in any direction from my starting point. We tried a few possible locations but the pilot had to turn back to Melbourne after thirty minutes as we'd chewed through a fair quantity of juice on the trip up.

"We've been in touch with the staff who operate the radar station at Mount William near Halls Gap, along with the tower at Tullamarine, but they weren't able to provide any data that was useful. Clearly the chopper which took off with Sergey was hugging the terrain and its transponder would have been turned off."

John hissed out the corner of his mouth, "Pity the bastard didn't fly *into* Mount William."

To his surprise the AC's hearing was razor-sharp. "Er John, we all wish that. It would save us an awful lot of paperwork." John grinned sheepishly as he checked around the table, confirming everyone was in full agreement.

The AC lapsed into considered thought before asking, "The hardware the terrorists used, how the hell did these guys get their hands on the stuff so readily?"

All eyes swung to Robert Mayne who didn't miss a beat, despite having been preoccupied checking that his bow tie was millimetre perfect. "I should have my report complete by the end of the day sir. No surprise the serial numbers on each of the weapons seized were ground off. While Sonia was being held in the chamber she managed to pass on her belief the mag capacity was thirty rounds, and"—he glanced at John, clearly impressed—"she was dead right. Well actually it was thirty-two rounds. Not bad for someone under so much pressure."

John acknowledged the compliment with a short smile as Robert added, "Uzis don't just fall off the back of a truck, which makes it clear The Board's reach into the black market knows no boundaries. The weapons were micro Uzis, so Mark, it may be worth checking whether Thor's Warriors have their hands on any more of these babies. They're a later model manufactured around 1982. The original of course was designed in 1949 by Uziel Gal. The micros weigh 1.5 kilograms and are 250 millimetres long with the stock folded. Their fire rate is an eye-popping 1,250 rounds a minute. A 32-round mag would be emptied in 1.5 seconds. Even a blind man could hit a target up to 40, 50 metres away with one of these darlings."

Robert licked his lips, prompting Delwyn to nudge Ballard in recognition that unless checked the ballistics expert was about to launch into one of his famous technical soliloquies, espousing +P grain loads, muzzle energy, and propulsion speeds. Fully aware of Robert's reputation the AC chose to bring the expert's briefing to an end. "Thank you Robert. Flick me your report as soon as you can, and yes Mark, if possible find out if more of these damn things are sitting on a shelf in some back room at the bikies' headquarters, or more likely in one of their homes. It's about time we put some additional heat on this particular gang."

Robert blinked several times, clearly disappointed he wasn't being permitted to go into more detail, but he consoled himself by flashing his pearly whites at Marjorie as he settled back down. Taking pity on him the psychologist returned the acknowledgement at the acute risk of conveying the wrong signal.

Next the AC focussed on Ballard, his cheeks ballooning as his look turned to disbelief. "Michael, all I can say is—no, all *anyone* can say is how the hell did you escape a trained Spetsnaz killer while handcuffed, wearing a hood, and trapped inside a helicopter flying to an unknown destination?"

After flashing a grin at Delwyn who rolled her eyes while attempting to maintain a straight face, Ballard turned serious before recounting his ordeal, neither downplaying nor overstating the sequence of events. At the point where he described shooting Sergey and grinding the knife into the pilot's thigh, both ACs, hardened street warriors though they were, couldn't hide their astonishment, ramping this up to incredulity when Ballard detailed how he made the life-and-death decision to force the chopper to crash. His relaying of the tragic shooting of the two police officers had everyone's features hardening as they channelled their anger towards Sergey.

The story told, there was a period of muted discussion which was broken by the AC who expressed zero sympathy for Sergey's injuries, adding, "Hopefully that'll keep the bastard out of circulation for at least a week or two. I'm told hospitals in the area have been checked out but it's obvious he's not stupid. The Board will have patched up his wounds privately."

He turned his attention to John, causing the seasoned detective to squirm uncomfortably. "I hear you managed to find the long-lost toilet in the ceiling of the cleaner's room in Parliament House?" A roar of laughter echoed throughout, relieving the tension which had been building; even so it failed to lessen John's discomfort, as always uneasy when subjected to direct attention.

The AC restored order. "Your assistance along with Sonia's during the crisis was incalculable. Without it we could never have achieved the positioning of the micro drones in the legislative assembly which gave us the eyes to see what was going on in there."

Ballard nodded to John, both men reliving the split-second timing and skill required by James's technical staff to fly the micro drone fitted with a camera into the chamber. The result was made possible by Sonia dropping her handbag in the doorway after asking to go to the toilet, her actions ensuring the massive doors into the chamber remained open long enough for the drone to be flown in undetected. Even now, despite the success of the mission it was clear John wasn't happy about the risk his fiancée took, but it was clear he was incredibly proud of her fearless determination to assist during the crisis.

A knock on the door saw the AC striding over. Two trolleys, one laden with sandwiches, the other with tea and coffee urns, together with cups and saucers were wheeled in. The AC acknowledged the delivery before turning back to the group. "As we haven't got to the guts of the meeting yet I thought a fifteen-minute break might be in order."

Unsurprisingly there was no need for a repeat offer.

CHAPTER
12

Sugar levels recharged and cups of steaming tea and coffee within arm's reach, everyone was back in their seats, with Delwyn and Marjorie eyeing John's overloaded plate of sandwiches with a disbelieving shake of their heads. Staring back John gestured towards Bernard's heaped plate, shrugging as if to say, "You think *I'm* over the top?"

Ballard took a bite from his chicken-and-avocado sandwich just as AC Gerhart Müller got to his feet, still swallowing what appeared to be a sizeable chunk from his own helping, making sure it was dealt with by draining half his glass of orange juice in the process. "To this point there are three people heavily involved with The Board who we believe are assisting the group's endeavours to gain control of the ports both here in Melbourne and in Sydney.

"Not wishing to repeat old news, we know The Board operates cells throughout the world, each cell involved in illegal activities netting them billions. Here in Australia we believe Dimochka Olegovich is the cell leader, and he just happens to be a diplomat with the Russian embassy. He lives high on the hog ensconced in a Toorak mansion, and his position means he has immunity for himself, his family, *and* his home."

"We know he blackmailed Vladimir Borisovich Bokaryov into financing the NPA robbery to pay back outstanding debts. Due to the efforts of a number of you only half of the one hundred and twenty million stolen has found its way to The Board."

Ballard glanced at Roger, noting the commander's grimace, aware he had been savaged by the NPA executive for not recovering more of the stolen notes.

Gerhart also recognised Roger's discomfort but didn't offer any sympathy. Being an old-school hardman who didn't waste energy on the niceties of life he declared, "This left Vladimir up to his neck in trouble with The Board and the reason he attempted to sting Malcolm Ferguson, the billionaire property developer, for a cool five hundred million, threatening Malcolm's wife Teresa as well as her mother if the dough wasn't coughed up."

Finishing the last of his orange juice in one extended gulp, Gerhart resumed, "As we all know, Vladimir pushed the envelope too far with Malcolm and somehow the billionaire managed to perform a citizen's arrest, with Vladimir's hitman Sergey taken in hours later at gunpoint inside the Eureka Tower by Tim and his team. As I mentioned, these men are the three principal players in this saga."

Flicking fingers through his curly grey hair, Gerhart pressed on. "Sergey's subsequent escape from the Melbourne Assessment Prison shows the scope and depth of The Board's reach, which of course contributed to the tragic circumstances at Parliament House. Separate to that, Command took a conscious risk in allowing Vladimir to be released with a locator chip in his backside, all on the undertaking he'd assist in identifying The Board members and with the threat he'd be exposed as cooperating with police if he didn't come to the party. Well, he demonstrated his true colours by having the chip removed and skipping town."

Gerhart continued to appear mystified. "Which brings me to Mr Bernard Winters and his son's private investigator agency which has proven to have considerable resources and managed to locate Vladimir swanning it up on a motor cruiser down at Portsea." Bernard began to stir in his seat but settled back when Gerhardt held up his hand. "Sorry Bernard, there's one more point I want to make before I pass over to you."

Bernard was more than relaxed, a veteran of thousands of similar briefings during his many years with the CIA. "No problem, Gerhart. I'm retired, remember?"

This generated smothered chuckles around the table.

"I'm convinced Olegovich was involved up to his neck in the siege at Parliament House. I've spoken with the federal attorney general and he's begun the process of having the Kremlin contacted to see if Russia will sniff the political wind and revoke the bastard's diplomatic immunity."

Ballard wracked his brains as he tried to remember what scope there was under the 1961 Vienna Convention on Diplomatic Relations to allow this. Gerhart beat him to it. "As I said, we have a fifty–fifty chance of getting the bugger's immunity revoked, not because Russia particularly likes us here in Australia, but because this episode has so much international air-play they'll want to appear to be assisting."

He massaged the side of his nose as he contemplated the best way to proceed. "I've suggested to Command and the attorney general we should progress with the withdrawal of Olegovich's immunity, but not let on the fact to the Russian embassy here in Melbourne or Olegovich himself."

The statement drew confused expressions throughout save for AC Thompson and Bernard, their years of political decision-making granting them foresight into the delicate path Gerhart was treading.

The counterterrorist officer didn't disappoint. "Were we to show our hand and let on his immunity was revoked he'd go into his shell, certainly not be as emboldened as he might otherwise be. At any rate it wouldn't be long before he was shipped back overseas, and we'd be back to square one regarding who the next cell leader would be. No, we need him to think he still has the cloak of protection and a job for that matter. That's where Vladimir comes into the picture and what he knows about the plot to take over the ports." He waved an encompassing hand towards Bernard who hopped to his feet with an agility contrary to his considerable bulk.

At ease in front of what had to be a room full of strangers despite the AC's previous introductions, he began by detailing his experience and credentials with the CIA. "The sole reason my wife Cheryl and I come to Australia each year is your summer, so we can thaw out from our American winter and to visit my son who runs the agency."

He propped the fingertips of one giant hand on the conference table's polished surface, the other hand resting nonchalantly in his trouser pocket. "For those of you who don't know, I have skin in wanting The Board brought to heel. The CIA has spent millions attempting to track down the group's members, but with no measurable success. Every time we get even remotely close to the people we have under surveillance they're executed by what James here euphemistically calls their death squad."

The ASIO officer stared up at Bernard, his face expressionless but taking in everything the American had to say, leaving no doubt the respect he had for the Texan.

"Because *I* have an interest in The Board, so too does my son. As a result, when Vladimir skipped town Bernard Junior offered his local contacts to put out feelers, flushing out where the Russian might be hiding."

Both ACs along with Delwyn made Ballard and John their focus, the two detectives ramped up their innocent stares.

Bernard noticed the exchange but continued without skipping a beat. "To cut a long story short, as AC Müller mentioned, Vladimir was spotted down at Portsea. To ensure it was in fact the man in question on the motor cruiser, one of my son's operatives who happens to live in the area went out in his fishing boat, armed with binoculars and a Wildtronics parabolic microphone, at the same time dropping a line over the side to mask the fact he was conducting surveillance."

Bernard hesitated, appearing embarrassed, which to Ballard bordered on a near impossibility. "It's when your SOG team came down in the two Zodiacs and arrested him that we stuffed up."

The AC leaned forward, curious. "How so, Bernard?"

"At the time my son was so chuffed at locating Vladimir he didn't conduct a debriefing with his operative until several days later. It was only when he listened to Vladimir's conversation on his mobile prior to his arrest, which the operative recorded using the directional mike, that he realised its significance. It's damn scratchy in places, but very revealing."

So intrigued was Bernard's audience, Ballard had to bite his tongue as he observed everyone straining forward, faces intense. With a dramatic flourish the American produced a micro recorder and positioned it on the table. Switching it on he adjusted the volume. As he warned the quality wasn't perfect, with wind gusts heard throughout, but the one-sided conversation was still able to be understood.

"Yeah, I know, I know . . . But this'll be one of Cobet's biggest gambles . . . Australia."

Bernard paused the recording. *"Cobet* is the Russian equivalent for *The Board."* He pressed Play again. A long pause was broken by *"Guess . . . this hostage thing"*—severe wind noise—*"raise quick cash. Shit, these port tenders . . . along more than once or twice in a goddamn lifetime."*

A considerable delay was followed by *"That's the thing . . . Melbourne and Sydney."* A ruthless chuckle could be heard then female laughter in the background. Bernard halted the recording once more. "I forgot to mention, Sergey had three ladies on board, keeping him company . . . or was it him keeping *them* company?"

Broad smiles broke out with the widest grin displayed by Marjorie as she eyed Delwyn knowingly, the two women having seen and heard it all before.

Bernard continued the recording.

"I've got the knife into a property developer . . . you'd know him . . ." The next word was unintelligible followed by *"Ferg—"* and despite the name being chopped off, it was obvious Vladimir was referring to Malcolm Ferguson. The group strained forward even more acutely so as not to miss a syllable. A cruel laugh was followed by *"I used to . . . his wife."* There was more static and wind noise. *"She's still . . . bloody hot."*

Ballard and John glanced at one another, John's complexion colouring on hearing Vladimir reminisce how he used to date Teresa until she discovered what kind of monster he was. Fleeing Sydney to avoid his clutches she began a new life for herself when she met and married Malcolm. The tape rolled on.

"Between us, we can raise seven . . . eight hundred . . ." The wind noise blanketed out the remaining numbers, causing Bernard to pause the recording. "I'd suggest that's seven or eight hundred million, ladies and gentlemen. This guy doesn't even *think* in thousands."

There was head shaking, with John's expression leaving little doubt as to his disbelief such figures could be discussed as though they were monopoly money. He strained forward.

"You leave that to me . . ." Vladimir was heard coughing several times. Bernard declared, "Talk about the high life—a sixty-foot Bertram, three lovely ladies to entertain him. He was eating what appeared to be caviar and smoking Cuban cigars like they were going out of production, I've seen the video the operative took." John's nod at Ballard and a quick point to his right hand was a clear reference to the nicotine stain they saw on Vladimir's fingers when they interviewed him before he was released.

Bernard's features hardened. "It's the next exchange which is most frustrating because a name is mentioned and we can't make it out. Even with my son's graphic equaliser wizgadgetry we couldn't clean it up. Let's see if anyone here can make it out."

The challenge had the room sitting to attention, heads cocked.

"I've run this past Ta—" The distortion was excessive, capped off with wind gusts most likely exacerbated by Vladimir turning away so the smoke from his cigar didn't blow in his face. Bernard produced a tight smile, his eyes flint-like. "Damn frustrating, don't you think?" He looked to Jordan. "Could your boys down at the DSTO enhance it?"

A number of curious expressions had the army officer explaining, "Maybe Bernard. The Defence Science and Technology Group have some serious cutting-edge goodies at their disposal. I'd suggest their Underwater Acoustic Laboratory would be the best place to start. Give me a copy and I'll see what I can do."

John's curiosity got the better of him. "Jesus, do we have that sort of James Bond techo shit here in Melbourne?"

Jordan laughed. "Closer than you think John. One of our DSTOs is here in Port Melbourne—Lorimer Street to be exact." John's eyebrows shot north, surprised at the disclosure.

Bernard held up his hand, drawing attention. "Now listen to the next exchange and tell me what you think." He flicked the Play button.

"She said if we can . . . the cash . . . chance to get in on the ground floor . . ." A pause. *"She just needs to fix . . . issues first. She's asked me to help . . . that score . . . this'll . . . more leverage in the group."* More chilling laughter.

Bernard paused the tape as he inspected his audience, raising his shoulders in an enquiring shrug. Peter took the bait. "So we have Bokaryov, Vladimir, Sergey, and now an unknown female in the mix—all with apparent knowledge of The Board's objective to gain control of the docks here in Melbourne and Sydney." He appeared thoughtful. "I'm assuming the guy Vladimir was speaking to isn't Russian considering everything except the reference to Cobet was in English." There was general agreement. "What about Vladimir's mobile. Can't we trace back through his calls?"

Tim looked disgruntled. "Just as my guys were about to board the cruiser, Vladimir ripped out the SIM card and tossed it along with the mobile over the side. The water police found the mobile but have been searching for the damn card ever since, even took down their broadband spectrum metal detector. However, for something as small as a SIM, which he probably broke in half anyway, well it was a hiding to nothing . . . no luck."

"Bugger." The AC's frustration was felt around the table. He leaned towards Peter and Delwyn. "Grill the bastard as soon as you can because he's playing us for fools." Kneading his forehead with clenched fists he added, "I'm going out on a limb here. I don't give a stuff Sergey's still on the loose and will probably try to put a bullet in Vladimir. I want him—Vladimir, that is—I want him out there helping us identify these buggers in The Board. And keep him on a tighter leash so he doesn't vanish like he did last time. If he won't

cooperate, threaten him with exposure to The Board again, and this time make him believe it. Keep him focussed."

Bernard adopted a ruthless expression, which caught the AC's attention, inviting the Texan to continue. "There may be another inducement you can employ . . . Vladimir has a child."

The statement drew whistles of surprise.

"A daughter, seventeen. She attends the Methodist Ladies College here in Melbourne."

"Where's her mother? *Who* is her mother?" The AC hung on the answer, aware this was Vladimir's Achilles heel.

Bernard obliged, very much mindful of the significance of his declaration. "A stripper from one of Vladimir's clubs in Sydney, now deceased, OD'd when her daughter was five."

Ballard looked at John, performing mental arithmetic, concluding the liaison must have occurred shortly after Teresa escaped Vladimir's clutches and fled to Melbourne. A check of John's expression highlighted he had arrived at the same conclusion.

The AC sat reflecting for several seconds before returning to Bernard. "You're certain about this?"

Bernard inclined his head, his face impassive. "While my son was hunting down Vladimir this piece of news surfaced. It's been checked out as valid."

"Does Vladimir ever see his daughter?" The suggestion of disrupting the life of an innocent child to further the efforts of revealing The Board members was disturbing to the AC.

"Most weekends Vladimir pops over to Box Hill where she lives with her adoptive parents. He pays their household running costs— food, power, water, rates, as well as all the daughter's private school fees and expenses." Bernard shrugged. "That'd make him a pretty popular guy in the adoptive parents' eyes I should imagine."

"Her name?"

Bernard hesitated. "My son only has a first name at this point: Erina."

The AC grunted as he directed a gun barrel gaze at Delwyn and Peter. "Use this threat against Vladimir as a last resort, but don't hold back if it's necessary to work him over." Clearing his throat he added, "Now the diplomat Olegovich." Taking everyone by surprise and emphasising just how frustrated he was, the AC hammered a clenched fist onto the table, resulting in cups and saucers jumping and rattling. "I'm copping heat from upstairs for questioning the guy, so we may as well go in boots and all. I still have a few spare credits considering our success at Parliament House, so bring the bugger in for another interrogation. Also, the moment his immunity's revoked I want eyes and ears in his pad in St Georges Road. Ladies and gentlemen, it's time to step things up."

Grabbing his cup he downed what had to be stone-cold tea, all the while staring defiantly at the group over the rim; there was no disagreement. Relenting he waved a grateful hand at Bernard. "Thank you. And pass on our gratitude to your son. Between the two of you it's helped us immensely." He directed a firm stare towards Ballard and John then back to the Texan. "I'll admit your engagement with us was a tad unconventional, but very welcome just the same."

John sat studying the crease in his trousers, fascinated by what he was observing.

Bernard pocketed his recorder and with a faint smile sat down, satisfied he and Bernard Junior had gone some way to helping unravel The Board's plot. Chomping through the last of his ribbon sandwiches he thumbed his nose at the twenty-chew rule. John nudged Ballard with an elbow. "A man after my own heart."

The AC took in his audience. "Okay James, time for an update on these port tenders."

Wiping crumbs from his mouth with a serviette, James glanced down at his open folder. "It'll be no surprise to anyone that ports throughout Australia have been plagued by criminal behaviour way before anyone here was even born."

He glanced across at the AC who volunteered a grin. "Yes folks, that includes me."

Brushing imaginary fluff from his tie, a habit which Ballard had noted from previous briefings to be James's only outward sign of unease, he continued, "While crime is rife throughout all Australian ports, the lion's share is still predominantly in Melbourne and Sydney. In terms of container movements, Melbourne is approaching three million annually with Sydney just behind, but catching up fast.

"Back in 2011 it was predicted the Port of Melbourne would reach full capacity by 2015. As a consequence the Victorian government pushed ahead to award a tender for a fifty-year lease of the port's commercial operations to a consortium made up of six companies, albeit the contract was signed well past what was initially declared to be the deadline." A tight smile was followed by, "And I might add the deal was for a tidy sum of just under ten billion dollars which if you do the maths isn't all that much considering."

Eyebrows shot up.

"It's also no surprise that due to this low figure and for a number of associated reasons the opposition screamed foul play, claiming rampant political corruption and unbridled horse-trading. They're now demanding IBAC, the Independent Broad-Based Anti-Corruption Commission investigate the tender process as a matter of urgency."

The AC twisted in his chair, nodding. "I can confirm the police minister has already warned the chief that resources, perhaps even a task force will be needed to kick off enquiries when the political time is deemed appropriate." He nodded at James, directing him to continue.

The ASIO officer took on a pained expression. "Rumours were rife criminal connections were embroiled in the tender process up to their eyeballs, but it wasn't until the events at Parliament House unfolded and Bernard's recording surfaced that we put two and two together and realised The Board was making a major play for the ports here in Australia."

The seriousness of the situation was reflected on everyone's face, especially Mark's as he arrived at the conclusion his investigations into bikie crime would almost certainly coincide with any enquiry into the ports, especially now it was known Thor's Warriors were a useful tool of The Board, albeit at arm's length.

"That Sydney is also on the radar *was* news to us, which brings me to the proposed Port Botany expansion, now on the drawing board to cater for increased container movement for the next twenty years."

Peter was unable to contain himself. "By any score the siege was an unprincipled dash for cash, and now that Vladimir with the help of a wealthy and still-unknown accomplice is rustling up the best part of a second billion to toss into the pot, he'll be ideally situated to ingratiate himself as a significant player in The Board's cell here in Australia."

James agreed. "Couldn't have put it better myself Pete. Vladimir's killing two birds with one stone, repaying the debt he owes The Board while making himself a real contender in their ongoing crooked endeavours, and he's ruthless enough and has the connections and resources to blend right in."

Peter waved a hand. "Tell me, what's the possibility the bastard's playing us for fools, pretending to be fearful of The Board but all the while negotiating with them like a double agent, convincing them that by cooperating with us he's a valuable resource? Jesus, is it too far-fetched to believe he was working hand in hand with Sergey regarding the attack on Parliament House? We're almost certain he financed the whole operation just as he did the NPA robbery."

A momentary silence punctuated the depth of thought Peter's comments engendered. The serious deliberations broken by the AC's next words which were more a statement than a reflection. "We think that's *exactly* what's going down here, so now you can see why it's not such a stab in the dark to push him back out onto the street so we can use him as a fox to lead us to the lair."

Ballard smiled at Delwyn and John, aware from first-hand experience the uncompromising temperament the AC displayed whenever the chips were down and difficult decisions had to be made. Again the officer nodded to James, inviting him to continue.

"So there we have it, almost irrefutable proof The Board has designs on our two largest ports. The real trouble will be proving it.

Even the *hint* of a threat from the group silences anyone contemplating breaking ranks."

"Are the Sydney police aware of The Board's intentions regarding their Port Botany expansion?"

Delwyn's question had AC Müller stepping up to the plate. "Not fully. We're holding our cards close to our chest on that one, but in some respects the NSW's police are ahead of us because they've already established a task force to monitor their ports." Furrowed brows had the officer raising an acknowledging hand. "In April 2013 the NSW's government granted a ninety-nine-year lease to a port consortium along with five other partners. Port Kembla was also included in the lease. Again there were cries of foul play by the opposition, so enough political pressure was brought to bear to have a task force established so the government would appear to be taking corruption and illegal activity at the docks seriously."

"Has anything come of it?" Ballard didn't appear confident.

"Minor stuff. Certainly nothing with any meat in it. The chief's been liaising with the NSW commissioner and promised to update him as soon as anything concrete comes to hand regarding illegal activities down here which may be repeated up there." He tugged hard at an earlobe. "To give you some idea of the personnel The Board will have at their disposal to corrupt or threaten if they do gain control, Melbourne Ports employs 850 workers. Sounds a lot but the number is down from over fourteen hundred prior to the strikes in the nineties. As for the Port Botany employees there's just on 320, so between the two ports it's clear there's a smorgasbord of dock workers The Board can coerce to ignore illegal activity in their day-to-day operation. If they get their way it's going to be an open-door policy for the group to move contraband in and out of Australia, injecting billions of dollars into their illegal accounts, right under our noses.

The AC stared at the wall clock and it was clear he was keen for the briefing to conclude. "Folks, this has been a lot to take in, but necessary to ensure you're all operating with the latest information."

John glanced at Ballard, his grin heralding his understanding that the senior officer was about to launch into micro management, something he was famous for but never criticised over due to the respect he engendered with everyone who worked with him.

The AC didn't disappoint. "Roger, keep me informed as to what your two investigators turn up in Switzerland, not that I'm expecting the bank executives to roll over after the execution of one of their own." The commander agreed.

"Tim, Jordan, again a big thank you for what you and your teams achieved at Parliament House, but with Sergey on the loose he poses a problem which may yet blow up in our faces. Stay on it and use whatever resources you need to track the bastard down. God knows what his next move will be if we don't get him behind bars." He focussed on Mark. "Anything your undercover lads can dig up via Thor's Warriors will be useful. Somebody *must* know where Sergey's holed up. Oh, and check out whether they have access to more of those micro Uzis. It's the last thing we need should there be another outbreak of gang warfare."

Mark gave Tim and Jordan a brief nod, conveying an understanding far more potent than words.

Next the AC directed his attention towards Peter and Delwyn. "Vladimir's been playing us for suckers. I've no doubt you could strap the bugger to a lie detector and he'd beat it every time. However, he along with Bokaryov and Sergey are the only ones we know of who have direct links to The Board's cell here in Australia. It's a certainty the head members in Russia are multiple layers removed, so we just have to accept identifying the Australian group is the best we'll ever achieve unless a miracle occurs and Bernard here has made it clear that's not likely to happen any time soon." After gritting his teeth he growled, "Probe Vladimir again then turn him loose minus a chip in his backside this time. I want him to think he has free rein. That *may* lull him into being careless and do something which gives us an edge."

The AC saw Delwyn and Peter's worried looks. "Yes, I understand releasing him without a tracking chip means you'll be chewing up mountains of surveillance overtime." The AC shrugged. "Any alternatives?"

Just as Delwyn was about to speak Bernard commented softly, "May I offer a solution?"

Everyone looked his way.

"As I mentioned, the only unfinished work-related issue in my life is bringing The Board to heel. While I may never see that achieved, I sure as hell want to catch *some* of them before I leave this planet, and I don't mean the bit players such as Thor's Warriors and the like."

The AC's furrowed brow encouraged Bernard to continue. "My son's a wealthy man in his own right, so financing around the clock surveillance on Vladimir with—and I apologise for assuming this—with more resources at his disposal than your police department, well, he'll be able to monitor the guy right down to every occasion he passes solids."

Bernard's pithy turn of phrase generated numerous smiles.

Everyone watched the AC with interest to see if he was prepared to outsource the surveillance role on such a critical investigation. Checking his whisker growth with a calloused hand, the officer mused, "Bernard, your son has very effective assets, no question about it. I doubt we could have found Vladimir as quickly without him so I see your offer as an extension of a service you and your son have already provided. Unorthodox, and if it goes south I can assure you I'll take full responsibility. But I must make it clear you'll need very well-defined communication lines with us so we can respond at a moment's notice. It's vital your role be surveillance and nothing more."

Bernard raised a giant paw in total agreement.

"Delwyn, Peter, liaise with Bernard and set up a communication protocol *prior* to Vladimir's release. This also raises the ongoing challenge of ensuring the safety of the billionaire property developer and his wife . . ." The AC hesitated.

"Malcolm and Teresa Ferguson." John blurted the names as he sat bolt upright, far from comfortable with the prospect of allowing Vladimir to roam the streets once more after he had already made every effort to extort money from Malcolm and might well attempt to do so again.

The AC did his best to appear relaxed with the arrangement but was far from convincing, his almost imperceptible head shake giving him away. Looking to Delwyn and Peter he stated the obvious, "You'll need to tread carefully on this one."

James shuffled in his seat. "The AC's made it clear Vladimir's not to be fitted with a locator chip because he wants him to feel he's a free agent, but we *can* put him on an electronic leash without him knowing he's being tracked."

James's comment piqued everyone's interest, but none more so than John who was still suffering a concerned look. James was aware of the detective's apprehension. "A guy like that will have an expensive watch, am I right?"

Peter glanced at Tim who responded, "When he was arrested at Portsea my guys commented he was sporting a Rolex dripping with diamonds. They thought he was a bloody drug baron, said they'd never seen anything like it."

James nodded. "My guess is it's an older-style piece, perhaps a gift from a business acquaintance and hopefully won't have an inbuilt GPS, so I'm suggesting we update it with some of our natty technology then give it back to him. That way we can keep him under electronic surveillance in conjunction with Bernard's human resources."

The Texan smiled his agreement, aware of the sophisticated gadgetry available to ASIO which was far above anything the public read about on Google.

The AC cleared his throat. "Hmm, I'm beginning to feel more relaxed by the minute." He stared at the notes he had scribbled in his unintelligible scrawl throughout the briefing. "Okay, one last hurdle to jump. Olegovich." He turned to AC Müller who took up the cause with enthusiasm.

"As mentioned before, the AC and I pushed the chief to convince the police minister that Olegovich's diplomatic immunity should be revoked without him or the Russian embassy here in Melbourne knowing anything about it. I'm told the minister has now agreed and is in touch with the Department of Foreign Affairs and Trade. They in turn have dealt directly with the Kremlin. At first, it was thought the Russkies would turn a cold shoulder but bugger me, it appears they've sniffed the political headwind and it's my belief they'll agree to casting Olegovich loose as a sign of good faith. And let's face it, he's a nobody to them so they're quite likely preparing a formal letter to cut him free."

His evil grin appeared for which he was famous. "Once that's received surveillance can head off to the mansion in St Georges Road and set up eyes and ears inside and out. I'm convinced this will generate invaluable intel." He addressed Peter while maintaining a half-smile, their interaction over the years lending to complete trust in one another's capabilities. "As soon as I get the letter I'll let you know to kick things off." Peter acknowledged the request.

AC Müller changed tack with the smoothness of an experienced professional. "Regarding the tender for the docks, we've begun sweating the ports minister, Laurie Davidson. I've been around long enough to know he's holding something back and appears to be a very anxious individual. We'll persist to see *if* he's being pressured and by whom."

AC Thompson took one last glance around the table. "Have I missed anyone? Oh yes Robert, your report as soon as possible please." He received a confirming nod as he turned his attention to the psychologist. "Now Marjorie, just in case you thought I've overlooked you it goes without saying these two . . ." He waved a dismissive hand at Ballard and John. "What can I say? These two dinosaurs need to participate in one of your famous counselling sessions to make sure they aren't emotionally damaged from their respective ordeals."

The snort from Delwyn was less than ladylike but backed up with gentle laughter from most at the table.

Marjorie acknowledged Delwyn's reaction, her expression reeking of sympathy for the superintendent given her long-standing attempts to manage the two senior detectives. "Rest assured, Mr Thompson, I'll do my very best."

John grimaced, nodding towards Ballard, mindful there was no escaping Marjorie's probing questions and insightful counsel now the AC had formalised the request.

"That's good enough for me Marjorie." Fixing the two men with an unwavering gaze the senior officer continued, "Despite everything that's going on and the actions we all need to tackle, I don't want to see either of you at work for the next few days. Our OH&S bill is exorbitant enough." His challenging look softened. "Be that as it may your assistance during the siege was incalculable, and we all owe you a great deal—the *public* owe you a great deal—so thank you both."

So rare was such effusive praise from the senior officer it left Ballard bemused and John open-mouthed.

Drawing himself upright in his chair the AC nodded meaningfully towards AC Müller before he demanded the group's attention, declaring in a measured voice, "Ladies and gentlemen we're at war with The Board and everything it stands for. If we don't get on top of the cell leaders here in Australia tragic events such as the NPA robbery and the siege at Parliament House won't be the exception— they'll be the norm. And our national and international reputation as a free and law-abiding society will take a hit from which it will *never* recover." He drew a lung-expanding breath. "Like Bernard, I have no desire to end my working career with a cloud hanging over my head because I failed to bring to heel the most dangerous, the most professional group of criminals I've ever encountered. But more importantly, as our sole duty is to protect the community by God this is what we're going to do." Eyes blazing he barked, "Daily updates on your respective tasks and more often if required."

As if by telepathy both ACs stood as one; after nodding to the group they strode from the room, the hush that followed them a clear display of the respect the officers commanded and deserved.

CHAPTER
13

Most in attendance made a rush for the door with the AC's words ringing in their ears. Bernard came over and shook hands with each of the detectives, winking at Ballard and John before announcing, "My son and I have a ton of work to do." Spinning on his heel he headed from the room.

Robert approached Delwyn and Marjorie, his eyes twinkling. "Ladies, it's been a pleasure as always." In keeping with his long-standing tradition, he took their hand and with a flamboyant flourish, planted a lingering kiss on the back of each, his expression devoid of any awkwardness or embarrassment. Straightening, he bounded off to comply with the AC's bidding.

Recovering Delwyn spoke briefly with Peter before turning to Marjorie, hooking a thumb towards Ballard and John. "I sympathise with you having to assess these two. As the briefing went longer than we thought, if you have the time could you spare them an hour this afternoon?"

"Not a problem Delwyn, and no need for concern. Michael and John have developed a great understanding with me over the past few months, haven't we gentlemen?" She smiled sweetly but her eyes challenged any objection from either detective.

The men stared at one another, feigning befuddlement, shrugging as they gesticulated with their hands like confused Italian immigrants disembarking at Station Pier.

Exasperated Delwyn barked, "For God's sake take this seriously. You've both been exposed to incredibly traumatic events, and I need to protect the department by having you evaluated for possible

PTSD." Uttering the demand she shook her head, appearing weary as she turned to Peter, seeking his support. The superintendent grinned from ear to ear as he raised his hands in mock defeat.

Delwyn's exasperation increased tenfold. "Why am I not surprised? You three stick together like glue. Thanks very much for backing me Peter—*not!*"

"Mission impossible Delwyn, but I understand you have to go through the motions. The AC made it pretty clear they need to take a few days off." Peter's expression became serious, underscoring how the senior officer's leave ultimatum wasn't negotiable.

Relenting, both detectives promised to behave, settling on a time to meet with Marjorie. The appointment agreed, Ballard and John requested they be allowed to interrogate Vladimir beforehand. Delwyn opened her mouth to protest but Peter's imperceptible nod changed her mind. "Very well, but don't be late for your session with Marjorie. I *mean* it."

Getting to their feet they headed from the room, stomachs rumbling, agreeing they needed to have a bite to eat first. Once in the stairwell Ballard motioned to Peter and John. "I didn't bring this up in the meeting because I'm still not convinced of what I saw, but John, when we were leaving the marina yesterday and you and Sonia had already headed into the car park . . . well, I *think* I spotted the Russian sailor we chased up the crane at the docks before Christmas."

"*What!* The prick who somersaulted off the deck of the container ship?"

"Yep, I'm almost certain it was the same guy."

Peter thrust both hands deep into his trouser pockets, heavy in thought. "Well the bugger didn't drown otherwise the Water Police would have found his body. The real issue is whether he managed to hang on to the iPad once he hit the water. It's at least twenty metres from the deck of the ship to the water. That's a pretty solid slap into the drink."

Ballard tugged at his earlobe while appearing uncertain. "The Search and Rescue lads claim there was no sign of the iPad in the mud, and we all know how thorough they are, so I guess he probably did manage to hold on to it. God knows how far he swam underwater to disappear the way he did."

Peter resumed his conjecture. "Well, if it *is* the same guy this possibly fits in with what The Board's attempting to do at the ports, and I'm certain whatever was on that iPad would have been very enlightening."

Turning they headed down to their floor, each mulling over the multiple scenarios that were swirling about like smoke on a windy day.

"Jesus boss, are they *really* going to let Vladimir loose again after he skipped town the first time?" Bobby was incredulous that such a proposition was even being contemplated. With eyes wide and demanding, the top of his head shone under the fluorescent lights as he sat bolt upright in the homicide team's meal room, imploring support from Susan and Ken whose munching on their respective sandwiches had slowed, equally troubled at the revelation.

Ballard and John glanced at one another, sympathetic to the trio's disbelief but aware there were bigger fish to fry. They relayed this reality to the three detectives who remained doubtful as to the wisdom of it all.

To emphasise they weren't far from the mark John growled, "I'm not happy about the situation either. One minute the bugger's extorting money from Malcolm to the tune of half a billion dollars while Sergey's hanging Teresa off the side of the Eureka Tower in a cleaning platform. Then to top it off Sergey escapes, holds Parliament House to ransom and is now wandering about God knows where in the state. But the real show-stopper is finding ourselves releasing Vladimir once more to help us catch the main prize, The Board's cell leaders here in Australia. No, you can be assured I'm not relaxed about *any* of this." He directed a stare at Ballard. "We're heading into uncharted territory Mike. A shitload can go wrong and probably will."

Interspersed between mouthfuls, Ballard and John updated the young detectives with the latest developments, emphasising the importance of presenting the department's line regarding payment of the ransom should they ever find themselves questioned by the press.

"Now as John stressed earlier, Malcolm and Teresa's safety is paramount." Ballard focussed on Susan and Bobby. "As soon as you've finished your lunch head up to the penthouse and break the news to them—without letting on about The Board of course. Emphasise how Vladimir's release is under tight surveillance. Even though we have him on a twenty-four-seven watch list and the chance of Sergey showing up anywhere near them is nigh on zero, Malcolm and Teresa won't be thrilled about the situation. And who could blame them, especially after what they went through? Suggest they go on a holiday or find alternate accommodation for the next week or so. If they wish offer them short-term witness protection."

No sooner had Ballard uttered the words than he shook his head. "Knowing Malcolm he won't have a bar of that." He caught John's pained expression. "Don't worry. He'll make certain Teresa flies under the radar until this mess is sorted out. He's not short of a quid so he'll draw on his limitless resources to make sure she's safe."

Despite giving his partner his reassurance, Ballard felt a stab of guilt that the department was placing two innocent lives in harm's way, as remote as the danger might be. Turning to Ken who was looking as hound dog as ever, Ballard directed, "Okay Ken, time for one of your famous profiling opinions." John rolled his eyes before staring up at the ceiling, mimicking the action Ken would undoubtedly adopt prior to commencing.

Ballard ignored him. "Vladimir was threatened with repercussions from The Board if he didn't toe the line the last time he was released, but he ignored the warning. Now we're going to set him loose again. The only difference this time is we're not fitting him up with any electronic tracking devices, the theory being he'll think he's even more of a free agent than before. What suspicions will he have with this, considering his known psychopathic tendencies? The real question is, will his suspicions stop him from acting spontaneously or will his supercharged ego override any caution?"

Sipping from his mug of ink black coffee, which for once he hadn't spilt as he placed it on the table prior to sitting down, Ken didn't disappoint John. He drew a lungful of air as he inspected the ceiling lights, his eyes closed. Bobby and Susan battled to contain themselves, recovering their composure by the time Ken looked back down. "I'm guessing that as a child, Vladimir would have been the one jumping off objects other boys baulked at, falling out of trees higher than others would dare to climb, riding his bike faster than anyone else while not holding the handlebars, always pushing the limits so he was the last man—er, boy—standing."

Ken leaned back in his chair, appearing to have completed his summary. Then just as everyone's expression grew doubtful he lurched forward again. "There's been a long-held belief that psychopaths mellow when they reach their fifties, but this is now thought to be a fallacy. There are dozens of examples of men around that age, even into their sixties still doing very bad things." He cocked his head sideways. "How old *is* Vladimir anyway?"

Ballard performed a Ken impersonation by checking out the same area of ceiling, cheeks ballooning before answering, "Er, approaching fifty but not quite there yet."

"Hmm, then I'd suggest his frontal lobe activity will still be working against him even though neuron behaviour *does* change over time." Ken grimaced. "Rest assured Vladimir's giant ego and self-assurance is such that while he'll suspect something's afoot . . . psychopaths aren't stupid—in fact, far from it—he'll be confident enough to believe he's capable of outmanoeuvring you no matter what you throw at him."

John growled, "That's what we're hoping for Ken."

Ballard reflected back to the first interview with Vladimir. He had observed him afterwards through the viewing window and witnessed the Russian's contemplative expression as he planned his next move, by no means panicking, clearly assessing his options. "Yes Ken, I think you've hit it on the head. Without doubt Vladimir doesn't rattle easily."

Susan was puzzled, her titian red hair glistening with good health as she shook her head. "Won't he just disappear again, perhaps head out of the country, this time for good?"

All eyes focussed on Ballard. "As I said, the surveillance on him will be a lot tighter and we'll be tracking him electronically—unless of course he finds the chip Pete's arranging our ASIO friend fit into his Rolex. On top of that he has a young daughter to consider, and for all we know she's the reason he didn't skip overseas the first time we cut him loose. None of us including the AC are happy about involving her, but the prize if we nail some or all the cell leaders is just too appealing not to give this a red hot go."

Eyeing Ken with a faint smile, Ballard continued, "Now young man, changing subjects, I want you to liaise with Peter and find out everything you can about our ports minister, the Honourable Laurie Davidson." A quizzical expression from the junior detective urged Ballard on. "He headed up the tender to lease Melbourne Ports for fifty years. I want to know everything there is about the guy. Is he under financial pressure? Is his family vulnerable? Are there any children? That sort of thing. Check out some of his performances in parliament. Analyse his strength of character. What are his weaknesses?" Ballard continued to direct his attention towards an attentive Ken. "Was Davidson coerced in any way to steer the tender in a particular direction? We're painfully aware the modus operandi of The Board is to apply emotional, financial, and physical intimidation against their targets. In other words have they made the minister an offer he can't refuse?"

The three detectives sat nodding like wise men, aware that should intimidation be proven a link back to some of the cell leaders may be a distinct possibility, as tenuous as the prospect might appear.

John lurched forward, taking up the commentary. "Susan, Bobby, when you get back from the penthouse, keep plugging away on Sergey's brief. Where are you with it?"

Bobby chuckled. "Up until Michael's escapades we were nearly there. Now we've another dozen charges to add to the list, which is already a mile long—or is that a kilometre?"

John ignored the pun. "Keep at it. In the meantime Mike and myself are about to have a character-adjusting heart to heart with Vladimir before he's—"

Susan and Bobby stared over John's shoulder, openly grinning, causing him to swivel around with Ballard following suit. Marjorie stood in the doorway, a Mona Lisa smile tweaking the corner of her mouth. "I hope I'm not interrupting. Well I guess I am." Her smile broadened. "Just checking we're still on for 3 p.m.?"

Her smile was matched and bettered by Ken, Bobby, and Susan, causing John to scowl at each in turn. "You'll be happy to know Marjorie, I was just informing Michael a moment ago how much I'm looking forward to our session this afternoon and hoping you were too."

Marjorie didn't miss a beat. "Oh rest assured John, I'm tickety-boo at the prospect and of course with you there Michael, it'll be icing on the cake. Your conference room I'm guessing?" Not waiting for an answer, and with a quick wink at the others she spun around and was gone.

With tasks assigned and dishes washed, Ken, Bobby, and Susan were on their way, jostling each other out the door. Ballard and John sat reflecting on the enormity of the forthcoming tasks, their experience prewarning them of the tribulations ahead.

"Vladimir's going to just sit there and laugh at us Mike—if not outwardly then on the inside." Using both hands John massaged his scalp, resulting in Ballard reflecting on the anomaly that his partner's hair appeared no more dishevelled post the aggressive attack than before.

"He may well Johno, but by the time we've finished with him and then Peter and James drag him through the wringer, he'll think twice about treating us like fools. Either way the AC's prepared to take the gamble, and the potential prize is just too inviting to ignore."

"Jesus Mike, I know the two ACs are dead set on nailing some or all of The Board's members, but Bernard and his son are taking it to a whole new level. They really seem to have an axe to grind." John shook his head, clearly bemused. "And the AC engaging them to track Vladimir while he's on the loose is nothing short of incredible. It just shows how far the brass are prepared to stick their necks out on this one." Shaking his head once more he added, "I'll make a quick call across the road and have Vladimir set up in an interview room before we get there."

While John was making the call to the Melbourne Assessment Centre, Ballard tucked his folder under his arm then poked his head into Delwyn's office, informing her he and John were about to head off to grill Vladimir.

Delwyn's brow knitted as she cautioned, "I'm not sure how you should tackle this Michael. I'll let your experience guide you but no matter what, Vladimir *must* be made aware if he pulls another caper like the last one he'll hit the can so fast his head will spin, never to breathe fresh air again—*ever*. He must know we have enough on him to put him away for life."

Throwing an acknowledging salute, Ballard turned and signalled to John to meet him at the lifts.

CHAPTER
14

Emerging from the crime building the two detectives stood at the intersection of Spencer and La Trobe streets waiting for the lights to change, the sun blazing high above them in a clear blue sky. A city circle tram thundered past packed with passengers, the majority of them tourists, most likely listening to the on-board commentary of Melbourne's nearby attractions.

On the opposite corner the Melbourne Assessment Centre loomed large, imposing, the burnt-orange brick building far from aesthetically pleasing but reeking of strength and impregnability. Commenced in 1983 and completed in 1989 at a cost of eighty million, the prison's role was to provide statewide assessment and orientation services for up to three hundred male prisoners. Originally built without steel bars fitted to the cell windows, the escape in 1993 by two inmates using smuggled explosives to blow out the armoured plastic panes saw the hasty installation of steel reinforcements, converting the prison to a more traditional high-security custodial centre.

Ballard glanced at the six-metre-high wall further along Latrobe Street, the top bristling with razor wire which enclosed the southern exercise yard from which Sergey was plucked to freedom. John noted the direction of his partner's gaze, shrugging expressively before growling, "If only we'd put a bullet in the bugger then and there Mike, I'm bloody certain the Parliament House fiasco wouldn't have got off the ground. Sergey was the glue that held that caper together. Hell, it was just another training day for him."

"Water under the bridge now John. All we can hope for is to track him down and nail the bastards behind this so it doesn't happen again."

The pedestrian signal broke both detectives' reverie. John raised his fist as a silver Mazda sped across the intersection towards Central Pier, having jumped the red light. He bellowed "*Shithead!*" after the vehicle as it crested the bridge, several pedestrians joining in with him. Ballard smiled to himself, aware John's outburst was unconsciously directed towards Vladimir and the frustration he was feeling regarding the Russian's impending release in the quest to catch much bigger prey.

Fronting the reception desk they displayed their identification, stating they were there to interview Vladimir Bokaryov. Escorted by a stocky prison warden they passed through the three-hundred-thousand-dollar Ionscan Sentinel II Contraband Detection Portal, Ballard noting with amusement John's hair swirling about as the puffs of compressed air blew around him. Gritting his teeth John remained silent, aware the security precaution was necessary but still peeved at the inconvenience.

Ballard clapped him on the shoulder. "An amazing piece of hardware John. It can analyse over forty different types of drugs and an equal number of explosives, and if it detects anything it snaps a digital mug shot."

John grunted, his feelings unambiguous.

The prison warden appeared apologetic but decided not to comment, leading them along a corridor until they came to the interview room. They paused outside the observation window, witnessing Vladimir sitting shackled to the table. Not in prison garb, it was clear the AC's directive had preceding them despite the Russian being classified as A2 maximum security. Dressed in a grey business suit and pale-blue shirt, the outfit costing more than either detectives' weekly wage, Vladimir was relaxed as though waiting to discuss a new business deal rather than fronting an interrogation that could put him in jail forever.

"Will you look at the prick!" John was furious that a ruthless criminal should be indulged in such a way, and from Vladimir's expression it was apparent he deemed it his right due to the critical information he possessed.

Observing John's reddening features Ballard thanked the prison officer as he led his partner to the interview door. "Now John, remember, this is videotaped okay? It's *not* twenty years ago in the St Kilda crime office."

John's disgruntled glare grew in intensity. "More's the pity Mike. Back then crooks knew how to show respect."

Pushing the door open both men entered and took up positions opposite Vladimir, neither acknowledging his presence as they set up their folders with John switching on his Olympus recorder and placing it between himself and the Russian. Extracting his favourite Montblanc pen from his jacket pocket, Ballard wrote the time and date on a blank page then pressed the button to commence the videotaping of the interview. Lastly, he fixed Vladimir with a direct gaze which was returned with an expressionless stare.

"It's 1330 on 26th March. For the record my name's Michael Ballard. I'm a detective inspector attached to homicide. With me is Detective Senior Sergeant John Henderson, also with homicide. For the record, in the room to be interviewed is Vladimir Borisovich Bokaryov." The Russian sat impassively, having heard it all before, neutral to the situation. His cold grey eyes reminded Ballard of Sergey's indifferent stare. Both men were calculating clinical killers but with very different temperaments and techniques.

After informing Vladimir of his right to remain silent Ballard turned to John, praying his colleague would control his loathing for the Russian and not lose it during the interview by mounting the table to choke him into submission or some similar career-ending action.

John opened proceedings in his typical no-nonsense hard-nosed fashion. "Did you in any way plan, finance, or support the recent siege on Parliament House in which four politicians were murdered?"

The delay in Vladimir's response was sufficiently protracted for both detectives to suspect he might have misunderstood the question—as impossible as that would seem—or, just as troubling, decided not to respond.

The grey eyes hardened. "I wasn't aware there had been a siege, or politicians had died. As you would know, I've been held in isolation with no access to TV, radio, or newspapers, plus no visitors. You'll forgive me if I'm a bit behind on the news of the day."

Vladimir's voice was ice-cold, measured, and dripping with contempt to the point Ballard continued to fear for John's self-control. His concerns were well founded. Leaning in to the Russian John's voice lowered as he stated with measured fury, "I fully understand how frustrating it must be not to be able to visit your daughter— Erina, is it? Oh, I forgot. She probably doesn't know you've been arrested."

Vladimir's reaction was immediate but remarkably unemotional. Other than a narrowing of his eyes and an involuntary clenching of his left fist shackled to the table, his demeanour remained unchanged. Ballard had to admire the man's capacity to absorb psychological pressure which highlighted the difficulty they were confronting to successfully negotiate any form of a deal. It was obvious Vladimir believed he was mentally superior to any challenge which may be posed by his interrogators, that his current situation was nothing more than a temporary inconvenience.

Ballard was aware the Russian's self-assurance had to be cracked with a wedge of uncertainty concerning his fate driven deep into his psyche before any meaningful information could be gleaned. "As I see it Vladimir, you have two options. One, go to trial and be locked away for life. Remember, there will be no parole. *Life* for you will be *life*." Ballard allowed the statement to mature. "There's just one catch. As we said at our previous interview, once The Board realises you're of no value to them you won't see out six weeks in prison."

"And the second option?" The question was delivered with incredible self-control, Vladimir's features as calm as though he were asking whether the sun was shining outside.

Ballard felt John stir alongside him. Both men were mindful that despite the Russian's apparent indifference to his current predicament, his love for his daughter, the threat of The Board, and a giant ego meant he wasn't ready to accept a lonely, un-newsworthy death in prison without offering something to improve his circumstances.

"You need to come up with information, and plenty of it. If it's valuable enough it may keep you alive." Ballard assessed the Russian before adding, "We need to know the name of the businessman you're negotiating with to raise a billion dollars, who and where The Board's cell leaders are here in Australia, the name of the woman you've been in contact with who has knowledge of The Board, what your involvement in the Parliament House siege was, and for the big one, how The Board is involved regarding control of the Melbourne and Sydney ports."

Try as he might, Vladimir wasn't able to supress the surprise in his eyes as to the depth of knowledge presented to him. He battled to maintain his impassive expression—again a clear demonstration of the man's ability to remain ice-cold under duress.

"And you believe I have this information?"

"Unless you want your nuts chopped off by The Board you'd better pray you do shithead, or if not, that you can find out in a hurry." John was making it patently clear he wasn't in the mood to mince words. He followed it up with "Let's break this down into bite-sized chunks shall we? Have you been in discussion with a second party to raise a substantial sum of money which may or may not find its way to The Board as further payment of your outstanding debts to them?"

As Vladimir opened his mouth to reply John halted him, raising a hand. "Think very, very carefully of what you're about to say because we already know the answer, and if you even *attempt* to deceive us this interview stops here and now. You'll be charged, processed, and will go to trial—it's that simple. The Board will deal with you after that."

John stared unblinkingly at the Russian, two hardmen facing off. Ballard prayed his partner hadn't painted himself into a corner and was relieved when they saw Vladimir give an imperceptible shrug. "It's no secret I owe The Board money. I told you as much last time. It's a substantial amount and I can't deny I pressured Ferguson for additional funding." In spite of the dramatic circumstances surrounding his brutal efforts to extort a massive sum from the billionaire property developer, underscored by the physical threat Sergey subjected Teresa to at the Eureka Tower, Vladimir's expression was devoid of any remorse, as though the incident was nothing more than everyday roughhouse business negotiations.

Ballard quickly eyed John to ensure he wasn't building a head of steam as Vladimir continued, "I also have partners whom I negotiate with regarding finance. Yes, I've been in contact with one of my associates to raise a specific amount of cash . . ."

"His name?" John's pen was poised.

"I can't give you his name."

John leaned forward aggressively, hissing, "*That's not your decision. You've got ten seconds to cough up the name or this interview's over, and so will be your chance of ever seeing your daughter graduate, get married, or have children. And don't forget all this is subject to whether The Board lets you live, which is very unlikely.*"

The bluntness of John's announcement had Vladimir hesitating for several seconds, appearing to retreat within himself before asking for a pen and paper on which he wrote a name. As he went to pass it back John barked, "*Mobile number and address.*"

Vladimir's eyes grew colder, were that possible, clearly fighting an internal battle whether to call his interrogator's bluff, but John's expression made it clear such a decision would be at the Russian's peril. Ballard sat back, observing his partner do what he did best.

After a further pause Vladimir wrote the additional details before thrusting the pen and paper back to John who read what had been written. Expressionless he slid the paper across to Ballard who flicked a look before placing it to one side. The name meant nothing to him as he registered the mobile number was scrawled alongside an apartment address in Collins Street.

That hurdle overcome John raised the next issue. "Okay, now that we have a deeper understanding of each other, what additional information do you have regarding who The Board's cell leaders are here in Victoria? Where do they meet? How often?"

Fatigue swept across Vladimir's face as he rubbed the nape of his neck. "I've already told you, Dimochka Olegovich is the cell leader. He's the bastard who forced me to get involved in the note printing robbery."

Both men recalled Vladimir describing the complex procedures the diplomat undertook to exchange instructions regarding the robbery, engaging cold war letter drop techniques in the Botanical Gardens to avoid leaving an electronic trail.

The detectives stared forcefully at Vladimir, making it clear they expected him to continue, with John urging the Russian along. "Is there any particular place where the cell members meet?"

"The Melbourne Club." The statement was blurted almost spontaneously, appearing to release some of the pressure the Russian was experiencing.

"*The Melbourne Club?*" Ballard and John glanced at one another, only partially successful in their efforts to supress their astonishment.

"There are monthly meetings in one of the boardrooms where the Cobet members discuss the status of various projects." Vladimir's tone was offhand, as though utilisation of the famous Collins Street club was a natural extension of its original purpose, that being the meeting of elite gentlemen to relax and discuss affairs of the state.

Ballard continued to do his best not to show his amazement at The Board's sheer audacity in selecting such a famous venue to collaborate on illegal activities and Vladimir's matter-of-fact reference to these pursuits as 'projects'. "Have you attended any of the meetings?"

For the first time the Russian exhibited a degree of extreme unease, reinforced by his inability to maintain eye contact. "Yes, once."

John smelt blood, realising this was perhaps the breakthrough in identifying at least some of the cell members. "Who was at the meeting?"

"I don't know."

"*What do you mean you don't know?*" John was incensed, his fierce glare letting it be known as he half rose out of his chair.

Vladimir gave another involuntary shrug. "The room I was ushered into had everyone sitting at one end . . . they had two spotlights directed at me. They were just voices in the dark."

"Did you recognise any of the voices?"

"Only Olegovich's."

"What was discussed?"

Vladimir's response was sufficiently delayed for both detectives to suspect he was refusing to answer, but when he did respond his voice was almost a whisper. "We discussed what actions were needed to achieve a successful ransom at Parliament House, along with what my involvement was to be."

This time, Ballard and John couldn't hide their stunned expressions. "You're admitting to being part of the ransom demand?" John's voice was at least an octave higher, so astonished was he at the revelation.

"I didn't have any choice."

"*Bullshit* you didn't. Good people died because of your caper." So enraged was John that spittle flew from his mouth, striking the table in front of the Russian's hand.

"They threatened to rape and murder Erina if I didn't cooperate." The statement was uttered sotto voce, Vladimir's expression leaving no doubt the threat was genuine and would have been carried out had he not cooperated.

John's mouth opened but his brain wouldn't engage. He turned to Ballard, signalling for the interview to be halted. Ballard responded by pressing the button to stop the video recording.

Recovering, John in his trademark pithy manner quipped, "Don't go anywhere. We'll be right back." Standing, he switched off the Olympus recorder, leaving it on the table.

Exiting the interview room the detectives grouped at the observation window, Ballard running his fingers through his hair as he stood watching the Russian. "Jesus John, talk about coming out of left field, and so too the thing about the meetings at the Melbourne

Club. I wonder what the captains of industry and the society high-flyers who frequent the place would make of it if they knew what was being discussed right under their very noses?"

John stared through the window, attempting to make sense of what he had just heard. "Do you believe him?"

"I do. You saw his face John. For a split second he was nothing more than a desperate father terrified as to what might happen to his daughter, and willing to do *anything* to protect her, illegal or otherwise."

John's eyes narrowed as he looked at his partner. "We can use this big time. That's why I wanted to get your take on things before we went any further."

Ballard hesitated, assessing the best option to adopt. "Clearly anything we threaten him with won't match what The Board's holding over his head, but the risk of him going to jail and how that exposes his daughter and the certainty The Board will finish him off in there is a close second—enough I'd wager to get him to play ball when we release him again."

"Do we get him to flesh out what his involvement was regarding the siege and just as importantly his involvement with Sergey? The Spetsnaz bastard must have known Vladimir had been released by us to gain dirt on The Board, yet he and the group went ahead and used his resources anyway. I guess they figured the threat would ensure he towed the line and as such they regarded him as a valuable informer as well as a cash cow—their guy on the inside so to speak."

Ballard nodded. "We may be treading on Pete's and James's toes with this but yes, it's still a murder investigation. So let's strike while the iron's hot and continue pumping him. And you're right Johno, the threat against the daughter was The Board's trump card in keeping him on a tight leash, simple as that. Sergey would have been operating armed with that knowledge."

Almost falling over each other in their haste, the two detectives re-entered the room to recommence the interview. Ballard activated the video recording while John reached forward to switch on his ever-handy Olympus recorder.

Both detectives flipped open their day books with Ballard directed his full attention to Vladimir who sat staring back, appearing confident but wary.

"Okay Vladimir, detail your involvement with the siege at Parliament House."

Sipping water from a plastic cup which he held in his free hand, the Russian took his time, aware the Note Printing Australia robbery alone was enough to see him put behind bars for life should the department so choose. His rat cunning also recognised that admitting his involvement in the siege was unlikely to jeopardise his current prospects of freedom and in fact could well enhance them by proving beyond doubt he had direct contact with The Board's hierarchy. Sensing his chance of being offered a second get-out-of-jail exchange was more than possible, his confidence in finding a way clear of his immediate predicament was reflected in his eyes, much to John's disgust.

Licking his lips, the Russian took his time, assessing the best way to answer Ballard's question. "My role was to raise money to finance the equipment and personnel required for the raid." His cheeks ballooned before declaring, "That's it."

"Were you in contact with any members of The Board during the preparation phase?" It was clear John wasn't hopeful of a positive answer, and he was correct.

"No, everything was channelled through Sergey."

"You were in direct contact with him?"

"I was." Vladimir's expression made it clear he was aware the detectives had significant doubts the Spetsnaz soldier trusted his boss, a consequence of the latter's arrest then subsequent release.

Ballard followed up his suspicion with "I'm assuming Sergey knows of The Board's threat to your daughter?"

A flash of anguish darkened Vladimir's features. "He *is* the threat."

Again the detectives stared at one another, attempting to comprehend the synergies at play between the two Russians, all this reinforcing their accumulated understanding of the incredible control The Board had over its contacts, fear being the driving force.

Ballard was the first to recover from Vladimir's heartfelt admission. "Once you provided the money what was your role then?"

"I didn't have one. As you'd have guessed, The Board arranged for the tracking device to be removed from my hip, after that I was ordered to make myself scarce, which I did until I was arrested."

John sought to clarify Vladimir's involvement in the siege. "You're telling us you had no further input to the planning or execution of the operation at Parliament House? It was all left to Sergey?"

A flash of annoyance exposed Vladimir's frustration regarding the detectives' belief he had more responsibility in the siege than mere funding. "Are you kidding me? *Sergey's* the soldier. Why would *I* have *any* say in the actual operation itself?"

Hesitating John deliberated on the answer before moving on. "Okay then, when is the next meeting to be held at the Melbourne Club?"

Vladimir gazed at the ceiling, again deliberating on the best response. "If it's a regular monthly meeting, which I'm certain it is, then within the next week or so."

Ballard scribbled a note in his day book then looked to John. Both men deliberated on who was going to ask the critical question, the decision line ball until John's imploring stare won out. Hunching forward he adopted an almost conspiratorial manner before asking, "Vladimir, just prior to you being arrested at Portsea you were on your mobile and you mentioned a lady's name who had knowledge of The Board's activities. Who is the lady?"

The question had Vladimir stiffening in his chair, assessing his options, his eyes narrowing as to how the detectives knew so much about the conversation. Guessing that if her name was known the question wouldn't have been asked, he chose to play hardball. "I can't tell you. Threaten me with whatever you like. Revealing her would be putting a gun to my head and pulling the trigger, with the same fate for my daughter. I won't do it." From the intensity in his voice it was obvious he wasn't going to budge.

John glanced at Ballard to determine whether Vladimir's non-compliance was worth pursuing. Noting his partner's deadpan reaction he decided to drop the matter. Scribbling notes in his folder before looking up he changed tack. "We know The Board has made moves to take significant control of both the Melbourne and Sydney ports, effectively making the docks their personal piggy bank." He paused and by watching Vladimir's reaction he was rewarded with the faintest facial twitch which denoted a raw nerve had been struck.

Pouncing on the imperceptible change in Vladimir's demeanour and armed with the snippets of conversation recorded by the operative at Portsea, John went for the jugular. "We need to know how the injection of your money, along with the ransom gained from the siege, will assist The Board to secure a foothold at the ports. In other words, who in the ports' management and for that matter in the government is being pressured, and how?"

Both detectives sat back, certain Vladimir would plead ignorance despite being aware he was walking a tightrope between saying nothing, which would result in him being thrown in jail with what that entailed and revealing too many specifics with serious repercussions on his wellbeing. Although prepared they were taken aback by Vladimir's resultant shrug and barely audible response: "I was just easy pickings. The Board intends to bleed me dry until there's nothing left. I'm also aware they have a politician in their pocket, but I don't know who." Such was his apparent broken spirit that the detectives would have accepted his words as genuine had it not been for their knowledge of the piecemeal recording supplied by Bernard. It was obvious a consummate liar was conning them, someone who had cheated and deceived his way out of a lifetime of difficult situations and in the majority succeeded.

Sensing the Russian needed to be softened up a whole lot more they nodded to one another, mutually concluding it was Peter and James's turn to tag-team the interview. Not uttering a word, they switched off the recordings and gathered their belongings before standing, noting Vladimir's attempt to appear unconcerned at the abrupt halt to proceedings with no mention of him being released. Leaving the room they moved to the window to watch the Russian assume a thoughtful expression as he inspected the ceiling, by no means panicked but far from relaxed.

"Hopefully he's got plenty to mull over. Jesus, there were a few surprises in that lot Mike."

"There was indeed Johno, and they won't be the last."

CHAPTER
15

"*The Melbourne Club*?" Peter's jaw dropped as he alternated his stunned gaze between Delwyn and Ballard. Sitting to one side, John appeared amused at the superintendent's dumbfounded expression.

"Yep, who would have guessed?" Ballard supressed a satisfied grin, enjoying watching his colleague lost for words.

Recovering Peter blurted, "And monthly meetings? Bloody hell, what is this, the public service for Christ sake?"

"It would seem that way." Ballard's supressed enjoyment broke free.

Delwyn seized on the importance of the revelation by addressing Peter. "Sweat Vladimir for all its worth. He has to find out *when* the next meeting is to be scheduled." Staring into middle distance she added, "We just might get there gentlemen. We just might . . ." Her mood was upbeat. "Peter, I'll get the AC up to speed while you and James continue grinding Vladimir for whatever intel you can." She thrust a forefinger skywards. "Oh, before I forget, James rang. He's good to go with the tracker in Vladimir's watch and Bernard has asked for sufficient notice prior to the guy's release so his son can position his surveillance teams. At least with this set-up if Vladimir *does* find the tracker and leaves it somewhere, or gives it to one of his cronies to fool us, we'll know soon enough as surveillance will realise his location doesn't match that of the tracker."

Turning to Ballard and John she stared at the wall clock with exaggerated purpose. "Excellent start you two, and now for a change of pace." She grinned wickedly. "Marjorie's ensconced in the conference room and tells me you're both looking forward to your chat."

John winced. "Indubitably." With a resigned shrug he clapped Ballard on the shoulder. "Might as well get this over with Mike." Winking at Delwyn and Peter, Ballard followed his partner.

Glancing up Marjorie greeted the detectives. Rising from her chair she shook hands. "So glad you could make it. I have to admit I was a trifle worried work pressures might get in the way so I appreciate you making the time."

Ballard noted her filigree gold clasp was nowhere to be seen, her shoulder length hair now free, softening her features. She spotted his look of approval but chose not to respond.

Settling on the far side of the conference table both detectives watched her flick pages in her diary. "I see the last time we spoke was just under a month ago. On that occasion I was discussing your penchant for living dangerously." She looked up, eying both men which caused John to shuffle in his chair.

Without warning her famous smile appeared, generous, exposing prominent front teeth. "Well this time you've got yourselves into even more of a scrape, but I'm glad to say you're both innocent parties drawn into what must have been a very frightening, *very* stressful situation."

John's reflex action was to inflate his chest, about to declare it was just another day at the office, but Marjorie's cautioning stare halted him in his tracks. "Take your situation John. Virtually a prisoner in a cleaner's room for nearly three days with little or no food, worried sick about what had or might happen to your pregnant fiancée—that had to be tough on you physically and mentally." She continued staring at him, defying him to pretend otherwise.

Surprising everyone including himself John replied, "Worst situation I've ever had to face Marjorie, and I'm pretty certain I couldn't go through anything as traumatic as that ever again. If something had happened to Sonia and the baby, I don't . . . I . . ."

He choked, emotional, dropping his gaze as he grew increasingly embarrassed.

Marjorie reacted. "You wouldn't be human if you didn't feel overwhelmed by it all." Leaning forward she licked her lips which she always did when she was about to expound on a specific topic. "Three days under the conditions you were subjected to would take its toll on even the toughest of detectives. Despite you and Sonia coming out the other side unscathed, you need to be mindful of potential flashbacks, panic attacks, a pounding heart, or even shortness of breath. Have you experienced any of these symptoms since the siege?"

John turned to Ballard, hesitant, wanting to be truthful but not keen to reveal emotional weakness in front of his partner. Ballard's brusque toss of his head was a nonverbal "Get on with it" directive.

"A bit of everything really." The words were mumbled, eyes downcast.

"Say again John?" Marjorie wasn't letting him off the hook.

"I said a bit of everything." John's glance switched to mild defiance, followed by "Nothing major, just every now and then I relive some of the events, trying not to image what might have happened."

"Sleeping okay?"

"Sonia says I am. I'm not dreaming, so that's a good sign."

Marjorie wasn't convinced. "Sometimes dreams can be a good thing." She eyed him closely. "At least you recognise you've been through the wringer in a most demanding way."

John straightened. "Not for anything which might have happened to me, but certainly for Sonia and the baby. Utter frustration at not being able to do anything the whole time she was in the chamber."

Marjorie shook her head, disagreeing. "From what I've been told being on the spot so to speak, unknown to the terrorists and being able to do what you did—along with Sonia's help of course—without both of your inputs the mission wouldn't have been as successful. In all probability your actions saved God knows how many lives."

Ballard stepped in to support the message being hammered home by Marjorie. "Spot on. Between John and Sonia we managed to get eyes into the chamber and verify Sergey was indeed the ringleader. As well John and Sonia were instrumental during the release of the gas—all vital actions which helped save the day."

Marjorie was almost conspiratorial. "John, I know I'm labouring this point but I want you to take two things out of this. Firstly, you couldn't have done *anything* more than you did. Bursting out of the cleaner's room prematurely to rescue Sonia would have placed you, Sonia, and the baby in a disastrous situation. End of story. The second point to be aware of is you need to take time off, even if you believe you don't. *Nobody* can go through what you did without needing a stint of R and R to mend body and soul. Be aware that running on adrenaline for almost three days while lacking nourishing food means your immune system will be shot to pieces. Quite likely you'll pick up the odd cold or two, so don't be surprised about that." She sat expectant of the detective, waiting for him to respond.

"I thought I might take Sonia to Queensland to meet Mum and Dad. It's about time we went up, so this is as good an excuse as I'll ever get. Just for three or four days. It's still a bit humid up there this time of year but we'll survive."

"And no work contact!" Marjorie attempted to look fierce, realising she was asking the impossible. John flicked a glance towards Ballard which didn't go unnoticed. "I mean it John. *Keep work out of this.* It's only for a few days."

John threw her a roundhouse salute which did little to placate her doubts.

Changing tack Marjorie focussed on Ballard. "Now *your* escapades up at Parliament House with Peter and John, then being held hostage and flown handcuffed in a chopper with Sergey to an unknown destination and an unknown fate . . ." She was momentarily lost for words. "My God Michael, a great story to frighten the hell out of your grandchildren, but like John it will have taken a huge toll on you. How are *you* sleeping these past days?"

Ballard pretended to be mystified, replying straight-faced, "With Natalie of course."

"*What?*" It was Marjorie's turn to be confused.

Again with a straight face Ballard replied, "With Natalie . . .oh, I see . . . *how* am I sleeping, not *who* am I sleeping with?"

John's braying laugh echoed throughout the room but was cut short by Marjorie's look of death. "Very funny. And I'm still waiting."

For a moment Ballard thought she was going to fold her arms and utter an unladylike *humph*, but she refrained.

"Like a baby."

"Really?" Open disbelief was evident.

"*Really.*"

Appearing serious Marjorie stated in a quiet voice, "The two police officers who stumbled into the crash site and were murdered by Sergey . . . that must have been appalling."

A black cloud swept across Ballard's features. Marjorie remained silent, her expression sympathetic but expectant.

"Such a tragedy. Innocent young lives snuffed out by a monster." Ballard went on to explain how he had expended too many rounds to control Sergey and force the chopper pilot to land, leaving him with only one shot to warn the officers. Marjorie pursed her lips at each disclosure, aware of the guilt wracking the detective.

"I hear you're going to their funerals." Ballard nodded, with Marjorie adding, "I can only support your decision. It'll show your respect to the officers' families and go some way to helping you heal from what had to be a shocking ordeal." There was silence for some time, everyone reflecting on the tragedies of the past days and the ongoing impact for those left behind.

Snapping her diary shut Marjorie took in both men, her expression one of respect and overwhelming admiration. "My report will state you've both come through this ordeal amazingly well, but you *must* be allowed to regroup which means taking some well-deserved time off. I just have one caution, gentlemen." She held their enquiring gaze. "Your recent actions have now moved into folklore. As such you're going to be surrounded by colleagues who believe you're bulletproof. Make sure you don't give too much credence to what *could* massage your egos into a false sense of invulnerability." Both men were thoughtful, aware the psychologist's words were on the money. They had seen similar situations over the years which often proved fatal—if not for the individuals then for those around them.

Jumping to her feet Marjorie shook both detectives' hands, the gesture prolonged. Her collaboration with them during the past six months had been such that her action appeared perfectly natural, albeit one which caused John to redden from the psychologist's extended attention.

The moment all three traipsed into Delwyn's office the superintendent sprang from her chair. Backing against the front of her desk she demanded, "Do we have a meeting of minds or do I still have to bang heads together?"

Marjorie chuckled. "Copybook answers Delwyn, and fully aware a period of rest and recreation is an essential part of getting back up to speed, not that they appear to have lost any to this point."

Delwyn viewed the detectives with more than a dose of cynicism. Shrugging she had to admit their contrite expressions were a model of compliance which only added to her suspicions. "Thank you Marjorie. Send me your report as soon as you can. I'll attach it to their files which are expanding by the day." The detectives' expressions of humility switched to exaggerated sympathy at causing their boss needless grief, their identical countenances appearing within milliseconds of one another.

"Yeah, yeah, make light of this you two, but as of now you're both on leave for the rest of the week. Go on. Get out of here." With that Delwyn repeated Marjorie's previous actions but added a hug for each man for good measure. Whispering to them both she muttered, "I've never been so worried in all my life." Turning away so they wouldn't see the welling in her eyes she brusquely waved them from the office.

CHAPTER
16

Their desks cleaned, they received numerous farewells from their colleagues. John informed the gathered throng that his leave was for a few days not months, so they better not get too comfortable. Minutes later, both detectives stood in the car park and shook hands. "Enjoy the sunshine John and give Sonia my love." Ballard paused. "It's great you'll be seeing your folks. You don't talk about them much. Come to think of it you don't talk about them at all."

John winced. "Queensland's a long way away, but the truth is I'm not all that close to them. Sounds shitty, doesn't it? But they taught me to be independent at a very early age . . . I think they might have done too good a job of it. Sonia's thrilled we're going to see them, she said she'll do everything she can to help rebuild bridges."

Ballard clapped him on the shoulder. "Whatever you do don't leave it too late John. Once your parents are gone they're gone forever."

Promising to keep in touch, the two men headed to their respective vehicles.

Emerging from the crime building onto a packed Spencer Street, Ballard rang Natalie's mobile, aware she had headed in to work for a few hours while he was at the office. Glancing at his watch he saw it was just after 4 p.m. On the second ring there was a cheerful "Hi, darling! Missing me?"

"Don't I always?" Judging it would take some time to drive to her Collins Street office with the congestion bumper to bumper, he asked, "Fancy a lift home if I can see my way clear of all this traffic?"

"Michael you read my mind. I was just about to pack up to go home so I could rustle up something for dinner. Where are you now?"

"Just turning into Collins. I should be outside your building in fifteen. I've been told to take a few days' leave so hopefully this meets with your approval?"

The gasp of excitement from Natalie was followed by "It's a date." With a chuckle she was gone.

Smiling, Ballard thought back to the first time he met her at the Ericsson & May law firm where she now worked as a legal secretary. It was a meeting which changed his life forever, throwing cold water on his long-held belief he was destined never to marry again after two failed attempts.

A stab of guilt swept over him as he acknowledged with regret their piecemeal honeymoon which involved a Pacific cruise to the islands followed by a trip to Paris and a seven-day riverboat journey down the Rhine, cut short by the Parliament House crisis. Eternally grateful for her unquestioning acceptance they needed to head home, he promised to make amends, but due to the current work pressures he wasn't sure when that would be.

Pulling into a vacant parking space near Natalie's building, Ballard saw her standing on the footpath searching the oncoming traffic. Opening the driver's door he stepped out, then reaching through the open window he tooted the horn, waving to catch her attention. Rising on tip toes she returned the wave before heading towards him, a broad smile forming. Ballard rushed to open the passenger door before encircling her waist and planting a flamboyant kiss, causing pedestrians to double-take.

"So Michael, it appears you really *are* glad to see me." Tucking in her Guangzhou Shandao floral summer dress so the fabric wouldn't catch in the door, she smiled up at him as she settled in her seat. Ballard darted around to the driver's side and slipped behind the wheel. Checking the mirrors he spotted a gap in the traffic, allowing him to ease from the kerb.

Natalie placed a relaxed hand on his thigh, a habit she adopted whenever they were driving. "Home James, and don't spare the horses." She laughed. "On second thoughts I'd better take that back. It wouldn't look too professional for an officer of the law to *cop* a speeding fine." She giggled at her mischievous use of the word *cop*.

Ballard squeezed her hand. "Your command is my wish, er, your wish is my demand . . . Ah, what the hell! Let's get out of this madness."

Surviving the bumper-to-bumper trip to the town house, Ballard headed upstairs for a shower before returning to help Natalie apply the finishing touches to a spinach-and-ham omelette. Pressing his lips to the back of her neck he peered over her shoulder as she carefully poured the mixture into the oiled fry pan, positioned the glass lid as she set the temperature to simmer. "You know you spoil me rotten Nat."

She spun around declaring, "Nonsense. We're just a great team, but come to think of it you do leave a bit to be desired in the cooking department." She laughed suddenly. "I feel sorry for Bradley. What he must have endured over the years growing up with you."

Appearing sheepish Ballard admitted, "There were times when he would tear out recipes from magazines and leave them on the kitchen bench."

"*Really?*"

"Really."

"So what did you do about it?"

"Stuck to my beef casseroles, along with ham-and-cheese jaffles for variety."

Natalie shook her head in disbelief. "*Jaffles?* The poor, poor boy."

"Poor boy my foot! Private school education at Ivanhoe Boys Grammar, a father who doted over him and, yes, gave him a strict upbringing—but he had a tennis court next door to use whenever he wanted a game with his mates—*and* bucketloads of vegetables and fruit every day, what more could he have asked for?"

"Meals that wouldn't repeat on him for hours after he ate them." Relenting Natalie reached up, kissing Ballard on the cheek. "Honestly

Michael you did a marvellous job as a custodial father, and now you can sit back and watch him excel in the army. About to be promoted to a captain at his age isn't to be sneezed at."

Ballard returned the kiss, looking on as Natalie busied herself preparing a Greek salad. Reaching forward he made to steal one of the cherry tomatoes but was promptly slapped on the wrist.

Turning to him Natalie's face lit up. "So you've achieved a minor miracle—time off—which means we can be together for at least a few days." Despite her light-hearted delivery Ballard felt a prick of conscience.

"Yep. Under threat of death from Delwyn who passes on her abject apology, insisting on taking the blame for what she describes as a 'disruption' to our honeymoon."

Shaking her head in clear disagreement, Natalie darted over to her handbag which was resting on the bench. She extracted two tickets and waved them above her head as though they were the winning numbers for the previous night's lotto draw. "Guess what I have here Michael?"

Ballard opened his mouth only to be beaten to the punch. "*Tickets to Her Majesty's Theatre!* One of the partners gave them to me this afternoon. I offered to pay but he wouldn't hear of it, said he had to attend a funeral instead. The poor man. He was really upset about it."

"What, not being able to make it to the show?" Ballard made out to be serious.

"Not funny." Natalie punched him on the arm, fully aware that his infamous black humour fostered from working with John for so many years was not meant to offend.

Ballard moved closer. "Okay Nat, what's on offer?" He established a positive expression, praying the tickets would be for something interesting, secretly hoping they were for the upcoming cricket match at the MCG.

"*Aladdin.*" Natalie's eyes sparkled, resulting in Ballard struggling to maintain his upbeat disposition, sensing from the outset Natalie could see through the charade. It was clear he was correct because her penetrating gaze brooked no dissent. "Trust me darling, you'll love it. It's a matinee session and the reviews have been fantastic. To quote one of them it claims the show is nothing short of 'shining, shimmering, splendid, and transports audiences on a magic carpet ride to a whole new world of kaleidoscopic intensity'."

Ballard's mouth dropped open. "Bloody hell Nat, did you *memorise* all that?"

Grinning, she ignored his amazed look with a nonchalant wave of her hand. "And what's more this will be our last chance to see it. The season ends in two weeks."

"Hmm, that *would* be a pity." Ballard took her in his arms, nuzzling her neck. "As I said, your command is my wish or something along those lines. No, it'll be fun, and even if I don't like it you'll never know."

Natalie poked out her tongue.

Ballard peered down at the tickets. "So when are we going?"

"Tomorrow."

"*Tomorrow?*"

"Yes, we have to be at the theatre by twelve midday for a twelve thirty start, which means we can sleep in just for once."

Ballard cocked his head to one side, reflecting, "I see, sleep in or perhaps occupy ourselves with another mutually enjoyable pursuit." Natalie mulled over the prospect with considered due diligence.

The city-bound tram was almost empty save for a grey-haired gentleman sitting opposite as Ballard and Natalie took in the shrine to their right, observing several joggers struggled past, their singlets dark with sweat. Natalie wore a peach-coloured Bianca Spender tailored suit and Moschino heels while Ballard maintained appearances in a navy-blue Armani wool blend suit, white shirt, and grey silk tie. Feeling unsure he asked a second time, "So you're *certain* we're not overdressed? It is a matinee after all."

Ignoring the question Natalie dug into her handbag, drawing out her mobile; within seconds, she glanced up with a triumphant smile. "Would you believe the land Her Majesty's is built on was bought in 1838 for—" She broke off, astonished. "Wow! Have a guess how much Michael."

Ballard pondered the challenge before blurting, "A thousand pounds?"

"*Wrong.* Try one hundred." Further flicking of the mobile's screen had her exclaiming, "This is amazing! The land was originally known as the Hippodrome and was used for open-air equestrian shows and circus acts."

Ballard shuffled closer, attempting to read the screen but gave up when Natalie held it to one side, wanting her disclosures to be a surprise. The elderly gentleman's imperceptible nod showed concurrence with Natalie's tactics.

"Incredible. It says here the theatre was built in 1886 for the princely sum of *forty thousand pounds?*"

Even Ballard was surprised at the figure, making a further attempt to read the screen.

"At the time Her Majesty's was the largest theatre of its type in the southern hemisphere."

"How many seats?"

More screen-searching ensued. "Er, originally eighteen hundred but that's been pared back to seventeen hundred. The theatre has had a number of renovations over the years, one of them the main auditorium which caught fire in 1929 resulting in a very expensive repair bill."

Bringing the screen closer as though unable to believe what she was reading she exclaimed, "Lordy, lordy, how's this for a quote? 'After adverse comments by Dame Nellie Melba in 1909 the auditorium and proscenium arch'"—Natalie crinkled her nose—"whatever that is, 'were extensively remodelled to improve the acoustics'. Then two years later in 1911 Dame Nellie made her 'Australian grand opera debut as Violetta in *La Traviata* on the 1st of November'."

Even the gentleman opposite was caught up in the revelations and said so, much to Natalie's enjoyment and Ballard's amusement. Warming to the task Natalie exclaimed, "The Russian ballerina Anna Pavlova danced there for a season in 1926 and this was followed by Dame Nellie's farewell performance in 1928." Eyes wide she looked up, reflective. "Who would have thought the place boasted so much history?"

Ballard backed up the rhetorical question with a less-than-convincing "Yeah, who would have thought?"

Ignoring him Natalie pressed on. "And it doesn't stop there." Open-mouthed she declared, "Dame Margot Fonteyn made her dance debut at the theatre in 1957." Continuing to thumb the screen she added, "Ahh, more shows . . . more shows . . . Oh! Here we go. The musical Cats opened in '87, and from the long list I can see international performances have played there ever since." Eyes widening once more she blurted, "*Michael*, even Pavarotti sang there when he was twenty-nine." Shaking her head she appeared puzzled. "Perhaps I was too busy over the years bringing up the kids to take much notice of what shows were on." A deep sigh preceded an almost wistful "And what's even more incredible is how many times we've walked past this grand old building and never given it a second thought."

Pressing the button to inform the driver of their intent to leave the tram, Ballard conceded, "I'll give you that. It must be a hundred times we've passed it over the years. While it may not have the history of the spectacular buildings in Paris, it's not doing too bad for 180 odd years." He then added in a muted tone, almost as an afterthought, "It's an arch framing the opening between the stage and the auditorium."

"Pardon?"

"A proscenium arch is the opening between the stage and the auditorium." The smug look on Ballard's face was countered by a slow head shake from Natalie, followed by the ghost of a smile.

Wishing the gentleman a safe journey they got off and hand in hand they walked the two blocks to Exhibition Street. Turning left they approached the theatre which was abuzz with hundreds of people milling on the footpath and even more in the foyer, many clasping drinks and snacks.

Scrabbling in her handbag Natalie produced the two tickets and, glancing about her, spotted a tall young usher who directed them up the staircase to the second level. On entering the theatre they were struck by the lavish burgundy seating that defied physics, the rows sweeping before them in huge arcs, seemingly suspended in mid-air. The circular lighting overhead and the Old World charm of the decor enhanced the interior's warm ambiance. After hunting for their seats they settled and leaning back, allowed the surrounding luxury to wash over them.

With less than fifteen minutes to show time, a mad rush unfolded throughout the theatre—patrons checking and rechecking seat numbers. Young children dashed about, excited, looking in all directions, their emotions redlining. Natalie pointed to one group of youngsters who came armed with booster cushions. "There was no such luxury in my day Michael. Whenever I was taken to a show I just had to peep left and right and hope for the best."

Ballard leaned across, feigning sympathy as he touched her cheek. "Well, I guess that explains quite a lot."

Natalie stared at him, unsure whether he was being serious, having missed his fleeting smile.

The moment the curtain rose an ear-splitting roar erupted from the audience; the elaborate sets, the brightly coloured costumes and the dazzling stage lighting assaulted the senses in a delightful way. Within minutes Ballard's trepidation as to whether he would enjoy what was essentially a children's story was swept away, with Natalie enthralled by his obvious pleasure.

The shrieks from the excited youngsters, some of whom were borderline frenetic, was deafening, and far from Ballard's initial apprehension that their presence would be distracting, he discovered to his surprise their exuberant enjoyment heightened the atmosphere which was nothing short of magical.

By the final curtain call Ballard was a convert, agreeing without reservation with the review Natalie had memorised. Leaning across he kissed her as other patrons scrambled about them, all dashing to the exits which by now were congested with shuffling bodies. "Thank you darling. I can't tell you how much I enjoyed the show."

Natalie flashed him a contented smile, glad she had been able to distract him from his work, if only for a few short hours, aware he needed to unwind for his emotional well-being. In her best southern drawl she declared, "You're most welcome."

Taking almost fifteen minutes to reach ground level, they strolled arm in arm to Bourke Street. Ballard glanced at his watch. "I'm famished Nat. Considering we saved on the tickets, how about a late brunch or early dinner at Florentino's?"

Natalie's face lit up at the thought but her anticipation was followed by a frown. "That sounds wonderful Michael but they're *very* expensive. I went there once with a girlfriend for a cup of coffee and a slice of cheesecake, I almost choked when I was handed the bill."

Ballard hugged her to his side as they crossed at the lights. "I'm starting to appreciate there's more to life than just work Nat, and while it may have taken me longer to realise this than most, the events over the past few days have well and truly hammered the reality home."

Glancing up at him Natalie could see the beginnings of a transformation, one she had prayed for but never thought would eventuate, a change to a softer and more relaxed husband and companion.

Catching her breath, she confessed, "I'm so glad Michael. This was something you had to come to terms with in your own time. No one else could do it for you. I'm just so grateful you didn't come to any harm. I . . . I don't know what I would have done . . ." She was unable to finish what she so desperately wanted to express. Ballard hugged her even tighter.

Settling at their table, they looked up at the smartly dressed waiter who was standing patiently in front of them, implying he had all the time in the world. Natalie tapped her menu. "Yum, just a main course for me. The *maltagliati di pane* thank you, with a glass of rose moscato."

Nodding an endorsement despite pinched lips denoting his silent disapproval of Natalie's failure to select a white wine with the fish, the waiter commented, "Excellent choice madam." Turning to Ballard who spotted the exchange, he raised his eyebrows questioningly.

"Er, yes, a main course for me too. I'll have the duck tortellini."

"Another excellent choice, sir, and to drink . . . ?" The eyebrows climbed higher, one brow more so than the other.

"Hmm, decisions, decisions." Ballard mentally bit his tongue at the waiter's air of superiority. "How about a tall glass of your finest Sauvignon Blanc apple juice, chilled, shaken, but not stirred?"

Almost reeling backwards in shock, it was clear the waiter wasn't predisposed to Ballard's brand of take-no-prisoners humour.

Natalie smothered a laugh as the man sped off, clearly unimpressed and more than a tad shell-shocked. "That was naughty Michael."

"Pretentious waiters get me riled up Nat. He's just an arrogant little shit."

"Be careful my sweet. Let's not forget he'll be bringing our meals out, and a lot can happen between the kitchen and our table." She let the comment mature, and as Ballard contemplated on what she was inferring, a lopsided grin formed.

"I'll scrutinise the plates when they arrive. Now your maltagli . . . er, maltagla . . ."

Natalie helped him out. "*Maltagliati di pane.*"

"Yeah, that. What is it?"

Natalie leaned forward, careful not to disturb her cutlery or the pyramid-folded serviette in front of her. "Moreton Bay bugs, *colatura*, and warrigal greens."

Ballard's eyebrows mimicked those of the waiter's. "I'm up to speed on the Moreton Bay bugs, but the rest?"

"Colatura is an anchovy sauce, and warrigal greens are, well, a type of wild spinach. Apparently the last meal on Captain Cook's *Endeavour* as it left Botany Bay was skate, a type of fish, and warrigal greens." Natalie smiled innocently. "Well according to the captain's log that is."

Laughing, Ballard suggested, "Hey Nat, what say you invite John and Sonia around for dinner sometime so we can bombard the poor guy with fine dining terminology to see how long it takes before he loses it?"

Natalie pretended indignation. "We'll do nothing of the sort Michael."

Ballard shrugged. "Seems like a good idea to me. I've lost count of the practical jokes he's pulled on me over the years."

"Maybe so, but right now I'd suggest he needs to recuperate and remain stress-free, just like you darling."

A thoughtful expression preceded "I guess you're right, but hey, the bugger's as tough as they come. He'll be fine, believe me."

Natalie didn't fully share Ballard's casual assessment. "Perhaps he is Michael, but everyone has their limit. And with Sonia now part of the equation you may well notice a considerable difference in John's demeanour."

Slow nodding, Ballard appeared reflective as he glanced about him, noting the three other tables with diners, putting the meagre clientele numbers down to the hour of the day.

The drinks arrived with a flourish, and ten minutes later their meals followed, with Ballard scrutinising the plates as they were placed on the table. Flashing a high-voltage smile at the waiter Ballard figured he was at least halfway towards mending burnt bridges.

Having enjoyed their meal they leant back, sipping their drinks as they contemplated whether to have dessert. Weakening, they settled on a serving of tres leches cake each, with Ballard requesting a side scoop of vanilla ice cream which returned the pinched look on the waiter's face with credit.

Twenty minutes later with the bill paid, which, as Natalie predicted, caused Ballard to swallow several times, they sauntered through the Block Arcade, stopping often as she inspected the array of wares on display. Following that they wandered back to Swanston

Street and caught the number 58 tram, arriving at the town house just as the sun began to dip in the western sky.

Taking her mobile Natalie spoke with Kayla and Josh for several minutes, then holding the cell phone to her chest, asked Ballard if he would like to have dinner tomorrow evening at her parents' house. Realising there was only one answer allowable he waved an acknowledging hand, hoping his apprehension regarding the grilling he would receive from Natalie's father wasn't obvious.

The call complete Natalie took his hand. "Thank you darling. I know Dad's bound to ask a few rough questions but you two see eye-to-eye on just about everything, so you'll be fine."

Ballard's expression was at odds with his inner thoughts, but he was satisfied he had set in place a convincing air of nonchalance; what he failed to catch was Natalie's fleeting glance of unease.

CHAPTER
17

"Bugger me Michael. The Ruskies came through after all." Peter's voice on Ballard's mobile was animated, the words clipped, with a hint of energised tension threaded throughout which was unusual as he was normally so measured and calculating in everything he said and did.

Ballard slumped into the lounge chair, having donned shorts and a T-shirt, glad to be free from the confines of his suit. "*And*?" He asked the question but realised it wasn't necessary. Peter's enthusiasm was on overdrive.

"A letter signed and sealed lobbed onto the AC's desk first thing this morning stating with typical Russian bluntness: 'Olegovich's immunity has been withdrawn forthwith'. The letter came from the chief after being hand-delivered from the minister's office."

"So the Russian embassy here in Melbourne, along with Olegovich, they're in the dark about this?"

"You betcha. An hour later we obtained a warrant authorising surveillance to fit up the St Georges Road mansion. Guess how many cameras the boys had to use considering the size of the place." Without waiting for a reply Peter blurted, "*Fifteen*. I've spoken with the guys since and they said they've established outer perimeter monitoring as well, just on the off chance it sheds light on who's coming and going.

"Olegovich headed off to work at 7 a.m. as usual, and the moment the good wife hopped into the Merc for her midday catch-up with the girlfriends in Toorak Road the guys went in. It's done and dusted my man."

Ballard smiled to himself. "This's got you fired up Pete. I can't remember the last time you were so gung-ho."

His partner chuckled. "You of all people don't need reminding what a breakthrough this may turn out to be Mike. Listening in on pillow talk of The Board's cell leader here in Australia, just think about it." He hesitated, his tone changing to one that was almost apologetic. "I know Delwyn's ordered you and John on leave, but I thought you'd want to know something as important as this. Do you want me to call John to get him up to speed?"

"No Pete, I'll give him the word. He's said all along Olegovich's ability to hide behind a cloak of immunity meant we were operating with one arm tied behind our back. This'll put him over the moon. Now what about Vladimir? I can't believe I'm asking this but is he back on the street again?"

"Yep, James arranged for the tracker in his watch, and Bernard's son is pulling out all stops to keep him under physical surveillance twenty-four-seven."

"Where is he now?"

"Sitting in his Docklands pad the last I heard."

Ballard's brow knitted. "He does know he's out there to dig up information for us?"

"He does indeed. I made it abundantly clear. That said, we're giving him rope to do his own thing."

"Just as long as it doesn't involve Malcolm or Teresa." Ballard knew there was no need to state the obvious but he felt compelled to air his thoughts.

"*Definitely* not involving them. Susan and Bobby have had their chat with Malcolm who just grunted, saying he'd make sure Teresa was safe, but clearly he wasn't thrilled with Vladimir being let loose again."

Ballard hesitated, unsure whether to scratch off the ever-present scab which was news of Sergey's current whereabouts. "Pete, what's the latest regarding our MIA Russian? Anything from Bernard or his son as to where the bastard's holed up?" Almost fearful of the reply, he felt his neck muscles tense in anticipation.

The tone of Peter's response hinted he was fully aware of Ballard's disquiet. "Nothing concrete. Well not yet Mike. Bernard's son believes it's possible he may be licking his wounds in Sydney. Said he was following up that line of enquiry while making sure he doesn't spook the bugger. Trust me Mike, Sergey will turn up at some point. Guys like him *never* fly below the radar for too long. If for nothing else he'll pop up to do another job, God forbid."

Peter changed subjects. "Now Mike, just to let you know we've been applying the blow torch to the ports minister's genitals, Laurie Davidson. Mate, there's *something* going down there. He's as guilty as hell, but we haven't been able to prise anything of value out of him—well not yet anyway."

"You think The Board's got to him?" Ballard saw Natalie in the lounge doorway and signalled five minutes; she gave a take-your-time wave before disappearing, her parting smile tinged with the shadow of uncertainty.

"Jesus Mike, there's no doubt about it, and who can blame him for shutting up shop?" Peter's laugh was brittle. "Ken's given me a profile of the guy. He's married, has two kids—a boy and a girl, six and ten. By that score The Board's got him by the nuts, I'm certain of that."

"What did Davidson say about the tender?"

"Just straight bat stuff. Everything was as it should be throughout the formal process—all meetings documented, government protocols followed, blah blah blah. These guys are so practised at dodging questions in parliament and with the press, it's nigh on impossible to separate the wheat from the chaff when we interview them."

Ballard laughed. "I wasn't aware you had farming aspirations in your blood Pete."

The superintendent snorted. "Mike there are days when I wish I'd taken up a country vocation in spite of all the fires, floods, and droughts I'd have to contend with."

Ballard reflected on his early years on his parents' property in Bordertown, South Australia where he and Kathryn grew up prior to leaving home, choosing not to remain on the land much to his father's displeasure and mother's disappointment. "I guess it's horses for courses and I feel yours will always be nailing bad guys to the wall, which you do rather well."

A resounding "Hmm" was his reply. "Yeah, no doubt that's going to be my lot. So what have you guys been up to? Or shouldn't I ask?" His braying laugh echoed over the line.

"If you must know we've just been to see *Aladdin* at Her Majesty's."

A brief silence was followed by "When you came down in the chopper, you didn't smack your head on anything hard by any chance?"

"Er no Pete, and this may come as a complete shock to you but I can highly recommend the show. One word of caution though. Don't choose the matinee—bloody kids all over the shop."

Both men laughed, with Peter promising to keep Ballard posted of any new developments.

Ballard sat reflecting on his colleague's update and how withdrawing Olegovich's diplomatic immunity had freed up the department, taking some of the heat off the AC for questioning the Russian while he was still officially an attaché. Hoping the grilling Olegovich had already received from Peter's team wouldn't drive the Russian to behave as a model citizen, Ballard pressed speed dial and was just about to hang up when John's breathless voice came on the line. "By Christ Mike, this had better be *really* important."

Fully comprehending his partner's meaning due to his continued heavy breathing, Ballard chuckled, "Sorry old son. Please pass on my apologies to Sonia. Would you like me to call back?"

The light-hearted sarcasm wasn't lost on his partner. "Mike at my age I very much doubt that would actually help."

John's pithy humour drew a bark of laughter from Ballard. "Okay, tell me when you've settled, and I'll . . ."

"*Just get on with it.*"

Ballard struggled not to burst out laughing a second time. As briefly as he could he relayed Peter's news and was rewarded with John emitting a whoop of joy. "Now we've at least a snowball's chance of getting on top of this thing."

While not wishing to dampen his partner's enthusiasm, Ballard cautioned, "We can only hope so John. Now tell me, how did the meeting with Sonia and your parents go?"

John was upbeat. "Mate really, really well. We're off to see them again tomorrow. Sonia and I can't believe how well Mum and Dad accepted her, so much so we said it was worth celebrating—"

"Which of course you appeared to be doing when I called." Ballard's face contorted into a smirk, seemingly with a mind of its own.

"*No, you silly bugger.* We decided we'd go out later this evening for a meal."

"To replace some of your expended energy?"

"Jesus Mike, keep throwing out wisecracks and I'm hanging up."

Ballard relented. "John you're up there to mend bridges as Sonia hoped, and just as important to recuperate, so carry on doing what you're doing."

Hanging up Ballard sat staring at his mobile, grateful his partner was enjoying his time with the woman of his dreams, the Parliament House tragedy and what could have happened to Sonia mercifully fading as a nightmarish memory.

"Flat battery Michael?" Natalie's cheeky question was backed up by her delivering him a vigorous neck massage, the result instant relief from the build-up of tension triggered by his previous discussion with Peter.

Tilting his head from side to side he revelled in the pampering. "Perfect timing Nat, and applied like a professional masseuse."

The massage increased in intensity as Natalie asked, "Everything okay at work darling?" The hesitancy in her voice heralded her fear their time together would be cut short as it often was.

Ballard reached up, grasping both her hands. With her cheek resting against his he knew he needed to reassure her. "Just Peter updating me on what's happening at the office. Then I rang John and guess what? Sonia met his folk and she's been welcomed with open arms."

Natalie moved to face Ballard, her expression one of righteous indignation. "And I should think so! Where Sonia's concerned she's top shelf Michael."

Ballard chuckled. "Calm down oh great defender. I'm sure she's more than capable of dealing with whatever's thrown her way, but from what John told me it's all smooth sailing."

Natalie relented, taking up position on Ballard's lap. "Just as well." Leaning forward she kissed him on the lips. "I'm glad you enjoyed the show. I wasn't sure when I was offered the tickets whether to accept them, but I thought it was—"

Ballard pressed a forefinger to her lips. "Darling, it was just perfect. I even enjoyed the thousand or so screaming kiddies. You'll be happy to know I recommended the show to Peter with the suggestion he not take the matinee option."

Natalie laughed, offering a more lingering kiss which Ballard accepted with enthusiasm. "Michael I was thinking, as we won't be having dinner we have time to catch up on other things we've been missing out on for the past week or so."

"Gosh, you read my mind." Leading her up the staircase he smiled to himself as he contemplated how fortunate he and John were in their choice of partners, but wisely refrained from any form of elaboration, instead savouring the intoxicating moment.

The next morning Natalie made it clear she wasn't getting out of bed before 10 a.m. for anything short of the town house catching fire, and even then she would have to be asked twice. Ballard supported her decision with more than a degree of enthusiasm, a designer grin developing only to have the laid-back start to the day disrupted by Peter's call.

Struggling into a fleecy-lined dressing gown one arm at a time while clutching the mobile to his ear, Ballard negotiated the stairs, almost tripping as he blurted, "Twice in less than twelve hours Peter. To what do I owe this level of attention?" He attempted to remain light-hearted but was experienced enough to know Peter must have something crucial to share to be ringing back so soon. Slumping onto a lounge chair, one bare leg propped over the armrest, Ballard braced himself for the answer.

"We've struck pay dirt Michael. Talk about pillow talk between Olegovich and his better half. I can tell you there was none of that last night—or any night it would appear. They don't sleep together. When Olegovich got back around eightish, his wife—her name's Tatiana by the way and a real looker, well Tatiana got stuck into him from the moment he stepped in the front door."

Ballard's interest redlined. "What was the gist of it?"

Peter's voice lowered as though fearful someone might overhear him despite Ballard being confident his colleague was making the call from the security of his office. "About an upcoming meeting."

The hair on the back of Ballard's neck prickled. "A meeting. Not *that* meeting surely?"

Peter's resultant laugh was staccato. "Well it sure as hell appears so. They referred to *the club*, and Olegovich mumbled something about women not being allowed in which got her fired up, snapping back that females *could* be invited. She then launched into a brutal character assassination."

"How so?"

"Said he was being openly criticised for not being tough enough, not pushing through agenda items and the like."

"Did she give details?"

"Nah, that's the annoying part. Everything was pretty vague."

"If she hasn't been to any of the meetings how would she know what others were saying about him?"

Peter's next laugh was one of pure joy. "Up until nine this morning I couldn't have answered that with any certainty Mike, but . . ." He let the sentence hang.

"*Jesus* Pete, enough of this John-like pregnant pause stuff. *But what for Christ sake?*"

"Have a guess who rolled up in his silver Aston Martin and drove into Olegovich's garage like he owned the place."

"Who?" Ballard was on the edge of the lounge chair, the mobile pressed so hard against his ear he felt it go numb.

"Vladimir."

"*What?*" The name was uttered so softly Ballard wondered if he had misheard but deep down he knew he hadn't.

"Yep, the very same. I know last night we talked about him not making any progress. Well I can tell you it took him about four minutes this morning to make some pretty significant moves on Tatiana. We've got the grunts and moans on tape to prove it."

"*What?*" Again Ballard thought he might have misconstrued what was being implied.

Peter snorted. "Stop saying *what* Michael. The truth of the matter is Vladimir and Tatiana are in cahoots and appear to have been for quite some time."

Ballard felt a shiver of expectation trickle down his spine. "Could Tatiana be the woman Vladimir was talking about just before Tim's crew arrested him down at Portsea?"

"Ah, very astute Mr Ballard. My thoughts exactly."

Ballard was puzzled. "What do you make of this Pete? When John and I interviewed Vladimir he absolutely refused to divulge the woman's name, almost as though his life depended on it. On top of that, from the recording of Vladimir's conversation on the boat it sounded like he was going to buy his way into the Australian cell's hierarchy and that this woman, whom we're now assuming to be Tatiana, was going to help him achieve that. But how?'

Peter's sigh was loud and clear. "Heaps of supposition there, but if *any* of it's true then we're on the cusp of a fairly significant breakthrough."

"How long did Vladimir stay at the house?"

"Oh just long enough to zip up his pants . . ." Peter's braying laugh was followed by "About an hour."

"Anything else discussed?"

"Nothing major, but just as he was leaving Tatiana made a comment which has us scratching our heads. She said she knows what she has to do regarding Olegovich and she's prepared to take Vladimir's advice and get on with it."

"That's it?"

"Yep, could mean anything, but there's no doubt it'll be something unpleasant for the guy's health. I'll bet my pay packet on it."

Ballard rubbed a bruise above his knee, a souvenir from the chopper crash, the injury turning a shade of purple. "Does it strike you as strange Vladimir would head straight around to Olegovich's pad knowing we may be following him?"

Peter uttered another throaty laugh. "I forgot to mention Michael. The bugger was like a Russian spy on the run prior to lobbing at St Georges Road—jumped red lights, turned up side streets at the last minute, led Bernard Junior's men on a right old chase. The Aston Martin's a brute of a machine in the same league as your father-in-law's Bentley Continental. In fact the spotters lost him at one point and only picked him up again after contacting James to request a current position from the tracker in the wristwatch."

"Bugger, not the most reassuring news I've heard today Pete, but between the physical tailing and the electronic tracking I guess Vladimir's not going to get too far without us knowing."

"That's as long as he doesn't decide to do an exploratory inside his watch." With that parting caution Peter was gone, leaving Ballard in a state of shock, amazed at how entangled the case was becoming.

CHAPTER
18

Ballard nosed the Chrysler onto Robert and Barbara's circular cobblestone lavender-bordered driveway. Pulling up opposite the impressive stone colonnade entrance, the solid-brick two-storey Hawthorn mansion towered beside them. Direct sunlight splashed over the ochre-coloured bricks not yet fully covered by the variegated ivy cascading down the west-facing wall. Natalie's parents stepped onto the porch just as Ballard switched off the motor. After giving them a wave Natalie rested a cautioning hand on Ballard's arm, quickly uttering, "Don't worry, Dad understands what your work entails and while he's concerned about the threat to the family, he knows it's your job."

"Yeah, right. But this isn't the first time I've had to deflect the Vietnam colonel mongrel in the guy."

Natalie giggled. "Perhaps calling my father a mongrel isn't the most advisable course of action darling." In a flash she was out of the car giving her parents a warm hug and a kiss on the cheek.

Alighting, Ballard fixed a broad smile in place, praying his eyes wouldn't betray him. "Good to see you Barbara." He hugged Natalie's mother before turning to his father-in-law who stood facing him at eye level. "Robert, it's been too long." Ballard held out a hand only to have it crushed in a Bernard-like grip.

An intense gaze was levelled his way. "You're looking well Michael, considering what you've just been through."

Ballard swallowed hard as he watched Natalie and Barbara head inside, their heads together in deep discussion, their love and affection for one another on full display. "Er, I got lucky Robert."

"Nonsense Michael. Spetsnaz soldiers aren't renowned for being pushovers." He took Ballard's arm as he ushered him along the driveway. "I saw first-hand what Russian military were capable of during the Vietnam War." His face grew reflective. "It's not a well-known fact but there were around three thousand specialist Russian soldiers operating against us during the war."

Ballard halted momentarily, surprised. "I never knew that."

Robert nodded as they resumed. "They were there to stop the air raids, and seeing the Soviet anti-aircraft missiles taking out the Americans along with our Aussie planes, well, it wasn't a pretty sight let me tell you. So as I said, your surviving as you did demonstrates it wasn't luck."

Taking into consideration Robert's military training and rank, Ballard felt comfortable detailing the main points of the helicopter incident while not revealing names or the current status of the investigation.

At the point where he described shooting Sergey in the thigh it was Robert's turn to halt their progress. "Gutsy stuff Michael. We're all thankful you came out of it physically and emotionally okay." His uttering of 'emotionally okay' had him fixing Ballard with a fierce, analytical stare.

"No Robert, all good. The department's shrink has already given John and I the all-clear. We're not going off the deep end any time soon."

"Glad to hear it which of course brings me to the matter of the threat made against you, Natalie, and the family."

Wincing, Ballard knew from experience Robert wasn't someone who would be satisfied with platitudes. "I've discussed this at length at my work and we believe it was a reflex comment considering what I'd just done to him, but you would have seen the footage on TV how he dispatched the politicians without a second thought. There can't be any certainties where this guy's concerned."

"Even more reason you and Natalie should stay here and not at the town house."

Due to the potential danger impacting the entire family, Ballard felt obliged to disclose additional details. "We believe the Russian's recuperating in Sydney and will be for some time. Natalie and I have discussed the circumstances and the truth of the matter is we have to live *somewhere*. And if anything should happen she's adamant she doesn't want to be near her children or you and Barbara. Even on the way over we did some pretty fancy driving to shake off anyone who may have been following us."

Once more Robert came to an abrupt halt, his expression one which had anticipated Ballard's reply. "I guess that's my daughter through and through Michael. And I know there's nothing I can say or do that will change her mind."

"I've tried and failed miserably."

Robert smiled at the admission. "Her personality can be a double-edged sword, and there's no doubt she got it from her mother."

Ballard half agreed. "I'd suggest she's been watching you for the past forty-odd years as well Robert, picking up a thing or two."

Becoming serious Robert stated, "Okay, so Barbara and I will continue to look after the children for as long as it takes. No problem there. Just find this bastard and put him away once and for all Michael. And by putting him away I'll leave that to your discretion and the circumstances confronting you."

Ballard glanced sideways and didn't see a seventy-five-year-old retired father but a ruthless Vietnam colonel who wouldn't hesitate to do whatever it took to protect his loved ones. There would be no second-guessing, achieving the required result with brutal efficiency—a trait which stood him in good stead during the Vietnam War unlike many thousands who succumbed to the mental and physical trauma.

In a soft voice Ballard promised, "I'll do my very best."

Robert squeezed his arm which was reply enough. Turning at the end of the driveway they headed inside to the coolness of the air-conditioned lounge.

Barbara and Natalie were seated side by side on the sofa. Looking up Barbara asked much to Natalie's amusement, "Well, have you two come to any consensus?"

Not missing a beat Robert responded, "If you're questioning whether Michael and I have unravelled the complexities of the female mind and arrived at a conclusion, no, the conundrum is ever present and as confounding as it has been for thousands of years."

Barbara's mouth opened before her brain had fully formulated a reply and was further disrupted by Kayla and Josh bursting in, their school uniforms less than pristine. They kissed Natalie and Barbara then shook Robert's and Ballard's hands, Kayla following her formal greeting with a brief peck on Ballard's cheek. Within seconds both teenagers had rushed off to their respective rooms to change, calling out they wanted a game of chess with Ballard before dinner.

The whirlwind over, Natalie commented somewhat dejectedly, "So much for missing their mother. I *think* they picked up that I was in the room."

Barbara patted her arm. "Of course they did dear, and they'll prove it as soon as their pocket money runs out."

"Which reminds me Mother. I need to transfer some money into your account for the mountain of food they must be eating."

"You'll do nothing of the sort. We love having them over don't we Robert?" Her stern look brooked no dissent.

"Er, yes Barbara, they are just . . ." He pretended to search for the appropriate word.

"*Delightful?*"

"Thank you my dear. That about sums it up." Robert winked at Ballard as he gave his newspaper a firm shake, pretending to immerse himself in it.

Barbara beckoned Ballard over to the carved ivory chess set positioned near the bay window, her disposition surreptitious. "No time like the present Michael. Before those precocious youngsters charge back in again I'm going to demonstrate two of Almira Skripchenko's most-played opening moves—the Sicilian and the King's Indian."

Accompanying her, Ballard was subjected to fifteen minutes of intense instruction which had his head spinning, and only on the fourth repetition did the complex moves begin to fall into place. "My goodness Barbara I think I've got it. The thing is if I *do* remember all these moves they're going to know I was coached by you."

"Won't do them any harm Michael. Winning all the time isn't healthy for teenagers."

Ballard nodded, thinking back to his own rearing of Bradley and the sports they used to play with Ballard victorious on most occasions. His belief centred on the need to instil in his son the reality that there were no favours in the real world despite modern parenting practices suggesting otherwise. As he reset the pieces he muttered, "I'll give it my best shot."

"You'd better Michael. I'm counting on it."

Glancing at Natalie, Ballard shook his head, understanding more clearly the iron will she possessed which had been instilled by parents who had refrained from choosing relaxed child-rearing options.

Forty minutes later, with three games completed and Ballard winning two of them, Kayla and Josh who had adopted their normal tag team technique sat stunned as they looked accusingly at Barbara who was beside herself with supressed delight. Kayla pointed a condemning finger at her grandmother. "Nanna, did you have anything to do with this?"

Straight-faced Barbara replied, "Today's the first time I've seen Michael since the last thrashing you gave him, and you were only upstairs a few minutes getting changed. I'm not *that* good an instructor."

Josh turned to Robert. "Pop, is Nan telling the truth?"

Robert pretended to be deaf, requesting the question be repeated while he thought over his answer. "Don't ask me Josh. I had my head stuck in the newspaper the whole time."

Both teenagers shrugged, aware they were battling superior minds, also conscious any request for their mother to grass on Ballard was doomed to fail.

All through their dinner which consisted of curried chicken, steamed vegetables, and basmati rice, Ballard caught the teenagers eyeing him covertly. He returned their gazes with deadpan neutrality.

"So Michael, Natalie tells me you really enjoyed *Aladdin* at Her Majesty's?"

"I have to admit Barbara I went along fully expecting to be bored out of my skull, but you wouldn't believe the incredible detail in the sets, the costumes, and the *energy* of the show."

"Yes, well I'd very much like to see it before the season winds up but Robert scoffs at the notion, says he won't go to a 'kids' show'. After hearing your recommendation I'm wondering if he might reconsider." Her prolonged stare at her husband meant only one response would be tolerated.

Rolling his eyes at Ballard in a silent reproach for inadvertently forcing the issue, he replied, "Darling, all I needed was an honest appraisal and now I have one, it'd be my pleasure to rustle up some tickets."

The triumphant look on Barbara's face was cautioned by Ballard, who advised, "Just avoid the matinee Robert. It may well push your tolerance to the limit."

"Er, thank you Michael for that piece of advice. I'll keep it in mind." The look on the veteran's face was anything but grateful; however the twinkle in his eye as he leaned across to kiss Barbara on the cheek belied any embarrassment at being outmanoeuvred by his wife. Adding to his woes was the look on Kayla's face, a firm indication she would love to see the production as well. By contrast Josh made it abundantly clear he would rather poke a fork into his eye than sit through what his Pop had referred to as a kid's show.

"There you have it Mum. You've at least one young contender wanting to go along with you. I'll pop some money into your account tomorrow." Holding up her hand Natalie declared, "No argument. Besides, I've already got your details from last time." The issue finalised she launched into a fifteen-minute recitation of the history of the theatre which had Josh battling not to appear open-mouthed at times. "Have you changed your mind young man?"

Natalie didn't attempt to hide her wish he should also go to the show with his grandparents.

The teenager hesitated, but realising it would diminish his appearance of being decisive, blurted, "Yeah right Mum. I'd *love* to be seen at a fairy tale—*not*."

"*It isn't a fairy tale.*" Kayla was adamant as she waved her fork at her brother much to the disapproval of her mother.

"Whatever." Josh maintained his firm resistance, aware any agreement now would paint him as weak, not something any red-blooded teenager aspired to.

Multiple conversations broke out around the table with Ballard winking at Josh as he asked in a lowered voice whether he was still hoping to be a policeman. In what was proof positive women could be across four topics at once, Natalie, who was in full description mode with her mother regarding her and Ballard's trip to Paris, suddenly hesitated. "Yes Michael, Josh *has* run that past me and I informed him it was a great career choice despite any future wife of his being worried out of her skull regarding the inevitable and ongoing dangers of the job."

Ballard watched on as Josh seemed to take a greater-than-usual interest in the tablecloth, attempting to straighten out a non-existent wrinkle. "As I mentioned Josh, *if* you do take that path you've got a lot of work ahead of you, but one thing's for certain, on graduation day your mother will be at the academy cheering you on as you march past."

Josh continued to flatten the invisible wrinkle, a half-smile forming as he winked at his mother.

Lemon meringue pie desserts appeared and were polished off in no time, and as it was a school night with homework to be completed, both teenagers uttered their goodnights before trudging upstairs. Natalie gave a longer-than-usual hug to each. Breaking free, Josh led the way to the bedrooms.

Attempting desperately to appear strong, Natalie busied herself with the dishes, not daring to look at her either of her parents or

Ballard. The latter sprang to his feet to assist, much to Barbara's protestations.

"If it's good enough for me to eat, it's good enough that I help wash up Barbara."

She smiled. "You see Natalie? Like I said, he's a good'un."

An hour later, after more hugs and another firm handshake from Robert, Ballard opened the passenger door for Natalie before settling behind the wheel. With a toot and a wave, they pulled out of the driveway.

Not ten minutes into the trip Ballard's mobile rang. Peter's voice boomed through on the speakers. "Michael, you're obviously in the car. Is Nat with you?"

With a sinking heart Ballard glanced across at her as he replied, "Yes she is."

"I'm sorry Natalie but work has gotten in the way big time. Michael how soon before you can get into the office?"

CHAPTER
19

The tension in the Serious Crime Taskforce's conference room was palpable as Ballard stepped through the door. At the head of the table with Peter was AC Thompson. Delwyn, Ken, Bobby, and Susan sat as a group with Tim and James to the side, the latter with a mobile to his ear.

After welcoming Ballard, Peter wasted no time pointing to the overhead projector. "Without going over old ground Michael I want your opinion as to what you're about to see. It's taken all of us by surprise and poses more questions than it answers."

If Ballard's curiosity wasn't peaking before it was now. Settling beside Susan who flashed him a brief but cautious smile, he frowned at the screen displaying a paused surveillance video of what he assumed was the St Georges Road property taken from the surveillance team's external wide-angle camera. Covering two enormous house blocks which in Toorak terms would equate to between ten and fifteen million for the land alone, the house was nothing short of gigantic, its two-story dimensions off the chart.

A wide, circular cobblestone driveway, similar to Robert and Barbara's but on steroids, swept beneath the front entrance portico dominated by four imposing colonnades. Enclosing the entire upper perimeter of the flat-roofed Roman-style building, including the portico, was a stone balustrade preventing any would-be revellers falling to their death nine metres below.

The dominant square design reeked of power and impregnability, the sandstone render adding to the sense of wealth, unbridled privilege and immense influence.

"Er, definitely one up from the Brighton bathing boxes. I'm guessing no change out of fifty million." Ballard's droll observation generated mutterings around the table.

"Our digging reveals Olegovich actually owns the place." Peter nodded towards several attendees who were staring in disbelief, their incredulity evident as to how a mere diplomat could have amassed such staggering wealth. "Yep, some pretty blunt pressure was applied to FIRB, the Foreign Investment Review Board executives. Because Olegovich had the place built on vacant land this proved to be in his favour as he sought initial council authorisation, and he didn't even have to take out a loan. Paid for the construction outright. Took two years to complete mind you." He shook his head. "As I said, we had to stand on a few toes to wheedle the information out of the respective authorities and yes Michael, fifty-two million Aussie dollars will get you an exact replica."

"Jesus, didn't this fact alone flag a warning to *someone* that the bugger's a crook?" Ballard was shocked.

"If it did it was knocked on the head by people in high places." Peter pointed to the screen. "Now watch carefully. What you're about to see took place forty-five minutes after Olegovich got home tonight, which by the way was earlier than usual. What you're going to see occurred around 7 p.m." Ballard checked the wall clock which showed 8.30 before refocussing his attention back on the screen.

The first sign of movement was that of a tall, dark-haired woman dressed in a cream blouse and black slacks approaching the balustrade to the right of the portico. Looking about her she appeared to slip something off her wrist which Ballard took to be a bracelet. Leaning forward she dropped the object onto the outer lip of the ledge which protruded from the bottom of the balustrade plinths.

At this point Peter halted the video. "You'll have guessed the lady's Tatiana, and we believe what she dropped was a bracelet or bangle of some sort. The other point which will make sense in a moment is where she dropped it, just out of arm's reach for anyone trying to retrieve it through the columns of the balustrade." He restarted the video.

Tatiana stood peering down at where she had positioned the jewellery then turning, walked out of the camera's field of vision.

Peter fast-forwarded the film. "There's a ten-minute elapsed time before there's further action." Returning to normal speed he focussed on the screen as keenly as though seeing the footage for the first time.

Once more Tatiana came into view, but this time she was followed by a thickset, silver-haired gentleman dressed in a dark suit; Ballard assumed he was Olegovich. Approaching her previous position Tatiana pointed to where she had dropped the bracelet. Stooping down, Olegovich attempted to reach the jewellery through the balustrade columns but he wasn't able to grasp it. Hesitant, he scouted around for an object to hook the bracelet but Tatiana shouted at him and unexpectedly began reaching over the balustrade in a vain attempt to secure the bracelet herself. Up to her waist and appearing to teeter on the edge, Olegovich grabbed her, pulling her back before leaning over himself. Positioning his waist on top of the balustrade he reached down with his left hand, his right grasping the balcony rail for support.

In a blur of motion which had Ballard disbelieving what he was witnessing, Tatiana glanced along the street then ripped Olegovich's right hand free while at the same time cupping an arm under his legs, allowing gravity to do the rest. In the split second it took Olegovich to complete the fall his body did a single cartwheel prior to crashing onto the cobblestones, motionless—without question, a very dead diplomat.

"*Bugger me.*" Ballard pursed his lips as he looked about him, noting all eyes were fixed in his direction, analysing his response. "If you want my opinion I'd say that wasn't a happy marriage."

His shot at humour was taken up by Bobby who proclaimed wide eyed, "I thought it was only Macedonians who were hot blooded. Remind me *never* to get mixed up with gorgeous Russian ladies any time soon." He lapsed into silence after receiving an elbow from Susan and a cautioning stare from Delwyn.

Pausing the video Peter asked, "So Michael, what do you make of it so far?"

"From what we heard Vladimir discussing in Bernard Junior's recording at Portsea and the bugger's subsequent refusal to divulge the lady's name, this footage now confirms the woman he was referring to is indeed Tatiana. Clearly she's desperate for Vladimir to be a paid-up member of the cell, and from what I've just seen, if he can pull off raising sufficient cash he's a shoe-in to be not just a *member* but the next cell *leader*. It's obvious he's utilising whatever support he can get from Tatiana in the process, which it would appear she's not backward in providing." Cheeks ballooning, Ballard realised he had rolled an enormous number of suppositions into one statement.

Staring hard at Peter he asked, "Mansions like that usually have at least four or five metre high solid front fences for privacy, so unless someone upstairs across the road spotted Olegovich going off the balcony no one walking past at street level would be any the wiser that a murder had just taken place, am I correct? What happened to the body?"

Delwyn couldn't remain silent any longer, her agitation hinting at more intrigue to come. "If what you just saw was unexpected wait until you see the next piece of footage." Her eyes widened, forewarning Ballard he was in for a bumpy ride. Recommencing the video, Peter gave his colleague an "Are you ready for this?" look which had Ballard's mind racing.

After pushing Olegovich off the balcony as calmly as though she were shaking crumbs from a tablecloth, Tatiana stood looking down at her dead husband as dispassionately as Sergey had when he shot the politicians on Parliament House steps. Turning, she walked out of view.

Peter fast-forwarded the video. "This time there's a shorter five-minute wait." Pushing Play once more he sat back, arms folded.

A black Mercedes van with tinted windows drove into view, stopping just short of the body. Four men in jeans and T-shirts sprang out and opened the rear doors. Withdrawing a grey body bag, two of the men hefted Olegovich inside. After zipping it up they literally threw it into the back of the van. The second two unwound from the reel a nearby garden hose and began spraying the pool of blood while the first two took a bottle of what was most likely bleach, pouring it over the cobblestones. On hands and knees one of the men attacked the stains with a scrubbing brush. More water was sprayed over the area then just as quickly the men hopped back in the van and drove out of the camera's range.

Peter halted the video. "Using the time stamp on the footage, from the moment the body hit the cobblestones the van arrived four minutes and forty-six seconds later. The clean-up took five minutes and twenty-two seconds. What do you make of *that* Michael?"

There was no doubt in Ballard's mind. "I'd say it was The Board's death squad doing what it does best—getting rid of evidence. By now Olegovich has been cut into manageable pieces and fed through a wood chipper or similar, the end result a burley trail in the bay. He no longer physically exists." Noting Susan wince, Ballard asked Peter, "Any luck on the van's plates?"

His question drew a snort of derision from the AC. "If only they were that sloppy. A false name and an equally false address—par for the course."

Ballard followed up with "And during all this, Tatiana sat polishing her nails?"

Peter shook his head in what could be mistaken as reluctant admiration of her ability to remain ice-cold. "Well not exactly. She made a call on her mobile not five minutes after the goon squad left and our Russian friend in his Aston Martin barrelled into the garage pretty soon after that. Foregoing the bedroom this time they made considerable whoopee on the dining room table—footage I don't need to show here." Ken and Bobby were disappointed while Susan sighed in obvious relief as she glanced at Delwyn. Peter continued, "The deed done, Vladimir zipped up before muttering something about not being able to stay and minutes later he was gone. The really chilling aspect that followed all this was Tatiana taking a glass of red and plonking down in front of the TV to watch the twenty-four-hour news channel as though none of this had even happened."

Delwyn began thinking aloud, a habit of hers which often crystallised everyone's thoughts. "The way I see it Vladimir put Tatiana up to it. His physical control over her is also dominating her mentally, whether she realises it or not. Hubby was old and boring. Along comes a vibrant Russian stud with a lot more money and sex appeal to boot. She goes for it hook, line, and sinker. She obviously has knowledge of the cell's doings and wants part of it for herself. Wise enough to realise in those rarefied circles it's a man's world, she cunningly assumes if she can hand pick the man leading the show then apply a degree of control over him she's partway to achieving her ultimate goal. Now for the death squad to arrive so quickly they must have been waiting nearby for her phone call. She's seen on one of the internal cameras making a call as soon as she went back inside the house, but she was too far away from the mike for us to hear what she said. So she either rang the squad directly or just as likely rang Vladimir who set things in motion." After taking a breath Delwyn pressed on. "Olegovich gets picked up and dropped off by the diplomatic car each morning and night so she'll have to admit he came home. My guess is tomorrow morning the driver will front and she'll be the distressed wife claiming he went for a walk first thing in the morning, which he apparently does quite often, getting up at 5 a.m. and strolling the nearby parks, but this time he didn't return. Tears will be flowing. She'll then make a call to the police."

"Do we know for certain he takes these walks?" Ballard wanted to be certain all the boxes were ticked.

"Surveillance have spotted him on at least four or five occasions smelling the roses, quite literally before returning home, obviously to have breakfast and get ready for work."

"So how do we handle a report of Olegovich's disappearance?" Ballard threw the question to the group.

Clearing his throat the AC assumed control. "Just to demonstrate how bizarre this case is becoming, witnessing a murder such as this would normally lead to an immediate arrest. It can't happen in this instance. When Tatiana makes the call uniform will attend as they would normally. Delwyn I want some of your team to drop by afterwards on the guise that as Olegovich is a diplomat the police department is giving the disappearance greater priority. Your team should also front up to the Russian embassy to fly the flag. Your thoughts?"

Delwyn gestured to the three junior detectives whose facial expressions were almost comical. "To be on the cautious side, Ken, Bobby, and Susan are the best choice to interview Tatiana as they haven't been seen by Vladimir. While I'm not expecting him to turn up at the house again until things cool down it's better to play safe than be sorry. The guys can then swing over to the embassy to show we're taking this incident seriously as you suggested sir. Obviously there won't be any mention they're from homicide."

Susan looked at Ken and Bobby before asking, "So you want us to straight-bat this as a missing-person call to see what story Tatiana comes up with?"

Delwyn's eyebrows did a round trip as she sanctioned the plan.

The AC addressed Peter, James, and Tim. "In the meantime the surveillance of Vladimir should continue as normal. I'd suggest with this latest development he's going to be a model citizen for quite some time, but the thing is, how will this affect the scheduling of the supposed meeting of The Board's cell members in the Melbourne Club? Will they cancel or go ahead anyway to elect a new leader? Either way we need to be ready to take them down when they meet. Peter, keep up the pressure on the ports minister. What we've just witnessed is an internal power play and not the main game. The Board securing control of the ports must still be our primary focus and taking out the cell members will put a hell of a dint in their operation, not to mention the intel it'll provide if any of the members squeal."

Tim joined in. "I've a team ready to raid the club the moment the word's given." He grinned ruefully. "No doubt any arrests will shake Melbourne's establishment to the core. My guys storming through those hallowed halls in full combat gear will be a first, that's for sure."

"It won't shake them up half as much as the publicity that'll be brought to bear once it's common knowledge terrorist activities have been planned in their premises for God knows how many years. *That's* going to put a dint in their pompous view of the world." The AC spat the last words in disgust.

Apologetic, Peter turned to Ballard. "Sorry to stomp on your days off Mike but I thought you'd be mighty peeved not to be brought up to speed on something as important as this. I'll leave it to you to let John know."

Just as Ballard was about to respond Delwyn shuffled in her chair. "Thanks Peter. I'll discuss this with Michael after the meeting and before he goes *home*." Her emphasis on the last word as much for Ballard as Peter.

The AC drew the meeting to a close. "You're all experienced enough to know we're on the cusp of nailing the cell members here in Australia. It's times like these when victory is within our grasp that we run the risk of not paying attention to the minor details and in the blink of an eye the prize slips through our fingers." His features softened. "A bit like Olegovich stretching for the bracelet. Folks, make sure we don't fall off the balcony of opportunity like he did." With the cryptic caution ringing in everyone's ears he strode from the room, the firm set of his jaw indicating he believed the case was nearing a critical phase and had to be won at any cost.

The moment the door closed a series of conversations broke out. James conferred with Peter and Tim regarding the ongoing surveillance of Vladimir and the need for the Russian to continue believing he wasn't being tracked, figuring his fancy moves in the Aston Martin were evasion enough.

Delwyn huddled with Ken, Bobby, and Susan, briefing them on their questioning of Tatiana along with their visit to the Russian embassy. Bobby appeared agitated, wanting to head off to St Georges Road then and there.

Ballard watched on, pensive, thinking ahead to the day when he and John would have to walk away from specialist investigations such as these, hopefully having convinced themselves the time was right to put their feet up and smell the roses. Deep down he knew the change would be tough, one he and John had discussed at length with Marjorie who suggested they prepare for retirement a number of years out.

So deep was Ballard's reverie he didn't notice Peter approaching until the superintendent clapped him on the shoulder. "Keeping you up past your bedtime old man?" While the ribbing was meant to be light-hearted it bit deep considering Ballard's current thoughts.

"No Pete, just wondering how someone at your stage of life manages to juggle so many balls in the air at once."

Peter laughed. "Touché. And a reality for which I don't have any firm answer. And to make matters worse I have a strong feeling from the look on Delwyn's face she isn't going to allow you to be a part of any of it for the next few days."

Fearing his colleague was right, Ballard focussed on the superintendent, noting her expression was indeed supporting Peter's prophecy. She confirmed it with her next comments. "Michael I had to be persuaded to allow you to come in this evening. Now I know you're hoping every day's going to be like today but you've been around long enough to know things will settle for a while before ramping up again. In the meantime I want you to take Natalie somewhere out of the state but close enough so you can be back within a few hours if need be. I don't care where you go, just do it for a couple of days. That way *I'm* covered, the department's covered, and you'll have recharged your batteries. It appears John's taken the message to heart so now it's your turn."

Ballard opened his mouth with what Delwyn assumed would be a rejection of the request. Instead he surprised her by claiming, "Nat and I have talked about going on a short trip to New Zealand. A couple of days in Queenstown, a drive down to Milford Sound, perhaps another day or two in Wanaka, tour the lakes, gaze at the long white clouds—that sort of thing. I'd suggest now's as good a time as any."

Reaching across Delwyn placed a hand on Ballard's brow as she addressed Peter. "Nope, no sign of a fever. Should I check his pulse?" Peter laughed.

Fifteen minutes later Ballard was in the Chrysler heading back to the town house.

CHAPTER
20

"*New Zealand*." Natalie's voice was amplified through the car's speakers. "Michael, that's fantastic! When do we leave?"

"Start packing my sweet. We head out tomorrow."

"*Tomorrow?* But what about tickets?"

"Done and dusted. According to our amenable travel agent Dave whom I dragged away from his favourite TV program, he said there's always spare seats to New Zealand midweek so it wasn't a problem. He did say the flight won't be until after lunch though."

"Oh well, in that case we'll be able to sleep in before we catch the bus to the airport." Natalie's unsubtle dig came across loud and clear.

Laughing, Ballard claimed, "Even that's sorted out. Considering the money I've tossed Dave's way for the honeymoon and the Paris trip he's organised for us to be picked up and driven out. He'll text through the flight and hotel details in the morning."

"Gosh, you've thought of everything."

"I'm guessing I've got enough brownie points in the bank to get us over the line. See you in ten minutes."

"I'll start making calls." Natalie was thrilled at the prospect of the holiday, albeit fully aware it would be a short one.

An early dinner was followed by suitcase packing which saw Natalie meticulously crossing off each item on her list. On completion both decided they needed to unwind and spent half an hour on the lounge sofa watching forgettable TV, then it was upstairs to bed.

The next morning Ballard made several phone calls, including one to his son. Natalie rechecked everything was in order which proved fortuitous as their ride arrived fifteen minutes early. Ballard returned from outside, confirming the driver was happy to wait. Once their luggage was stowed in the boot of the Lexus they sat back with Natalie commenting, "We should do this more often Michael."

"What, go on holidays?"

She laughed. "Yes, that too. No darling, I mean being chauffeured to the airport. It's *sooo* much more relaxing than a bus."

"You can say that again."

"It's *sooo* much more—"

"Very funny." Ballard kissed her, much to the approval of the driver who glanced in the mirror.

Flying into Queenstown between the mountain ranges is breathtaking, but during periods of high wind and low cloud for which it's renowned it can be dangerous, striking trepidation into the hearts of many novice airline pilots. On this occasion there was little or no wind, the carpet of white cloud the Airbus A320 was descending through mirroring the nearby peaks topped with snow, not a normal occurrence this time of year. Sitting in the window seat Natalie clung to Ballard's arm, wide-eyed, taking in everything with computer-like efficiency.

"It's just so beautiful Michael. I checked the weather forecast and for the next four days it'll be around twenty-one degrees, perfect for sightseeing."

Straight-faced, Ballard added, "Oh I forgot to mention, the temperature here in Queenstown plummets at night which explains why its birth rate is so much higher than the national average. Couples have to cuddle a lot."

Natalie began to denounce the claim but a doubtful look came over her, aware that every so often Ballard slipped in the odd truth amongst his numerous outrageous assertions.

After piercing the low cloud and experiencing a near-perfect landing, they waited at the carousel to collect their luggage before traipsing along a corridor bustling with passengers, all hauling suitcases of varying shapes and sizes. Arriving at the car rental area Ballard suggested Natalie choose which she did without hesitation, stabbing a forefinger towards the photo of a bright-red Mazda 3. Paperwork complete they eventually located the vehicle in the outdoor rental area. Behind the wheel, head cocked to one side, Ballard listened to the motor, likening it to a cheap lawnmower, accustomed to the throaty V8 rumble of the 300C. Shrugging he pulled out into the traffic while Natalie keyed in the hotel's address. In a much shorter time than it would have taken on Melbourne's congested roads they arrived at their destination, the Waterfront. After unpacking, Ballard took Natalie in his arms, his kiss lingering, almost urgent. "Welcome to the land of the many long, *low* white clouds."

"I *know*. Weren't they fantastic? I've seen dozens of photos in various magazines but in real life they seem to hang in the sky just out of reach." Fearing the glint in his eye would turn to something more physical, robbing her of precious sightseeing time, she asked innocently, "So what have you planned for us?"

Taking the hint with a designer drooping lip, Ballard quipped, "You're right. We can catch up on cuddles any time back home. Thankfully you're wearing slacks and flat shoes because we have a mountain to climb."

"Michael, no, not in these clothes."

Ballard laughed. "Don't worry. You'll be sitting down all the way." Taking her hand he led her outside, pointing to the mountain towering over the Queenstown CBD. "Up there my darling is Bob's Peak, the top 450 metres above where we're standing, and as you can see the Skyline Gondola takes us there in total comfort."

Natalie craned her neck, noting the multiple gondolas snaking up the side of the mountain, her mouth dropping open in the process. "You scared the life out of me in the Blue Mountains on the scenic railway. Is this ride going to be more of the same?"

"Would I be that cruel?" Ballard dropped into a Fonze impersonation, arms apart, fists clenched, thumbs vertical. "Aaayyy!" He grinned. "Come to think of it I did read somewhere the Skyline is the steepest ride of its kind in the southern hemisphere."

"Of course it is." Natalie shook her head, in no doubt the next four days would expose her to adventures which would remain locked in her memory for years to come; secretly she relished the thought, knowing her man was by her side.

After a short five-minute walk they bought their tickets then stood waiting for the approaching gondola to sweep them around in an arc on the anchor wheel before lurching vertically up the mountainside. Facing outwards they gazed at the houses in Queenstown spreading before them, along with Lake Wakatipu which stretched to Kingston in the south and Glenorchy in the north.

Pointing in the distance Ballard declared, "That mountain range is the Remarkables where they ski in winter, and over there"—he pointed to his left—"that's Arrowtown. I guess you could call it a gold mining *village*, and it's where they filmed segments of the Lord of the Rings trilogy."

So fascinated was Natalie she forgot to be nervous as the ground dropped away at an alarming rate. To add to her experience Ballard began rocking the gondola back and forth, only stopping when punched on the arm by a clenched fist. "You know how you loathe grey hair Michael, those sort of antics just added another twenty to my collection."

Alighting at the top they strolled to the observation deck, staring in awe at the panoramic views which lay before them, appearing to stretch forever. Natalie whispered, "Our honeymoon cruise to the islands was fantastic Michael, and Paris along with the few days we had down the Rhine were just a fairy tale, but this is every bit as breathtaking. Thank you my darling."

Grinning, Ballard muttered, "You can thank me in your own special way tonight sweetheart. Right now, let's nip over to the chairlift. There's something I want to show you." He pointed to his left where couples were taking a cable chair further up the mountain.

Nervous but happy to go along with Ballard's almost childlike excitement, Natalie allowed herself to be led over to the ride and together they hopped on. As soon as they began their ascent she realised what was in store as she stared beneath her. "You've got to be kidding me! *A luge ride?*"

"Yep, got it in one. I bet you didn't know the luge was invented right here in New Zealand. Now we can take the bumpy, faster ride or the relaxed, scenic route." Ballard didn't have to wait long for the answer.

"The scenic will do just fine thank you."

And scenic it was as they glided in their separate carts, the bends wide and sweeping. Within the first minute Natalie was laughing aloud at the experience, Ballard right behind her. "*We should have taken the faster route Michael. This is so much fun.*"

Reaching the bottom they hopped onto the chairlift once more and for the second descent opted for the more daring ride, with Natalie proving to be a natural, beating Ballard to the bottom. Breathing hard she pointed an accusing finger. "You let me win."

"I'd love to say that was the case Nat but you did me front and centre with your blocking manoeuvres."

Returning to the restaurant they booked a table with an uninterrupted view of Queenstown and the lake. Eyeing the menu Ballard blurted, "A six-course selection no less. Aren't you glad you did the fast lap to build up an appetite?"

Natalie drew in a lung-expanding breath. "The fresh air does it for me. There's no pollution over here and I doubt there ever will be."

Concentrating on the menu she ordered a bowl of spring vegetable soup with Ballard choosing the pumpkin and a shared plate of antipasto, both settling on a flame-grilled Scotch fillet with salad for their main course. Fast reaching overload they threw caution to the wind, selecting the goat's-cheese-and-lemon-curd cheesecake for dessert, Ballard's serving including his mandatory scoops of vanilla ice cream. Natalie sipped on her shiraz, a twinkle appearing in her eye. "Methinks later on we're going to have to work off some of these calories Michael, and you're right, I do feel a distinct chill in the air."

Almost choking on his last spoonful of ice cream, Ballard could only manage a watery-eyed nod, albeit an enthusiastic one nonetheless.

Not wishing to leave the warmth of the restaurant but realising they needed to head back to the hotel for a good night's sleep, they struggled to their feet. After Natalie paid the bill they took the gondola back to street level, the lights from the town twinkling like fireflies beneath them as they descended. Cuddling against Ballard, Natalie whispered, "Just magic."

Settling into their room they were glad they had adjusted the heating before leaving. Ensuring all the blinds were drawn Natalie shed her clothes and with a cheeky smile headed for the shower. The moment she stepped from sight Ballard ripped off his own clothing and hearing the shower running, crept into the bathroom.

Due to the poor excuse for a fan the room was fast filling with steam so it wasn't until Ballard had joined Natalie in the shower that she realised she had company. "There you are. I was *certain* I'd given enough of a hint."

Ballard stood behind her, arms encircling her waist, the water cascading over them. "Yep, picked up the signal loud and clear."

Snuggling back against him she murmured something unintelligible which Ballard didn't bother to clarify. Instead he took the soap and gently lathered her breasts, a jolt of desire rippling through him as he caressed her silky skin, her nipples hardening with his touch. Kissing her he felt the tension and stress of the past days draining from his body, leaving him light-headed.

"Just what the doctor ordered."

"What's that, darling?"

"I said, just what the—" Natalie's lingering embrace halted Ballard's remaining words.

CHAPTER
21

The next morning Natalie and Ballard climbed aboard the glass-topped tour bus emblazoned with "Milford Sound Select" in large letters on the sides and rear. Ballard confirmed his decision to sit back and take in the scenery rather than drive to the world-famous attraction was the correct one as it spared him from having to concentrate on other tourist traffic on the often-narrow roads. Accidentally brushing Natalie's breasts as he helped her with her seatbelt, he took in the "You just can't help yourself" stare which was returned with a "Whatever do you mean?" grin. None of the twenty passengers filing into their seats, many yawning due to the early hour, were aware of the exchange much to Natalie's relief.

Slinging his backpack onto the overhead shelf, Ballard dropped alongside her. "Settle back Nat. We've got a long day ahead, but I promise it'll be a goodie. The trip to Milford Sound, the cruise, then the return leg I'm told is around twelve hours. You can nap on my shoulder on the way home."

"Not likely buster. I'm here to see everything."

Clearing the outskirts of Queenstown they headed through what appeared to be the only flat stretch of countryside before staring gobsmacked at mountain ranges that rose vertically from the edge of the road, stretching hundreds of metres upwards towards the low-slung clouds. Natalie's head swivelling and photo snapping matched that of the Red Bus tour in Paris, only this time she was witnessing the awesome power of nature and what it had created as opposed to the bricks and mortar of world-famous buildings.

Throughout the trip Ted the coach driver, who obviously enjoyed his work, provided a non-stop commentary of the points of interest, his silver hair bobbing left and right as he spoke. The passengers responded with oohs and aahs while snapping away. Just under two hours into the trip they pulled into Te Anau, stopping at one of the many restaurants. Stretching their legs everyone grabbed a bite to eat which for Natalie and Ballard was a mere snack due to their previous night's overindulgence.

Aboard once more and after a thorough headcount by Ted to ensure he wasn't leaving passengers behind they drove on, witnessing more roadside mountains and deep ravines with bubbling streams threading through the countryside. In the distance the Remarkables had everyone leaning across in their seats, cameras clicking away with Natalie in the thick of it.

With obvious pride, almost as though he had discovered the mountain himself, Ted pointed out Mount Christina, 2,500 metres high and perennially snow-capped. The frenzy of camera snapping revved up a notch. Rounding a sharp bend he announced, "Up ahead is Eglinton Valley, carved out by glaciers thousands of years ago. The sides of the mountains are covered in native beech and on the flatlands you can see golden tussock growing wild for kilometres. Not surprisingly, running parallel with us is the Eglinton River." Chortling at his own joke he continued, his audience hooked. "The first Europeans to explore the area arrived in 1861, naming the river and valley after the British Earl of Eglinton. The road was built in 1935 which allowed more visitors to enjoy the valley's natural beauty."

Taking a deep breath which was heard over the mike he announced, "Eglinton Valley is within the Fiordland National Park which is listed under the banner of UNESCO World Heritage. It has over thirty endangered species of wildlife not found anywhere else in the world. It's also where a number of scenes from *The Lord of the Rings* were filmed."

Additional oohs and aahs burst forth, with Ballard whispering in Natalie's ear, "He's getting worked up to the point I just hope he concentrates on his driving, which I might add has been excellent up to this point."

Natalie squeezed Ballard's hand. "I'm sure he knows what he's doing Michael. Besides, you never were a relaxed passenger."

Ted launched into another salvo of fresh information as he manoeuvred the bus with the dexterity of a Formula One driver, as though he had overheard Ballard's concern and was responding. The countryside rolled by and the ever-changing vista delivered a panoramic smorgasbord of diversity, all lapped up by an appreciative audience.

Ted took up the microphone once more. "Folks, the next stop's going to be a real treat—Lake Matheson, better known as the Mirror Lake. The water's almost black due to the humus and algae growing in it and on the right day it produces a perfect reflection of mounts Tasman and Cook." Pulling alongside several tourist buses already parked, he asked everyone to be back within fifteen minutes.

With a sense of urgency Natalie headed down the steps and was five paces ahead before she stopped, embarrassed, allowing Ballard to catch up. "Sorry darling, I'm hoping this won't be like when we tried to photograph the Mona Lisa and had to wait twenty minutes to get even remotely close enough to take some shots."

Ballard smiled, remembering how he had to physically restrain Natalie from punching a rude tourist who repeatedly attempted to elbow her out of the way.

She laughed at the recollection. "I trust there won't be the same pushing and shoving."

Arriving at the side of the lake they were stunned by the ink black colour of the water, the reflection of the two mountains quite spectacular as attested by the gathered crowd. While the wait to reach the railing for an uninterrupted view wasn't long, it was sufficient to have Natalie checking her watch multiple times until she was able to loose off a barrage of photos. Satisfied, she took Ballard's arm and headed for the bus.

Performing his methodical headcount Ted asked if the lake was clear. The chorus of "Yes, it was magnificent" widened his already-broad smile. Merging with the passing traffic he announced the next stop would be Knobs Flat, four kilometres up the road, giving him time to explain the attraction's history. "During the last Ice Age rivers and streams deposited gravel into ice caverns and when the glaciers finally melted, the gravel was left behind." Ted went on to detail more archaeological specifics before pulling the bus to the side of the road and opening the doors for the passengers to exit.

Stepping out Natalie marched over to several piles of incredibly smooth, almost polished stones, firing off more photos, including shots of hills of varying sizes in the distance which according to Ted had been carved out by the sheer brute force of the glaciers. Confronting Ballard, eyes wide with wonder Natalie declared, "It's just impossible to imagine the raw power and the *noise* there must have been as the glacier made its way down the valley."

"Physics Nat, sheer weight of frozen water, there's nothing quite like it." Picking up one of the flat stones Ballard skimmed it across the surface of the stream running alongside. "Damn, only four skips. When I was a young'un I could manage at least six."

Natalie giggled. "Oh, I don't know Michael. Your efforts last night got six skips out of me so I'd say you haven't lost your touch at all."

Swivelling his head left and right to check she hadn't been overheard, Ballard grinned. Seeing her momentarily shiver in the cool mountain breeze he placed his arm around her shoulders, leading her back to the bus while whispering, "And I can assure you they won't be the last skips you'll be enjoying this holiday."

After recounting his passengers, Ted swung onto the highway with precision, his driving skills convincing Ballard they were in safe hands.

"Ah, decisions, decisions, folks. We need to be at Milford Sound by 1 p.m. to allow everyone time to enjoy a well-deserved lunch before your cruise. Because the traffic's been heavier than usual I'm going to forego several of the points of interest we normally stop at but after Homer Tunnel, which is about forty kilometres up the road, we should be able to drop by the Chasm for a quick peek."

Taking a sip from his water bottle, which Ballard quipped to Natalie was more than likely vodka, Ted launched into a barrage of facts about the upcoming tunnel. "It's purpose was to afford easier access to the Milford Sound area. This meant piercing through a massive rock formation known as the Homer Saddle discovered naturally enough by William Homer in 1889." Another quick sip was followed by "Work didn't begin on the tunnel for forty-six years. In fact it was 1935 when five government employees armed with picks, shovels, and a wheelbarrow began the task."

This revelation brought gasps that such a monumental undertaking would even be considered with such meagre equipment. Ted answered the numerous doubtful mutterings with a simple shrug which preceded "Relief workers during the depression, happy to find any form of work but it came at a cost." A pregnant pause fuelled the audience's expectation as it was designed to. "Does anyone fancy living here in tents in the winter where there's no direct sunlight for six months of the year?" He followed the question with a quick glance in the mirror at his attentive onlookers who were shaking their heads, even Natalie joining in.

"No, it was back-breaking, slogging work and dangerous because of the falling rocks and avalanches. Adding to this pumps had to be installed to remove up to forty thousand litres of water an hour which flooded through fissures in the rock from the melting snow and rain."

Pausing as though only now appreciating the enormity of the task, Ted added, "The saddle was breached in 1940, but the official opening wasn't until 1953. Even now it's basically one way at a time, although a bus and a car *can* pass. Two buses negotiating the tunnel together and we lose our mirrors." There was general laughter at the mental picture.

"Folks I've bored you enough . . ."

Cries of *"No, no!"* rang out.

Ted laughed. "In about fifteen minutes you'll see what I mean about the tunnel being a Herculean effort, and as I said, we'll almost certainly have to wait our turn prior to passing through." With that he pushed the mike to one side as he settled into the drive.

As predicted they arrived at the eastern end of the tunnel and had to stop in line with other vehicles until the traffic light turned green. Easing the bus forward, Ted resumed his commentary. "A total of one point two kilometres long. Amazingly it was 2004 before roof lighting was installed." Ballard noted with amusement the studious nods from some of the passengers, amazed there would be anything but an urgent need for adequate lighting; he also observed several tourists glancing about them, uneasy, the claustrophobic nature of the tunnel momentarily halting what had been to that point total enjoyment for all.

Emerging on the far side everyone sat back, experiencing the ongoing beauty of the heavily wooded mountain ranges left and right. Chuckling as though experiencing a private joke, Ted explained, "A word of warning: should any of you decide to travel through this area in your own car and leave it unattended for any period of time, be aware of the Kea Mountain parrot's rather nasty pecking habits." Inquisitive expressions abounded. "Intrusive, some say cheeky, it's known to strip the rubber trim from around windscreens causing very expensive repair bills, and if you don't believe me pop Kea Mountain parrot into Google and watch some of their antics." Ending with a further chuckle he lapsed into silence which was replaced by animated discussion amongst the passengers.

Natalie turned to Ballard, amused. "I'm assuming you've committed all of Ted's commentary to memory so you can infuriate poor John at some point in the future?"

Ballard grinned evilly. "*You bet I have.*"

Just eight kilometres further on Ted pulled into a parking bay, informing everyone they had twenty minutes to explore the natural wonder of the Cleddau River which had carved weird and wonderful rock formations through what was known as the Chasm. Not to be left behind Natalie burst from the bus like a greyhound with Ballard not catching up for at least twenty strides.

"Er, I think Ted said it's just strange rock shapes Nat. He never mentioned anything about panning for gold or tripping over loose uncut diamonds." Natalie ignored him as she set a cracking pace, passing other tourists like they were stationary with Ballard attempting to keep up.

Meeting the return deadline they dropped into their seats, having marvelled at the rock creations carved over millennia, concluding the power of running water combined with time was a thing of wonder and a sombre consideration when reflecting on one's own existence.

As they pulled up at the Milford Sound Visitor's Centre, Ballard's mobile rang. Glancing down he saw it was from Peter. Squeezing Natalie's arm he mouthed "Work" as she headed inside to purchase snacks and drinks.

"Well Pete, as always your timing's spot on. We've just stopped for lunch before heading out on a cruise on Milford Sound."

"Sounds like you guys are doing it tough Michael. I'll bet Nat's enjoying every minute of it and taking her usual kitbag of snaps?"

"Bloody hundreds of them. Christ knows what capacity she's got on her phone. I've just realised we could start a new business when I retire—holiday film nights for a fee. Tell me, is John back at work yet?"

"He most definitely is not. I can't believe it, but he's really enjoying his time in Queensland. I rang him yesterday to give an update on Olegovich's acrobatic dive off the balcony and other than being amazed, he just grunted and said, 'Serves the bastard right'."

Ballard decided not to comment on his own surprise at his partner's reluctance to return to work. "Okay Pete, what's the latest?"

The superintendent exhaled, as though he had been holding his breath. "Well it appears Vladimir really *does* believe he's a free agent and isn't being monitored. When we brought him in yesterday morning he admitted he had heard on the grapevine that Olegovich had vanished, but no mention of Tatiana and his involvement with her, *nothing*." Peter gave a short laugh. "It's amazing how these buggers can lie through their teeth and think nothing of it. I decided to give the prick a heart starter by putting to him that with Olegovich off the scene he wasn't much use to us and why shouldn't we just chuck him in the can. Well I'm telling you Mike, he spluttered like a badly tuned rent-a-bomb and said a replacement cell leader would have to step up and take the reins, very soon and he could do some digging."

Peter laughed again. "Ratchetting up the pressure a few more notches we told him we wanted a date and a location of the next cell meeting or he'd be dragged off the street and locked up."

"So no mention of Tatiana's involvement in any of this, *or* his involvement with her?"

"Not a peep. I guess the good news about all this is with him believing we're just a bunch of dicks, it increases the chance he'll slip up at some point down the track."

Ballard watched on as several tourists emerged, clutching a variety of refreshments, his stomach rumbling at the sight. "Has Vladimir been back to St Georges Road since Olegovich's cartwheel?"

"Hell no! He's too smart to get caught there should the police turn up again to interview Tatiana."

"So how did the guys go with her after the uniforms did their initial report?"

"Susan said it was nothing short of an Academy Award performance. Real tears, attempts to be stoic, breaking down multiple times, sobbing through a pretty disjointed expression of 'If only I'd gotten up earlier and accompanied him on his walk, everything would be ok'."

"So officially Olegovich is a missing person but in reality Tatiana, Vladimir, and the death squad know better. What about the Russian embassy?"

"Same thing. A bloody unhelpful bunch of clowns they turned out to be Mike. Robotic, in fact all they gave was one-syllable answers and they couldn't get rid of our guys soon enough. Talk about not caring about their own."

"Back on Tatiana, you don't think she suspects anything with our people arriving after the uniform boys?"

"No, it was explained that with Olegovich being a diplomat it was the department's policy to have plain clothes investigate the circumstances." Peter sounded convinced Tatiana hadn't been spooked.

"What about the ports minister, Laurie Davidson?"

"Getting a right old grinding from my guys and the cracks are beginning to open up. I'm guessing another couple of sessions and something will give."

"Maybe, or he'll wind up a very mutilated corpse."

There was a pause. "Yes Mike that could well be the sad consequence, so we need to work fast and smart." Another pause was followed by "So Mr Fifty Questions, anything else you'd like me to elaborate on?"

Ballard laughed as he racked his brains. "No, you appear to be on top of everything, Superintendent."

There was a return chuckle. "When are you two lovebirds flying back?"

Ballard waved at Natalie who was approaching, her arms laden. Heading over to assist her, the mobile still jammed to his ear, he replied, "Two more days here Pete. Make sure you keep me posted."

"I will. Say hello to Nat for me."

Pocketing his mobile Ballard took the two bottles of water wedged under Natalie's arm and led her to a free table overlooking Milford Sound.

"Everything okay at work?" Natalie appeared uncertain, fearful a new development might force them to abandon their remaining days.

"No, all good. And yes, our holiday will be continuing." Natalie smiled a contented smile.

Glancing at their watches they attacked their food so as not to be late boarding their waiting cruise ship, all the while staring in wonder at the majestic scenery.

Standing with Natalie on the starboard side of their passenger ship, Ballard looked on with interest as the vessel was manoeuvred away from the jetty, curious to glean any tips which may assist him when handling *Whatever It Takes*. It didn't take long to confirm that steering much-larger craft was fundamentally similar in principle. Deciding the afternoon breeze was a tad too cold to be on deck they moved inside, choosing a seat which offered an uninterrupted view of the passing scenery.

Grasping Ballard's hand Natalie snuggled alongside him, a smile in place and her mobile at the ready. No sooner had they cleared their mooring than the cruise director came over the speaker and began detailing the many astonishing aspects of Milford Sound.

"Good afternoon boys and girls, ladies and gentlemen. Let me begin by saying the water beneath us is 500 metres deep." Passengers muttered amongst themselves at this disclosure, with Ballard convinced several glanced about them to determine the closest location of the life jackets.

In a voice filled with pride the director announced, "Rudyard Kipling once described Milford Sound as the eighth wonder of the world. As if that wasn't promotion enough, an international survey in 2008 listed this location as the world's top travel destination."

Allowing the disclosure to be digested, the director declared, "The two main mountains you see ahead are Mitre Peak and Pembroke Peak, 1,700 metres and 2,000 metres respectively, each snow-capped for the majority of the year. Milford Sound is some 15 kilometres in length with the depth at the mouth where it meets the Tasman Sea a mere 70 metres, a result of the rock-laden glacier that carved it melting at that point, dumping its material at the mouth. In fact so narrow is the opening that Captain Cook didn't venture in as he was concerned the steep mountains on either side would create wind conditions that might prevent sailing ships from escaping. Just think what he missed out on in terms of the incredible spectacle."

Appreciative head nodding resulted. Natalie's face was transfixed as she gazed out the window, lost in a world of serenity and breathtaking beauty.

"Now the rainfall in Milford Sound is one of the highest in the world at 6,400 millimetres *each* year, or in the old measurement, 256 inches."

Gobsmacked, Natalie stared at Ballard who thought back to his teenage years on his parents' property and how he would look up at a cloudless sky, praying for rain so the crops could be sown, a situation which had a lifelong impact on him, so much so that whenever it rained he felt an overwhelming sense of relief and contentment.

The director pointed to where several areas of the rainforest had dislodged due to the soaked soil, collapsing into the Sound, new growth emerging in its place. Natalie fired off a short barrage with Ballard smiling as he reflected on his conversation with Peter.

It was the director's next announcement that had everyone sitting on the edge of their seats. "Seals, bottle-nosed dolphins, hump-backed whales, and southern right whales frequent these waters." This resulted in a minor stampede as many of the tourists crowded forward, requiring Natalie and Ballard to seek alternate seating. Ballard gently grasped Natalie's arm in the subtlest of hints to prevent her from becoming physical as several passengers blocked her view; her polite but pointed "*Excuse me*" resolved the issue.

The cruise director continued. "As of 2006 only 120 people lived in Milford Sound but the area attracts between six hundred thousand and a million visitors each year. To ease road congestion there are plans afoot to make it easier to get here from Queenstown with a tunnel mooted as one option, along with a monorail. Time will determine which is chosen, if any." With that the director welcomed those on board to sit back and take in the sights.

And take in the sights they did, the highlight being the close encounter with Sterling Falls where the captain nosed the vessel into the swirling mist created by the 150-metre drop of glacial water three times the height of Niagara Falls, and the location where Hugh Jackman purportedly jumped off in the movie *Wolverine*, these details breathlessly announced over the speakers.

Returning from the bow of the cruise ship partially soaked but excited, Natalie told Ballard the experience was one of the highlights of her life. Taking her word for it, having chosen to remain dry, Ballard took out a tissue and began dabbing her face.

Thirty minutes later they were back on the bus. Ted declared the return trip would be a quiet one so the passengers could hunker down and nap, or watch the movie which was about to start. Several tourists indicated they would rather hear more "stories" but Ted stuck to his word, and even Natalie, despite her earlier resolve to remain wide awake, succumbed to the rigours of the trip and within an hour was fast asleep on Ballard's shoulder.

CHAPTER
22

From Queenstown there are two main roads to Wanaka, and for reasons Natalie had no difficulty appreciating, Ballard chose the more challenging which traversed the Crown Range. The twists and turns at times were tortuous, demanding undivided attention. The Mazda 3 proved it was up to the task despite continuous gear changes as opposed to what would have been brutish, effortless cruising by the 300C.

Looking across Natalie smiled as she watched the concentration on Ballard's face. Driving was one of his purest pleasures in life which once behind the wheel meant the only thing that mattered was total attentiveness, having fronted too many horrific road fatalities in his early police career to believe otherwise.

Descending the range they toured along the Cardrona Valley with the open farmland of the Crown Range on their left and the Criffel Range to the right. Thirty minutes later they pulled up at the Cardrona Hotel and with stomachs rumbling they chose to have lunch.

Armed with Dr Google's endless facts Natalie revealed, "The hotel was established in 1863 and is one of only two remaining buildings from the gold rush era." She sat gazing at the off-white weatherboard frontage, the windows and door trims a dusty rose hue. The words 'CARDRONA HOTEL' were emblazoned in capitals across the entire frontage. Above the door leading into the restaurant was an old metal sign which read, 'Gaelic Whisky'.

Eager to absorb the hotel's ambience, Natalie gave Ballard a hurry-up nudge before stepping from the car. Aware they were experiencing history they entered and were immediately transported back in time. Memorabilia abounded on the walls and ceiling, the assortment astonishing, ranging from old-fashioned scythes for slashing grass to multiple rabbit traps and early-style wooden snow skis. One section of the ceiling was covered in currency notes of every conceivable denomination from countries across the globe. On the floor near the bar an old mining shaft was glassed over so patrons could stand over the pit and peer down to where workers would have toiled away with picks and shovels all those years ago, the dangers of the undertaking clear to see.

The interior of the hotel was warm due to the crackling log fire, the heat trapped in by the low ceiling. Natalie unbuttoned her cardigan and spotting a spare table, steered Ballard towards it. "Isn't this just something?" Her head swivelled left and right as she took in the surrounds.

Perusing the menu she settled on the Cardrona ale-battered blue cod and salad, topped with tartare sauce, declining the chips. Ballard chose the rib-eye steak, also with salad and no fries. Rubbing his stomach he declared sheepishly, "I probably need to cut back a bit considering what I've eaten over the past few days." Natalie eyed him with a degree of envy, fully aware he could devour mountains of food with little or no change to his weight.

The meal complete and foregoing dessert, Ballard posed, "Fancy a short horse ride?"

"What, on a full stomach?"

"Do cowboys wait before hopping back into the saddle after a belly full of beef stew?"

Natalie conceded his point but countered, "Yes Michael, but most cowboys have the skill to sleep in the saddle and not fall off."

"Well the good news is there's a family-friendly horse riding farm just two minutes up the road. I saw the sign before we got here."

"But I've never been on a horse *in my life*."

"Not a problem. These nags trudge around at their own pace. It wouldn't matter what you did. They mosey along a set path and afterwards you can boast to your kids you're an experienced horsewoman."

"Hardly, but ok, let's give it a go." Natalie attempted to appear positive but it was clear she harboured vivid images of a bolting steed and her being dragged along with one foot trapped in the stirrup as her head bounced off sharp rocks.

Thirty minutes later, helmets in place and astride hand-picked horses with gentle temperaments, Ballard and Natalie followed their guide Beck as they splashed across a shallow, slow-flowing Cardrona River. Shuffling about, they did their best to secure a more comfortable position in their Syd Hill half-breed saddles, in the main achieving the desired result while accepting only so much satisfaction was possible.

Maintaining a running commentary Beck provided a history lesson on the 1860s gold rush, informing them that after the precious metal ran out the area switched to farming, this detail underscored by the mobs of merino sheep grazing nearby much to Natalie's fascination. Admiring her perky posture in the saddle and chuffed at how she had taken to horse riding like an experienced equestrian, Ballard gave his gelding a gentle nudge to catch up. At that exact moment his mobile rang.

Embarrassed he peered at the screen, intending to turn it off but noting with a degree of disquiet it was from John. Apologising to Natalie and Beck he added, "Keep going. I'll be right behind you, but I *have* to take this."

Reins clutched in one hand and the mobile pressed to his ear with the other, he asked, "Are you back at work yet?"

"Yeah, clocked in this morning."

"And about bloody time. Pete and I were contemplating sending a team up to Queensland to drag you and Sonia back home."

"Not likely. And what's wrong with your voice Mike? You sound like you're standing on one of those bloody vibrating platforms they have in gyms."

"You're spot on John. My testicles are getting a right old workout being slapped against a leather saddle as this nag I'm trying to control continually breaks into a trot. I can tell you it's bloody painful. Yep, as crazy as it sounds Nat and I are horse riding as we speak."

"*Phew*. For a second there, testicles and slapping leather in one sentence had me wondering if you'd swapped camps."

"Very funny. Now what's the latest?"

"I've just finished chatting with James and Pete and bugger me we just *might* have a date for The Board's next cell meeting. To everyone's surprise Vladimir snuck around to Tatiana's late yesterday and stayed overnight. The resultant pillow talk has revealed the cell members are holding their monthly get-together in four days' time—this coming Thursday, around nineish."

Ballard checked he couldn't be overheard. "Christ, is it still being held at the Melbourne Club?"

"It is. And guess what."

Ballard didn't wait for John to adopt his usual delay routine. "I'm on a bloody horse John, remember?"

Laughing, his partner relented. "Not surprisingly the first hot topic will be selecting a new cell leader, and from what Vladimir was boasting in between grunts and moans is he's managed to cobble together a pretty handy sum of money. The bastard believes he's in with a real shot."

Ballard gave his horse a gentle kick along with a tug on the reins to prevent it from stopping and munching on a patch of grass. "Did he say how he got the money? It can't have been from Malcolm so he must have called in favours from his other contacts, quite likely the guy he was on the blower with down at Portsea."

"I'd say it's a distinct possibility." The tone in John's voice was one of frustration brought about by Vladimir's current carefree actions. "Mike, despite the predicament the bastard is in it would appear he's managed to secure finance without any apparent effort."

"Electing a leader tells me the remaining cell members *know* Olegovich isn't going to be walking through the door. What did Tatiana have to say about all this?"

"*That's the thing Mike.*" John's voice became breathless. "She's going to be at the meeting to sing Vladimir's praises. It's as though she has a degree of say in the whole shebang. Perhaps she *was* pulling strings behind the scene when Olegovich was running the show while giving the impression he was in charge." John went silent for several seconds and Ballard could picture the expression on his partner's face as he strove to make sense of the multiple power plays unfolding in the male-dominated group.

"Maybe, even though women *can* be invited into the club this is a strange one."

"And we now have proof positive that Vladimir regards us as a bunch of idiots Mike. The bloody arrogant prick!"

"How so?"

"James contacted him this morning and as a test aired the question about when the next cell meeting would take place. The bugger mumbled something about at least a couple of weeks off."

"The bastard. He really is getting cocky which may be a problem. The last thing we need is for him to go feral and take too many risks for The Board's liking, ending up being put down by the death squad. While we have him on the ropes we've at least a chance of getting closer to the cell members and denting the Australian wing of the organisation."

After nodding at Natalie to reassure her all was okay, he asked John, "Now changing subjects. Our man Sergey . . .?" There was no need to explain.

"Still nothing. Other than it's almost certain he's in Sydney. For all we know he's checking out the port situation up there while he's recuperating. Bernard Junior's still on the case though, along with maintaining physical tabs on Vladimir."

"What about the mobile I took off the chopper pilot? Have the analysts come up with anything there?"

A moment's hesitation followed. "I don't know Mike. I'll chase it up."

Ballard saw Beck pointing in the distance and while he wasn't within earshot it appeared she was drawing Natalie's attention to

Mount Cardrona and the Crown Range in all its sunbathed mid-afternoon glory.

John brought him back to the moment. "Assuming the cell meeting at the Melbourne Club goes ahead on Thursday evening I made it clear to Tim and James I wanted to be sitting off while they stormed the club. I'm assuming you'd like to be there as well?" Almost a plea, his next question was uttered in a soft voice, "When do you guys plan on getting back?"

Ballard laughed. "Don't worry old son. I've no intention of missing the fun and games, believe me." With a guilty glance at Natalie, Ballard added, "We fly back late afternoon the day after tomorrow, arriving around sevenish."

"Thank God. We're nearly there Mike. Pete mentioned he was grinding away at the minister so that might shed light on how far The Board's muscled their way into the ports' hierarchy. Jesus, imagine if they do get control, the flood of black market goods in and out of the country would be unbelievable."

"Hopefully we can knock this on the head sooner rather than later John."

"Okay, I'm off." A barking laugh preceded "Pass on a hello to Nat for me, and look after those testicles Mike. They come in handy every now and then." Before Ballard could reply his partner had gone.

Giving his horse a gentle nudge, Ballard caught up to Natalie and Beck who had stopped and were gazing at the scenery which was every bit as breathtaking as the promotional brochures.

"Everything ok, darling?" Natalie maintained eye contact.

Ballard leaned across and reaching her lips their helmets bumped. "Couldn't be better." Addressing Beck, he added, "I can see why you love your job—fresh air, stunning scenery, and a mobile office. What more could a young lady want?"

Laughing they headed back to the stables and after feeding each of the horses a bucket of mixed grain and lucerne, Natalie and Ballard thanked Beck for an enjoyable ride, promising they would do it again if ever they returned to the South Island.

As Ballard negotiated the last kilometres into Wanaka, Natalie checked out Dr Google. "Not a big town Michael, a smidge under eight thousand residents. Lake Wanaka itself is the fourth largest lake in New Zealand at 45 kilometres and a whopping 311 metres deep. And no wonder, with the Clutha River flowing into the lake at the rate of 560 cubic metres a *second*."

Ballard's eyebrows rose as he grumbled, "At least in there I wouldn't be touch-parking the bottom of the Riviera like I did near Point Gellibrand."

Natalie smiled at how Ballard hated making what he called amateur mistakes when driving a car or boat. She continued. "The population may not be high, but the annual number of tourist nights is over eight hundred thousand." This revelation had Ballard glancing sideways, curious how such a small town could cater for so many visitors.

Pulling up at their hotel, the Edgewater, Natalie hauled her case into reception with Ballard close behind. Minutes later they flopped on the king bed in their room, Natalie appearing exhausted. "Isn't it amazing how tiring horse riding can make you feel? And all we did was sit in a saddle."

Ballard rolled her onto her stomach and began massaging her lower back. "This should help circulation. If nothing else it'll reduce your stiffness."

Looking over her shoulder Natalie quipped, "A likely excuse, Doctor. But don't stop. It feels wonderful."

After a quick shower and a change of clothes they headed out, strolling the two kilometres to the town centre. Natalie was delighted as she spotted historical plaques embedded in the footpath, each one displaying a different date and a short description of important events beginning at the time of the Crucifixion. Reading them all, their progress into the town centre was slow but informative, arriving at the shops and restaurants around 5 p.m.

Over the next hour they window-gazed. Then, after a light meal in one of the nearby hotels they took in a film at the Paradiso

Cinema, amused there was an intermission which allowed them to cast caution to the wind and buy a choc-top ice cream each. Strolling arm in arm back to their hotel Natalie glanced at Ballard, wistful. "Tomorrow's our last day. Why is it our holidays fly past so quickly?"

"I'd suggest because this one's only four days long my love. I promise our next venture will be more substantial. They tell me Rome's not bad this time of year."

"Michael you don't have to apologise. This was a wonderful surprise, and I've loved every minute." She stared at him, unsure whether he was serious about the Rome suggestion, hesitant to admit it was second on her list of top five places to visit.

Ballard held her tighter, hoping he wasn't passing on his impatience at wanting to be back at work to progress the case, aware it was at a critical stage and could go either way.

The following morning, they were up at 7 a.m., determined to make the most of the hours they had left before flying back to Melbourne. First on the agenda was a short cruise on Lake Wanaka, passing Roy's Peninsular and the islands Mou Tapu and Mou Waho; the round trip just under two hours. Next, after visiting the local supermarket so Natalie could buy nibbles for a picnic, they drove alongside Lake Hāwea for thirty minutes before pulling over at a secluded spot, choosing a grassy ridge overlooking the expanse of water; snow-capped mountains Corner and Dingle were majestic in the background. Setting out the picnic they tucked in, washing everything down with apple cider.

Glancing about her Natalie was amazed at their isolation, not a vehicle in sight. "All this scenery to ourselves Michael. Where else in the world is this possible?"

No sooner had she uttered the words than a four-wheel-drive pulled alongside the Mazda and a family of four hopped out to admire the view. Smiling at one another, Ballard and Natalie were stunned by what happened next. Over the next fifteen minutes a cavalcade of cars arrived, their occupants spilling forth, clearly assuming this was a tourist hotspot. Many set up for a bite to eat while others stood gazing at the vista, cameras clicking.

"Er, you were saying about the isolation Nat?"

Smiling, she confessed, "It's beginning to feel a tad like we're at an old-fashioned drive-in. Perhaps we should move on." Packing the remnants of their meal and nodding at the late arrivals, they headed back to the Mazda.

"Next stop—the Blue Pools just up the road." Ballard checked his watch. "Afterwards we'd better head back towards Queenstown and the airport. I checked this morning and our flight is still scheduled for five thirty."

Natalie nodded as she twisted in her seat. "When you mentioned visiting the Blue Pool last night I looked it up and apparently we have to walk across a swing bridge that spans the Blue River. The pool itself is best seen on sunny days." She glanced out the window. "We may be in luck. *And another thing.*" Staring sternly at Ballard she demanded, "The bridge only holds a half dozen people at any one time so no rocking it about as you usually do, okay? That'd frighten the life out of me and the other tourists."

Ballard gave an exaggerated shrug, his manner innocent. He followed it with a wink as he formulated a cunning plan to achieve what he was commanded not to. They drove on, each with their own thoughts, Natalie's hand resting on Ballard's thigh, both admiring the passing scenery.

Arriving at the car park Natalie led the way, tossing Ballard one last warning glance before beginning her cross of the cable bridge, resigned to the inevitable. As feared, at the midpoint she was subjected to not only sideways motion but several bounces, causing her to hang on for grim death. A group of onlookers weren't amused, their attitude such they believed they were witnessing mental and physical cruelty. Ballard approached, encircled Natalie's waist as he planted a lingering kiss which went some way to pacifying the bystanders.

"You just can't help yourself. Such a child." Natalie headed off so Ballard wouldn't see her broadening smile.

Minutes later, staring down at the pool she exclaimed, "My God, it really *is* blue. And *look, look* Michael!" She thrust a forefinger at the various rainbow trout circling in the water. Levelling her mobile she fired off several shots.

Moving on they approached the river's edge and observed tourists stacking polished stones from the riverbed in a variety of weird-shaped monuments. Hundreds had already been built, each unique, all to be washed away by the next flood.

Glancing at his watch, Ballard took Natalie's hand as he led her to the car. "Best we start back, darling." Reluctantly she agreed.

The trip to the airport was uneventful but did include a brief stop at an old gold mining site. Witnessing a diversity of ingenious but antiquated equipment used to wash away veritable mountains of soil in search of the precious metal they contemplated how most of the workers would have left heartbroken and destitute, a fortunate few attaining incredible wealth.

At the airport they hauled their luggage inside and checked in before relaxing in the departure lounge, waiting to embark. Ballard's mobile rang, startling him as he was deep in thought, reflecting on the holiday and everything they had experienced in their four short days. "Pete, great timing. We're about to hop on a plane to come home. We both miss you."

Ignoring the obvious sarcasm Peter got down to business. "That's what I'm ringing about Mike. The funeral for the two policemen is being held at the academy tomorrow at 11 a.m." There was a pause with Ballard sensing something more personal was about to be revealed. "Michael, both parents have asked if you would say a few words at the service."

Ballard swallowed, recognising the holiday was now little more than a distant memory, harsh reality overtaking what had been a delightful interlude. Sitting alongside Natalie felt the mood change, Ballard's work persona now locked in place. Maintaining his unblinking gaze with her he replied, "Pete, pass on I'll be there. It'll be an honour to commemorate the policemen's lives."

CHAPTER
23

The chief commissioner's voice broke momentarily as he ended his eulogy, hesitant, wanting to say more but the words weren't forthcoming. Stepping forward the police chaplain shook his hand then turned and signalled to Ballard.

As he got to his feet Ballard felt Natalie squeeze his arm for reassurance. Buttoning his suit coat he strode to the microphone before turning to look out across the chapel, noting every seat was occupied. The majority of those in attendance were in full dress uniform, many displaying medals. Behind him the two coffins were draped with the Australian flag and surrounded by a sea of flowers.

Taking a deep breath he glanced up at the massive domed ceiling above him, as though seeking guidance, all the while fighting to control his emotions. He cleared his throat. "Two brave policemen, Trent and Mark, going about their lawful duty by rushing to the aid of someone whom they thought was seriously injured, only to be betrayed in the most despicable and cowardly manner. These young men now join the long list of police members killed in the line of duty, undertaking a job which demands courage, dedication, and sacrifice. Collectively, these fine policemen have contributed to making our society a much safer and more secure world in which we live.

"Tragically they paid the ultimate price in doing so. We can only thank them, honour them, and pray their fellow officers facing the same risks in their day-to-day duties remain safe. To Trent's and Mark's parents, siblings, partners, and friends, the police department and the community bear heavy hearts as we offer our sincerest condolences. We can only imagine the immense grief the passing of these wonderful young men has created for those who knew and loved them. We will always remember and respect Trent and Mark, praying their memory remains alive for their families and friends who I know will forever regard them as heroes."

Feeling inadequate and now understanding the commissioner's hesitation, Ballard began the difficult walk back to his seat, stopping to clasp hands with the parents and immediate families. Both mothers wiped tears from their face while the fathers attempted to remain stoic, only partially succeeding. Ballard's own eyes welled up, experiencing the now-familiar stab of guilt that he hadn't done enough to protect the two young men. Forcing the thoughts to the back of his mind he continued to his seat.

Settling alongside Natalie he kissed her cheek, her look of compassion and concern helping him through the wave of emotion threatening to overwhelm him. Whispering in his ear she murmured, "Just perfect darling." Not trusting his voice he managed a tight-lipped nod. Holding her hand he drew strength from her presence, grateful she had accompanied him.

The police chaplain read a passage from the Bible then led the congregation in the singing of "How Great Thou Art" which reduced the majority in the chapel, including Natalie, to tears, her distress continuing as the coffins were carried from the chapel to the haunting strains of the Police Pipe Band. The drivers of the two hearses parked near the front steps stood to attention in a dignified sign of respect.

Ballard looked on until the vehicles had passed through the front gates. After commiserating with several colleagues, some of whom he had graduated with, he led Natalie to the Chrysler. In a low voice shaking with rage he snarled, "I'll get the bastard who did this Nat. Take it as my promise to those families."

Natalie gripped his arm tighter, choosing not to disclose her mounting fear for his state of mind, aware he would leave no stone unturned in his efforts to ensure justice was meted out to the offender whom she knew little about other than what she had witnessed on television.

Dropping Natalie at her work where she left him with a consoling hug, Ballard headed to the crime building and after waiting for the steel entrance barrier to descend into its recess, drove in and parked in his allotted space on the second level. Arriving on his floor he discovered Ken, Bobby, and Susan head down, absorbed in preparing briefs of evidence.

Observing him searching for John, Susan lifted her chin towards Delwyn's office. "He's with the boss and Peter. I'm not sure what's going on but it seems something pretty significant is being discussed."

Bobby was desperate to join the fray but knew he would have to temper his enthusiasm; by contrast Ken displayed a contemplative expression, his profiling, analytical brain working overtime. Ballard grinned. "Bobby as soon as I get up to speed you'll *all* be the first to know. How are the briefs coming along?"

The three detectives gave individual accounts of the state of play regarding their evidence gathering for Vladimir and Sergey. Although not necessary Ballard added, "It's not a matter of *if*, but *when* those two front court, so treble-check everything. Remember the golden rule, at the end of the day it's all about points of proof. You can just imagine what John will do if either crook gets off on a technicality." All three faces left little doubt of their fate at the hands of their senior sergeant should such an occurrence eventuate. Ballard strode to Delwyn's office where she offered a silent question, her eyes sympathetic.

Ballard shrugged. "As far as funerals go it was as dignified yet tragic as they come."

"The chief was there?"

"Yep, did his bit."

John shook his head. "On top of all the political hassles the brass have to contend with, dealing with the emotional stuff has to be a real bummer." His head shaking became more pronounced.

Eyes narrowing Ballard took in the mood, glancing across at Peter and Delwyn, then back to John. "For the three of you to be huddled together like this I'm assuming there's been a development."

Peter scoffed. "Thank Christ your holiday has sharpened your wits. A bit back I was worried you might be losing it." A smirk materialised but didn't reach his eyes, signalling a serious issue was indeed afoot. "You're spot on Mike. An hour ago I received a phone call which I can only describe as attention-grabbing."

If his intent was to augment Ballard's already-burgeoning curiosity it succeeded. "The pressure we're applying to the ports minister is clearly worrying The Board big time." Peter appeared mystified as he raked both sets of fingers through his hair. "A lady rang me, *demanding*—not asking mind you—*demanding* I meet her tomorrow morning at a location in Altona."

Ballard's curiosity ramped up a notch. "Jesus, was it Tatiana? And how did she get your number?"

Peter's ongoing bafflement matched Ballard's escalating curiosity. "I can't be certain but hey, how many women ring me demanding I front up at a secret rendezvous in the middle of the night?"

John couldn't help himself. "Mate, the rumour mill has been in overdrive for years about your romantic shenanigans."

After a withering stare that ended in a weak shrug, Peter continued, "As to how she got my number, well, I'm supposing Vladimir's got something to do with it. I've heard the pillow talk tapes and while they're not studio quality I'll bet my pension the woman on the phone *was* Tatiana."

Ballard digesting the ramifications of the call as Peter continued.

"I'm to pull up alongside a black Saab on the passenger side no less. It'll be in one of the parking bays overlooking the beach at the intersection of the Esplanade and Mount Street, Altona. She was insistent I not get out, just lower the window. If any effort is made to arrest anyone in the Saab the ports minister will be executed. Coincidentally, Altona is where the minister lives with his wife and two kids."

"Bloody hell. What time is this rendezvous supposed to take place?"

"At 3 a.m. Not a minute either side."

"You're joking." Ballard saw from Peter's face he wasn't in the mood for anything remotely light-hearted.

"Nup. I asked what it was all about and there wasn't a moment's hesitation—she gave it to me right between the eyes. Calm as you like, said it was 'to discuss the port minister's ongoing health'."

Ballard's mouth dropped open. "Christ, The Board must be panicking the minister's about to break ranks so they're slapping a muzzle on the situation. But if it *is* Tatiana, what's her connection to them and why would she be exposing herself like this? For all intents and purposes she's the grieving wife who's coming to terms with her husband going missing with the strong possibility there's been foul play. She'll be unaware we know otherwise."

"That's the point Michael," Delwyn was animated. "She doesn't know *we* know. My guess is the Saab will have tinted windows and one of them will be lowered a few centimetres. Peter will be given an ultimatum—take it or leave it." She grew contemplative. "I may be wrong but with hubby out of the way Tatiana appears to be enjoying playing super villain assuming it is her who made the call. Also, if she can swing Vladimir into the top job she'll be sitting pretty, not that she isn't now. We did some digging at the Land Titles Office and her name is on the deed for the property. She's one wealthy lady is our Tatiana."

Again John couldn't resist. "Even more reason for Pete to make his amorous moves tonight. Who knows what he might pull off if he plays his cards right? But then again he *does* have Vladimir to contend with."

The superintendent reached across, pretending to strangle his colleague.

"Okay you two. So how do you see this going down Peter?" Delwyn's question was delivered with a degree of trepidation.

"There's no doubt I need to front up. If nothing else it'll show we're taking the demand seriously."

"I'm driving." John's flat statement made it clear he expected opposition from his superintendent but it was obvious his mind was set on backing his partner.

"Great, that means I'll have to ride shotgun." Ballard chuckled. "Come to think of it Nat and I watched the remake of *The Magnificent Seven* the other day, so I know what to do."

"Dear God will my nightmare never end?" Delwyn was fully aware her concerns wouldn't be taken seriously. "In that case have Tim's lads back you up Peter. For Tatiana to give such early notice of the meeting it smacks of her being super confident. She'll have her own protection in place and that can only mean the death squad, or similar."

Peter shook his head. "If there's even a hint of us attempting to ambush this meeting it'll turn into a bloodbath. The tone of her call made that very clear. No, this *must* be handled as she directed. As you said Delwyn, it's all about hammering home that we're to back off interviewing the minister, simple as that. Control of the ports is such a massive prize for them they'll stop at nothing to get what they want. With the minister as The Board's puppet, a lot of underhand deals can be pushed through with no hard questions being asked. We need to listen to Tatiana's demands, appear to consider them *then* act accordingly."

Delwyn wrestled with the logistics, troubled by the whole scenario. "Okay, you may not want backup close by, but Tim's team *has* to be within a few streets should the situation go south."

Appearing to relent Peter confessed, "You're right. It'd be nice to know someone's got our backs, just in case. Okay, I'll talk to Tim and organise for some of his boys to be on standby."

Delwyn nodded, relieved but still troubled by what the detectives would be walking into. "We're at a tipping point with The Board's Australian cell. They've been emboldened by their achievement at Parliament House despite losing out on their second cash grab. They now believe they can manipulate the police department by adopting threats we know they'll carry out without hesitation or regard for human life. If we don't get on top of this mob and soon we may as well shut up shop because the more wins they pull off the more brazen they'll get. Our job will become intolerable."

The detectives pondered her words, silently agreeing. In all their years they had never faced a group of criminals with such diverse skills and utter ruthless intent to achieve their goals. It was now clear Australia had joined the rest of the world where brutal, professional felons operated with no regard for law and order, and equally, no respect for the organisations endeavouring to enforce it.

CHAPTER
24

Driving along Mount Street towards the intersection with the Esplanade the dashboard clock flicking over to 3 a.m. with John the first to spot the Saab parked facing the bay. "There it is boys and girls, right on cue."

Peter sat in the back behind John, positioned so he would be near the Saab's passenger window, assuming Tatiana would also be sitting in the rear of her vehicle. Ballard sat alongside John. He touched the Smith & Wesson snug in its shoulder holster for reassurance, a reflex action, aware his partners were also armed. Tim had previously arranged for his SOG team along with himself to be on standby several streets away, and while not happy with the situation, agreed it was the best that could be arranged under such short notice.

The parking bays on either side of the Saab were empty, as was the immediate beach area itself, not surprising considering the hour. On the sand near the water's edge a four-sided marquee cast a forlorn image, and while it appeared to have been abandoned, it generated a degree of speculation amongst the detectives. For the moment it wasn't their immediate concern.

The fronds on the palm trees stretching left and right across the beachfront were almost motionless due to the light wind. Above a three-quarter moon had completed its climb into the cloudless sky, casting a dappled glow across the sand, glinting on the incoming waves as they massaged the shoreline.

John eased alongside the Saab on the passenger side as instructed while Ballard wrote down its registration number. The vehicles were now less than a metre apart. John switched off the ignition and sat with both hands in clear view, gripping the steering wheel. His action was deliberate, displaying a neutral position. The Saab's windows were heavily tinted as Delwyn had predicted, and still raised.

Out the corner of his mouth Ballard whispered, "And now we wait."

Seconds later Peter stiffened in his seat, his face transfixed in alarm. "Guys, no sudden moves, okay?"

Ballard twisted around, instantly comprehending his colleague's unease. A laser dot was locked on the back of John's seat along with one on his own, while another danced briefly on Peter's headrest. Searching the properties behind them they saw a laser flash in a ground floor window of a two-storey house across the Esplanade. It was from this vantage point that at least three snipers had them fixed in their sights. All Tatiana had to do was issue the command and a volley of high-powered rounds would penetrate the vehicle's glass, plastic, and metalwork, converting the car's interior into a slaughterhouse.

"Jesus! I'd say this sets the tone of the meeting gentlemen." Deep-seated rage augmented Peter's words. While not shocked by the precaution Tatiana had taken, his resentment at how the police department was being held in contempt was on clear display.

After rechecking the snipers' location Ballard faced his partner. "Take it easy Pete. We're here to gain intel, nothing more. Let them play their goddamn games."

Grunting, Peter lowered his window. Looking across at the Saab he waited for a response.

A full thirty seconds passed before the rear passenger window lowered halfway, the interior in total darkness making identification of the passenger impossible. The glow of what was thought to be a cigarette could be seen but within seconds the aroma of an expensive cigar wafted into the police vehicle. It took Ballard back to his youth and memories of his grandfather who every Christmas would indulge in his one simple luxury in life, Montecristo No.4 cigars.

Snapping back to the present, Ballard watched John twist around, attempting to gain a clearer view. "Steady on. Don't do anything unexpected for Christ's sake."

John grunted his compliance.

The female voice from the Saab was silky, educated, with no hint of an accent and unhurried, as though the meeting were nothing more than the gathering of old friends. "I'm assuming we have mutual appreciation of where we stand?" It was obvious the question referred to the snipers.

Peter chose not to respond; the question rhetorical. Ballard watched the cigar glow brighter as a lungful of the aromatic smoke was drawn in; seconds later it was expelled in a wisp through the open window. "Now gentlemen, there's an immediate problem requiring a very simple solution, and it involves the ports minister. I'm led to believe the police department is continuing to ask a lot of annoying questions, and the minister has asked that something be done about it."

Again Peter remained silent, foreseeing the inevitable directive; he didn't have to wait long.

"The questioning will stop—as of now."

The silence that followed the blunt statement grew louder until Peter tonelessly asked, "And if we don't?"

"Then one of the minister's children will meet with a very nasty accident coming home from school. Should the minister and his family disappear because you've placed them in witness protection, the minister's mother, father, or sister will meet with an equally unpleasant accident. Your department doesn't have the resources to protect them all."

Ballard watched as Peter's jaw clenched, his inner rage growing to an alarming level which for him was out of character.

The voice resumed, as calm and precise as ever. "As I said, the resolution is simple and *will* be followed."

Peter opened his mouth to answer but was cut short.

"There's nothing more to discuss. Remain parked for fifteen minutes. If you leave earlier or I even *suspect* I'm being followed I'll give the order for you to be executed. At the fifteen-minute mark, *and no earlier*, I suggest you inspect the marquee on the beach." There was an agonising pause. "As you will have guessed it hasn't been abandoned by an absent-minded sunbather. What you'll need to do will be obvious when you get there, but remember one thing gentlemen, the questioning of the minister ceases or his family suffers. As an added incentive if my demand is ignored a *very* disagreeable incident will occur in the CBD that will see many innocent people die. Remember what happened at Parliament House and think what *could* have happened."

No sooner had the words been uttered than the window rose and the Saab backed out of the parking bay, its headlights flicking on as it travelled west along the Esplanade and out of sight. To punctuate the order for the detectives to remain where they were the laser beams remained rock steady, the rifles clearly tripod mounted.

"*What a bitch!*" The venom in John's voice matched Peter's earlier rage, his sense of total impotence alien to his customary "can do" personality.

Ballard tapped the Saab's registration number into the mobile data terminal, muttering, "This'll be an exercise in futility." His premonition proved correct less than two seconds later, the details returning with the registered owner listed as Beryl Baker, the licence photograph revealing an elderly lady with an address in Laverton. "I'll guarantee the location's a vacant building lot or a bloody car park."

All three detectives stared at the screen, John shaking his head in disgust. "The bastards are treating us like bloody halfwits." He slammed the heel of his hand against the steering wheel, frustration boiling over. "We're sitting here like castrated dummies."

"Careful John, we're still being targeted." The three laser beams underscored Ballard's warning. "Okay Pete, your thoughts on whether that was Tatiana?"

His colleague cocked his head sideways. "Oh I'm certain of it. The inflection on certain words was identical to the surveillance tapes. Yep, that was Tatiana all right, and clearly she was enjoying every minute of her drama-packed theatrics."

At the fifteen-minute mark as though flicking a light switch, the laser dots disappeared. Each of the detectives checked his partner, confirming they were no longer a target. "We *could* call in Tim and his boys but if the shooters are still in the house it'd end up a bloodbath. I suggest we let sleeping dogs lie on that score."

Peter agreed with Ballard's summation.

"We're not going to like what we see down there are we?" Arming himself with a flashlight, John waved an accusing hand towards the marquee which by now had waves lapping at its base.

Peter flung his door open. "Let's find out shall we?"

Cautiously they approached the marquee, the dry sand firm under their feet. All three detectives levelled their weapons, unsure of what they would encounter. Switching on the torch John focussed the beam to a tight, bright disc, directing it over the marquee's entrance. With a nod from Peter and John, Ballard reached out, grasping the entrance flap, drawing it back to peer inside. Although prepared for the worst the image confronting him took his breath away, with John blurting, *"Holy shit!"* Peter stood stock-still, open-mouthed.

Facing them and buried up to his neck in the sand, blindfolded, and gagged was the ports minister. Seawater lapped about his neck causing him to crane his head up and away. His face was distorted in terror, nostrils flaring in rapid, panicked breaths. A primal moan emitted from deep within his throat.

As each new wave rose higher he became increasingly frantic, desperate to move his head but unable to do so. The detectives' presence was an additional fear for him and a further torment.

Rushing forward Ballard dropped to his knees, ripping off the blindfold. "Minister you're safe. We're police officers." After peeling back the grey duct tape the minister gasped, sucking in much-needed air but also collecting a mouthful of saltwater as a fresh wave swept in. Choking, he cried, *"I don't want to drown!"* He continued to cough up water and sand, eyes wild, his head tossing back and forth.

Ballard did his best to reassure him, fearful he was on the verge of a panic attack. "We'll get you out I promise." Peter knelt and began scooping sand as John looked around, spotting two spades off to one side of the tent.

"Would you believe the bastard's left their shovels behind? The pricks are messing with our heads Mike." He threw one to Peter then positioned his torch on the sand to best illuminate the marquee's interior. Following that he began the delicate task of drawing away the packed sand with his own shovel, careful not to inflict any injuries.

The tide kept rolling in, flooding the cavity that was being created, frustratingly drawing in additional sand. The minister's teeth began to chatter uncontrollably, as much from shock as from the chilling waves. His shirt and suit coat were saturated; water and sand swirled around and over his upper body which he twisted back and forth in a vain attempt to extricate himself.

Ballard halted his digging. "Minister, stop struggling. It's making you sink further."

Mumbling incoherently the minister did his best to comply, still shuddering violently. Ballard and John concentrated their efforts in front while Peter worked near the minister's back, glancing at the ever-rising tide as it washed under the marquee. The torchlight cast chaotic shadows as they worked frantically, the water and sand swirling relentlessly around them. Within minutes they had excavated to below the minister's hips and managed to free his thighs. Grabbing an arm each and with John hauling on a trouser belt they dragged him moaning from the sand's clutches and what would have been a watery grave.

They collapsed exhausted alongside the hole which was filling with water and sand, John's torch now floating freely. He reached out and secured it. In a combined effort Ballard and John dragged the minister to his feet, slinging an arm each over their shoulders. From there they carried him between them towards the police vehicle. The tip of one of the politician's shoes furrowed the sand, the other missing, having been sucked from his foot when he was extricated from the hole. A chilling southerly had sprung up and the palm fronds were on the move, casting ghostly shadows in front of them, the moon at its peak.

John grunted with exertion. "Mike I've got a blanket in the boot. We can wrap him in that. Do you think we should call an ambulance?"

Ballard managed a half-smile as Peter quipped, "Forever the Boy Scout Johno." He appraised the minister's condition. "Nah, he'll live, no need for an ambulance. Besides that'll end up generating a shitload of questions. No, just wrap him up."

The minister's teeth continued to chatter non-stop, underscoring the need to raise his core temperature as a matter of urgency. Ignoring Tatiana's blunt warning Peter asked, "Minister, did you see who did this to you?"

There was hesitation followed by a halting "No . . . they pulled a hood over my head."

"Where were you when this happened?" It was clear John's curiosity was on overdrive.

"Parliament House. I was working back . . . I'd texted my wife I'd be late, perhaps around midnight or just after. As I was walking to my car it . . . *they* came from behind—" His voice broke, followed by a retching sob as the shock of his ordeal took hold of him. "They jabbed me with something. I . . . I don't remember anything until after I woke up . . . in the sand. *It felt like I'd been there for hours.*"

John winced, imagining the overwhelming horror the minister must have felt on waking to discover his predicament. Foregoing their questions due to the politician's weakened state they reached the police vehicle. Peter took over John's position as the latter popped the boot to extract a blanket. Doubling it, he wrapped it around the minister's saturated body. Slowly the minister began to calm, his breathing returning to normal.

Appraising his own wet clothing in distaste, Ballard reached forward to open the passenger door just as he heard Peter draw a sharp breath. "Christ, the bastards have us back in their sights."

Spinning around, Ballard saw the familiar laser beams targeting Peter and John as well as a third sweeping over the minister's back; a quick glance confirmed they were directed from the same house. The headlights of a car appeared from their right, approaching at speed. It slid to a halt, smoke pouring from protesting tyres. With sinking hearts the detectives realised the Saab had returned.

The boot opened remotely as the rear passenger window lowered partially. The female voice this time was icier, even more demanding. "Put him in the boot then back away. You've got five seconds or you'll all be shot." The window rose again.

Cursing, John reluctantly grabbed the minister's legs while Peter and Ballard took his upper arms. Hefting him into the boot of the car the minister struggled weakly, his look of disbelief combined with abject terror on display. He opened his mouth to plead to the detectives but was cut short by the boot closing. With a screech of tyres the Saab accelerated away, brake lights flashing momentarily as it took a corner and disappeared.

John slammed the boot shut on the police vehicle, kicking savagely at the rear tyre. Ballard placed a hand on his arm. "No choice John. If they were going to kill him they would have done it earlier, leaving us to find the body. No, this is an in-your-face warning to the minister to keep his mouth shut and for us to back off, proving they can do anything they want—*any time* they want."

"Tell me about it. That's *exactly* what they're doing, and there doesn't appear to be anything we can do to stop them."

A howl of tyres had them spinning around to see a black van bursting from the driveway of the house the snipers had occupied, taillights flashing on as it headed along the Esplanade away from the police vehicle. John kicked at the rear tyre once more, but much harder. "Ahhhh! This just gets worse and worse! What the bloody hell is the world coming to?"

Ballard took out his mobile and contacted Tim, indicating he would explain all when he and his troops arrived. Minutes later the SOG officer pulled up followed by the Balkan containing five of his men. After a brief discussion Tim directed the house be searched, assuming it was now unoccupied but warning they should take every precaution. While this was happening the three detectives walked the SOG commander through the sequence of events, with Tim exclaiming, *"What, buried up to his neck?* Have they been watching bloody *Pirates of the Caribbean* for Christ sake?"

Just as Ballard was about to continue the account, Tim's mobile sprang to life. Answering, he tensed, staring at each detective in turn, his features like stone. Hanging up he snarled, "Our death squad have struck yet again gentlemen. There's an elderly gent and a woman on the sofa in the lounge, dead, both shot in the back of the head."

CHAPTER
25

"What time did forensics say they'd get here?" John addressed his question to Ballard who was contemplating how much dry cleaning the department would accept of his work clothes. He glanced at Peter who was sitting in the rear of the police car with Tim.

"Around the same time I mentioned five minutes ago John—four thirty, give or take."

John glared at his watch, willing a different time. "If nothing else we've ruined the 7 a.m. knock-off for Ken, Bobby, and Susan." His comment was a caustic reference to having requested they "pull their finger out" and attend the grisly scene Tim's officers had discovered; the three young detectives having arrived twenty minutes later, their nightshift in tatters. After being briefed they got to work analysing the crime scene while the senior detectives and Tim waited for the forensics team to arrive.

Settled in his seat Peter commented, "Other than taking a few photos I'd suggest there won't be much to collect by way of DNA in the marquee. The saltwater will have done its thing and the shovels won't have prints of any value, not after we finished using them. This also explains the timing of the meet, right when the tide was coming in. Guys, can you believe these bastards?"

"It worked. Got our attention and with Tatiana's threat there's bugger all we can do about it. What do you think she meant regarding the CBD warning?" John's expression indicated he feared it involved explosives or something equally lethal.

Ballard hunched around to face him. "Whatever it is you can bet they'll follow through on it with God knows how many innocent lives being lost if we don't comply. As for the minister I'll stake my pension he's being dropped back at Parliament House as we speak so he can clean himself up, put on a fresh set of clothes then drive home to a wife who'll accuse him of being unfaithful." He sat reflecting on the difficulty the badly shaken minister would face, explaining the last four hours to a suspicious spouse. "You said Missing Persons confirmed she reported him missing Pete?"

Recalling his previous contact with the bureau just after he got in the car, Peter responded. "Yep, and she was given the stock-standard answer that a few more hours had to pass before it could become an actionable report, minister or no minister. I was reminded by some snotty-nosed staff member that around seven thousand people go missing in Victoria every year." He added with a savage undertone, "We *really* need this meeting at the Melbourne Club to go ahead so we can scrape these bastards off the shit heap of society."

Ballard looked hard at his partner, one eyebrow raised. "Couldn't have put it better myself. All we need is to be able to . . ." He broke off as a crime scene vehicle pulled into the parking area and two investigators jumped out. Climbing from the police car Ballard shook their hands before introducing his colleagues. Together they walked across the beach to where the marquee was now under a foot of water and looking the worst for wear, the tide rising by the minute.

Divulging only basic information which avoided mentioning the ports minister, Ballard stated, "Just photos of the general area and after pulling on some gum boots, perhaps a shot or two inside the marquee. Include where it's located in relation to the intersection behind us." He hooked a thumb over his shoulder. "From there I'd suggest pack the bloody thing up and take it back to your office. God knows if it'll prove of any value later on." The officers confirmed they were to investigate the murder scene in the house; Peter nodded, indicating three homicide detectives were already on site.

Set to their task the forensics officers returned to collect their equipment then headed back across the fast-shrinking beach.

Peter chuckled. "Guys if we'd been another ten minutes getting down there they'd be using an underwater camera to photograph a bloody head sticking out of the sand attached to a very dead minister."

"*Ten minutes.*" John scoffed. "Pete I'd have given him ten seconds, at which point he'd have had to sprout gills."

Peter's grunt emphasised his general frustration at the situation.

Thirty minutes after arriving the forensics team had gathered all the evidence they could, with the area now fully submerged. Packing their equipment along with the marquee they acknowledged the detectives with a brief wave then drove across the street to the house to begin their gruesome analysis.

Yawning, John fired the motor and glancing at his watch added with tongue firmly in cheek, "My troops will be here for at least another hour. That being the case it's home for us and a good night's sleep before we meet up again at seven this morning."

AC Thompson made no effort to hide his displeasure as his eyes roamed the Critical Incident's conference table, an imposing figure at any time but more so in full uniform. Peter John, and Ballard had just completed their briefing on the incident at the beach, including the two callous murders. They highlighted the difficulty the department now faced in progressing their investigation involving the ports minister, along with the CBD threat should the department continue its efforts to thwart The Board's agenda at the docks.

Delwyn stared at all three detectives, incredulous that such an audacious warning was enacted so blatantly. "Up to his neck in the sand. *Really?*"

John obliged. "Yep, another minute or two and he wouldn't be sitting in parliament ever again, or anywhere else for that matter."

The AC cleared his throat. "So that highlights our conundrum folks. If we pump the minister for any more information we run the certainty one of his children will be murdered. Place him and his immediate family in witness protection and his extended family gets the chop. Leave him to sit in parliament and Christ knows what deals he'll be forced to push through which will strengthen The Board's control." Cursing under his breath he viewed the assembled group, his eyebrows arched, an unspoken demand for options.

Sitting beside the AC, James rose to the challenge. "I listened to the pillow tapes earlier this morning and yes, it *was* Tatiana in the Saab, and wasn't she stoked when she recounted the beach episode to Vladimir while engaging in other things." He grinned, leaving his audience to visualise what 'other things' might be.

"In fact she was *so* upbeat she boasted she'd be able to advise at the meeting the problem concerning the minister had been dealt with and we, the police, no longer posed a threat."

The AC leaned forward. "Did she confirm the meeting's date and time?"

To everyone's relief James nodded. "She did indeed. They're bringing it forward by three days."

"So that's . . . ?"

"Tonight, 9 p.m." James uttered a frustrated snort. "We contacted Vladimir after he'd left St Georges Road and he's still pushed the line the meeting's *possibly* happening in a week or so. The lying bastard. What he doesn't know is when he attends, being the star recruit he's certain to be there, we'll know about it because of the tracker in his watch and Bernard's son's surveillance. The good news regarding his fabrications is they prove he's still in the dark about being watched or he wouldn't be continuing to lie through his teeth."

"Jesus *tonight*." The AC ran his fingers through his hair. "It doesn't leave us much time to prepare."

James pressed on. "Regarding your initial question Kevin, about the minister's safety, if we do manage to round up all the cell members then the problem of what to do with him *should* be resolved in the short term." He allowed his statement to mature, his countenance implying there was unpleasant news to follow.

Ballard thought hard about interjecting, aware the Melbourne Club resolution wasn't going to be the finale everyone was praying for, deciding to relieve the ASIO officer of having to explain why. "James you're correct about the issue being resolved in the short term. Unfortunately there's nothing to stop The Board from rolling out another cell in its place in a 'here's one we prepared earlier' move. They're bound to do just that considering what appears to be their unlimited resources."

James dropped his head in agreement. "Thanks for shouldering the bad news Michael. Yes, that about sums it up. The Board will undoubtedly have a duplicate cell on standby for just such an eventuality."

The AC glared at Ballard, not because of what he had said but in bitter realisation the likelihood of a replacement cell was now almost a certainty.

Sporting a grim smile Ballard added, "That being the case then we've no choice but to murder the minister."

John shot upright, as though waking from a deep sleep. "*My thoughts exactly.*" Despite his outburst his expression matched the majority around the table, but not Bernard, who sat slowly nodding.

"Ah, the 'charred body in the burnt-out car after running headlong into a tree' scenario."

The AC sighed, aware that what was to follow threatened to be a white-knuckle option which he would be requested to approve.

Ballard elaborated on Bernard's pithy description. "As we're all fearing sir, should we manage to arrest this mob at the Melbourne Club and another cell is slotted in its place, we can't permit the minister to remain free to do God knows what in parliament. He's utterly compromised and could never be trusted again. Further to that Tatiana has slammed the door shut on us pumping him for additional information, and we can't hide him and his family away in witness protection." He smiled at the Texan. "I'd suggest what I'm about to recommend wouldn't be the first time Bernard has heard of such a proposal or been part of orchestrating a similar scenario."

Bernard nodded with a hint of a smile, confirming what was to be revealed was indeed stock-standard CIA protocol.

Ballard continued. "In short, The Board must be convinced the minister is dead. To achieve this we need to source an already unrecognisable charred body and have it found in his vehicle which will have met with an accident and caught fire. For authenticity we'll have to bring the coroner on-board to ensure that any identifying features that can be traced to him are included in the coroner's report. There's no guessing how far The Board's tentacles reach. We can't leave anything to chance."

The AC winced. "Thanks for nothing Michael. If you're not proposing gassing Parliament House which I'm happy to say proved a master stroke, you now want me to countenance taking a burnt cadaver, stuffing it into the minister's car, then crashing the car into a tree and setting it alight." He looked to the ceiling while muttering, "I've got a snowball's chance in hell of *ever* collecting my pension haven't I?"

Ballard took in the stunned expressions of Delwyn and Roger, only Peter sat grinning, enjoying the exchanges. "Yes sir, that about sums it up." He stopped as he observed the AC's expression. "No, not about your pension. I'm sure that's safe." He continued on a serious note. "There doesn't appear to be any other way to pull this deal off. Sadly, for complete authenticity the minister's wife and children must also believe this scenario and can't *ever* be told otherwise. In fact we'll need to plant a suicide note somewhere to highlight the minister wanted out of this whole cock-up. That's going to be horrendously tough on the family, but it's the only way we can be sure The Board will buy it, assuming they do. There's always going to be the risk they'll carry out their threat regardless, tying up loose ends so to speak, all we can do is try and mitigate it."

"And how do we convince the minister to go along with a lifetime of witness protection?"

Ballard cleared his throat. "After this morning's shenanigans he must be aware the group will only allow him to live while he's useful. The moment they've pumped him dry of parliamentary favours he's a dead man walking. The minister doesn't have too many options once we point out to him the reality of the situation, and the risk he poses to his own family should he appear to remain alive."

Peter supported Ballard's supposition by adding, "There's no doubt The Board hasn't survived this long without being able to plan ahead, perhaps decades in advance. They're sure to have one or two additional ministers in their back pocket as we speak. I'm certain we're going to be amazed when we see the 'Who's Who' at their little shindig."

The AC focussed on Tim who had been sitting quietly beside Delwyn, taking in the ever-changing landscape of the briefing. "Knowing how thorough you are Tim I'm assuming you've already prepared an operational order to raid the club?"

Tim sat upright, lack of sleep lining his face but not diminishing the fire in his eyes. "Yes sir, our warrants are good to go and surveillance has deployed drones to take shots of the garden area out the back should the action spill outside the club rooms. We also sent in one of our guys dressed in his finest to enquire about joining the club and he was given a brief tour of the more common areas. He managed to take a few shots with a concealed camera but they don't help us an awful lot, though at least we have *some* idea of the internal layout. That said, he wasn't allowed upstairs which'll be where the action takes place—if not, perhaps in the basement. Either way we'll sweep in both directions." He grinned. "No matter what it's going to cause quite a ruckus when we go in."

The AC agreed. "That's what I'm afraid of. I can see the headlines now: 'Melbourne Club Harbours Criminal Syndicate'. The first thing the chief will do is ring and ball me out as to why the hell the arrests couldn't be made somewhere else. For this very reason I won't be briefing command about the raid until it's over." He was silent for a moment, picturing the facade of the heritage-listed building, trying not to imagine the possible carnage about to unfold within its walls before admitting to everyone as much to himself, "Just as well I've got a thick skin." He turned to Tim. "Try not to shoot anyone *inside* the club if at all possible."

Tim shrugged, not entirely comfortable with the AC's dry humour but adding some of his own. "I'll do my very best sir, but if I *do* have to shoot someone I'll endeavour to see it's done outside in the garden area."

Ballard held up a hand. "Pete, John, and myself will sit off around the corner so when you've finished your sweep through the place

Tim, we'll pop into the club. I've always wanted to see inside." As an afterthought he added, "Ken, Bobby, and Susan will also be there. You'll need numbers to collar anyone who might try to scatter during the raid."

The AC assumed control. "Good, that's settled then. Folks this group is the most brutal, money-hungry bunch of professional criminals I've ever had the displeasure of investigating, and remember, this is just the *cell* we're talking about not the true masterminds. The CIA, Interpol, Scotland Yard, ASIO . . . despite being the pinnacle of the world's law enforcement agencies they've all attempted to crack the upper echelon and failed. Our friend Bernard can attest to that. We now have a better-than-even-chance to bloody The Board's nose but if we *can't* crush it, we can be guaranteed they'll stop at nothing to gain a foothold in the ports. That's if they haven't done so already, reducing us to mere spectators in terms of curbing their criminal ambitions." A tight smile appeared. "No pressure folks, just make sure you get these bastards."

He fixed everyone with piercing cobalt-blue eyes, his faith in his colleagues a double-edged sword. Giving a curt nod, he strode from the room.

Ballard drew Bernard's attention. "Any update on Sergey's whereabouts?" While he was striving to appear nonchalant, it was clearly threaded with underlying tension.

Guessing as much, Bernard responded, "Glad you asked Michael. I *was* going to update you after the meeting. Bernard Junior rang me last night and he was more than a touch excited I can tell you. His intel has Sergey holed up somewhere in the Crows Nest area on Sydney's North Shore, just off the Pacific Highway." Bernard noted the look of expectation in Ballard's eyes. "We're closing the net. One of the operatives was tailing him but because he had to hold back so as not to be spotted he lost him at the last minute. It's now just a matter of time before we get a fixed address."

Delwyn also witnessed Ballard's expression of hope. "I've a counterpart in the NSW homicide whom I've known for years. I'll call him as soon as we determine Sergey's exact location and have him request their Specialist Operations Command scramble a team and arrest the brute. We're nearing the end game Michael. I feel it in my bones."

While Ballard didn't share Delwyn's optimism, he was appreciative of her positivity.

Delwyn followed up by asking, "Tell me, how's Natalie faring with all this?"

Ballard was reflective. "Once she offloaded her two youngest to their grandparents, in her mind it's as though there isn't a threat, which is good *and* bad as you can imagine."

Delwyn reaffirmed Bernard's previous positivity. "It's just a matter of time before we have an address Michael. Then he'll be arrested I promise you."

"I appreciate your confidence but every day that goes by the bastard's recovering from his wounds, if he hasn't already."

During the next hour they went over every aspect of the forthcoming raid, ending with Delwyn declaring to the detectives, "By my count you got about three hours' sleep this morning. Go home and take a power nap, but be back here for a final briefing at 19.00." She turned to Tim. "I'm guessing you fared no better in the shut-eye department?"

The SOG commander grinned wryly. "Hmm, I guess the difference is I'm nowhere near as old as this bunch of codgers, so it's not such a problem. Plus my 2IC will be part of the team going in so that eases the load."

John's middle finger was the last thing visible as he and Ballard left the room.

Resisting Delwyn's plea to leave work immediately, settling on a compromise of two thirty instead, Ballard and John updated a very tired Ken, Bobby, and Susan as to what was expected of them during the raid, followed by some urgent paperwork. The task allocation complete, John indicated he would kip down in the building's living quarters which were available for country members attending court, claiming he couldn't be bothered driving to his unit in Keilor.

Ballard phoned Natalie and asked if she could get off work early and was informed without the slightest hesitation it wouldn't be a problem, and of course she would make sure he was well nourished before he returned to the office. She refrained from enquiring as to the reason for his callback.

An hour later, after negotiating the surprisingly light traffic in Collins Street and Punt Road their arrival at the town house saw him almost bowled over in the garage by Natalie scrambling to get to the kitchen. In no time he was tucking into a reheated veal schnitzel and salad while she sat picking at her meal. "When do you think you'll be back tonight, darling?"

Swallowing, Ballard hesitated. "I'll give you a ring if it's too late. Don't wait up."

Natalie dug a little. "I guess John will be with you?"

"And Peter."

"Ah yes, the terrible trio. Will you be in any danger?"

Ballard ensured there was no hesitation in his reply. "None whatsoever my sweet. Just dull, boring stakeout duties we detectives have to contend with from time to time." He washed down the last of his meal, careful to avoid her eyes.

Far from convinced Natalie knew well enough there was no point pushing any further. Reaching forward she touched the back of his hand. "Go. At least have a lie-down. I'll wake you at six thirty."

She shunted him towards the stairs and minutes later, shoes kicked off, he stretched out on the bed and in no time was sound asleep.

CHAPTER

26

"Would you believe John, the Melbourne Club was kicked off by twenty-three gentlemen property owners on the seventeenth of December 1838? Displaying its British heritage, the building itself is a classic example of a nineteenth-century purpose-built clubhouse in the Victorian Renaissance style." Ballard grinned roguishly as he paused to take a breath from his formal recitation.

Sitting behind the wheel of the police car John glanced at his watch, growling in disgust as he hooked a thumb towards Ballard before peering over his shoulder at Peter reclining in the back. "Christ, it's only eight thirty. He's got at *least* another half hour to bore us witless while he waffles on endlessly about the history of this place." His thumb changed direction as he spoke, now aimed towards the five-metre-high brick wall alongside them which ran parallel with Ridgeway Place, leading off Little Collins Street between Spring and Exhibition Streets.

Peter leaned forward, conspiratorial, winking at Ballard to urge him on.

Encouraged by the superintendent, Ballard resumed his deliberate commentary. "That wall John protects the privacy of the club's courtyard garden at the rear of the building." Peering upwards he took in the mass of foliage on the tree which rose majestically above the wall. "The garden itself is maintained by a famous arborist-horticulturist whose name escapes me, but the primary focus of the guy's maintenance schedule is to check the ongoing health of that tree up there which is the largest plane tree in Victoria, perhaps Australia." Ballard shook his head. "And ensuring the health of that sucker is bloody crucial because a tree that big in any London park would be worth nearly two million dollars."

"*Bullshit.*" John's head craned forward, squinting as he attempted to gain a better view. "*Two million?* Jesus the world's gone nuts. On top of that where the hell do you dig up this stuff?" He sat staring ahead, refusing to look directly at Ballard so as not to encourage further onerous dialogue, feigning interest in the cars flashing past the end of the lane on their journey down Little Collins Street. On the far side a multi-storey car park loomed large, headlights winking as cars wound their way to higher levels in search of vacant bays.

Ballard adjusted the volume of the police radio which was set on channel 36, making it the third time he had performed the action, a sign of his growing tension. They heard Tim issuing instructions to his team while maintaining contact with the surveillance officer situated further along Collins Street, the member operating a tripod-mounted camera with a sophisticated zoom lens. Pretending to take shots of the streetscape he was in fact snapping people entering and leaving the club.

Determined to reduce the mounting anxiety Ballard pointed to his right, focussing his colleague's attention on the glass entrance of a second club. "That gentlemen is the Lyceum Club, a women-only establishment catering for Australian arts, literature, and social activism." The latter description produced a typical deep-throated grunt from John but no pithy outburst, spurring Ballard on.

"The aim of the organisation is to promote a spirit of goodwill and understanding within the association and provide opportunities for contact and friendship between its members—"

John shuffled around in his seat. "Yeah, yeah, enough Mike. Thanks for passing the time on yet another deathly dull stake-out, but *you* know that *I* know what you're up to. I'll even go so far as to say it's worked—to a degree." He shook his head again. "Two million dollars, *really,* for a single bloody tree?"

"Apparently so. Crazy isn't it? And we can be thankful it's not between October and December because the trichome fibres it drops during those months are bloody hell for asthmatics."

"You just can't help being a smart arse can you?" John's declaration was accompanied by a wry smile which he battled to suppress.

They fell into a companionable silence, their thoughts turning to what was about to unfold and the consequences should they fail. Ballard watched with mild interest as two moths circled the nearest street light. The insects' ever-diminishing rotations became more frenetic as their flight path closed in on the shimmering glow.

Peter snorted with amusement as he punched the back of John's seat, animated. "Can you imagine what the looks on the high court judges, captains of industry, church leaders and businessmen of every persuasion who frequent the place will be when Tim storms in with his troops?"

John agreed, adding dryly, "It might wake them up to the reality a bunch of professional crooks have been operating under their very noses for a bloody long time. They should be ashamed of themselves for being so naive."

"John I'd suggest their egos wouldn't factor in shame of *any* kind—well not for most of them. They didn't get where they are by having thin skins." Ballard's words drew an unsubtle burst of profanity from John as he rolled his eyes, supporting his partner's summation.

Peter joined in. "Perhaps they're not so much naive as prepared to turn a blind eye. Who knows? A bunch of them may even be copping a healthy sling on the side."

Ballard looked across at John. "What time did your guys finish with forensics this morning? I clean forgot to ask when we checked on them earlier." His reference was to when they walked down Little Collins Street to where Ken, Bobby, and Susan had backed their police vehicle into Club Lane which was on the far side of the Melbourne Club courtyard. The bluestone lane was occasionally used by members as a back entrance as well as an exit; the detectives' presence a precaution Tim believed was worth adopting under the circumstances.

John laughed at Ballard's query. "Around seven this morning. I told them not to come in until after ten, but come to think of it they didn't fare any better in the sleep department than we did. *Tough.* They're young and used to holding down crazy hours." Changing subjects he checked his watch again before asking, "Christ, the cell members *must* be in place by now. Did Tim say how he was going to tackle storming the club?"

Peter took up the query. "I spoke to James before we got here. He said he'll let Tim know when Vladimir's tracker shows he's in the club. Bernard's surveillance teams will also advise whether Tatiana's going along for the ride, but after last night's caper I don't think there's any doubt about that. So all we have to do gentlemen is hang tight and—"

"*Move in. Move in.*" Tim's controlled order over the radio caused all three detectives to stiffen in their seats, aware the raid was underway.

John's smirk at having guessed the time the raid would commence was replaced with a snarled "Christ I hate this, being away from the action and just an onlooker." He paused, his face showing mounting frustration as the heel of his hand struck the steering wheel. "Bloody hell, come to think of it, sitting here in this shitty lane we can't even consider ourselves *onlookers.*"

Fifteen minutes passed at an agonising pace as the detectives waited, on edge, John fidgeting non-stop. Ballard attempted to reassure him with an occasional sideways glance and a nudge on the arm. Peter remained quiet, reflecting on his age and the passage of time, very much aware the days of being the first on the scene were long gone, replaced by Critical Incident Response Teams and SOG personnel. He was resigned to the fact the specialist squads were better equipped and trained to handle high-risk, dangerous situations such as these.

Ballard's mobile broke the silence. Snatching it he saw it was from Susan. He pressed the phone hard against his ear. "Talk to me."

"Michael, just a few seconds ago the deputy commissioner of Specialist Ops came out the rear door behind us. He seemed pretty shaken up. As he came along the lane he spotted us and was in two minds whether to run or acknowledge us. After composing himself he nodded but kept going even though Bobby called out to him.

The DC then turned right at the end of the lane and is now heading up Little Collins towards Spring Street. Just before he went around the corner he did a double take in our direction. What do you want us to do?"

Ballard made a snap decision, aware of the politics involved. "Susan, you and the lads get on after him. We'll try to cut him off at our end."

On hearing the urgency in Ballard's voice Peter and John bolted from the car, all three sprinting towards Little Collins Street, Ballard shouting, "If you see DC Salisbury *stop him*."

Reaching the end of the lane they saw Bobby in full flight with Susan close behind and Ken bringing up the rear. Pointing towards the car park as he reached them Bobby declared while breathing hard, "*He went in there boss*." He appeared perplexed, desperate for an explanation but realising now wasn't the time.

Ballard assessed the situation as he directed his younger colleagues. "Each of you take one of the top three floors and see if you can spot him. We'll search the lower levels."

"What if he's in his car and won't stop?" Susan was uncertain how far she should impede the movement of a deputy commissioner.

John left her in no doubt. "Shoot out one of his goddamn tyres."

Susan blinked at his words but offered no argument.

Ballard was about to moderate John's directive when his mobile rang. "*Yes Tim*."

"Michael, I can't believe I'm saying this but keep an eye out for Deputy Commissioner Salisbury. I *think* the bugger is part of the cell . . ."

"Tim we already have him somewhere in the car park in Little Collins."

"Good, I'll send a couple of my boys over. Make sure he doesn't get away. We can't—"

Ballard disconnected mid sentence.

Peter was on the move. "I'll prop at the exit and stop anyone entering and check all those leaving." Bobby, Susan, and Ken sprinted off to begin their search of the upper levels.

John snatched Ballard's arm, eyes wide, a cruel grin forming. "Let's do this. I've *always* wanted to nail a deputy commissioner."

Ballard cautioned his partner. "For Christ sake John don't shoot him. It'll make for very nasty headlines and embroil the department."

With Peter at the car park entrance and the three younger detectives racing to the top floors, Ballard and John began a systematic inspection of each of the parked cars, starting on the ground floor level.

"I tell you what Mike, if the bastard really *is* part of the cell I'll . . . I'll . . ."

"You'll arrest him and read him his rights. That's *all* you'll do." Ballard's eyes roved over, around, and under each vehicle as he continued to check, eyes narrow, wondering whether he should draw his firearm. Deciding on caution he indicated John should do the same. Several members of the public heading towards their vehicles saw the detectives' weapons and needed no further encouragement after being ordered to leave the area.

"Can you believe what we're doing Mike?"

"Concentrate John, we can't—" Ballard broke off, dropping to a half crouch along with his partner as three shots rang out near them in rapid succession. This was followed by a series of explosions reverberating in the confined space. A ball of flame mushroomed in front of them, rising from the tray of a nearby Land Cruiser; the flames struck the concrete ceiling and spread in all directions, the source appearing to be multiple gas bottles stacked in the rear of the vehicle. Black acrid smoke billowed throughout, reducing visibility just as the overhead sprinklers began spurting water.

"*What the hell!*" John's alarm was cut short as one of the gas bottles fizzed through the air, smashing the windscreen of a nearby Volkswagen Golf. Additional explosions forced the men to duck again as they came to the realisation the commissioner had created a diversion by shooting the bottles then igniting the escaping gas. Their experience prewarned them he was about to make his escape.

Angrily pumping a round into the chamber of his weapon John snarled, "If the prick thinks he's getting past us he's sillier than I thought."

"Careful John. We don't know if there are other motorists on this level or whether your guys are behind him."

The sound of a car engine revving and the squeal of tyres alerted them of the commissioner's approach. Standing side by side in what would be the path of any oncoming vehicle, both men raised their weapons as they went into a combat crouch in one of the few areas not being soaked by the sprinklers.

Out the corner of his mouth Ballard warned, "This is pure bluff John. We can't shoot the bugger for fear of hitting bystanders. If the prick won't stop get out of the bloody way. We can always pick him up later. There's no sense getting run over just to prove a point."

"Bullshit! I'll be . . ."

Tyres shrieking a black sedan rounded the corner at speed, emerging through the billowing smoke, heading straight for the detectives. Ballard felt a charge of adrenaline as the hair on the back of his neck prickled and his heart pounded in his chest. In the instant he was about to shove John to one side the car braked hard, tyres protesting, the sedan slewing sideways on the concrete's wet surface.

The deputy commissioner slumped in his seat, both hands gripping the wheel. Raising his face his expression was one of total capitulation, comprehending that life as he knew it was over. The windscreen wipers continued to operate as water from the sprinklers cascaded over the vehicle. John stood to one side, his weapon aimed while Ballard ordered the officer from the car. Bobby approached, panting, eyes disbelieving. Pulling out his handcuffs he offered them to Ballard. Susan and Ken brought up the rear with Ken on his mobile to Communications demanding the fire brigade attend *"Now"*, pointing out that if more petrol tanks ignited the whole car park would erupt in flames. With those words, Susan and Bobby grabbed a fire extinguisher each and bracing themselves, headed towards the Land Cruiser. John's caution followed them despite no additional bottles exploding.

Ballard snapped the cuffs on the deputy commissioner who bowed his head just as Peter arrived, open-mouthed at what he was witnessing. "Jesus guys, I turn my back for three seconds and all hell breaks loose." John rattled off the commissioner's rights, the words hissed through clenched teeth.

Ballard drew Peter aside and was about to explain the events when a grunt of pain had them spinning around to see the commissioner slumped on all fours, moaning between ragged breaths. John was straight-faced. "I read him his rights like you said Mike. Then somehow his groin connected with my left knee—twice!"

Ballard grabbed his partner's arm, dragging him away. "Yeah, subtle John. Now *enough*. The last thing we need is to get embroiled in an assault charge."

John grew serious. "Sorry, I just snapped. To think this prick's been divulging departmental secrets to The Board for God knows how long. People have *died* because of this bastard."

"I know, I know, but we have to *prove* his involvement. There's still a lot of water to pass under the bridge before then." Ken stood to one side, smirking at John's previous action.

The sound of fire engines could be heard in the distance and it was clear they were heading in from the East Melbourne depot, but not before two cars adjacent to the Land Cruiser ignited in a burst of noise and flame, the sprinklers unable to prevent the eruption. John called out to Susan and Bobby to stand clear and leave the firefighting to the experts.

Three fire trucks parked in Little Collins Street, lights flashing, blocking all west bound traffic. Firemen armed with large-capacity foam extinguishers went to work isolating the burning vehicles to prevent more ignitions.

Tim arrived with two of his officers and after speaking briefly with Ballard and Peter, instructed that the deputy commissioner be led away. Turning towards John he quipped, "So . . . twice in the nuts?"

John did his best to look bashful but the steel glint in his eyes gave him away. "Nothing the bastard didn't deserve, just wait until the AC hears about this. I wouldn't be surprised if he doesn't front up and give him two more."

Ballard clapped Bobby on the arm. "We'll send the crime scene lads over and they can do their thing. When they've finished get them to move the DC's vehicle out of the way so it can be picked up as evidence. After that you three come over to the club and see how the other half . . ." He hesitated. "What am I saying, see how the other *fraction* of the world lives."

The senior detectives accompanied by Tim headed from the car park towards the club. On the way Ballard and John attempted to rearrange their damp suits into some semblance of respectability as Tim commented, "I just can't get my head around the fact a DC in charge of Counter Terrorism, the Crime Department, Forensic Services, Intelligence and Covert Support—*Christ*, half the bloody police force could get to his rank and be an out-and-out crook. I spoke with my chap taking photos out the front and he's certain the bugger didn't come in the front or he'd have seen him. He must have snuck in the back way *before* your guys got into position." He shook his head once more.

Peter chipped in, equally frustrated. "This isn't the first or the last time we've dealt with bent cops Tim, and senior ones at that."

All four men trudged along Ridgeway Place, deep in thought at what had just taken place, fully aware of the political fallout it would generate.

Ballard turned to Tim. "I take it no one was hurt in the arrests?"

Tim's eyebrows rose as he explained the raid. "It was all a bit of an anti-climax. We stormed in and discovered the cell meeting was downstairs. Tatiana was in full flight in front of seven other guys, including Vladimir. When she spotted us she let off some very non St Georges Road linguistic gems. Then after kicking and fighting like a banshee she was cuffed and led off with the others."

He expressed his displeasure. "The DC was sitting near one of the exit doors and before we knew it he was through. *Poof! Gone.* We had our hands full with all the other guys who put up varying degrees of resistance, and I have to admit my time to check out the

DC was limited. I was so stunned at seeing him that for an instant I questioned whether my eyes were playing tricks. That's when I rang you guys."

Ballard agreed. "I can't blame you. I felt the same when John and I saw him coming at us in his car. For a split second I thought he was going to run over the top of us. I'm guessing the last vestige of conscience he possessed must have come to the fore."

John disagreed, scoffing, "Perhaps the fact I was about to put a bullet in the bugger might have sharpened his reasoning also."

John's tone had Ballard glancing at his partner, unsure whether he would have shot the DC; he was aware he would go to his grave never knowing.

They walked up the steps into the elegance of the Melbourne Club's reception area, Ballard noting the huge gold-framed mirror in the hallway which reminded him of the Hall of Mirrors at Versailles. "Just think how many prime ministers must have stopped in front of that very mirror to preen and check their bow ties Johno."

"And I'll bet my left testicle quite a few of them asked the question 'Mirror, mirror, on the wall, who's the dandiest of us all'?"

Laughing, the group swung left, taking in the ambiance of the lounge, the wealth in the room washing over them as they observed the abundant leather Chesterfield sofas and armchairs. Mahogany woodwork was evident throughout, highly polished and expansive. The apricot walls and teal ceiling, resplendent with massive cornices and mouldings added to the atmosphere of privilege and power, subduing the detectives' previous light-heartedness.

John's face twisted into a mask of disdain. "And our DC thought it was okay to hobnob here while honest coppers were out on the streets risking their necks?" He didn't look for an answer but Peter obliged anyway.

"No point railing against what's been the status quo for thousands of years Johno. All we can do is root out the baddies one at a time and hope it makes a difference."

Crime scene and forensics officers swarmed throughout, with several of the club's management being interviewed to one side, their expressions one of utter shock that their privileged world could be shattered so abruptly, so publicly.

Through one of the windows Ballard could see reporters milling, held at bay by several uniform officers. Grunting, he commented, "I see the vultures are circling gentlemen. Perhaps when we leave we might take the DC's route out the back."

Fifteen minutes later Ken, Bobby, and Susan joined them to inspect the room where the cell had been conducting its meeting. Ballard took one last look before suggesting it was time to leave. John muttered, "Good move, the last thing we need is to have our faces plastered across the front pages so The Board's death squad can use us as target practice."

His words were a sobering reminder as to the reality of the situation.

CHAPTER
27

If the AC's face had shown anger at the briefing the day before it was now scarlet as his furious glare swept those gathered in the Critical Incident room. "I never liked Salisbury, even when we were in the academy together." He wiped his mouth after taking a hurried sip from his cup of steaming tea. "I liked him even less as the years went on, but I put that down to the fact he got promoted to DC and I didn't." His face cracked into a faint smile as everyone sat fascinated by his free-flowing disclosure which for him was as rare as summer snow.

"After this caper now I *know* my slime detector was transmitting true-to-life signals about the guy all these years." Appearing sheepish which was unchartered territory for his audience he added, "All I can say is if the justice system prevails he'll never breathe fresh air outside of four walls topped with razor wire ever again."

The AC nodded towards the three senior detectives as well as Tim, all sitting as a group, while Delwyn eyed them with undisguised admiration.

Clearing his throat the AC declared, "Well done gentlemen. As predicted I copped a phone call from the chief who made it clear that while the Melbourne Club was a tad public, he understood the need for seizing the moment. The remainder of the conversation centred on how Salisbury appears to have succumbed to greed big time. The chief did request however, that when the DC's questioned we need to determine beyond *any* shadow of doubt that his involvement with the cell isn't a result of coercion from The Board. We don't want a last-minute defence thrown up in court which could see him walk."

He became reflective. "What I'll never understand is how seven high-profile men and one woman could ever think they'd get away with such insidious crimes as the Note Printing Australia robbery and the siege at Parliament House. How they could *live* with themselves after watching innocent lives being snuffed out is just beyond me."

The wall clock showed five minutes past midnight as the AC's frown transformed to a full-on beam. "You've all performed way beyond my expectation, and as you well know, my expectations are never easy to live up to. Taking out the cell is a major step in the ongoing battle against The Board. While I'm aware the cell may be replaced over time, this must shake head office to the core." He grinned boyishly, eyes shining with uncharacteristic mischievousness. Then in a remarkably accurate Churchillian growl he rumbled, "Whatever happens we'll fight them on the beaches. We'll fight them in the streets. We'll fight them wherever they are, and we'll *never* surrender." Chuckling at his own loose portrayal the AC was joined in celebrating the victory by a spontaneous round of applause, a triumph which had been a long time in the making and despite it being transitory, an excellent fillip for morale.

"People, it's late. Go home to your loved ones and give them a big hug. Thank them for their collective understanding and forbearance. This has been tough on them, something we must never forget."

There wasn't any need for a repeat request as all present shot to their feet and made a rush for the door.

While Ballard peeled off his somewhat-bedraggled suit to take a well-deserved shower, Natalie insisted he hurry downstairs where a hot Milo and homemade shortbread would be waiting for him. Refreshed and wrapped in a navy dressing gown he happily chomped through a mountain of the biscuits, washing them down with two cups of steaming Milo. With the TV in the kitchen switched on they watched the twenty-four-hour news channel which was showing the exterior of the Melbourne Club with crime scene and forensics officers swarming in and out of the building. A reporter armed with a mike was doing his best to appear as though he had something of substance to say but in reality he could only relay that an incident involving SOG personnel and plain-clothed detectives had occurred earlier in the club.

Natalie guessed from Ballard's intense concentration that he had been involved and as such being aware John and Peter had been with him she was unsure whether to broach the subject. Throwing caution to the wind she asked, "So that's where you all were?"

Ballard chuckled. "Indeed we were, along with Ken, Bobby, and Susan. It was more like a family affair really. We all wanted to see inside what is possibly one of the most exclusive clubs in Melbourne."

"And did you?"

"Yep, and pretty flash it is too."

Returning her attention to the screen Natalie knew this would be the extent of the details revealed, content to leave it at that, just relieved her man and his colleagues were safe.

Bernard's voice was excited, which for a man who had experienced much in his professional career meant something significant was about to be revealed. "Bernard Junior has locked in an address for Sergey. As we thought Mike, Crows Nest on the North Shore. I'll text the details through as you sound like you're in the Beast." He laughed at his own joke, his reference clearly directed at Ballard's 300C.

Ballard contemplated what the Texan would think of Robert's Bentley Continental and the astonishing brute power it was capable of unleashing, as demonstrated by Natalie's father at the Calder Thunderdome several months earlier. "I just don't know how to thank you and your son Bernard. Putting Sergey behind bars for good will be an emotional weight off Natalie's shoulders and I have to admit, off mine. Delwyn has the NSW police on standby and has been waiting for an address to set in motion the Russian's arrest as a matter of priority." He paused. "Has Bernard Junior got operatives watching the address now?"

"You bet your ass Michael, twenty-four-seven. You'll be the first to know if anything changes."

"Great. I'm only ten minutes out from work so I'll ring you the instant the NSW boys are ready to swing into action. Text me the address and we'll do the rest."

Ballard checked the Chrysler's clock, estimating he would be in the office by 8 a.m., feeling refreshed from a good night's sleep.

Delwyn almost leapt from her chair at Ballard's news, her reaction copied by John and Peter who had been in deep discussion with her when Ballard arrived, John breaking off to wish him a sarcastic "Good afternoon". Without hesitation Delwyn snatched up the phone and rang her counterpart in NSW who advised her he would mobilise their Specialist Operations group to form an arrest team while notifying his assistant commissioner of developments. Delwyn then surprised her audience by declaring, "Toby, give me two hours' warning prior to the raid as my colleagues and I want to be there when this bastard is nailed to the wall. That way we can bring him back to face the music on home soil."

John turned to Ballard, brows raised as Delwyn ended her call and sat considering the three detectives. "Who fancies a quick trip to Sydney so we can drag this bugger back home?" They were all speechless, which for them was a rarity. "As I said before, I've known Superintendent Toby Richards for years and he has a copy of the warrant for Sergey's arrest. As soon as Bernard told us he may be in the Sydney area I flicked Toby a copy. Thank you section 82, sub para one of the *Service and Execution of Process Act* 1992." She smiled conspiratorially. "An hour and a half up, affect the arrest, a quick appearance in the local magistrate's court then back to the airport and home again. All over red rover." She made a dusting motion with her hands, clearly on a high. Ballard prayed it wouldn't be in vain.

Her next move was equally impressive as the detectives watched her contact the Air Wing. "Yep, a flight to Sydney. Today. *Yes today damn it*. Within the next hour. What have you got? Uh-huh . . . Hmm, uh-huh." She scribbled furiously on her notepad then hung up, beaming from ear to ear. "Done. They have a Hawker Beechcraft on standby, juiced up and ready to roll. They lease it for critical incidents, and as you just heard I was able to convince them this was just such an incident."

Ballard winked at Peter then blurted for John's benefit, "Ah the 400XP, a nice little unit. I'll explain more when we get in the air Johno."

His partner twisted in his chair. *"The hell you will."*

Still grinning Ballard rang Bernard and informed him of the plans. "Just keep me posted if Sergey looks like he's on the move."

Bernard's deep chuckle vibrated through the phone. "Unlikely. The bugger was out boozing most of the night wearing a pretty convincing wig and glasses God forbid. He's now crashed back at his pad and I'll wager he'll be there most of the day. But yes, you'll be the first to know should anything change." The line clicked dead.

Delwyn became serious, her previous jocularity dissolving. "Is all this just a bit too straightforward? First the cell members are picked up, now Sergey's located and with any luck he'll be arrested before the day's out. We have a crooked DC behind bars along with a mastermind femme fatale. Vladimir whom we know financed the NPA robbery and the siege on Parliament House is also in the can. Suddenly it all seems *too* easy. What are we missing, gentlemen?"

Peter shook his head. "I know what you're thinking Delwyn, but up till now we haven't had too much go our way. The law of averages meant we had to strike it lucky at some point, and as the AC mentioned, The Board won't sit idly by. Word of the Melbourne Club raid would have reached the Russian hierarchy by now which means they're already looking for replacements. It's just—"

"Yes, thank you. I'm glad I asked Peter. I mean after all, why should I enjoy a moment of celebration when I could be assessing all those shitty options?" She grinned to remove the sting. "I still say we've bloodied their nose and it feels good." There was complete agreement.

The trip to the Air Wing at Essendon Airport was fast, with Delwyn choosing to drive her departmental vehicle. Activating the car's red and blue lights once she was on the freeway she fell short of switching on the siren, despite being tempted. Peter was ensconced in the front passenger seat while Ballard relaxed alongside John in the rear. The detectives were impressed with Delwyn's consummate driving skills with John frequently nodding to highlight his appreciation.

Toby Richards had rung twenty minutes prior indicating an arrest team would be in place by 1 p.m. This gave the detectives an hour and a half of flight time and another hour to negotiate the Sydney traffic. He informed them he would meet their plane on the tarmac at Sydney's Kingsford Smith airport then shadow the special operations team who would be apprehending Sergey at the address in Lane Cove.

Pulling into the Air Wing's parking bay, no sooner had Delwyn got out than Inspector Bruce Walters the unit's OC approached. Taking her hand he shook it enthusiastically while sporting a broad smile. Turning, he acknowledged the three detectives. He went on to explain a flight plan had been filed and approved by the Essendon Control Tower, along with confirmation from Sydney's Kingsford Smith Airport. Ballard thought back to the inspector's contribution at the initial NPA briefing, describing his ongoing acquaintance with Malcolm Ferguson and the billionaire's love for his two vintage Iroquois helicopters which had been hijacked and used in the robbery. Ballard's attention was drawn to Malcolm's hangar in the distance, the giant doors closed; exchanging looks with John he jutted his chin meaningfully in that direction.

Wasting no time the detectives were escorted to one side of the police hangar as the Beechcraft was towed onto the tarmac.

John grunted his disgust. "*Bloody hell*, just as I expected. A white-knuckle ride in a toy aeroplane. Why does it always have to be me copping this shit all the time? If it's not Malcolm's Eurocopter dropping out of the sky like a stone with us on board at the Williamstown Yacht Club, it's flying in this kiddie plane to Sydney."

After climbing aboard and buckling into their seats, John's head a mere inch from the cabin's roof, Ballard gestured to his partner. "Now regarding your belief this baby is a toy." John's exaggerated groan sounded remarkably like the auxiliary power units which had just spun over the twin jet engines, his staged disinterest failing to discourage Ballard. "For starters this 'toy' costs the wrong side of two million dollars. The Pratt and Whitney turbo fans can push this thing over one thousand six hundred kilometres at a cruising speed of around seven hundred and eighty kilometres per hour." He grinned at Peter before continuing. "Oh I forgot to mention, the cruising altitude is a tad under fourteen thousand metres and our two friendly pilots up front." He waved towards the smartly dressed aircrew who acknowledged them with a brief glance and a thumbs up. "They're running through their checklist on the Rockwell Collins Pro-Line 4 avionics system as we speak."

Delwyn twisted in her seat, adjusting her headset as she directed her question to an exasperated John. "Good God man! Is this what you have to put up with every day?"

John continued to milk the sympathy he was being offered by perpetuating his hound dog expression.

Eyes twinkling Delwyn suggested, "If it's any consolation I *could* team you up with one of the younger detectives if that'll ease your pain."

Massaging his chin, John realised he was ensnared in a catch-22 conundrum.

Ballard asked the pilots how long before take-off and was told five minutes. Ringing Bernard he was informed Sergey was still in his apartment and due to the lack of movement in the unit appeared to be sleeping off his late-night carousing. At the same time Delwyn contacted Toby, relaying their ETA at Kingsford Smith Airport.

Arrangements made they sat back and waited for the Essendon Tower to announce they were clear for take-off which came three minutes later. Everyone except John commented on the luxury of their surrounds which for high-flying businessmen and women was just ho-hum everyday reality.

The thrust in the middle of their backs as the jet engines hurled them along the runway and into the air was breathtaking, which

Ballard informed an agitated John involved 1,350 newtons of vectored thrust.

"Keep this up Mike and I swear I'll jump out of this tin can just to put an end to your ranting." Eying Delwyn he sought her sympathy but came up short as she and Peter made no attempt to hide their amusement. Hunkering down he scowled at Ballard before fixing a prolonged stare out his window, taking in the shrinking landscape.

The detectives sat back and reflected on Delwyn's decisive action, appreciating how she had arranged an Air Wing flight as this meant they could retain their weapons, thus avoiding the procedural delays a commercial flight would have entailed. Peter hooked a leg over his armrest as he swivelled in his seat, a satisfied smile lurking. "Not long now folks. Once Sergey's nailed we'll have a clean sweep of these buggers, and not before bloody time."

Ballard nodded but his thoughts were far from positive, having first-hand experience of the Russian's incredible physical and mental capabilities. He knew he wouldn't feel comfortable until the man's hands and feet were handcuffed and he was hog-tied for good measure. Even then he would be keeping a watchful eye until the man was behind bars.

As was often the case when all four detectives were together for an extended period, anecdotes from their past exploits flowed thick and fast. Ballard contemplated with a degree of remorse a major lack of judgement when he was a young constable at St Kilda. Having stopped the divisional van on three separate occasions at the intersection of Alma and St Kilda roads he remembered warning a fourteen-year-old boy not to sell newspapers amongst moving vehicles. A week later he attended a road accident at the location and discovered to his horror the lad had died at the scene, having been hit by a truck. "Why I didn't grab him by the scruff of the neck and haul him off to his parents, reading all of them the riot act is an eternal regret. I just didn't do my job." He took a deep breath, lamenting his lack of experience at the time, the only action available to him now being to offer advice to younger colleagues as to what should have been done.

Everyone reflected on their guilt of at least one incident in their careers they were less than proud of, but were now thankful they had achieved a degree of salvation over the years, despite their remorse never truly leaving them.

An hour and twenty minutes after take-off the pitch of the jet engines altered as they began their descent into Kingsford Smith Airport. Severe turbulence caused John to clutch his armrests, knuckles white as they descended far more steeply than the average commercial jet. "Jesus, just what I thought, Maverick and Iceman at the controls."

CHAPTER
28

Stepping from the plane they were hit with a temperature variation of at least five degrees from what they left in Melbourne, along with substantially higher humidity. The men hooked their jackets on a forefinger while Delwyn appeared as cool and composed as ever in her pale-grey suit and white linen shirt with upturned collar.

On the tarmac a tall man with cropped grey hair and a film star smile approached them, his pale-blue business shirt, magenta tie and navy suit pants projecting the image of a homicide detective comfortable in his own skin and not afraid to show it. Taking Delwyn's hand he drew her in for an affectionate kiss on the cheek. "Good to see you again Delwyn. It's been . . . what, eighteen months?"

"At least Toby, and yet for some reason you don't look a day older."

John rolled his eyes as the two superintendents exchanged small talk before Delwyn introduced her colleagues. Toby offered a firm handshake and a direct gaze. "So we have a particularly nasty Russian to put behind bars. The havoc he unleashed on your Parliament House was pure evil, and you're right Delwyn, this guy's a one-man militia."

He turned to Ballard, inclining his head. "And you must be the action man. Achieving what you did in the chopper is beyond me. Delwyn gave me a rundown over the phone and Michael, I'd have soiled my pants."

Ballard quipped, "When we crashed I nearly did."

Everyone laughed.

Toby switched to business mode. "The Specialist Ops are en route and will be in position around the corner from your man's unit. They'll go in on my word." Indicating the unmarked police car behind him he growled, "So let's do this."

Ballard, John, and Peter crammed in the rear with John in the middle, elbowing his colleagues to secure additional space while Delwyn sat regally in the front seat. Once on Southern Cross Drive Toby exhibited comparable driving prowess in the heavy traffic to that shown by Delwyn. Within thirty minutes they had entered the Sydney Harbour tunnel, with John appearing uneasy as he considered the volume of water above him. Ballard chose to add to his disquiet by declaring the harbour at that point averaged eight to ten metres in depth, receiving a sharp elbow for his troubles.

Toby viewed them in the mirror. "You're right Delwyn. They *are* out of control."

Exiting the tunnel they travelled north along the Cahill Expressway and were close to St Leonards Park when Ballard's mobile chirped. Noting it was from Bernard he snatched the phone to his ear, his heart sinking. "Yes Bernard."

"The bastard is on the move."

"You're saying he's left the apartment? Where is he now?" Ballard tensed in his seat.

Deducing the context of the conversation Delwyn and Toby exchanged a silent look. Veering into the left lane Toby pulled up at a bus zone alongside the park, the vehicle's emergency lights flashing.

Bernard's usual drawl was clipped and professional. "Bernard Junior's with me on the line and he's in radio contact with his surveillance team. He'll give you an exact sitrep." He paused, allowing his son to respond as Ballard switched his mobile to speaker.

"Sergey's travelling east in the Lane Cove tunnel, just short of the Gore Hill Freeway. If he maintains that route he'll be in position to either cross the bridge or take the harbour tunnel into the city."

"Where are *you* Michael?" Bernard's voice was edgy but controlled.

Ballard looked to Toby who announced, "Stationary alongside St Leonards Park, facing north."

Bernard Junior heard the response. "At the speed this guy's travelling I'd suggest you've got less than four minutes before he's level with you on the Warringah Freeway."

Toby spun in his seat as he spoke into Ballard's mobile which was being held towards him. "What's he driving?"

Bernard Junior responded. "A grey four-door LS400 Lexus."

"Rego?"

"'Fraid not."

Toby made a snap decision. "We have to get on the other side of the freeway."

With the vehicle's police lights operating he accelerated hard, taking the Falcon Street exit before turning sharp right, passing beneath the freeway. His passengers braced themselves as tyres howling he made three illegal turns which had oncoming vehicles honking furiously. Swinging back onto the freeway he headed towards the city. Suddenly stomping on the brake he pulled into the service lane before grabbing his mobile and barking a series of orders to the Specialist Operations team, explaining the situation and for them to head towards the bridge.

Taking advantage of the stop Ballard requested that Bernard Junior advise when Sergey was half a kilometre back so Toby could merge into the freeway traffic ahead of the Russian, the police vehicle's lights now off so as not to draw attention.

Toby stared at Delwyn before refocussing on the detectives in the rear. "How do you want this to play out? My guys won't get here in time so it's up to us. I could run the bastard off the road and the five of us arrest him. But from what you've told me Delwyn this prick doesn't take kindly to being cornered, so we face the prospect of innocent people being injured or killed."

Delwyn spoke over her shoulder. "We're damned if we do and damned if we don't gents. If he gets away he'll be up to his neck in another plot that'll see God knows how many more people dying before it's over."

Ballard took a deep breath, his previous concerns returning as the events at Halls Gap replayed in his mind. "Run the bugger off the road Toby. We *can't* let him get away again."

Everyone agreed.

Ballard spoke into his mobile. "Bernard, where is he now?"

There was a short pause as Bernard Junior questioned his surveillance team. "About a kilometre behind you and still on the Warringah Freeway. Hopefully he's heading for the CBD and won't branch off to Neutral Bay at the last minute because if he does you won't be able to cross over to those lanes from where you're positioned."

Praying Sergey would remain on their section of the freeway, Toby accelerated into the traffic. "Where do you want me to broadside him?"

Peter responded. "Do it on the bridge if that's where he's going. He'll have less options to get away there." Consensus was reached once more.

Seconds later Bernard Junior barked, "He should be four hundred metres behind you and yes it appears he's taking the bridge. He's in the left lane so pull one across so he'll be on *your* left." Having heard their decision to run Sergey off the road Bernard Junior added, "Travel parallel with him then wedge him into the Armco railing. Traffic will bank up behind him so he won't have anywhere to go."

Peering out the rear window John snarled, "Right on schedule Toby. As Bernard Junior said, he's on the outside lane . . . fifty metres back and closing fast."

All except Toby pumped a round into the chamber of their weapons. Ballard cautioned, "This is self-defence only. There are too many pedestrians on the walkway to start blazing away." Deep in his heart he was certain Sergey would challenge them, but he couldn't think of an alternative in the remaining seconds they had left.

The Lexus drew alongside with Toby matching it in speed; Sergey was staring ahead, concentrating on the traffic. Sensing the police vehicle alongside he glanced to his right, his eyes widening as he recognised Peter less than a metre away. Jaw thrusting he went to accelerate but was prevented by a car in front. Alternatively there was no room for him to brake.

Toby swung the wheel hard left as he snarled, *"Hang on."* The sensation and sound of the collision was phenomenal, the ongoing screech of tortured metal as the Lexus slammed against the railing like a giant fingernail scraping across a blackboard. Jaw clenched, Toby maintained his hard lock on the steering wheel, preventing the Lexus from breaking free. The combined friction of the guard rail and the police vehicle braking brought both cars to a halt in less than thirty metres.

Peter aimed his weapon out of his window, unable to open his door as it was jammed against the driver's side of the Lexus. Fearing Sergey would unleash a barrage of shots, Ballard was amazed to see the Russian dive across to the passenger seat and with two sharp elbow jabs, shatter his already half-lowered side window. Heaving himself upwards he crawled from the Lexus. Desperate to exit their vehicle the detectives had to wait frustrating seconds for motorists to hurtle past before they could scramble out, all having to alight on the driver's side.

Traffic chaos ensued as cars banked up behind them. Drivers tooted horns as they leaned out their windows, hurling abuse; two nose-to-tail accidents had the detectives spinning around, relieved the collisions were minor. Racing across the front of the Lexus they spotted Sergey vaulting the safety rail while looking along the single inbound lane to his left. Realising there was no time for a carjacking he dashed between vehicles to cross the roadway.

All five detectives bellowed variations of *"Police!" "Stop!" "Stay where you are!"* with John throwing in *"shithead"* for good measure. They might as well have bayed at the moon as they watched the Russian vault the second guard rail and front up to the pedestrian walkway which was fully enclosed in mesh and topped with barbed wire. Shouting to passing pedestrians John warned them to back away which they did in haste when they saw the detectives' weapons. Additional cars swept past, further delaying them from crossing the single lane.

To their surprise Sergey turned and stared momentarily at a point behind them. Ballard swivelled, spotting the *Sea Princess* cruise liner approaching the bridge from Barangaroo Wharf. The ship was less than two hundred metres away. An omen shook Ballard to his core, his mind in turmoil at what he believed the Russian was about to attempt. "I think the bastard's about to jump onto the cruise ship as it passes underneath us."

"*Bullshit!* The idiot will kill himself." John was adamant, adding seconds later, "But it'll save us a shitload of paperwork if he does."

Aware the detectives couldn't fire for fear of hitting nearby onlookers, Sergey sneered in their direction before turning away. In just a few eye-popping seconds he scaled the walkway's wire mesh canopy, utilising one of the supporting metal arches. Negotiating the barbed wire across the top with ease he clambered down the other side and dropped below the walkway.

Ballard noted with regret the injuries he had inflicted appeared to have little or no impact on the Russian's freedom of movement. Sightseers pressed against the security mesh to gain a clearer view of what to them was a madman attempting a very public suicide, their mobiles held high to capture the incident unfolding before them.

Peter, along with Delwyn and Toby gaped at his performance. "Jesus Mike, how the hell does he plan to get onto the ship?"

Ballard watched the liner's approach beneath them, predicting the next sequence of events. "The clearance between the gangway either side of that thing's radar is less than four metres from the underside of the bridge. *I know what the bastard's going to do*! He'll climb down to the lowest point of the bridge and by hanging from the bottom girder his feet will be less than a metre from the walkway." Ballard's lips curled into a snarl. "Providing he times it and doesn't lob onto the radar, his landing will be softer than most parachute jumps."

Delwyn spat out an unladylike profanity. "What in God's name do we have to do to nail this bastard?"

Shaking his head Toby declared, "This is bloody unbelievable." The detectives waited for a gap in the traffic then dashed across the lane, climbing onto the Armco railing, clutching the pedestrian walkway security mesh for stability. The *Sea Princess* was now directly beneath them as pedestrians lined the far side, equally curious as to the fate of the Russian.

Travelling at what Ballard estimated to be eight knots, the bow of the ship came into view and the resultant cries from the gathered crowd on the walkway foretold that Sergey had either fallen to his death or successfully made the transition. Seconds later the gangway appeared, so too Sergey who was leaning back against the railing, one leg crossed over the other, casual and supremely arrogant. Looking up he threw a mocking salute to where he knew the detectives would be standing.

Risking life and limb Toby sprinted back to the police car, popping the boot before returning with two pairs of binoculars. Thrusting one towards Delwyn he peered through the other as the *Sea Princess* began to alter course, progressing across the harbour towards the Heads. Sergey was nowhere to be seen. Toby contacted the Water Police radio operator, organising for the police launch to rendezvous with the *Sea Princess*. The operator advised that the launch was currently clearing Potts Point. Relaying his mobile number to the operator he requested the launch captain call him immediately. After disconnecting he waited, agitated, looking towards Delwyn whose frustration mirrored his own.

Moments later he was rewarded, going on to explain the circumstances to a disbelieving water police captain. "I'm telling you the prick dropped onto the bloody boat *as it was going under the bridge*. I'll explain how he did it when things calm down. Contact the Sydney Port Authority and have them notify the captain of the *Sea Princess* he has an intruder who literally dropped onto his upper deck if he doesn't know already. This is going to cock up the ship's schedule but insist the Port Authority order the ship to stop, heave to, or whatever the bloody hell the naval term is. Also have them advise the *Sea Princess* captain this guy's ex-Spetsnaz and was responsible for the Parliament House siege in Victoria. Get the message across loud and clear this prick won't hesitate to slaughter anyone who gets in his way.

"I'll arrange for a team from Specialist Ops to head down to your office so they can be taken out to the liner. Flushing him out of a cruise ship that size is going to be a task and a half. Your role in the meantime is to remain with the ship and monitor the situation—*nothing more.*" Toby followed this with a call to the Specialist Operations headquarters, relaying the basic details yet again, adding the boarding party was to take every precaution.

An extended screech of tyres and the unmistakable crunch of vehicles colliding heavily had all four detectives spinning around to see two cars skewed sideways on the bridge's inside lane, the following traffic banking bumper to bumper behind the crash site. Two men leapt out of the damaged vehicles and began arguing furiously while the drivers in the trailing cars honked their horns, a number leaning out their windows, shaking fists to vent their anger.

John shrugged, motioning to his colleagues. "I guess I should make myself useful sorting out this bloody fiasco until the uniforms arrive." Making a move forward he was halted abruptly by a sudden explosion as the petrol tank on one of the impacted cars exploded.

Rocked backwards by the blast of scorched air, one of the feuding drivers tripped, landing heavily on the road's surface. In an act of bravery and in sharp contrast to their argument moments before, the second driver grabbed the fallen man's arm and hauled him unceremoniously from the petrol fuelled inferno. The cars behind attempted unsuccessfully to reverse, creating further collisions and confusion.

Galvanised into action, the detectives raced back to the police vehicle, Toby popping the boot and snatching a fire extinguisher. John accompanied him to the burning Mazda, having grabbed an extinguisher from a driver who had stepped onto the roadway. Both detectives attempted to halt the fire from spreading under nearby vehicles; the smoke and heat generated making the task hit and miss. Additional drivers, along with several passengers joined the fray, all armed with extinguishers, focussing on the rivers of ignited fuel streaming in every direction, the scene one of utter chaos.

Ballard, Peter and Delwyn did their best to divert the remaining lanes of traffic around the Mazda, with Ballard snarling, "I tell you what Delwyn, that bloody Russian has a lot to answer for."

Seconds later the Lenco Bearcat armoured car arrived, nosing in behind the Lexus. Specialist Operations officers piled out, their expressions one of understandable confusion as they approached Toby who had returned to the police car. Utilising the police radio he urgently requested the fire brigade before resuming his coordination of the Specialist Ops boarding party heading out to the *Sea Princess*.

John switched from fire fighter to backup traffic controller by assisting his colleagues direct cars around the charred vehicle, his extinguisher long since empty, the flames now limited to the immediate vicinity of the Mazda's burnt-out shell. It was a full ten minutes before a uniform van arrived with lights flashing and siren blaring to clear a path through the congestion, the officers taking over the traffic duties much to Delwyn's relief, fearful that John's overzealous directing would result in him being run over by an inattentive rubber-necking motorist.

A quick series of photographs were taken of the Lexus and police vehicles in situ while John confirmed none of the panels on Toby's car were sufficiently damaged to prevent it from being driven. Aware that the Major Collision Investigation unit would normally attend before they could move, they knew this wasn't the time for departmental procedure. Leaving the uniform officers to continue directing traffic, the detectives piled into Toby's vehicle, the next stop his office at police headquarters.

Gazing out the car window at the fifteen-storey Curtis Chang building in Charles Street, Parramatta, John took in the glass facade of Sydney's Police Headquarters with a slow nod directed at Ballard, both men reflecting on the vulnerability of the structure to a terrorist attack. They left their concerns unspoken, Sergey's escape their immediate priority.

Parking the car inside the building, Toby rushed the detectives to his office. All watched on as he took a phone call, his expression changing from concerned to relieved, then almost jubilant. He ended the conversation with "Just make bloody sure you treat this bastard as though there were ten of him, okay?" Eying each detective in turn he revealed, "That was the launch captain. Don't ask me why but Sergey just dived off the side of the cruise ship into the harbour."

John's mouth dropped open, confused. "You're kidding me."

Toby shook his head. "Nup, the launch is about to pick him up. The police chopper's overhead and streaming vision of the arrest into our Major Incident room."

Alarm bells reverberated in Ballard's head. "How many members are on the launch?"

"Why, er . . . the captain and two crew."

Ballard saw Delwyn and Peter staring at him, equally troubled. "*Think* about it Toby. Sergey would know a Specialist Operations team is being scrambled as we speak. Generally how many would be in the boarding party?"

"At least ten."

"How long will it take for them to get out to the *Sun Princess*?"

"I've just been told they're five minutes away from the Water Police headquarters, so by the time they load their gear into the inflatable and get mobile I'd say at least fifteen minutes before they're alongside."

"There you go—ten or so Specialist Ops fifteen minutes away. Sergey would know if he remains on the ship he'll be arrested, even if it takes a day for the team to flush him out. By jumping in the water he's figuring the police launch will only have a basic crew on board which swings the odds in his favour."

Ballard's sense of alarm peaked. "Toby, get the captain on the mobile and have him circle Sergey until reinforcements arrive. Tell him *not* to let the Russian on-board *no matter what*."

The comprehension that dawned on Toby's face said it all. Snatching his phone he barked, "*Follow me.*"

Traversing the stairs two at a time, with Delwyn outperforming her colleagues, Toby led everyone up two flights before bursting into a corridor on the sixth floor. Pounding past several doors, they entered a room which could have been the twin of the Critical Incident room in the crime building in Melbourne. Multiple flat-screen monitors were located on the walls along with overhead projectors; computer screens were strategically placed throughout. Six police officers sat at the conference table, two in uniform the rest in plain clothes. All were glued to a screen displaying an aerial shot of the *Sea Princess*, alongside it the Steber police launch rolled gently in the half-metre swell.

The occupants spun in their chairs, taken aback by Toby and his group's abrupt entrance, introductions not even contemplated. Waving a reassuring hand Toby and the four detectives grabbed spare chairs each, focussing on the screen above them.

They saw Sergey swimming towards the launch, his strokes effortless, now less than thirty metres away.

"*Pick up. Pick up.*" Toby rocked back and forth in his chair, frustrated as he clasped the mobile to his ear. He barked to the group at the table, "Can you get radio contact with the launch?"

They all stared, paralysed with indecision.

"I need to speak with the captain. *NOW!*"

The urgency in his voice galvanised a young sergeant who grabbed a UHF radio transmitter off one of the tables beneath the screens and began issuing the call sign for the launch.

Fixated on the screen, Ballard watched as Sergey drew alongside the police boat. A sickening foreboding flooded his senses, matched by the expression on his partners' faces. Delwyn's hand was clasped over her mouth in an identical gesture to that when she had witnessed Sergey executing the politicians on Parliament House steps.

Ballard heard the sergeant continue to repeat the call sign but the image on the screen showed all three officers positioned near the launch's stern, two of them with drawn weapons.

"*Goddam it.* The captain's focussing on arresting Sergey." The mobile still in his hand, Toby pounded it against his forehead in helpless frustration.

Hissing to John who was beside him, Ballard declared in a voice shaking with emotion, "This is going to be another Halls Gap massacre." He felt light-headed, the overwhelming sensation numbing his consciousness even more confronting than the earlier tragedy. In this instance he knew in advance the hideous action that was about to unfold.

John responded. "Jesus Mike, this is a bloody nightmare, and there's *nothing* we can do to stop it."

Paralysed with fear for the three police officers safety, all in the room stared transfixed as Sergey held up a hand to be pulled on-board. The two armed crew stood apart, bracing against the waves, their weapons directed at the Russian. The captain's grip was wrist on wrist, hauling Sergey onto the swim deck.

For a split second it appeared a successful arrest was about to be achieved, but without warning the Russian collapsed, appearing to faint. What followed was a sickening textbook take-down by a highly trained military soldier.

Instinctively the two crewmen moved closer, one of them within easy reach of Sergey's sweeping kick as he lay on the deck. Dropping the officer onto his back, the Russian pounced on him, seizing the man's weapon. Because of Sergey's proximity to the fallen officer the second crew member couldn't fire, appearing uncertain what to do. The captain leapt onto the Russian's shoulders but was flung backwards. Teetering on the edge of the swim deck he lost his footing and fell overboard.

Sergey fired two shots, the first taking out the crew member still standing, the second killing the officer lying on the deck. Sergey then aimed at the captain scrambling to get back on-board. Two shots found their mark and the policeman rolled over, floating face down, blood pooling around his undulating body.

The entire action took less than ten seconds leaving everyone in the room in shock, senses numb, forgetting to breathe. Cries of disbelief eventually burst from dry lips as everyone glanced amongst themselves, helpless rage boiling over. The image of the police launch came into sharper focus as the chopper dropped to a lower altitude showing Sergey dumping both slain policemen overboard as though discarding rubbish.

Ballard looked to Toby whose face was ashen, matching the expressions of those around the table. "How many crew members are in the chopper?"

The homicide detective nodded before answering, as though confirming the facts in his own mind. "The pilot, an observer, and a rear crew member."

"Armed?"

Another nod. "But only with Glocks which Sergey now has two of."

"I can understand why the aircrew wants to get closer to put a bullet in the bastard—he's just shot three of their own—but the Russian's a crack marksman. Unless they have rifles and can sit off and take him out from a distance they'll need to keep well clear. Sergey will hit them long before they hit him."

Ballard's comments proved prophetic as everyone watched the Russian drop to one knee, bracing against the side of the launch as he fired systematically at the chopper. The image on the screen swung wildly as the chopper banked hard and climbed out of range, reestablishing its position at a much safer distance.

The sergeant at the radio transmitter turned questioningly towards Toby who barked an order. "Get PolAir on the blower and warn them to maintain their altitude. They're to observe and track only. The last thing we need is to have a chopper and its crew taken out."

Contacting the Water Police radio operator, Toby was informed the boarding party was good to go. Passing on the current situation while watching the screen, Toby informed the operator that Sergey had now taken control of the police launch and was heading across the harbour in the direction of Taronga Zoo.

Peter leaned across and placed a hand on Delwyn's arm, speaking softly so Toby wouldn't hear yet loud enough for Ballard and John to catch his words. "The bastard's outsmarted us yet again. The chance of the Specialist Ops catching him is bugger all. The best the chopper can do is track him but once he hits the shore he'll disappear. All we can hope for is he doesn't add to the body count."

Toby finished his call, slumping in his chair. "I saw the footage of this prick and what he did at your Parliament House." Appearing shell-shocked he shook his head. "But seeing first-hand what he's capable of over the last forty-five minutes is staggering. There doesn't appear to be any way of stopping him." He added, "VKG is coordinating units to try to corner him, but from what I've just witnessed that's not looking promising." The four detectives could offer nothing to lift his negative thoughts. "Those poor men. They were like lambs being led to slaughter, and in reality that's what it was. VKG is sending out a recovery team for the bodies."

The Halls Gap wave of guilt flooded Ballard's consciousness once more, a voice in his head challenging him to accept some of the blame for what had just taken place.

As though reading Ballard's thoughts, Delwyn placed a comforting arm around Toby's shoulder, her voice low with pain. "I feel equally to blame. Sergey's *our* problem yet we've driven him across the border to your patch, and now this has happened."

Toby attempted to shake free of his justifiable grief. "I don't need to remind you Delwyn, crooks of this bastard's calibre don't respect borders. As coppers our job is to lock 'em up. We just got outsmarted."

John chipped in, "What I want to know is *how* are these Spetsnaz soldiers trained? I mean the man's superhuman. He shows *no* self-doubt, *no* fear . . . doesn't even appear to feel pain. Christ, imagine any of us hanging under the Harbour Bridge and dropping onto a bloody passing cruise liner."

Peter was furious, unable to take his eyes from the screen which showed the chopper still tracking the police launch as it headed towards Taronga Zoo. "*Nothing a bloody bullet in the bugger's skull wouldn't fix*, and if I'm ever given the opportunity I won't be hesitating." His tone made it clear his outburst wasn't an idle threat.

The sergeant drew their attention by increasing the volume of the UHF transmitter so everyone could hear the interaction between the chopper and VKG. All eyes focussed on the screen with renewed intensity as they heard the PolAir pilot advise that Sergey had swung the police launch to port in the direction of Curraghbeena Point.

Toby cursed as he pinched the bridge of his nose, contemplating various scenarios. "Bugger me, if he gets ashore there it'll be nigh on impossible for PolAir to track him. That suburb has wall-to-wall homes throughout and he's sitting pretty to steal a car from any one of them, not to mention undercover car parks in the nearby shopping centres. The chopper crew won't have a clue which vehicle he's in." Raking his fingers through his hair he turned to the detectives. "I don't want to sound defeatist but my guess is the show's over for today. This guy's about to vanish into thin air."

Unwilling to accept an arrest wasn't still possible John offered, "VKG will concentrate uniform and plainclothes units in the area. Toby it's *not* a done deal yet, we may get lucky."

The homicide detective shook his head, despondent, wanting to believe in John's optimism but experienced enough to know the unfolding scenario was going to end badly. "Armed with two Glocks and God knows how many rounds and a heap more if he stripped spare clips off the officers before dumping them overboard, Christ he could unleash a shootout the likes of which this state has never seen."

This was a scenario no one could deny considering the devastation Sergey had wreaked to this point. From their eye in the sky, they continued to watch as the Russian skilfully manoeuvred the launch to the edge of a small jetty. Jumping off he abandoned the craft, allowing it to drift from the shore. He began loping along a side street at a speed that was testimony yet again to the man's incredible physical ability.

The chopper maintained a visual up to the point the Russian entered an underground car park as feared by Toby. The detective sat with his head bowed, appearing overwhelmed. Police units swarmed within minutes but not before at least twenty cars had emerged from the car park exit and driven off in all directions, presenting the crew on board PolAir with an impossible dilemma.

For the next twenty minutes they sat watching the coverage. The Specialist Operations team disembarked from their inflatable to commence their search of the car park as well as the shopping centre. As the minutes ticked by John conceded Sergey had indeed slipped the net.

Delwyn rang the pilots on the Beechcraft and after conferring with Toby, notified them to obtain authorisation for a return flight leaving at 5 p.m. Double-checking the time she was dumbfounded that all they had experienced had taken place in just under four hours.

Everyone stood, abject weary, with Delwyn reiterating her regret. "Toby I can't tell you how sorry I am to have dragged you and your poor officers into this debacle. Not that you weren't aware earlier, but now you know first-hand what we're up against with this monster." She quickly ran over the arrests made at the Melbourne Club and the hope this had disrupted The Board's plans to take control of the ports in Melbourne and Sydney.

"And Sergey was the final piece in the puzzle."

"Yes Toby, and a very vital piece but John's right. If not now, at some point in the future we'll get him, and we'll put him in jail where he'll die of old age or more likely from The Board putting a hit on him. Personally I'd rather the latter as this will save the taxpayers a heap of money."

The flight back to Essendon Airport in the Beechcraft was a melancholy affair, in sharp contrast to the expectant mood on the flight up. Each detective reflected on the events which cost three innocent lives and achieved nothing in return. John swore at regular intervals while describing what he would do to Sergey, aware the laws of the land didn't allow for such barbaric actions.

Peter made a heartfelt attempt to be philosophical, but his words fell on deaf ears. Delwyn kept her eyes on the passing horizon, contemplating the explanation she would have to provide the AC, mindful of what his reaction would be.

Ballard resurrected his dark thoughts at Halls Gap where for agonising seconds he had been a squeeze of the trigger away from executing Sergey. In hindsight this would have saved innocent lives and given the identical circumstances he was in two minds whether he would be able to resist his primal urge to put Sergey down like the mad dog he was. His bleak thoughts occupied him for the remainder of the flight, intermingled with Marjorie's earlier words of concern for his state of mind.

CHAPTER
29

The AC's clenched fist struck the Critical Incident table with such force that cups rattled in their saucers, water trembled in glasses and attendees jumped in their seats. Eyes blazing, his attention was focussed above all their heads, as though castigating the gods who had allowed Sergey to evade arrest yet again and in the process murder three policemen. "While I'm not advocating a formal shoot-on-sight order, the time has come that should we *ever* get this guy in a position where we can arrest him and he looks like adding to his already horrendous body count, this may be our only option."

Peter's impassive expression as his eyes met Ballard's spoke volumes, while the others sat nonplussed, unsure whether the AC was thinking aloud or deliberately sending a less-than-subtle message. Tim was particularly conscious of the ramifications of the AC's comment, aware his team would in all probability be responsible for bringing the Russian's reign of terror to an end.

The AC broke from his momentary musings. "That said, on the positive side the arrests at the Melbourne Club have at least bloodied The Board's nose so we need to maintain our momentum by keeping on the front foot." James Patterson who was sitting alongside the AC took up the senior officer's ceiling-gazing pose, deep in thought. Both Ballard and John were certain the ASIO officer was dubious The Board's nose was as bloodied as the AC proclaimed.

Undeterred the senior officer continued. "However, before we progress on any further"—he smiled at Bernard who was on his right, clapping a grateful hand on the Texan's broad shoulders—"on behalf of everyone I want to thank you and your son for the tireless work you've done. Your contacts flushed out Vladimir when the Parliament House siege was at a critical stage, then you located Sergey holed up in Sydney. We couldn't have asked for more, and notwithstanding the unbelievable tragedy of the police officers' deaths at Halls Gap and now on Sydney Harbour, we came within a blink of catching the bastard."

Bernard was sombre but defiant in his confidence the Russian was on borrowed time. "He can only pull off so many circus acts until his luck runs out. I'm assuming you'd like Bernard Junior to continue tracking him?"

The AC grunted his confirmation. "*Too bloody right.*"

The surveillance requirements confirmed, the AC turned to James, Peter, and Delwyn, a ghost of a smile forming. "So, who drew the short straw to interview DC Salisbury?"

Peter held up his hand. "I believe I've been granted that privilege sir. Perhaps you'd like to sit in on proceedings?"

The AC flashed a cold smile, appearing to contemplate the offer before disappointing the gathering. "No, I'm almost certain I'd lose it and end up punching the bastard on the nose, and that wouldn't help our case nailing him in court."

Peter chuckled. "I understand but let me know if you change your mind."

The AC turned serious. "Who's got Vladimir?"

Ballard and John received a confirming nod from Delwyn before Ballard pointed to himself and John. "That'd be us."

The AC grunted a second time. "Good." He locked eyes with John. "Speaking of punching offenders on the nose, just keep your hands in your pockets, there's a good chap."

Despite the subdued mood, the mental image of John launching across the interview table and choking Vladimir had spirits lifting, reducing the tension in the room which was the AC's intent.

John duly mumbled his compliance, pretending his dignity was injured but understanding his actions over the years negated any possibility of sympathy.

"So that leaves five other high-profile offenders and our favourite Russian diplomat's wife Tatiana, to face the music."

Delwyn added dryly, "As you'd be aware sir, Tatiana's currently enjoying three very basic meals a day by her standards at the Dame Phyllis Frost Centre. I'll be conducting the interview regarding her murdered her husband, and I've asked Marjorie Otterman to sit in with me. She'll pick up anything I might miss from a psychologist's point of view." She paused. "As for the three businessmen, plus the retired admiral and the former magistrate, I'll divide them up between Ken, Bobby, and Susan who'll knock the interviews over in the next couple of days." There was collective head shaking at the impressive social standing of the arrested cell members, accompanied by mystified looks at how so many could be involved with such a treacherous group of criminals, demonstrating the far reach and intent of The Board.

The AC raised the issue of prisoner security. "I've been on the blower with the Commissioner for Corrections. He assures me each of the prisoners have been isolated at the remand centre, *and* they're under twenty-four-seven video surveillance."

Peter drew the AC's attention. "Now that Vladimir, Tatiana, and the rest of the cell members have been arrested, I'd like to have one final crack at the ports minister. It'll be low-key of course to maintain his safety and that of his family. I believe if we can assure him Tatiana's threat no longer exists, we *may* be able to convince him to unload something worthwhile to pin on those we arrested at the club. We need this because other than Vladimir and Tatiana we've actually got bugger all on the rest of them."

The AC pondered for a moment, fiddling with the teaspoon resting on his saucer, evaluating the personal and political ramifications while mindful of the potential threat still hanging over the minister's head. Within seconds he made his decision. Clearing his throat he barked, "*Go for it*. You saved his life so he owes the department big time. Plus he's got a hell of a lot of explaining to do if he wants to stay out of the can. Yes, keep it low-key as you said but make him an offer he can't refuse." There were smiles all round.

Checking the wall clock, the AC was surprised it showed 7.30 p.m. "Folks it's been another long day and even longer for some." He directed his comment to the four detectives who were beginning to show the strain of their disastrous interstate trip. "Go home, make sure you get a good night's rest then come back in the morning ready to keep these bastards behind bars for the rest of their lives."

Natalie took one look at the fatigue lines etched deep into Ballard's face. She hugged him for longer than usual, hoping the stress he was feeling would ease. Reaching up on tiptoe she brushed his cheek before leading the way into the kitchen where he sat down to a plate of leftover roast chicken and vegetables. "Now eat! You can have your shower later. Afterwards, it's straight to bed with you."

"Am I on a promise?"

Natalie's exasperation put paid to that proposition. "You'll be lucky to stay awake during your shower let alone make offers you can't fulfil." She eyed him, unsure whether to raise the Harbour Bridge incident, which she had followed on the news channel, including the amateur footage of all four detectives in pursuit of Sergey climbing under the massive structure.

Ballard guessed her thoughts as he finished a mouthful, putting down his cutlery. He held her gaze. "I'm sorry to say he slipped our net yet *again*." The last word was spat in frustration.

Natalie sighed as she stood behind him, massaging his shoulders. "Darling I'm just glad you and the others are okay, but I feel so sad for those three poor policemen and their families."

Ballard kept eating but for once the meal wasn't registering, his continued consumption pure reflex, aware he had to maintain his strength for the long days ahead. In spite of his obvious distress at the events in Sydney, to Natalie's bewilderment he finished his meal then winked at her as he suggested, "Ice cream?"

Shaking her head she dug into the freezer and in no time presented him with three scoops of pecan caramel ice cream drizzled with dark chocolate, enough calories to raise the cholesterol level of an ox. Hesitant, she asked, "Will he *ever* be caught?"

Ballard's laden spoon remained suspended on its journey, the chocolate topping threatening the lace tablecloth. "This may sound trite darling, but yes, he *will* be. Guys like that always come unstuck eventually—or end up dead."

Natalie's eyes watered. "I know you can't answer this with any certainty Michael but I miss having the children here with me. And I know it's for their own safety they're with Mum and Dad, but when is this nightmare *ever* going to end?"

His spoon returning to the bowl, Ballard sighed as he squeezed her hand, a deep sorrow running through him. "I know sweetheart. This is the question we're all asking ourselves. When *will* it end? Thankfully he appears to be holed up in Sydney for now and doesn't look like heading south any time soon."

Natalie's supreme effort to smile wasn't convincing. "I guess that's some consolation."

Ballard returned the hug she had given him earlier, attempting to reassure her. Holding her hand he led her to the lounge. Attentive, he listened as she brought him up to speed on family news, her smile returning as her enthusiasm grew, her love for her children restoring her to something near her usual positive self.

Deciding to give the transformation a helping hand, he stared deep into her eyes. "When, not if this hiccup in our lives is resolved, let's take a trip to Italy like I suggested in New Zealand. Rome, Florence, Venice, and Milan. Two weeks. A bit like our Paris trip, short but a goody."

Natalie's eyes widened before she lunged forward, flinging her arms around his neck. *"Michael, that sounds wonderful.* I'll start packing right away."

Laughing they trudged upstairs with Ballard admitting he was near the end of his reserves. Minutes later, as Natalie had predicted he was fast asleep. Remaining on the edge of the bed as she gazed down at him, her thoughts continued to jumble in her head.

CHAPTER
30

Ken, Bobby, and Susan sat straight backed in the homicide conference room, absorbing the advice being offered to them by Delwyn, each point accentuated with a stab of her forefinger. "These people have substantial standing in the community. They have egos. They're used to getting their own way, and other than Vladimir and Tatiana, we don't have anything concrete on them apart from their association with those two whom we're nailing for murder, armed robbery, blackmail, and extortion. Getting anything to stick in court on the other five will be as difficult as getting a magnet to attract plastic."

Ballard and John smiled at one another, mildly amused at Delwyn's left-field example.

"Oh, I don't know Delwyn. It's amazing what they can do with plastic these days. I wouldn't rule it out entirely." John's lopsided grin widened. "But you're right about how hard it'll be nailing this lot to any charges which will stand up to a high-priced barrister." He allowed his gaze to fall on each of the young detectives. "You'll have bugger all options if they don't play ball, and they won't because they didn't get to where they are by being pushovers. That being so, you'll have to play your trump card and threaten them with The Board at some point in the proceedings."

Susan was doubtful. "Won't bringing The Board into play make them clam up even more?"

John nodded. "It will if it's all we're threatening them with. In this instance you'll need to get across to them that if they don't cooperate they'll be listed for court and more than likely The Board will weigh up the risk of them talking and have them taken out long before they even get to the witness stand. What they must be convinced of is *if* they're prepared to share intel which amounts to something of value, we *may* offer them witness protection. If not, they go to jail, and their chance of survival in there is pretty well zero."

Ballard joined in. "I agree. These guys are The Board's weak link at the moment. The fact they're in custody will have members in the upper echelon of the organisation *very* nervous. We need to act fast and wring every shred of information out of them as soon as possible."

Bobby nudged Ken who was looking even more serious than usual. "If our powers of persuasion fail what are the chances we can dabble in some short-term waterboarding?"

Ballard raised one brow. "Bobby if you'd been in the conference room yesterday and heard the AC you may well have gotten a nod. I can't remember the last time the boss was so gung ho. The news of the three police officers being shot doesn't fare well for Sergey's ongoing health from the AC's perspective."

Delwyn brought the conversation back to an even footing. "Okay, there you have it. Crucial interviews coming out of our ears and very little time to conduct them." She addressed the three senior detectives. "When are you going to interview the minister?"

Peter answered. "No time like the present. I'll make a call to arrange it."

Everyone prepared to leave, with Bobby leading the charge, his enthusiasm on overdrive.

The three detectives sat on the 86 tram, agreeing that the trip to Parliament House would be faster using public transport than if they were to drive and have to locate parking within the parliamentary grounds. Watching shoppers in the Bourke Street Mall go about their business John remarked, "If they only knew how close the big house on the hill came to being blown to smithereens."

Peter stared at his colleague, the words conjuring a horrendous image. In deep thought he added, "I guess we can thank Michael for distracting Sergey when it mattered." John winced, remembering too well the agonising hours during which he was convinced Ballard would die at the hands of the Russian.

Ballard felt the need to break the mood. "Tell me, was Davidson okay with us meeting him?"

Peter nodded and followed it with a ruthless smile. "He wasn't excited about it but like the AC requested I made him an offer he couldn't refuse."

"What did you say?"

"I told him there'd be far less publicity if we came to *his* office, no fuss, no bother, or . . ."

John chipped in, curious. "Or what?"

"Or we'd send a marked car up to Parliament House and he'd be escorted to *our* office."

Ballard's lower lip pursed as he gave a considered smile. "Yep, that'll do it every time for the average pollie. They love publicity, just not the wrong kind."

Piling out at the Spring Street tram stop the detectives crossed at the lights then mounted the imposing Parliament House steps. Pausing on the first landing they studied where the explosives truck had parked and near where Sergey had executed one of the politicians using a charge of C4. Several of the ornate lights remained damaged from the shockwave but the shattered windows on the ground and first floor had been replaced. Acknowledging the armed Protective Security officers they continued on up the steps.

Having left their weapons at the office, all three passed though the security scan without incident. Fronting the reception desk Peter indicated to a stocky security officer that the ports minister was expecting them. After handing them their passes, a phone call was made and they didn't have to wait long before Laurie Davidson approached, looking very different to when they had last seen him buried in the sand. Dapper in a dark suit, pale-blue business shirt and charcoal-grey tie, and with his full head of hair slicked down he appeared every bit the successful politician. What put paid to that outward appearance was his cautious disposition. Having difficulty maintaining eye contact with his visitors it was obvious he knew the meeting wasn't going to be a pleasant one. Offering an indecisive handshake he indicated the way.

The detectives followed the minister along a wide corridor and up a carpeted flight of stairs to his office where chairs were set out in front of his desk. He chose to join them rather than sit behind the ornate mahogany masterpiece. John cast an appreciative eye over the intricate carving. To break the ice the minister expounded on John's obvious curiosity. "A gift from my grandfather when I was first elected." John ran an approving hand over the polished woodwork, clearly impressed.

Peter made it clear he wasn't in the mood for pleasantries. Adopting a blunt persona he launched into his first question. "After your little incident at Altona Beach the other night are you still married?"

The minister swallowed hard, and it was clear he was near emotional meltdown. "Yes I am, but things aren't good on the home front as you can imagine." He appeared beaten, slumping low in his seat, his breathing ragged, almost a shudder. "I just pray we both get through this. I don't know how but we're trying for the kids' sake."

Peter gave the impression he was sympathetic but his next words were far from compassionate. "You'll get through it if you take our advice, something you've refused to do up to this point. While your private life is of no interest to us we need to know where you stand on the marital front while we attempt to dig you and your family out of this mess." He leaned forward, closing the gap between himself and the minister. "Because of your involvement with these criminals I can pass on *some* information which normally I wouldn't be able to for confidential reasons."

He gave Ballard a sideways glance before continuing, "We've recently made a number of arrests and they include the woman who was responsible for you being buried up to your neck down at the beach."

Ballard couldn't be sure but he thought he observed the minister tremble, shuffling to mask the action, there being no doubt now as to his emotional fragility.

Peter continued, ruthless, giving no quarter, "I don't know what deals you've set in motion to allow these criminals access to the ports here in Melbourne but we *do* need to know the extent of it, and right away. That'll involve you being interviewed by contract specialists and our Legal Services Department who are more qualified in these matters than we are. Our job"—he waved at Ballard and John before pointing to himself—"our job is to deal with the threats made against you and your family which we assume resulted from you getting tangled up with this mob in the first place." He dragged his chair even closer, now fully in the minister's face. "I accept their intimidation is the *reason* for your involvement. What I don't accept is it being an *excuse* for you not reporting their coercion to us. Had you done that we could have protected you and your family if need be in witness protection."

Ballard maintained a neutral expression, as did John despite both weighing up whether they would have reported the threats to police were it them in the firing line. The decision would have been line ball, notwithstanding both men were aware Peter had no option but to push the department's official line.

The preamble over, the superintendent came to the point of the meeting. "Prior to interviewing the criminals we arrested—"

"Were the arrests those at the Melbourne Club?" The minister blurted the question and by the look on his face he appeared certain of the answer.

Again Peter glanced at Ballard and John before replying. "Yes, they were. Now we need to know who approached you and forced you to make alternate contract decisions." He waited expectantly.

"Nobody approached me."

"*What?*" The detectives exclaimed as one.

"Nobody *approached* me. Everything was done by snail mail. At first I received envelopes at my office. They contained photos of my wife and my two children—at the shop, being dropped off at school, in the park, along with a typed letter directing I *not* go to the police." The minister's eyes welled, but he forced himself to continue. "Next I received letters demanding I steer the contract negotiations in a certain direction."

"When was the first letter?"

"Almost a year ago at the beginning of the tender process." His face twisted. "I've been living under this threat ever since."

"Does your wife know about any of this?" Ballard posed the question, guessing the answer.

The minister shook his head, miserable. "No, I was told awful, *terrible* things would happen to her and the kids if I so much as breathed a word of this. Of course I haven't been myself at home and Sheree, my wife, she's certain I'm having an affair."

The detectives looked amongst themselves, impressed how the cell had eliminated the risk of the wife becoming aware and perhaps going to the police should she have learned her husband was being threatened. It was also clear the cell had avoided creating any electronic footprint by adopting cold war techniques to make their demands.

Peter decided to press the point. "You're telling me *no one* . . . *not a single soul* physically approached you, or contacted you over the phone regarding the port tenders?"

The minister looked back at him, defeated, not bothering to reply, emotionally crushed by the life-threatening predicament he now found himself and his family in.

"Did you by any chance keep any of the letters or photos . . . copies of them?"

A head shake preceded an emphatic, "No, each one ordered me to burn or shred everything, even the envelope."

"Which you did?" John appeared resigned.

"Which I did."

Peter hesitated, preparing to ask the major question, aware it would change the minister's life and his family's forever. "Are you prepared to go into witness protection if we deem it necessary?"

The minister's eyes widened as his mouth dropped open, words failing him.

Peter waited, aware of the gravity of his question.

"How long would I need to be in . . . in"—he struggled with the concept—"*in witness protection?*" He tensed, fearing the worst, clearly wanting the detectives to wave a magic wand.

Peter didn't provide one. "Worst-case scenario for life."

The minister slid even further in his chair if that were possible, hands washing over his face, ageing ten years in as many seconds. "I . . . I just don't know. My life will . . . *our* life will be turned—"

Peter cut him short. "Yes, your life will be turned upside down but you'll still be alive, and your wife and your children can get on with theirs."

The silence was excruciating, the detectives aware witness protection wasn't as convenient as the casual throwaway lines delivered by smooth talking TV detectives to victims of crime. Rather it was a harsh life sentence, one which shaped an individual's future forever, and rarely for the better.

The minister was ashen, appearing near collapse. "I . . . I just can't conceive not having my wife and children in my life. I . . . it would *kill* me!" He broke off before pleading, "Is there any *immediate* threat to myself and my family?" His anguish was palpable, a panicked look flooding his eyes.

Peter relented. "You're still of value to the criminals, so no, not that we know of."

"*Not that you know of?*" Incredulous, the minister's voice rose. He was stunned Peter couldn't be more specific and was desperate for something positive to grasp on to.

"Our case is very fluid, but hopefully when we've conducted more interviews with those we've arrested things will become clearer. There's no point in blowing smoke at you. Believe me there's still an incredible number of unknowns in this investigation."

There was a sharp rap on the door and an aide poked his head in. "Minister, you've been summoned in chambers for the divisional vote." In the distance a bell could be heard ringing. The head retreated, and the door was closed softly, the aide sensing something grave was afoot.

The detectives rose, followed by the minister, his expression implying he had more issues to discuss but was aware there was no time to broach them.

Peter held out his hand. "We'll be in touch to arrange a time for the more contractual interviews I mentioned." He took out his card. "Contact me day or night if there's *anything* you think I should be made aware of.

The minister nodded, his eyes haunted. After slipping Peter's card into his breast pocket he shook hands before leading them back to the foyer. Handing in their passes they emerged into bright sunlight. Descending the steps each was in deep thought and not without sympathy for the minister and the predicament he now found himself and his family in.

Breathing in the warm summer air John summed up the meeting in his usual blunt manner, "In the wrong job at the wrong time and knee deep in the wrong tender."

Ballard turned to his partner. "Yep, that's about the tall and short of it."

CHAPTER
31

Delwyn glanced up as the three detectives approaching her office. By the time they had entered she was backed against the front of her desk, arms braced, her expectation unmistakable.

"*Well?*" The single word demanded positive news but she was prepared for the worst and wasn't disappointed.

Peter scoffed. "These bloody Russians, they think the cold war never ended, and their sixties tactics haven't changed either. The cell utilised letter drops to direct the minister's actions which meant he never set eyes on *any* of the group's members. On top of that threats of pretty awful things happening to his family guaranteed he dare not speak to anyone about this whole sordid affair, *including his wife.*" He conveyed the impression he wanted to punch someone, anyone, exasperated at not having an immediate target.

Delwyn agreed that interviewing the five businessmen was now significantly more difficult without incriminating evidence from the minister. She stated the obvious, "So there'll need to be secret follow up interviews with Davidson."

Peter confirmed what had been requested. "Yes, we made it clear that from a contractual perspective he has to detail what strings he pulled to get The Board's nominated company or companies ensconced in the Melbourne port's tender process."

"Considering the threats do you think he'll cooperate?"

"He bloody well will if he wants to stay out of jail." John's gruff tone brooked no sympathy for the minister and his current predicament.

A smile appeared on Delwyn's face as she looked over the detectives' shoulders. A double tap on the door caught all three men's attention. Marjorie stood in the opening, immaculately dressed as ever in a cream blouse, navy skirt and sling-back sandals, her bare arms and legs lightly tanned.

"Perfect timing Marjorie." Delwyn moved around her desk to her seat as the detectives scrambled to offer their chair to the psychologist. Ballard indicated his would be more comfortable than John's, while his partner was adamant his offer was first therefore should be accepted.

"Cut it out you two." Delwyn winked at Marjorie who smiled back, finally settling on John's proposal.

Grinning triumphantly at Ballard, John hitched a trouser leg as he propped on the side of Delwyn's desk.

The superintendent got down to business. "Marjorie and I are about to head off to grill Tatiana."

Peter's tone was blunt. "Take no quarter Delwyn, our Ms Tatiana is as hard-nosed mentally as they come."

Delwyn held aloft a pink USB drive. "I'm guessing after she sees the let's-push-hubby-off-the-balcony footage she may be a tad more conciliatory."

Peter wasn't convinced. "Normally that'd be a slam dunk, but I'm telling you she's one tough cookie. She's just as likely to claim he slipped and she was only trying to catch him."

Marjorie smiled at Peter, inquisitive. "I hear you're tackling Salisbury. How do you think that'll go?"

Peter shook his head. "He'll attempt to intimidate me by playing the seniority card. He'd be aware our evidence is weak regarding his involvement with the cell." He grimaced. "In fact our case is all but non-existent. What we do have however, is him setting off gas bottles in the car park and attempting to run down these two fine detectives in a department police car." He added, "Even that's a problem because a good barrister will hammer home no one actually saw him shoot the gas bottles despite his firearm being short the same number of rounds we heard let off. And for that matter, why did he have his police issue weapon with him in the first place? On the flip side, regarding almost running Michael and John down—it'll be a case of Salisbury not spotting either of them until the last moment due to the smoke and the water raining down from the sprinklers. I hate to harp on the reality our case is paper thin with not much prospect of that changing I'm afraid. That's why something substantial from Davidson to tie Salisbury into this unholy mess would have wrapped this thing up rather neatly."

"You'll think of something Peter. You always do." Marjorie swung her attention to Ballard and John. "Vladimir?" She didn't elaborate.

John's levity over the musical chairs charade was long gone. "Yep, only this time there's no offers on the table. Twice we've been suckered in by this slippery shit. It won't happen a third time. He's going down for the count."

Delwyn began gathering everything she would need for the interview. "Even so John he's still a crucial link to The Board so we need to keep him on side. Let's face it, he and Tatiana were adamant in the love tapes he'd be the next top dog. It shows they must have *some* link with the central Russian arm of the group so tiptoe as much as you need to in order we get something of value out of him."

Shoving everything into her briefcase she scouted around to see if she had missed anything. "Ken, Bobby, and Susan are at the assessment centre as we speak. They're divvying up the other five." She paused, eying her audience. "In your wildest dreams who would have thought a retired admiral and a *magistrate* for God's sake would be wound up with this lot? The businessmen I understand. Greed 101. But an *admiral* and a *magistrate?* The criminal axis in this country is tilting at an alarming rate. I just hope we can get on top of it before we're overwhelmed."

CHAPTER
32

The Melbourne Assessment Centre loomed large on the opposite side of the intersection. The imposing structure appeared the embodiment of a fortified prison, shrieking impregnability in every sense of the word. The three detectives stood gazing at it on the north-west corner of La Trobe and Spencer Streets, waiting for the traffic lights to change.

John appeared thoughtful. "With our crime digs on this side they should think long and hard about building a tunnel under La Trobe Street to link the two so we can move prisoners with complete security."

Ballard and Peter measured their colleague's comment, giving his suggestion thoughtful consideration with Peter commenting, "You know John, there *are* times when you come up with some pretty rational ideas. As you said, the crime building's here to stay, so with the new police headquarters being built alongside, your tunnel suggestion is a damn sight more than just a thought bubble."

John aimed a smirk at Ballard, the expression lasting until Peter added, "Blowed if I can work out why you bugger up your good suggestions with so many dud ones."

Ballard laughed, punching the button for the traffic lights. The rapid-pulse pedestrian signal activated seconds later, and as the green man lit up the detectives strode forward three abreast.

Nudging Peter as they went, Ballard asked, "Following up on Marjorie's query, how do you *really* think you'll go with Salisbury?"

Pausing on the opposite footpath Peter lamented, "Not too well I'm afraid. Bugger me, even the chief rang yesterday to pass on background information regarding the guy, said he'd had doubts about him for years. That dovetailed into our AC's suspicions. The chief made it clear Davidson's a tough, old school copper who'll sit there and lie through his teeth to the extent you begin to doubt whether your own mother loves you."

John chuckled. "Mate, we've known for years your mum's been dead keen on distancing herself from you. The problem is she doesn't know how to go about it." He continued to cackle at his own joke.

After directing a withering glare his way, Peter led them into the remand centre. Having left their weapons behind as they had for their Parliament House visit, Ballard and Peter passed through the electronic security screen without triggering the alarm, but not so John, who, after much pocket slapping, produced a small bunch keys he had absent-mindedly picked up at the office.

Peter drawled out the corner of his mouth, "Serves you right."

The reception desk was occupied by a giant of a man whose speckled grey hair had been reduced to a buzz cut. His lantern jaw was sufficiently prominent to have the detectives double taking, something the guard appeared to be used to. Introducing themselves, Peter stated he had rung earlier to have prisoners Vladimir Bokaryov and Deputy Commissioner Cliff Salisbury secured in separate interview rooms.

The guard tapped keystrokes with sausage-like fingers then sat squinting at the screen, one meaty hand stroking his jaw while he deliberated. Just when the detectives feared there had been a mix-up the guard announced triumphantly, "*Here it is*, interview rooms 1 and 2 on the ground floor." He pressed a button and before long another guard appeared who was as physically dissimilar to the man behind the desk as could be imagined—at least a foot shorter, thirty kilograms lighter, and sporting a receding chin which was masked behind a weak excuse for a greying beard. By way of further contrast, this man was in a constant state of flux, a bundle of bustle and energy. It was all John could do not to laugh; a smothered snort erupted instead, resulting in Ballard elbowing him in the ribs.

Recovering John read the smaller guard's name tag. "I'm assuming we'll need to go through the huff-and-puff gizmo, Leonard?" Confused, Leonard stared at each detective in turn.

Ballard helped him out. "My partner's referring to the walk-through biotech scanner."

A light bulb moment materialised on the guard's face. "Ah, yes . . . huff and puff." He cackled long and hard. "Very funny. I'm going to call it that from now on." Spinning on his heel while still chuckling he took the lead along a tiled corridor to where the scanner was located.

Ballard grabbed Peter's arm, whispering, "Watch John's hair as he goes through." Both detectives stood back, allowing their partner to pass through first, nearly collapsing with laughter when they saw his shaggy locks standing on end as he was subjected to the strong jets of air.

"Okay smart-arses, let's see how dignified *you* look now it's *your* turn."

Scanning complete they were escorted to a dark-blue security door. Extracting a key attached to a lanyard, Leonard unlocked the door, holding it ajar for the detectives. Signs indicating interview rooms 1 and 2 were fixed to corresponding doors with associated viewing windows. Through the closest they saw Vladimir in room 1, dressed in civilian clothing, as usual sitting unperturbed, his expression composed, almost reflective, his left wrist shackled. John muttered an obscenity, unable to rein in his contempt for the Russian.

In room 2 the deputy commissioner's manner was the exact opposite. Dressed in the tuxedo he had been wearing when arrested at the Melbourne Club he was clearly furious, on several occasions testing the strength of the handcuff shackling his wrist which amused the detectives.

Ballard addressed Leonard. "Our colleagues are currently interviewing other prisoners." Pointing upwards he queried whether they were in the interview rooms on the next level.

Leonard nodded, his chin disappearing on each downward journey. "Yes, do you want to see them?"

Without waiting for a response he led off, the detectives following him through another security door and up one flight of stairs. Arriving at interview room 3 they watched Ken through the observation window. The admiral was sitting on the far side of the table, also wearing a tuxedo, his left wrist handcuffed to the table. Ken sat opposite, relaxed, appearing almost bored.

John scoffed, "I'll bet the navy guy thinks this is a pushover. That'll be a mistake. Ken'll tie him up in knots. Bugger me if I know how he does it, but he pulls off these heavy confessions one after another."

Ballard noted his partner's obvious pride for his younger charge, a pride John revelled in but would never relay to Ken, claiming too much praise often proved to be a demotivator. The next window showed a grey-haired man in his mid to late fifties being ferociously grilled by Susan and Bobby. The man's pinstripe suit was at least one size too large for him as he slumped in his chair, sporting a darkening bruise under his left eye.

John nodded. "Yeah, come to think of it Tim did mention one of the group cut up rusty when he was arrested, swinging punches all over the shop. Tim's guys must have clocked him one. Serves the bastard right. I'm assuming that's the magistrate. Gee, what I'd have given to be able to thump the bugger on the nose myself. As Delwyn said, the social makeup of this cell is incredible."

With Leonard standing patiently to one side they continued to watch Susan interact forcefully as she hammered home a crucial point, stabbing a forefinger onto the table top. Bobby hunched forward in his seat, enjoying his role as backup cop.

Ballard turned to his colleagues. "Before we get stuck into our two I'd like to hear what's been admitted by the admiral and this guy, not that I'm holding my breath."

John and Peter agreed.

Ballard tapped a short text to Ken, requesting he halt the interview unless he was in the middle of securing an admission. Within seconds the young detective reached forward, reading his mobile's screen.

Looking up he spoke briefly to the admiral then got to his feet, heading for the door.

Acknowledging the senior detectives, Ken could only shake his head. "I've been hard at it for just over an hour and I can tell you this guy's no pussy."

John was impatient. "Anything at all?"

"I started with irrefutable facts—that he was at the club in the same room as Tatiana and Vladimir, along with the DC and a number of businessmen."

"And?" John posed the question even though he knew the answer.

A shrug. "Well, he couldn't deny it and didn't attempt to. As a response he said, 'So what?' I then tried to find out whether he'd been to previous meetings. All I got was a vague 'Can't remember, I go to the Melbourne Club all the time . . . I'm retired in case you hadn't realised.'"

"Has he admitted to knowing Tatiana or Vladimir?" Peter's question was also delivered with minimal expectation.

"Nup, straight-batted me all the way."

"Does he show any concern his standing in the community is in tatters?" Ballard felt certain such a high-profile figure would have to feel remorse now his reputation was shot.

Ken put paid to the notion. "He's not giving *anything* away in that department, well, not on the face of it." Dropping into familiar profiler mode he added, "Quite often people in his position only have a small group of friends they consider to be their intellectual equal. As such they don't really care what the rest of us mere mortals think or say about them. More often than not their friends have lived on the grey side of the law at some point in their careers, so these guys don't see what they've done, or are doing, as all that terrible."

"So this means you've no alternative but to adopt full-blown in-your-face character adjustment to break him down." John's blunt statement didn't need explaining.

Ken summed up John's direction just to be certain. "I'll be making it abundantly clear The Board has him as a marked man, and it would only need us to release that he's cooperating with our enquiries for a red dot to appear between his eyes the next time he steps into the exercise yard."

John smiled evilly. "Attaboy Ken. Stick it up the bastard big time. Guys like him who've had a silver spoon in their bloody mouths all their lives think it's okay to go and shit on society because they believe it's their right."

Ballard and Peter were mildly amused, noting the rising anger in their colleague which Peter tempered by quipping, "Very philosophical John, and I have to agree, not only *should* these buggers know better, the sad fact of the matter is they invariably *do* know better. And the same goes for the damn magistrate next door. Christ, can you imagine someone of his standing getting mixed up in this mess, of all people?"

Ken stepped back inside to resume his battle while Ballard forwarded an identical text to Bobby's mobile, all three detectives now at the adjacent interview window. Like Ken, Bobby checked his phone and after whispering in Susan's ear, stared at where he knew he was being observed, an imperceptible nod ensuing. Seconds later he joined them while Susan remained locked in combat with the magistrate.

"Jesus boss, she's like a dog with a bone."

John chuckled. "Is there any meat on the bone worth chewing?"

Bobby's head gleamed under the fluorescent light, his upper lip sporting a sheen of sweat. "I can safely say he's one terrified magistrate, and also *very* aware of the deep shit he's in. From what he's told us he was coerced into the group for the sole purpose of influencing the odd committal hearing and to make rulings that went in favour of any cell members should they ever front him in court."

Ballard and Peter seized on the comment, with Ballard beating Peter to the obvious. "You're telling us he's admitting to being part of the cell?"

"It would appear so." Bobby grinned at the surprised looks on the senior detectives' faces.

"You said *coerced*, so he wasn't a willing member? *How* was he coerced?" John posed the questions while watching Susan toil away.

Bobby loosened his shoulders as he too observed his partner's efforts through the viewer. "That's what we're attempting to find out, and hopefully we'll see through any lies he might throw up to lessen his sentence."

Ballard had heard enough, now keen to begin his own interview. "Work him over and find out what specific knowledge he has of the Note Printing Australia robbery and the siege at Parliament House. As John mentioned to Ken next door, use The Board as a bargaining chip. We *have* to break these buggers down and fast."

Bobby was halfway through the door before Ballard had finished speaking, the three detectives smiling at the young man's passion. Peter was the first to turn away, shrugging, not looking forward to his impending task. "Okay, time to sort out our two heavies."

Signalling to Leonard they followed him to the floor below.

CHAPTER
33

Peter inwardly braced himself as he prepared to tackle Deputy Commissioner Salisbury, the man's rank and standing an obstacle he had to thrust from his mind. Ballard and John clapped him on the shoulder, wishing him well. Peter gave a tight smile as he entered the interview room. Watching him settle they saw him address the senior officer whose belligerent countenance foreshadowed the difficulty the superintendent was about to experience.

John massaged his forehead. "Rather him than me tackling the arrogant prick."

Turning away from the window, Ballard took a deep breath. "Okay, now for Vladimir, only this time as you pointed out John, *no* concessions."

His partner's jaw jutted. "You betcha. It's about time the bastard was given a dose of reality."

The Russian took little notice as the two detectives entered the room and settled. Clearly he had been expecting at least one of the senior officers to conduct the interview. John took out his trusty Olympus recorder and set it on the table. Vladimir eyed it with disdain, causing John to move it closer to further annoy him. Activating the video recorder, Ballard stated everyone's name, along with the time and date.

Hunching forward, Ballard led off, getting straight to the point. "No more deals, Vladimir. You've been caught with your pants down, literally, once too often. As a consequence, our assistant commissioner has directed us to process you for all your offences leading from the NPA robbery, the siege on Parliament House, right through to the Russian diplomat cartwheeling off his balcony."

Vladimir inclined his head, feigning confusion, but his eyes gave him away, opening a fraction wider. He said nothing.

John lunged forward, startling Ballard who feared his partner was about to strike the Russian. With a supreme effort John controlled himself, but his eyes blazed. "*Not good enough, Vladimir.* We've had St Georges Road wired up with eyes and ears for some time now, and you've been starring with Tatiana day *and* night. Your phone call before the murder, and your lust-charged romp *after* the diplomat was chucked off the balcony have all been recorded—audio as well as visual."

Ballard watched John draw breath, nostrils flaring. "Those issues aside we know it's your aspiration to become The Board's next cell leader, so that's where we're focussing our attention for the time being. Who have you been dealing with to make you and Tatiana so confident you could be the next contender?"

Vladimir's eyes narrowed, but it was his "Whatever I say won't really matter" brashness that set off alarm bells in Ballard's head, although he wasn't sure why.

The Russian sat upright, defiant. "I've got nothing to gain by admitting anything to any of you."

"*Really?*" John was about to explode. "Do we *have* to go down that road again? You've already told us threats have been made against you to cooperate or your daughter will be harmed, but that's losing some of its potency considering your actions since we released you the second time."

Vladimir gave another indifferent shrug, causing John to shift gear. "As you'll be going away for life"—he stabbed a forefinger at the Russian, very much in his face—"Erina will be taken into foster care now her mother's dead, and it's on *your* head because of *your* actions, no one else's."

The Russian's jaw clenched as he reflex-wrenched his shackled arm, almost as though he had forgotten it was restrained. John leapt on the mood change, taunting him, determined to capitalise on the man's discomfort. "I said you're going away for life, but you and I know that will never happen. You're too far up the food chain for The Board to let you live. You know that. *We* know that." He leant back in his seat, punctuating the comment with an assured lift of his chin.

The Russian's jaw clenched tighter but he maintained his stony silence.

About to pursue his argument, John was interrupted by the harsh screech of a siren. Initially believing it was a fire drill, both detectives realised within seconds it was the prison alarm system. It's on–off nerve-jangling pulse made the hair on the back of their necks stand, but it was Vladimir's impassive demeanour that caused the most disquiet; he sat perfectly still, unperturbed, appearing to have predicted the situation.

Ballard dragged John to one side, hissing in his ear, "The bastard knows something. *Look* at him. There's no way this is a drill or we'd have been notified over the public address. A prisoner *may* have lit up his mattress, or stabbed a guard, but my guess is we're under attack from The Board. They're here to kill everyone we arrested at the club."

Colour drained from John's face as full realisation hit home. Nodding in the direction of Vladimir he snarled, "By the way the prick's just sitting there I'd suggest he thinks it's more a rescue than an execution." He cursed. "I'm not so sure about the DC, the admiral, or the magistrate. I doubt they're important enough to be saved. No, it'll be a bullet in the back of the head for each of the other lot, and the danger is Ken, Bobby and Susan are in the firing line, along with Pete next door."

Their mobiles in hand they were about to dial the respective detectives when Leonard burst into the room, eyes wild, gasping. He blurted the obvious. "We're under attack. I've warned your superintendent."

"*Where is he now?*" Ballard's voice was anxious.

Leonard unlocked Vladimir's handcuff as he spoke over his shoulder. "Outside with the prisoner, about to take him to the safe room on this floor." John grabbed Vladimir by his lapels, literally hauling him to his feet, delivering a vicious punch to his stomach to gain his immediate compliance. The Russian doubled over, dry-retching as he was hauled towards the door.

Ballard ordered Leonard to lead the way. The guard wrenched the door open and stepped into the corridor, almost colliding with Peter who had the deputy commissioner in a half nelson as he frog-marched him along the passageway, the superintendent's face ashen.

Taking one hurried look at his colleagues Peter hissed through clenched teeth, "This is going to turn into a major blood bath if we're not careful."

John took up position behind him, with Vladimir continuing to moan from the savage blow.

Racing ahead, Leonard called out unnecessarily, *"Follow me."*

He halted in front of a metal door which he fumbled to unlock in his haste. He finally swung it open by leaning his shoulder against the heavy panel, which by its weight appeared to be bullet and bombproof.

"Get in. Get in." All the while the guard checked left and right along the corridor, fear sharpening his voice.

Shoving Vladimir and Salisbury inside, the two were quickly handcuffed to securing rings bolted into the wall. Leonard slid across the three internal bolts on the door before rushing to a keyboard, tapping in commands. He stared at the multiple screens on the wall which monitored the corridors in the building, including the one they were on.

Ballard grabbed the guard by the shoulder. "Is there a safe room on every floor?"

The man's beard disappeared several times. "Of course, OH&S insisted they be installed. The walls and doors can withstand a shoulder-mounted rocket—"

"Okay, okay, our three colleagues on the floor above, how do we get them into the safe room on their level?" While staring at the respective monitor they saw to their relief a guard sprinting along the corridor above, stopping at both interview rooms to pound on the doors, his left and right glances mimicking Leonard's movements moments before.

John shouted, redirecting everyone's attention, his outstretched finger pointing accusingly at the monitor displaying their own level. Two men dressed in black military fatigues, miked, wearing thigh holsters and carrying what Ballard believed were SIG MCX semi-automatic carbines were running along the corridor. Halting at the interview rooms they kicked the doors open. The instant the attackers realised the rooms were empty they moved cautiously towards the safe room, one of them taking out several small packs of what the detectives feared was C4, slapping the explosive against the door's hinges.

Peter hissed out the corner of his mouth, "Leonard, here's praying your theory about these bloody doors holds true." He reached across and relieved the guard of his Glock, much to the man's dismay. Peter confessed, "Not that we stand much chance against military weapons, but I'll be stuffed if I'm going down without a fight." Gritting his teeth he signalled his intent to Ballard and John. They all moved back from the door and to the side as a precaution.

The tension was unbearable. All eyes were glued to the screen as the two figures retreated from the blast zone, disappearing from the camera's vision. Seconds later a muffled explosion shook the entire room, dust particles showering from the ceiling. John swore he saw the reinforced door buckle, but it held firm. He grunted, "Thank Christ for that. We're stuck in here with one piss-ant handgun which is about as effective as a knife at a gunfight. I'm guessing that's the death squad in action out there?"

Ballard could only nod as he concentrated on the second screen which covered the floor above. It was obvious the guard on that level had mobilised the three detectives who were shoving the admiral and the magistrate towards their own safe room which the guard had unlocked as he urged the group to hurry.

The detectives and the two prisoners disappeared inside. To Ballard's horror the guard turned, making a fatal mistake by taking one last glance along the corridor the moment two assault team members came into view. A short burst from one of the carbines caught him, dropping him to the floor.

What happened next was breathtaking in its bravery. Keeping out of the line of fire, the detectives dragged the shot man inside, slamming the door shut. The two assailants grabbed the handle to haul it open, but it was clear the bolts had been slid in place. Within seconds two more assault team members appeared.

"Are they the guys who were on our floor?" John strained to identify them but the balaclavas covering their faces along with their helmets prevented any form of identification. He took out his mobile and rang Bobby while Ballard did the same for Ken.

Six rings passed and Ballard was on the verge of giving up when he heard a hesitant, "Mike, are you guys okay?"

Ballard couldn't help but smile. "We're fine Ken. We're in the safe room downstairs, below you. Are you three okay?"

A weak reply followed. "We got inside just as the shooting started."

Ballard followed up with "We saw you on the monitor. The guard was hit. How is he?"

There was a long pause during which Ken sighed. "He's dead Mike. He copped a couple in the chest and one in the head."

"Ah Jesus, the poor bastard." While Ballard felt relief wash over him, knowing his colleagues hadn't been harmed, the elation was tempered by the news of the guard.

Ken continued in a low voice charged with emotion, "He saved our lives Mike. If he hadn't turned up when he did we'd all be dead." The statement was delivered as a monotone, shock setting in.

Ballard attempted to reassure his colleague. "Ken hang in there. You did everything you could and thank Christ you managed to secure the bolts in time."

There was an emphatic "*Bloody oath.*"

Ballard agonised how to deliver his next piece of news, deciding there was no option but to lay it on the line. "With the guard dead there isn't time for us to talk you through how to activate the monitors in your room so we'll have to be your eyes as to what's going on around you. Currently there are four of the assault team outside your door. They *may* try to blow it in—"

"*Jesus!* What can we—"

"*Ken, Ken!* They tried the same on our safe room and the door stood up to it. Just make sure the bolts are fully secured and stay back from the door." He hesitated. "I'm assuming your guard's armed?"

Ken took several seconds to reply. "He is . . . or was."

"Good. Take his weapon just in case. I'll have Peter contact Tim to find out when he can get up to your floor. Make sure you stay on the line."

Holding the mobile to his chest Ballard was about to request Peter make the call when he saw the superintendent already in animated discussion with the SOG commander. Seconds later Peter held up three fingers, indicating three minutes.

John mirrored Ballard, clutching his mobile against his body as he growled, "Bloody hell Mike, there has to be *something* we can do other than sit cooped up here like rats in a drainpipe."

Despite his words he knew there was nothing that could be achieved other than provide intel until the SOG teams arrived. He was also fearful that against a disciplined death squad it was going to prove a monumental task for Tim's group, and one which may well result in SOG fatalities. All three detectives considered one another, their haunted eyes exposing their deep concern for Tim and his group's safety.

Furious, John's sense of complete impotence triggered his emotions to boil over. Asking Ballard to hold his mobile he crossed to the deputy commissioner, landing a vicious blow to the man's solar plexus, even more savage than the one he gave Vladimir. Tight lipped he added, "*That's courtesy of our AC.*" The senior officer doubled over, slumping to his knees. Unprepared for John's action, he was unable to speak as he gasped for air, his handcuffs preventing him from collapsing outright onto the floor.

Peter's casual look at Ballard implied he saw nothing. Ballard reciprocated the stare as he handed John's phone back, muttering, "Now you've got *that* off your chest, let's keep our mind on the job shall we?" John rolled his shoulders, allowing himself a satisfied smile.

Checking the screen once more, to everyone's relief the four assailants decided against blowing the door. Instead they moved from the floor, realising they had limited time before the SOG teams arrived. Ballard passed the news to Ken who advised Bobby and Susan of the lucky break; their whoops of joy echoing in the background.

Peter indicated that Tim had assembled ten of his squad and they had begun their systematic sweep of the prison, the SOG officer revealing the lantern jawed guard at the reception desk had been fatally shot while still in his chair.

The detectives stared at Vladimir and the deputy commissioner, their anger directed towards the two criminals, channelling the blame for the guards' deaths squarely at the men's feet. Ballard maintained a close eye on John to ensure he wasn't tempted to repeat his previous actions and dish out further rough justice.

CHAPTER

34

Several minutes passed before they spotted Tim and four of his team on the monitor, all moving cautiously along the corridor outside their safe room, their weapons sweeping front and rear. Rechecking the screen to ensure the SOG team wasn't under attack, John unbolted the door that had been crucial in saving their lives.

The reunion was brief but emotional, Tim claiming the assailants had started a fire in the exercise yard as a diversion prior to entering the remand centre. He explained how multiple fire trucks had to wait in the street until it was known the entire assault team had been terminated.

John was astonished. *"What? You killed all of them?"*

Tim brushed it off. "They weren't going to surrender, and two of my guys can thank their body armour for being able to walk out of this place, notwithstanding with badly bruised chests."

Intense relief swept over Ballard, identical to that which he had felt for the young detectives earlier. "Thank God Tim. You can be bloody proud to have taken out this mob because this is the first time *anyone's* been able to touch them. What your team has achieved is nothing short of a miracle." His relief switched to acute concern as he caught his breath. *"Delwyn and Marjorie,* at the Dame Phyllis Frost Centre. What if more of this mob are attempting the same down—"

Tim placed a reassuring hand on his shoulder. "Take it easy Mike. I rang the centre and warned them to lock down all the prisoners. Then I spoke to Delwyn and she told me they'd wrapped up their interview with Tatiana and were heading back to the office. But you're right. An attack there was a distinct possibility so I've sent some of my guys over. The prison's Security and Emergency Services Group have also been made aware of the situation and are mobilising a squad."

Ballard relaxed, while John and Peter clapped Tim on the back in heartfelt celebration. Compliments over, John was agitated to get upstairs to check on his team. Leaving two SOG officers to guard Vladimir and the deputy commissioner, they piled up the stairs, Tim's officers leading the way as a precautionary measure. John hammered a fist on the safe room door, calling out it was okay to open up.

In spite of his bellowed assurance it took a full thirty seconds before the door was inched ajar, Bobby's face appearing. "Christ, are we glad to see you guys. This has been some scary shit."

John growled, pretending to be dismissive. "Stop whining. It's what you get paid for."

Stepping inside they saw the detectives had positioned the deceased guard against the wall in as dignified a manner as was possible under the circumstances. Susan stared down at the body, her lip trembling as she fought back tears, the mounting shock of the preceding terrifying minutes overcoming her. Ken placed a comforting arm around her shoulders as he led her away; she returned the gesture with an appreciative hug.

As was the case for the DC and Vladimir, the admiral and the magistrate were handcuffed to the wall rings; the admiral defiant, demanding to be released. The magistrate appeared a broken man, his head hanging low, too ashamed to take in his captors.

Ken turned to Tim. "Are your guys okay?"

Tim nodded. "A couple of close calls but yes, they came through. Sadly the reception guy was killed, along with three other guards. Prior to that the assailants forced one of the guards to open the cells for the five businessmen. They then shot the guard *and* the businessmen, double-tapping each in the head."

In spite of his years of operational experience John was shocked at the ruthless efficiency of the assault team, his expression imploring better news but aware it wouldn't be forthcoming.

Tim nodded. "'Fraid so John. It's a miracle your guys were able to keep these two alive as well as Vladimir and the DC."

On hearing this the admiral stiffened, his head cocked to one side, contemplating what might have been. The news that they had narrowly avoided being executed by The Board left the magistrate emotionally shattered.

Ballard aired his concerns. "There has to be something fundamentally wrong with security in this place for the assailants to have just waltzed in here. How many were there all up?" He looked to Tim.

"Six."

Ballard shook his head in frustration. "There you have it. Six kitted-up assassins bursting in the front door of a major prison. What the hell does that tell you?"

Tim cleared his throat. "They didn't come in the front door Mike."

There were mystified stares. Tim moved into the corridor with everyone following, out of earshot of the two prisoners. "Folks you're not going to believe this but a couple of my guys have checked out a tunnel leading off the major storm water drain which runs under La Trobe Street . . ."

"*Oh, you've got to be shitting me!*" John shook his head from side to side, his expression turning to stunned acceptance as he noted Tim's steadfast gaze.

"By the professional manner the secondary tunnel was bricked up it may have been there for months, if not years." His smile was enigmatic, almost secretive. "And guess where it ended up. The opening was only exposed when the group broke through just prior to the raid kicking off."

Bobby and Susan shook their head, unsure whether to proffer what was an obvious answer, with Ken opting to spoil Tim's suspense. "Oh that's easy, in one of the exercise yards."

"Bingo! The south-west yard near where Sergey escaped over the bloody wall. Go to the top of the class young lad."

John had difficulty getting his head around the situation. "You're telling me the tunnel was in place for God knows how long with only the last bit opened when they broke into the prison?" He was dumbfounded by the extent of The Board's forward planning.

Peter added his thoughts. "With the access in place it meant they could breach the assessment centre whenever there was a need to take out anyone who may prove to be a security risk for the group. When you think it over there's solid logic to it." He became reflective. "By my estimate the distance from the outer edge of the storm water drain to inside the yard is less than twelve metres. Johno could dig that far in a couple of days—*on his own*. Like I said, it was good business sense having the bloody thing ready to go."

John was unimpressed. "Yeah, 'good business sense' for a bunch of lunatic psychopaths."

Peter wasn't unconvinced. "I suggest you go a wee bit lighter on the 'lunatic' angle and a whole lot heavier on the 'psychopath' aspect." He laughed suddenly. "Besides John, wasn't it you who suggested a tunnel should be dug between the crime building and the assessment centre? There you have it, The Board's already done half the work for you."

"Just not via a storm water drain thank you very much." John's inverted finger increased Peter's already growing mirth.

Members of the Critical Incident Response Team arrived shortly after to escort the prisoners across La Trobe Street to be interviewed later in the day at the Crime Department offices. The detectives along with Tim moved outside to inspect the exercise yard and the ragged hole boxed up with rudimentary timber near the edge of the grassed area. It was through this opening the assassins had sprung, their first violent act to shoot the two guards on the wall's observation walkway.

John snapped several photos on his phone, all the while muttering his disbelief, "If I wasn't seeing this with my own eyes I'd never have thought it possible. Talk about balls."

As they turned to walk back inside, Ballard's mobile rang. To his relief he saw it was from Delwyn. Snatching it to his ear, he exclaimed, "Thank God Delwyn. Where are you?"

The response caused a chill to run the length of his spine as he recognised Sergey's voice, halting him in his tracks. In typical abrupt style the Russian dispensed with any introduction or preamble, instead delivering a blunt message delivered devoid of emotion. "You have something *I* want. I have something *you* want." With that he was gone.

Everyone stopped, alarmed at the dramatic transformation in Ballard's demeanour. Seconds later his mobile signalled receipt of a text. Trepidation flooded him, fearing what the message would reveal. A photo materialised. Feeling weak as the air left his lungs his limbs became leaden. He fought to comprehend the image confronting him—brutal in its delivery, misogynist in its concept. He couldn't speak, his face wracked in disbelief.

Once more he questioned his decision not to execute Sergey when he had the opportunity. He weighed up the ever-mounting loss of life instigated by the Russian. He related this with the associated trauma and heartache for the survivors and the lifetime of guilt he would have had to endure had he put the Russian down, along with the genuine prospect of going to jail, a result of the department's rigid rules of engagement. His thoughts were line ball what he would do were he ever presented with the opportunity a second time.

When he displayed the photo to John, his partner's guttural growl was pure primal rage. In turn Peter crowded alongside, the image registering like an electric shock, causing him to gasp in dismay.

Observing the detectives' reactions, the three junior detectives pressed closer, forcing Ballard to pull away, refusing to show them the photo. Instead he steeled himself to take a second look despite not wishing to confirm his initial fears.

Delwyn and Marjorie's faces were contorted in abject terror, eyes wide, frantic. They were strapped to wooden chairs, their hands drawn behind them, their legs bound, mouths taped. The surroundings were brightly lit but devoid of any features that might reveal the location.

Emotions raged as the image burned deep into Ballard's psyche, numbing his senses, clouding logical thought. It was evident both women had been demeaned by their captor, the photograph displaying them naked. Their upper bodies were bruised and covered in blood, both degraded in the extreme, defenceless, denied any hope of liberation.

His face a mask of controlled fury, eyes blazing, Ballard snarled, *"Sergey, you've just signed your own death warrant!"*

The End

Ballard and John return in *Dead Man Walking: Whatever It Takes.*

Acknowledgements

The alter egos of the four key support characters in 'Payback', 'The Heist', 'End Game' and 'The Siege' are as strong and dynamic as ever. My thanks goes once more to Glenys Reid, Ken Sproat, Bobby Dzodzadinov and Susan Dodd for their ongoing interest in my novels and their encouragement and involvement. In 'Whatever It Takes', Glenys' character Delwyn goes operational bigtime, showing Ballard and John a thing or two on Sydney Harbour Bridge! Ken, Bobby and Susan continue to have an affinity for action in and around the Melbourne Remand Centre while providing their ever youthful energy to the storyline.

Natalie's honeymoon in Paris proved to be a hit-and-miss affair due to Ballard's work commitments, as such a short holiday in New Zealand was a pleasant interlude and a way to ease her concerns regarding the stresses her husband was experiencing. As always Natalie's character is based on my wife Leanne, with her good humour, affection and street smarts— not to mention her ever cheeky nature always at the fore.

Ballard's work colleague John, continues to feature in every perilous escapade in the novel, and has now matched Ballard in the hero stakes. Unfortunately, it is with immense sadness that the real life gentleman the character is based on (yes, also named John), died suddenly this year, leaving me with an emotional ache in my heart that will be with me always. The laconic larrikin that you were in real life John will live on in deed and spirit, which I promise to keep alive in future novels. I miss you buddy.

Peter Donelly, my former boss is ever present, continuing to provide me with vital grist for his fictional character, that being a very stylish and capable detective superintendent. On this outing his persona is up to his eyeballs in the nuts and bolts of the case, taxing even his considerable expertise. Thanks Pete for being such a complex, funny and interesting individual whose namesake stands as a shining example as to what we all wish our senior police to be.

One of Leanne's closest school friends Diane Howden has raised the bar and her 'take-no-prisoners' sharp, perceptive suggestions have added considerable value to the flow, pace and readability of the story. Her suggestions have made this book 'slick' and a far more enjoyable as a read than it would have been. Beware Diane, book six is on the way!

My son's father-in-law, Don Wyer (looking and sounding more like Sean Connery than Sean Connery ever did!) provided some very astute advice in which he told me I had written too many adjectives and adverbs. After looking up what they were (joke!) I had to agree and went to work with an axe. Thank you Don, and remember, I can NEVER publish a novel unless you give it the once over.

A new comer to my acknowledgements is Myra from Xlibris who was technically brilliant editing the manuscript, introducing me to rules that I never knew existed. Just ease up on the commas on the next novel Myra. Many thanks.

Mr Joel Cobb, Xlibris Design Consultant has done a fantastic job on the novel's cover and after all, the cover is what draws readers to reach out and lift the book off the shelf. A great job Mr Cobb!

Ms Joy Daniels, Xlibris Author Services Representative and Ms Mary Lopez, Xlibris Senior Marketing Consultant provided me with the guidance and direction that I needed to give this novel, and several previous books, the oomph they needed. I'm forever grateful.

Finally, as always a big thank you to you the reader for choosing this novel and allowing yourself to be immersed in a world that most people never experience.

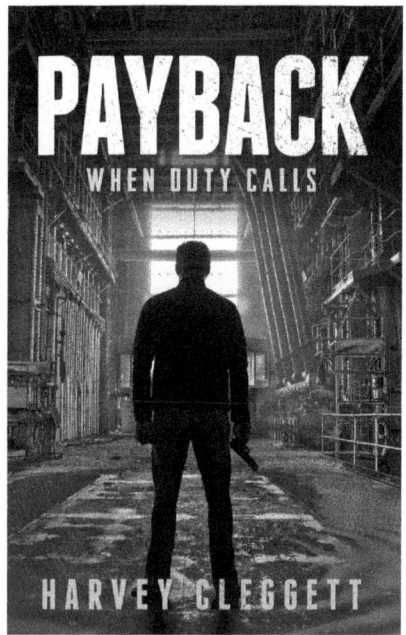

PAYBACK
WHEN DUTY CALLS

Homicide Detective Inspector Michael Ballard is vigorously resisting retirement, not wishing to walk away from investigating and solving complex criminal cases.

The brutal murder of a factory owner has him and his partner applying their 'old school' policing skills to hunt down the killer. But while Ballard is hunting the killer—is the killer hunting him?

An absorbing murder mystery set in the often violent world of modern day law enforcement.

THE HEIST
WHEN DUTY CALLS (part 2)

An audacious robbery that breaches the Note Printing Australia building with fatal consequences, sees homicide partners Michael Ballard and John Henderson pitted against ruthless professionals who will stop at nothing to retain their ill-gotten $130 million in uncut bank notes.

A pulsating country raid, followed by a heart pounding boat chase in Port Phillip Bay has Ballard and John in the thick of the action. Throughout, Ballard fights to ensure his love for Natalie his fiancée, doesn't place her in harm's way.

'The Heist' returns the characters from Harvey Cleggett's first novel 'Payback', catapulting the reader on a wild roller coaster ride, culminating in a traumatic climax no one could foresee.

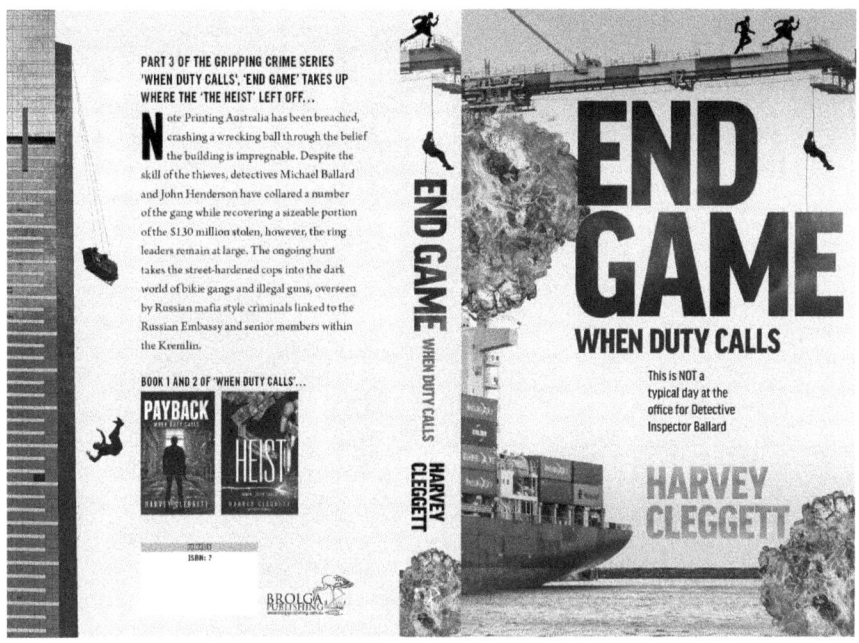

END GAME
WHEN DUTY CALLS (part 3)

Note Printing Australia has been breached, crashing a wrecking ball through the belief the building is impregnable. Despite the skill of the thieves, homicide detectives Michael Ballard and John Henderson have arrested a number of the gang while recovering a sizeable portion of the $130 million stolen, however the ring leaders remain at large.

The ongoing hunt takes the street hardened cops into the dark world of bikie gangs and illegal guns, overseen by Russian mafia style criminals linked to the Russian Embassy and senior members within the Kremlin.

'End Game' takes up where Harvey Cleggett's second novel 'The Heist' left off, turbo-charging the reader's adrenalin rush.

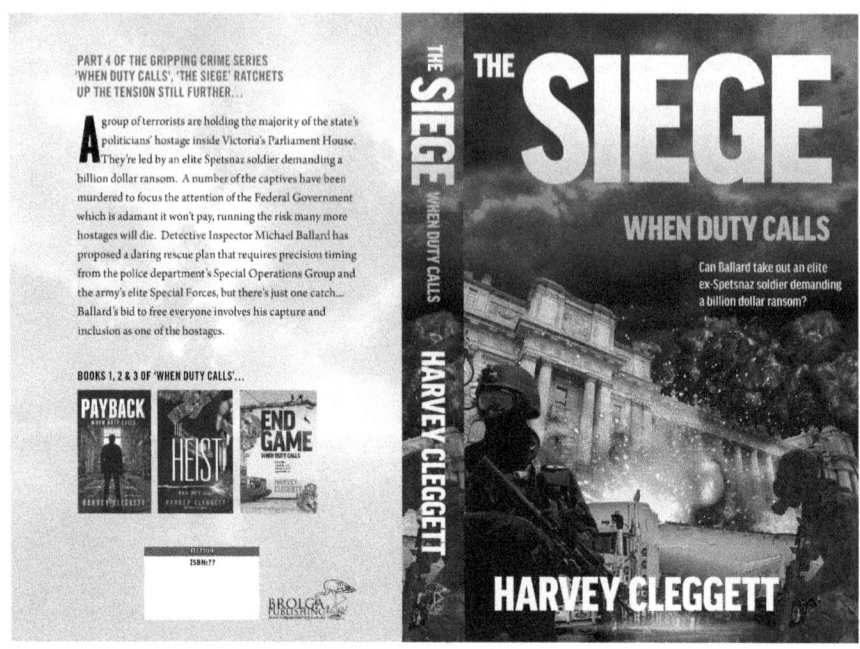

PART 4 OF THE GRIPPING CRIME SERIES
'WHEN DUTY CALLS', 'THE SIEGE' RATCHETS
UP THE TENSION STILL FURTHER...

A group of terrorists are holding the majority of the state's
politicians' hostage inside Victoria's Parliament House.
They're led by an elite Spetsnaz soldier demanding a
billion dollar ransom. A number of the captives have been
murdered to focus the attention of the Federal Government
which is adamant it won't pay, running the risk many more
hostages will die. Detective Inspector Michael Ballard has
proposed a daring rescue plan that requires precision timing
from the police department's Special Operations Group and
the army's elite Special Forces, but there's just one catch...
Ballard's bid to free everyone involves his capture and
inclusion as one of the hostages.

BOOKS 1, 2 & 3 OF 'WHEN DUTY CALLS'...

THE SIEGE
WHEN DUTY CALLS

HARVEY CLEGGETT

Can Ballard take out an elite
ex-Spetsnaz soldier demanding
a billion dollar ransom?

THE SIEGE
WHEN DUTY CALLS (part 4)

A group of terrorists are holding the state's politicians' hostage inside Victoria's Parliament House. They are led by an elite Spetsnaz soldier demanding a billion dollar ransom. A number of the captives have been executed to focus the attention of the Federal Government which is adamant it won't pay, running the risk many more hostages will die.

Detective Inspector Michael Ballard has proposed a daring rescue plan that requires precision timing from the police department's Special Operations Group and the army's Special Forces, but there is just one catch . . . Ballard's bid to free everyone involves his capture and inclusion as one of the hostages.

Lightning Source UK Ltd.
Milton Keynes UK
UKHW01n2120240718
326229UK00001B/1/P